THE
WRONG SIDE
OF PARIS

HONORÉ DE BALZAC

THE WRONG SIDE OF PARIS

A new translation by Jordan Stump

Introduction by Adam Gopnik

Notes by James Madden

THE MODERN LIBRARY

NEW YORK

2005 Modern Library Paperback Edition

Published in the United States by Modern Library, an imprint of
The Random House Publishing Group, a division of Random House, Inc., New York.

MODERN LIBRARY and the TORCHBEARER Design are registered trademarks of
Random House, Inc.

This work was originally published in hardcover by Modern Library,
an imprint of The Random House Publishing Group,
a division of Random House, Inc., 2003.

LIBRARY OF CONGRESS CATALOGING-IN-PUBLICATION DATA
Balzac, Honoré de, 1799–1850.
[Envers de l'histoire contemporaine. English]
The wrong side of Paris/Honoré de Balzac; a new translation by Jordan Stump;
introduction by Adam Gopnik; notes by James Madden.
p.   cm.
ISBN 0-8129-6675-9
I. Stump, Jordan, 1959–   II. Madden, James.   III. Title.
PQ2165.E494E5 2004
843'.7—dc22   2003059942

Modern Library website address: www.modernlibrary.com

Printed in the United States of America

8   9   7

HONORÉ DE BALZAC

Honoré de Balzac, often said to be the greatest of French novelists, was born in Tours on May 20, 1799. His father was a civil servant who had survived the Revolution and prospered under Napoleon; his mother came from a middle-class Parisian family. Raised by a wet nurse until the age of four, he was later sent to study at the Oratorian college in Vendôme. In 1814 the family moved to the Marais district of Paris, where Balzac attended the Lycée Charlemagne. Following three years as a legal clerk he earned a Bachelor of Law degree in 1819, but soon decided to pursue a literary career. His first effort, *Cromwell*, a verse tragedy, was a complete failure. During the 1820s Balzac supported himself as a hack journalist, turning out sensational novels and potboilers under various pseudonyms. He also tried to make money in several publishing ventures, all of which failed and left him saddled with debt. The appearance in 1829 of *Les Chouans*, the first work published under his own name, along with *La Physiologie du mariage*, marked the beginning of Balzac's success as a novelist. *Scènes de la vie privée* (1830), a collection of short stories, quickly enhanced his reputation.

"Salute me for at this very moment I am in the throes of becoming a genius," Balzac announced to his sister in 1833, when he conceived the idea of pouring all his creativity into writing one great chronicle of the age, *La Comédie humaine.* "[It] was at first as a dream to me," he later explained. "French society would be the real author; I should only be the secretary. By drawing up an inventory of vices and virtues, by collecting the chief facts of the passions, by depicting characters, by choosing the principal incidents of social life, by composing types out of a combination of homogeneous characteristics, I might perhaps succeed in writing the history which so many historians have neglected: that of Manners. By patience and perseverance I might produce for France in the nineteenth century the book which we must all regret that Rome, Athens, Tyre, Memphis, Persia, and India have not bequeathed to us: a history of their social life."

Balzac devoted the rest of his life to this monumental task. Clothed in a white dressing gown that resembled a monk's robe and imbibing huge quantities of strong black coffee, he began writing at midnight and continued until midday. Famous for composing an entire work on successive galley proofs instead of submitting a finished manuscript to printers, Balzac published five or six books a year, with as many others in various stages of completion. Over a period of two decades he produced ninety-two tales filled with some two thousand characters. Among the most outstanding are *Eugénie Grandet* (1833), *Le Père Goriot* (1835), *César Birotteau* (1837), *Illusions perdues* (1837–1843), *Ursule Mirouët* (1842), *La Cousine Bette* (1846), and *Le Cousin Pons* (1847).

Yet in many ways Balzac's own life became his most extraordinary creation. An exuberant, flamboyant man who pursued married women and unsuccessful business schemes with equal ardor, he was constantly in debt, forever unable to control the follies of his own passionate impulses. In *Story of My Life,* George Sand offered this telling remembrance of him: "One evening, when we had dined on a strange assortment of food at Balzac's—I believe we had boiled beef, a melon, and whipped champagne—he tried on a brand-new dressing gown, showing it off to us with girlish joy, and wanted, thus appareled, to accompany us, candle in hand, up to the Luxembourg gate. It was late, the place was deserted, and I pointed out to him that he would get murdered going back home. 'Not at all,' he told me. 'If I meet some thieves, they'll take me for a madman and will be afraid of me. Either that, or they'll take me for a prince, and pay me homage.' It was a calm, beautiful night. He accompanied us thus, carrying his lighted candle in its pretty holder of chased vermeil, speaking of the four Arabian horses he did not yet have, that he should have soon, that he never did get, and yet firmly believing he sooner or later would have. He would have walked us to the other end of Paris, if we had let him."

During the last years of his life Balzac traveled throughout Europe, often in the company of Madame Eveline Hanska, his longtime mistress. The two married on March 14, 1850, in the parish church near her vast estate in the Ukraine. Honoré de Balzac died just five months later in Paris on August 18, 1850. "Balzac [was] the master unequalled in the art of painting humanity as it exists in modern society," judged George Sand. "He searched and dared everything. . . . Childlike and great; always envious of trifles and never jealous of true glory; sincere to the point of modesty, proud to the point of braggadocio; trusting himself and others; very generous, very kind, and very crazy, with an inner reserve of reason which controlled all aspects of his work; brazen yet celibate; drunk on water; intemperate regarding work, but sober in the other passions; materialistic and romantic to equal excess; credulous and skeptical; filled with inconsistencies and mysteries— that was Balzac."

Contents

THE WRONG SIDE OF PARIS

INTRODUCTION

Adam Gopnik

Balzac is a hard case for the modern American reader. Undoubtedly a classic, he is also a puzzle, and the puzzle rises from knowing where to place him, knowing exactly what kind of writer he is, and what kind of reading his writing demands. Reading literature in translation—even more or less modern literature from a more or less familiar country in a more or less idiomatic translation—we seek first to find the thing in our own language which it most resembles, and then start up the hill from that. *What book that we know is this book that we don't know like?*

Reading Proust, for instance, we sense first that it is a beautifully long-winded, high-society, fin de siècle, Jamesian kind of thing, and though we later discover that it is less Jamesian than it seemed at first (Proust being no pragmatist but an unbending systematizer, as firm in his relativistic conclusions as Einstein), we are not wrong in beginning there, and it helps us reach the end. The footholds may not get us all the way up the mountain, but without them we can hardly start.

With no other unquestioned master are the footholds so familiar and the ascent so hard as they are with Balzac. Even the casual reader probably knows of Balzac as the author of one of the monuments of nineteenth-century literature, *La Comédie Humaine,* a sequence of eighty-one (eighty-one!) more or less linked texts that he placed into semiscientific categories: the philosophical, the Parisian, and so on.

As the superintending novelist of the first half of the French nineteenth century, pinning its types Darwinianly in categories, he instantly invites a mental comparison to the contemporary masters of the English novel, whose world-encompassing ambitions he seems to share. Balzac, we decide, is the French Dickens. And indeed he shares, as few other writers ever have, Dickens's appetite and energy, his verbal floods, his ability to turn a whole world over as if it were an anthill and name the scurrying creatures beneath. Balzac also has the ability, which perhaps only Dickens has ever equaled, of making pure industry and invention an acceptable, and in some ways preferable, substitute for artistic perfection, the ability to make sheer productivity into a strictly literary virtue, a fecundity that rivals God's. And then he has Dickens's confidence, that wonderful nineteenth-century belief that whole worlds can be held in view in single books.

In the novel before us, for instance, we are delighted by an introduction that announces the romance of the great urban novel—the kind of opening that a modern writer can only envy; it is so sure in its command of whole cities and societies. "One fine September evening in the year 1836, a man of about thirty stood hunched over the parapet of a quay by the Seine." Balzac begins and then goes on to summon up the whole of the Seine, the Île de la Cité, its history, and the particular vantage of one young man who we know instantly will become the novel's consciousness. This is, in fact, the classic Balzacian opening: the urban opening that invites the reader into a world through the vessel of a personality. Balzac is the great master, and in some ways the inventor, of the kind of "epic" urban opening that Joyce parodied out of existence in *Ulysses*, eliminating the supply without eliminating the demand. "The young man on the bridge might have seen . . ." That kind of opening is Balzacian before it is anything else.

Yet, begun with a confident promise of an all-seeing omniscient survey of a world, *The Wrong Side of Paris*, as so often in Balzac, suddenly takes an abrupt turn into the dark, the magical, and the just plain weird. A little monastery of religious devotees turns out to be hidden in that sweeping urban panorama, and the peculiar lives of its inmates, devoted to the mystical text *Imitation of Christ,* becomes its ostensible subject. This always seems to happen in Balzac. We expect the world-as-it-is but get the world-as-only-Balzac-can-imagine-it. Strange skins radiate magical effects; apparent desperadoes turn out to be the hidden emissaries of government; the world is secretly ruled by an order of thirteen sinister/wise men. Conspiracies and occult wonders are everywhere. Even in *Lost Illusions,* the most wonderfully sour and cynical of Balzac's Paris books, we can never entirely, or even remotely, credit the sudden intrusion of the Cenacalo, the little group of perfectly good artists who, briefly, rescue Lucien from his course of corruption. Dickens, we realize, is a humorist and satirist, who rises or falls into melodrama, employs it as he needs to, but is most entirely himself as a writer who sees even the absurdities of his own inventions. Balzac, by contrast, is an essentially romantic and even melodramatic writer who occasionally can't help being funny.

In fact, it soon strikes the searching Anglo-American reader, a little troublingly, that the real parallel for Balzac in nineteenth-century English letters is not really with Dickens at all but with Dickens's strange—and had he not become prime minister of England, *weird* would be an appropriate word here, too—contemporary Disraeli: the same bizarre mixture of wild romantic fantasy and shrewd social observation, and the same obsession with a reactionary royalist-cum-Catholic restoration. For the other thing that strikes one throughout Balzac's *Comédie Humaine,* and in this novel particularly, is his wholehearted embrace of a reactionary politics so bizarre and overextended that one almost feels that they are not meant to be taken quite seriously. Yet one also recognizes at once, of course, that Disraeli is a minor figure in English literature, while Balzac is as big as they come, big enough to have inspired, in different ways, Henry James and Émile Zola. So what in his gift and circumstances made this particular mix of imaginative over-reach and sharp observation work so potently?

As with most things in writing, it's partly Him, partly Then, and partly Us—what Then made Him into, what He made Then look like, and what we make of it all. More specifically, it has to do with the peculiar nature of France, and particularly with the Paris of the first half of the nineteenth century. For Balzac, though as universal as they come—his subject was the human comedy, not the French predicament—lived and mastered a place which, uniquely, and still to our own day, was a kind of testing ground for wild acts of the imagination, a city where it took a melodramatic, surreal imagination simply to mimic the mundane.

———

Balzac was born in 1799, ten years into the Revolution, just at the moment of the turn toward Napoleon, and died, quite young, in 1850, and so is literally a creature of the first half of the French nineteenth century. We tend to see that first half through the splendors of the second half, and, if we know that the years from 1852 through the Second Empire and the Third Republic were, as they used to say, "tumultuous," what with the Commune and the Dreyfuss case, still a stubborn small part of our minds thinks "Well, give me tumult like that." We expect a Paris novel, even a bitter one like Maupassant's *Bel Ami,* to have a pleasure-giving setting, to take pleasure as one of its subjects, however disabused the narrator is about it.

But the history of France in the first half of the nineteenth century—Balzac's half—more closely resembled that of Chile or Argentina in the twentieth century: a constant struggle, on the writer's part, not just for legitimacy but for life. That list of regimes, stretching back into pre-history and stretching forward into Balzac's present day, with which this novel begins, is not meant to be charming or reassuring, as it might be in a French novel today, if anyone wrote such novels. It is meant to suggest how unsettled French history is, how the physical unity of Paris gives one an illusory sense of historical unity. From the point of the Cité, beautifully compared to the stern of a ship—you can still stand there today, surrounded by young lovers from Holland and Scandinavian backpackers—one sees a city where everything looks settled and everything is precarious. And what had produced that precariousness was a war of romantic ideas, from Jacobinism to Bonapartism, a series of attempts to remake the world in radical ways which, even after their failures, still had a glow for the people who had seen them explode and burn out. (This afterglow is one of Stendhal's great subjects.)

At the same time, amid that idealizing precariousness, a new kind of practical society was coming into being. It was the society that we now call "bourgeois" (though, as the scholars have recently insisted, no one at the time referred to it, or themselves, quite that way). Balzac saw both—the romantic ideal that had failed and the bourgeois idea that was ascendant—and his question was always the same: How, in a society devoted to getting and spending, do you build structures of romance, not just of benevolence but of glamorous benevolence? In *The Wrong Side of Paris* he pursues this theme in what is, for him, a uniquely single-minded manner, and the surprising conclusion he comes to is that you can only remake religion from *within* the city.

The novel is set in 1836, six years into the regime of the "bourgeois king" of whom Balzac and the caricaturist Grandville are the two leading artistic figures. Every schoolboy knows—as every schoolboy used to say—of the Revolution of 1789 and the Reign of Terror, but it was, oddly, this later Revolution of 1830 that gave Balzac's life its central event—the revolution that put in place the "bourgeois" King Louis-Philippe, but accidentally made it plain that the symbols of monarchy were not enough to sustain a kingdom. For the next twenty years, Balzac, and indeed the French generally, searched not just for a "strongman" but for a strong idea—for authority, something with the assurance and dignity and common assent of the old regime. (A struggle that, in a sense, only ended in France with the establishment of the Fifth Republic by de Gaulle, whose presidential pomposities, rooted in the authority of the State and the dignity of a national myth of France, could embrace left and right alike. Paradoxically, it was only the utter humiliation of the Occupation that could produce a national myth large enough to encompass everyone.)

In this way, the elements in *The Wrong Side of Paris* that seem reactionary are, at least, searching. Balzac, without question, was a royalist, and particularly a "legitimist," i.e., someone who believed in the true line of the old Bourbon Kings rather than in an Inflato model from another family or even from the Bonapartes. But he was not reactionary at all in the sense of defending an inherited interest. Just the contrary: Balzac's own interests were entirely with the bourgeoisie whose vices he pilloried and whose virtues he embodied. Industry, diligence, the ability to pull oneself upright by pure energy, even a love for fashion and for dandyism (it is the aristocrats who dress in old clothes and sit in old chairs). These were all Balzac's defining characteristics. But he felt also—as every bourgeois sooner or later does—the absence of any principle, any virtue larger than that of greed, in the society around him and perhaps in his own life. (Heroic materialism only looks heroic in retrospect; at the time, it just looks like materialism.)

Balzac's hunger for an ancient order (in both senses) is moving because he dramatizes so vividly the alternative. Chaos and horror, anarchy and terror, were not bogeymen scared up to terrify timid bourgeois: they were true things that had happened in living memory when the old order gave out. It was not the Terror alone, which had lasted only months and years, that haunted his imagination, but the way the entire ship of French society—at one moment radically Jacobin, then the next resolutely Bonapartist, then Orleanist, then Bourbon again—could list and tip over. The price for guessing wrong about the next change of direction was your life, or the lives of your children. In this historical context, Balzac's search, which governs his books, for an order not only better but more reliable, more *orderly*, than the bourgeois order of buying and selling, is not nostalgic but, in its way, progressive—life as it was presented to his half century was either a casino or a charnel house, either the gaming room of bourgeois capitalism or the abattoir of idealistic politics. What certain thing, he asked, again and again, could lay between? Although the satiric element is not uppermost in this book, his satiric flights rise from the same fascination. His satire of bourgeois corruption and instability, the fantastic figures who appear often throughout *The Human Comedy*—most famously Rastignac and Vautrin—who change allegiances and masks instantly, and at one moment are figures out of Rowlandson and the next moment figures out of Fuseli—these were real types who filled the life of France. (Vidcoq, Napoleon's legendary secret policeman, who inspired the character of Vautrin, was every bit as duplicitous as his fictional equivalent.) We need only recall how so upright a figure as Tocqueville was tortured by the decision of where to place his loyalties after the 1830 Revolution to get a sense of how easily the ground under everyone's feet was not just likely to shake but to drop right away. It wasn't just living on a fault in the plates; it was life lived on top of an active and temperamental volcano.

It is this sense of utter instability that makes Balzac's novels "real" even in their wildest flights. For this novel is almost a fairy tale or fable of that kind of volcanic instability and the search for responses to it. *The Wrong Side of Paris* makes the case for retreat, but retreat of an odd kind. A small band of invisible do-gooders—a favorite Balzacian fantasy—exists at once outside and inside modern Paris. Devout Catholics, though of an oddly sectarian kind (one doesn't see them answering to Rome or even to a local cardinal) live in a rooming house on the Île de la Cité. They radiate out into Paris to do quiet good deeds—they loan money to the indigent, circulate among workingmen to save them equally from destitution and the unions, just then emerging for the first time. It all seems improbable, not to say ridiculous—but then the histories of these pious do-gooders emerge. Each life—particularly that of the seemingly cold and formidable Madame de La Chanterie—is a study in horror: we discover a daughter, for instance, who is executed, and who has written post-dated letters to her mother in prison to make her believe that she is alive. Each has come to this place in Paris and to this faith only after these horrors, and it is the hero Godefroid's initiation into this history, the "back story" as a modern screenwriter would call it, that gives the book its meaning.

Throughout Balzac, this melodramatic sense of background and foreground is essential, and in this book, though it lacks the world-devouring urban scene of *Père Goriot* or *A Harlot High and Low*, much less *Lost Illusions*, still has a dignity of its own that comes from the paring down of the Balzacian question: How do we live decently in a world without decency? Balzac would become a regular little God of the Action Française, the reactionary royalists who did so much harm to the French Republic in the 1930s, but their reactionary Catholic royalism was rooted more in acts of vengeance than inconspicuous charity: we'll get the bad guys. Balzac's imagination was still stirred—as in life, he perhaps never was—by the idea of inconspicuous urban charity. We may (I at least, don't) quite believe in the goody-goodness of this little house on the Seine, but if we are sensitive at all, we must feel some empathy with Godefroid's feelings about it—his belief that a higher calling rests not outside the city but within it, and the way forward may lie in burrowing in the city, and we may come to admire the romance and glamour of this depiction of the secret life of the good within the city.

The oldest spiritual opposition is of the City and the Garden, the rural retreat and urban corruption. But Balzac proposes that you can only remake bourgeois society from inside: the solution to the sins of Paris can only be found in Paris. If our hearts quicken more in the presence of Balzac's immoral and evil characters, we still have to be at least a little stirred by his commitment to realizing some idea of goodness. "While the ignorant and foolish fretted and chafed and made their usual uproar"—Dickens escorts Dorrit out of the Marshalsea with those words, and that image—of the quiet good people going on with their lives amid the madness of the modern city—was as important and moving an image to the mid-nineteenth century as the idea of escape from the city into a pastoral surrounding had been a hundred years before. It is typical of Balzac's appetite that he would actually have tried to imagine, rather than just imply with a gesture, what such a life would be like, and even if his imagination cannot quite persuade us of the tangible possibility of his good people, the emotion that produces it stays with us even if we are not Catholic reactionaries, or, for that matter, particularly nice ourselves.

I have mentioned Grandville as being a true contemporary of Balzac's in his marriage of satire and surrealist-seeming fantasy. Yet in Balzac, the evident "surrealism" is always in tension with his social observation, and in this way, we may finally find the right parallel for his work not in the work of his time but of ours. His situation, and the art he produces, finally reminds us most urgently of the late-twentieth-century South American writers García Márquez, Vargas Llosa, and even Borges—all those other masters in whose work folktale and the modern novel and outright fantasy coexist in a way that seems to mirror the condition of their countries and people better than a narrowly realist novel ever could. For Balzac's circumstances anticipate theirs. A South American reader and writer, a Chilean or Peruvian audience, knows just what it feels like to pass, in the compass of thirty years, from middle-class security to the ravages of a fascist dictatorship through a communist insurrection, only to return to middle-class comfort at the end—this kind of kaleidoscope of constant change and insecurity was the common experience of Balzac's first audience, too. Balzac shares with the great Latin American writers the constant sense that *anything can happen,* anything at all, and, like them, only long before, he grasped that the right novel for a society in which anything can happen is one in which any style might contain the truth. The sudden switches from plain tale to folktale, from the credible to the frankly incredible—all of this makes Balzac closer to the late modern novelist than he is even to the most gifted of his contemporaries. Balzac himself knows how much is ridiculous in what he is writing, but he still makes it plausible. Its plausibility depends on the larger implausibility of the experience of his audience. Balzac wrote in a time, and for a public, which had been made and scarred by the free play of possibility—by the force of romantic ideas. His art is a tribute to the power of a romantic imagination to go wild and still be sane, and he remains for us the first, and far from the least magical, of all the magic realists.

—

ADAM GOPNIK is the author of *Paris to the Moon.* He writes often on various subjects for *The New Yorker.*

TRANSLATOR'S PREFACE

Jordan Stump

Wander into the fiction aisles of any moderately sizable public library in this country and you will almost certainly find at least one imposing set of matched volumes bearing the enticing title *The Human Comedy* and a date from the late nineteenth or early twentieth century. A kind of melancholy may descend over you as you gaze on that neat, often unbroken row of spines, embossed and gilded in high Victorian style; you may for instance fall into a wistful nostalgia for an age when librarians in Lima, Ohio, or Lincoln, Nebraska, thought it worthwhile (and found it possible) to invest in the almost complete works of a still relatively recent foreign author, when at least two publishing houses believed it would be profitable to have those works translated into English, when Balzac's very French tales could safely be counted on to arouse such considerable interest so far from Paris. Now glance at the nearby shelves, and your eye will no doubt light on an extensive array of more recent translations—renderings not of the entire *Human Comedy* but of individual novels from that collection, *Louis Lambert*, perhaps, or *Lost Illusions*—which may cause you to muse that, not only for authors but also for translators and even for readers, the days of the monumental undertaking are over, vanished with the sort of leisurely and reflective life that is a prerequisite for all vast labors. You may notice, too, that these individual volumes show signs of much more frequent use than the complete collections, more recent readings, a much livelier existence. In short, those aged matching sets will very probably strike you as the physical manifestation of something lost, something slowly but ineluctably fading from visibility, relics from a dusty past—still present, of course, there on the shelves before you, but nonetheless mute and unnoticed amid the clamoring masses of fresher books that surround them. You may even find yourself reflecting on the lives of the little band of translators who, alone or in concert, produced those rows of matching volumes: Katharine Prescott Wormeley, for instance, or Clara Bell and Ellen Marriage, all long since disappeared from this earth, along with the joys and torments they must have felt as they toiled away; today, their very work seems to be disappearing, increasingly superseded by the labors of later generations. Now look through the titles that make up those collections; some, such as *Father Goriot* or *Eugénie Grandet*, will of course be instantly familiar, but you may discover a great many others that mean nothing to you, *Ferragus* or *Jesus Christ in Flanders*, and you may find yourself reflecting that these less celebrated elements of Balzac's oeuvre seem themselves to have been cast into shadow by the glittering renown of the titles around them, and you may once again feel a little regretful to see them sitting there on their shelves, silently telling their stories, unseen and unheard by the passing crowd. Page through a few of these lesser-known volumes, and at some point you will come across a curious little book translated as *The Seamy Side of History* or *The Brotherhood of Consolation*: a novel of half-vanished people living extraordinary lives unbeknownst to those around them, engaged in great and arduous works of good-heartedness that society will never see, lost in secret sorrows that their world has in one way or another chosen to ignore, a novel of forgotten existences and unacknowledged virtues. This is the book that I found one day on just such a dusty shelf, under its original title of *L'Envers de l'histoire contemporaine*; I now offer it to you in my own translation, as *The Wrong Side of Paris*, with an enthusiastic urging that you consider it more closely than it has been considered so far.

I do not have specific figures to back up this claim, but I would venture to guess that *L'Envers de l'histoire contemporaine* must be among the least read of Balzac's books. In every way, it seems almost to have been fated from the beginning to occupy a position outside the mainstream of *The Human Comedy*. This was the last novel Balzac completed for his great, unfinished project, but we may assume that its completion involved some considerable difficulty or hesitation, if the chronology of its genesis is any guide: the first half, "Madame de La Chanterie," was finished and published in serial form in 1845, but another three years elapsed before work was begun—and hastily concluded—on Part 2, "The Initiate." Two years after that Balzac was dead, and still the work's two halves had never appeared under a single title; only in 1854, after a delay caused by the precarious financial state of French publishers in the wake of the 1848 revolution, did *L'Envers de l'histoire contemporaine* see the light of day. Balzac had long planned this as the last volume of the "Scenes of Parisian Life" subsection of *The Human Comedy*, so as to end that bemused portrait of a deeply cynical society on a note of celestial purity and selflessness; by the time he began work on the second half of this culminating novel, however, he found himself in declining health and, far worse, stricken by the sense that his talent was deserting him—an impression echoed in the dismissive, even disdainful reception the novel was given in the French press. The intervening years have done little to better its lot; its sole English translations to date are those found in the dusty, long out-of-print collections just alluded to, and it has garnered only a sporadic and desultory sort of attention from the academic community (the Modern Language Association's bibliography of scholarly literary criticism lists nine printed references to it since 1981). There is no way around it: this is a book that has long proven easy to ignore.

So much for the objective facts of this novel's relative obscurity, which in all subjectivity I find both incomprehensible and unjust. I confess that I had never heard of *L'Envers de l'histoire contemporaine* before I first came across it in the fall of 2001; from the first moments of that first reading, however, I found myself fascinated and entranced, and that pleasure has not faded since. I still wonder at the cunning narrative structure Balzac erects in this text, and the perfect coherence that lies behind its apparently disordered surface: two equal halves telling two very different stories, revolving around two very different sorts of Parisian boardinghouses that mirror each other in subtle and intriguing ways, each with its own secret life, its own taboos, its own rather unlikely potential love interest for poor Godefroid, the young protagonist. I admire the way the focus of the novel's attention is continually shifted away from Godefroid and toward those around him, a narrative strategy that is also an ethical or philosophical stance intimately bound up with the message the novel seeks to convey. I delight in the familiar little emblems of modern existence that occasionally flash into view in this distant early-nineteenth-century world (herbal medicine, the specter of communism, the grumbling of an unhappy investor checking the interest rate in the morning paper as he sips his cup of coffee) and marvel at the profoundly odd atmosphere—almost Gothic, almost even Expressionist—that overtakes the novel in its second half. I enjoy the absolute sincerity and seriousness—but also the verve and the playfulness—of the voice that recounts these extraordinary events. And, not least, without sharing in any way Balzac's political and religious sensibilities, I cannot help but be moved by the blissful refusal of cynicism that emerges from this dark and twisted tale, and by the novel's unquestioning faith in the virtue and power of goodness, compassion, and forgiveness.

In short, from the beginning I was in every way charmed by this book, mystified that it should so long have remained a forgotten dark corner of Balzac's bright tapestry, and unwilling to see it languish any longer as a relic known only to specialists, and—to be frank about it—eager to possess it in the way that only a translator can. (This is a translator's guiltiest secret: we, or at least I, translate not simply out of a sense of devotion to the text but also for the pleasure of possessing it, a pleasure that reading alone can never quite match.)

I realize, of course, that to offer a new translation of this novel is in some sense to wrest it from the hands of its previous translators, and I do so not without regret. I have only respect and admiration for the work done by my predecessors so long ago, but the fact is that the two existing translations, whatever their qualities may be, are not really ideal renderings of the original. They strike me as less alive than Balzac's novel, less sternly exuberant, and considerably less readable—

and that, I think, is a wrong crying out to be righted, for, more than anything else, this is a wonderfully exciting, eccentric, and intriguing novel, and deserves to be made available as such to the American public. Those are the qualities that first compelled me to translate it, and I have done all I could to carry them through into my own version. From one point of view, *The Wrong Side of Paris* is a part of a much larger whole, *The Human Comedy;* from another, it is a representative of a vast literary movement, Realism; but from a third, it is simply a novel, and a marvelous novel, and it is as that that I have attempted to translate it. This is no doubt the moment to confess that I am not a scholar of Balzac, or of nineteenth-century fiction in general; my own training and tastes tend more toward contemporary writing. Thus, my translation is not a specialist's translation. It is the work of an enthusiastic reader of novels, and intended for others of the same persuasion, offered in the hope that they will find in it the same pleasures as I found in the original: a gripping and complicated story, remarkably intense characters, a series of haunting images memorably expressed, a little world both strange and familiar, and a notion of human goodness impervious to easy cynicism.

Or, to put it a bit more strongly, I hope that this volume will offer its readers the same pleasure I found in translating it. One remarkable quality of Balzac's voice is its distinctive intermingling of density, detail, and liveliness, to which, in this novel more than in some others, is conjoined a kind of somber gravity that verges unashamedly on the grandiose, even the melodramatic. I feel a great affection for that voice, and I find its translation peculiarly invigorating, which is not to say easy. Let me cite just one example, but not a minor example, of the difficulties Balzac presented me: the problem of the title. *L'Envers de l'histoire contemporaine* might be directly translated as "The Underside of Contemporary History." The "contemporary history" in question is that of the turbulent years just after the Revolution, but it also refers, I think, to the Paris of the 1830s, the setting of the novel's present tense. As for "underside," it should be understood literally as the tail side of a coin or the back side of a piece of fabric (often called the wrong side) and metaphorically as a reference to the revealing of a whole series of hidden stories, one involving the tragic events of

Madame de La Chanterie's past, another the mysterious association that she now oversees, another the hidden, secretive existence led by Vanda's family, still another the very different sort of seclusion suffered (or perhaps enjoyed) by Vanda herself. A remarkably complex and eloquent little phrase then, and one difficult to render naturally in English. Clara Bell's title, *The Seamy Side of History*, is a neat formulation but a slightly deceptive one, most particularly because *seamy*, although an irreproachable choice in its literal sense, nevertheless has connotations of sordidness that are not entirely suitable here. Katharine Prescott Wormeley chooses to call her version *The Brotherhood of Consolation*, a fine title in itself but one that implicitly reduces the novel's complex interweaving of multiple tales to one single story. Mind you, I could not do better myself; I owe this translation's title to David Ebershoff at the Modern Library, who to my delight and relief came up with a euphonious little phrase that is as rich as Balzac's, and endowed with as many multiple senses, which I will allow the reader to unravel for him- or herself. I will say only that I find it a wonderfully adept solution, for which I am genuinely grateful.

Let me conclude by citing a number of other friends and fellow readers without whom this translation could never have been what it is. I am happily indebted to MJ Devaney, for her confidence and encouragement; to Judy Sternlight, for her enthusiastic guidance; to Susan M. S. Brown, for her excellent copyediting; and most of all, as always, to Eleanor Hardin, for her patience, her lucidity, and her keen and discriminating ear. There are still others I would dearly love to thank but to whom circumstances prevent me from expressing my gratitude directly. Nevertheless, for whatever it may be worth, I'll attempt to do so here: thanks, then, to Honoré de Balzac, for having offered me the great pleasure of reading and of translating this novel, and thanks especially to any reader who might one day come across this volume on a shelf somewhere, pick it up, and find it as fascinating as I have.

THE
WRONG SIDE
OF PARIS

FIRST EPISODE

MADAME DE
LA CHANTERIE

One fine September evening in the year 1836, a man of about thirty stood hunched over the parapet of a quay by the Seine. Facing upstream, he could survey the riverbanks from the Jardin des Plantes to Notre-Dame; downstream, his gaze followed the water's majestic course all the way to the Louvre. There is not another such prospect in all the Capital of Ideas. Standing here on the Île de la Cité, one imagines oneself in the stern of some sea vessel grown to colossal proportions. The view summons up dreams of Paris, the Paris of the Romans and the Franks, of the Normans and the Burgundians; the Paris of the Middle Ages, the Valois, Henri IV and Louis XIV, Napoleon and Louis-Philippe. Each of these regimes has left some mark or monument hereabouts, insistently recalling its creators to the observer's mind. Sainte Geneviève watches over the Latin Quarter, spread out beneath her dome. Behind you rises the magnificent apse of the cathedral. The Hôtel de Ville speaks to you of Paris's many upheavals, the Hôtel-Dieu of her many miseries. From here you can glimpse the splendors of the Louvre; now take two steps and you will have before you that wretched huddle of houses between the Quai de la Tournelle and the Hôtel-Dieu, toward whose disappearance the city fathers are working even now.

Another edifying sight graced that wondrous tableau in those days: between the cathedral and the Parisian at his parapet, the Terrain, for such was the name of that deserted plot of land in times past, was still strewn with the ruins of the archbishop's palace. Standing where the Parisian now stood, contemplating this inspiring prospect, with Paris's past and present laid out together before your admiring gaze, you might think that Religion had chosen to settle on this island in order to reach out toward the sorrows of both banks of the Seine, from the Faubourg Saint-Antoine to the Faubourg Saint-Marceau. We can only hope that a setting so sublimely harmonious will one day be made complete by the construction of an episcopal palace in pure Gothic style, replacing the drab hovels now enclosed by the Terrain, the Rue d'Arcole, the cathedral, and the Quai de la Cité.

This, the very heart of old Paris, is the city's loneliest and most melancholy spot. The waters of the Seine clap against the quay, shrouded in the long shadows of the cathedral as the sun sinks in the west. Such a setting gives rise to serious thoughts, particularly for one in the grips of a spiritual affliction. No doubt fascinated by the sympathetic harmony of his private preoccupations and the thoughts awakened by this panorama, the stroller stood with his hands on the parapet, lost in a twofold contemplation: of Paris, and of himself! The shadows grew longer, lights flickered to life in the distance, and still he stood motionless, caught up in a meditation pregnant with thoughts of the future, made solemn by the presence of the past.

It was then that he noted two figures approaching, their voices wafting to his ear from the stone bridge that links the Île de la Cité to the Quai de la Tournelle. No doubt they thought themselves quite alone, for they would never have spoken so loudly in a more frequented spot, nor if they were aware of a stranger standing close by. The voices from the bridge betokened a discussion which—from the few words reaching the ear of the involuntary witness—clearly involved a loan of money. As they drew nearer, one of the two men, dressed in the fashion of a worker, abruptly stalked off as if in despair. The other whirled around, calling the worker back to him, and said, "You haven't even a *sou* to pay the bridge toll." Handing him a coin, he added, "Take this, and remember, my friend, that it is God Himself who is speaking to us when virtuous thoughts come into our minds!"

The meditative Parisian gave a sudden start on hearing these last few words. Their speaker could not have known that his maxim had, as they say, killed two birds with one stone, that he had thereby addressed two separate miseries at once: on the one hand the despair of a defeated schemer, on the other the sufferings of a soul adrift; one a victim of what Panurge's sheep call Progress, the other of what France calls Equality. These words, so simple in themselves, were made great by the speaker's intonation, for his voice possessed a sort of mesmerizing charm. Are there not certain voices, calm and gentle, that strike the ear much as the color ultramarine the eye?

A glance at this stranger told the Parisian he was a man of the cloth; in the last glimmers of the setting sun he made out a pale face, noble but careworn. The mere sight of a priest emerging from the beautiful Saint Stephen's Cathedral in Vienna, on his way to give extreme unction to a dying man, was enough to bring the celebrated tragic author Werner to Catholicism. The Parisian was not far from a similar transformation as he gazed at the one who had unknowingly offered him solace; against the threatening horizon of his future, he glimpsed a long ray of light shot through with the blue of the ether, and he followed that gleam just as the shepherds in the Scriptures pursued the voice crying to them from on high: "The Savior is born!" The speaker of the healing words was now walking along the cathedral's northern flank, heading—purely by chance, which is sometimes no inconsequential thing—toward the very street that had brought the wandering Parisian to this place, a street to which he would now return, lured ever onward by the many missteps of his life.

This wanderer went by the name of Godefroid. The reader of our story will soon understand why its actors must be referred to by their Christian names alone. Now, here is why Godefroid, who lived near the Chaussée d'Antin, happened to find himself by the apse of Notre-Dame at this hour.

The son of a shopkeeper whose frugality had earned him a sort of fortune, he was the sole vessel for his parents' ambition, which was to see him one day made a *notaire* in Paris. Thus, at the age of seven, he was placed into Father Liautard's academy, along with the scions of many distinguished families, who chose to educate their sons in this establishment out of devotion to a religion too widely ignored in the public schools of the Emperor's reign. Among his school friends he remained blissfully unaware of the notion of social inequality; but in 1821, his studies at an end, Godefroid was placed in a *notaire*'s office, and here he realized how great was the gulf between himself and those with whom he had once lived so familiarly.

Forced into the study of law, he found himself submerged in a vast herd of bourgeois youth, who, with neither fortune nor hereditary distinction to their names, have no choice but to place their faith solely in personal merit or tireless work. His father and mother, now retired from business, conferred all their aspirations on Godefroid, encouraging his self-confidence but preserving him from vanity. His parents lived simply, like Dutch folk, spending only a quarter of their twelve-thousand-franc yearly revenue; the money thus saved, along with half of their capital, would be used to purchase a situation for their son. Oppressed by the laws of this domestic economy, and finding his present circumstances so distant from his parents' dreams and his own, Godefroid lost heart. Among those of weak temperament, disheartenment soon gives way to envy. His fellows, for whom need, tenacity, or diligence took the place of natural talent, marched resolutely ahead down the path of bourgeois ambition; but Godefroid rebelled, yearned to stand out, to shine. Wherever things were bright and glittering, there he was inexorably drawn, but the light only hurt his eyes. He strove to reach the pinnacles; his efforts brought him nothing more than the revelation of his own inadequacy. Recognizing at last that his station would never match his desires, he conceived a hatred for social hierarchies, remade himself in the guise of a Liberal, and sought celebrity through the authorship of a book. But at his own expense he came to see Talent in the same light as Nobility. Having aspired successively to a career as a *notaire*, an attorney, and an author, and having each time met with the same disappointment, he finally resigned himself to a life in the magistracy.

It was then that his father died. His mother, in her old age, found she could easily survive on two thousand francs per annum and so ceded virtually the whole of the family fortune to him. Endowed at age twenty-five with an annual revenue of ten thousand francs, Godefroid thought himself rich, and so he was, compared with his younger days. His existence thus far had been composed of acts without will, of longings without consequence; but now, hoping to take his place in the world at last, to act, to play a part, he set out to find his way into some serious field of endeavor with the help of his newfound fortune. He first thought of journalism, whose arms are always open to anyone possessed of a bit of capital. To own a newspaper is to be an important figure, one who lives off his fellows' intelligence, sharing in its fruits while assuming none of its labors. Nothing is so tempting to an inferior mind as this possibility of rising on the talent of others. Paris has known two or three parvenus of this ilk, and their success is a disgrace both to our times and to those who lent them the strength of their shoulders.

But here too, through the crude machinations of some, the prodigality of others, the wealth of his rival capitalists, the caprices of his editors, Godefroid was once again undone. At the same time, he was dragged into the many compromises of literary or political life, the habit of jeering from the sidelines, the endless distractions required by men whose intellects are never allowed to rest. He thus found himself in bad company, but at least he learned that he had an insignificant face, and one shoulder greater than the other, and no unusual gift for ruthlessness or special generosity of spirit to compensate for those flaws. The right to be rude is the salary that artists exact for telling the truth.

Short, ill-formed, with neither wit nor direction, our young man had little to hope for in an age when the finest mind has no chance of success without the concurrence of good fortune, or the sort of doggedness that makes its own luck.

The Revolution of 1830 came as a balm to Godefroid's wounds; his hopes for the future renewed, he took heart—for courage can be born of hope no less than of despair—and, like so many other obscure journalists, found his way into an administrative post. But, confronted with the exigencies of a new political regime, his liberal ideals made of him a rebellious instrument; deeply committed to liberalism, he found he could not simply adapt his beliefs to suit his new circumstances, as so many superior men have done. Obedience to ministers he thought an abandonment of his principles. Worse yet, the new government seemed to be breaching the rules set out at its creation. Godefroid declared himself for the Party of Movement just as the Party of Resistance was in the ascendant, and he returned to Paris very nearly a poor man, but still faithful to the doctrines of the Opposition.

Frightened by the unbridled ways of the Press, more frightened still by the violence of the Republicans, he saw retirement from the world as his only choice, as the only existence suited to a man of imperfect faculties, too frail to withstand the jolts and shudders of political life, a man whose struggles and sufferings had produced not the slightest spark, wearied by a succession of abortive endeavors, without friends because friendship requires distinctive qualities or flaws, possessed of a nature given more to dreams than to profundities. Was this not the only course for a young man so often deceived by this world's pleasures, a young man grown old from too much contact with a society as unsettling as it was unsettled?

His mother now called her son back to the peaceful village of Auteuil, where she was living out her final days. To be sure, she wanted him at her side; but at the same time, she hoped to set him on a path toward the simple, uneventful happiness that a soul such as his must require. She had taken stock of Godefroid, finding him at twenty-eight years of age with a fortune reduced to 4,000 francs interest income per year, his dreams withered, his potential come to nothing, his energies stilled, his ambition humiliated, and his hatred for any other's legitimate success grown all the more bitter for his own failures. She hoped to marry Godefroid to an eligible young person, the only daughter of two retired shopkeepers, who might serve as a nursemaid for his diseased soul; but the girl's father's many years in trade had given him a calculating turn of mind, which he made no attempt to quell for the business of matrimony. After a year of frequent visits and careful cultivation of the prospective in-laws, Godefroid was finally turned away. For one thing, these thoroughly bourgeois parents were convinced that his former livelihood had led him into the depths of turpitude, from which he had likely not yet emerged; for another, he had once again dipped into his capital over the course of that year, as much to bedazzle the parents as to charm the daughter. This display of vanity—quite understandable, let it be said—ensured Godefroid's dismissal by the girl's family, who in their pious hatred of dissipation were profoundly shocked to learn that his capital had shrunk by 150,000 francs in six years.

To make this blow all the more painful for his bruised and battered heart, the girl was not even beautiful. Nevertheless, under his mother's tutelage, Godefroid had come to recognize in his intended the merit of a serious soul and the immense advantages of a well-formed mind; he had grown used to her face, he had studied her physiognomy, he liked her voice, her ways, the look in her eyes. He had risked his life's final stake on this liaison, and now he succumbed to the most bitter despair. His mother died, and he found himself—he whose desires had always followed the currents of fashion—with no fortune to his name but an annual revenue of five thousand francs; worse yet, he knew he would never recover any future losses he might incur, finding himself simply incapable of the activity implied in that terrible phrase *earning one's fortune!*

This morose, restless inertia is not an affliction to be cured overnight. Thus, still in mourning, Godefroid returned to Paris in hopes of meeting with some happy stroke of luck: he dined in public restaurants, he struck up reckless alliances with total strangers, he sought out the company of his fellows, but he found only further occasions for expense. As he went strolling along the boulevards, his inner torment was such that the sight of a mother accompanied by a daughter of marriageable age filled him with intimate pain, and he suffered a similar pang each time he spied a young man on horseback riding toward the Bois de Boulogne, or a parvenu in his elegant finery, or a civil servant with a decoration on his breast. His sense of his own impotence told him that he could aspire neither to the most blandly respectable of subordinate posts nor to the most mediocre and untaxing sort of Destiny; and he had enough will to be continually aggrieved by this, and enough wit to pour out his rage in private elegies of the most bilious character.

Ill-equipped to struggle against the world, imbued with a sense of untapped powers but without the energy required to set them in motion, feeling himself incomplete, too feeble for great undertakings, powerless to combat the tastes dictated by his former life, his education, or his heedlessness, he was devoured by three illnesses at once, any one of which would have been enough to inspire a deep loathing for existence in a young man grown distant from religious faith. Thus, Godefroid showed the world a face so prevalent in our society that it has become the very emblem of the Parisian: a face scarred by traces of failed or exhausted ambition, of inner poverty, of disgust kept in abeyance by the distraction of the city's superficial daily spectacle, of satiety forever desperate for new sensations, of complaint without talent, of forced vitality; a face scarred by the sting of disillusion, whose venom compels its victims to smile on any mockery, to sneer at any greatness, to mistrust the most necessary powers, to rejoice in their difficulties, and to disdain all civility. This Parisian illness is to the active and relentless conspiring of people of energy as a tree's sapwood is to its sap; it protects it, feeds it, and conceals it from view.

One morning, wearying of himself, Godefroid sought to give some direction to his life by renewing his acquaintance with an old friend who, in the terms of La Fontaine's fable, had played the tortoise to his hare. In the course of one of those conversations ensuing from the reunion of two schoolmates, pursued during a sunlit stroll down the Boulevard des Italiens, he was crushed to learn of the glittering successes of a boy who, by all appearances endowed with fewer aptitudes and a lesser fortune than he, had simply begun to desire every morning precisely what he desired the night before. The dejected Godefroid vowed to emulate his friend's single-mindedness.

"Society is like the Earth itself," his friend had told him. "It provides for us in direct proportion to the efforts we put forth."

Godefroid had now fallen into debt. As a first step toward redemption, he assigned himself the task of withdrawing from society, of living quietly and saving enough from his yearly revenue to repay his obligations. For one accustomed to spending six thousand francs when he has five to his name, learning to make do with two thousand is no small undertaking. Every morning he read the private notices in the newspaper, hoping to find some retreat where his expenses could be fixed at an unvarying rate, and where he might find the solitude necessary for one yearning to look deep into his own soul, to examine himself, to find a calling. The way of life in the private boardinghouses of the Latin Quarter shocked his delicate sensibilities, the atmosphere of a convalescent home struck him as insalubrious, and he was about to sink once more into the fatal indecision of the man without will when he came across the following advertisement:

To let, a small apartment, seventy francs per month, suitable for a clergyman. A lodger of quiet habits is desired; full board will be offered, and the apartment may be furnished for a moderate price should the arrangement prove mutually satisfactory.

INQUIRE AT THE GROCERY OF MONSIEUR MILLET, ON THE RUE CHA-
NOINESSE NEAR NOTRE-DAME; HE WILL PROVIDE ALL NECESSARY PAR-
TICULARS.

Charmed by the warmth faintly discernible beneath this text, and by
its perfume of bourgeois respectability, Godefroid appeared at the
grocer's door around four o'clock that afternoon. He was told that
Madame de La Chanterie regularly dined at this hour and received no
visitors while she was at table. She could be seen in the evening after
seven o'clock, or in the morning from ten to noon. Monsieur Millet
closely scrutinized Godefroid as he spoke, submitting him to what is
known in juridical parlance as a first-degree interrogation. Was Monsieur a bachelor? Madame wanted a person of orderly habits; the
doors were locked no later than eleven o'clock. "Monsieur," he said by
way of conclusion, "seems of an age that might suit Madame de La
Chanterie."

"And what age do you take me to be?" asked Godefroid.

"Something like forty, I should say," the grocer replied.

This naïve response threw Godefroid into a fit of misanthropic
chagrin; he trudged off to dine on the Quai de la Tournelle, then returned to contemplate Notre-Dame as the last gleams of the setting
sun flooded over the stone, its beams filtering through the flying but-
tresses. At that hour, the towers stand resplendent in their halo of light
while the quay is plunged in shadow, a contrast by which Godefroid
was greatly struck as he ruminated the bitter thoughts stirred up by
the grocer's unwitting cruelty.

This young man thus found himself adrift, between the dark voice
of despair and the moving, sacred harmonies of the cathedral bell. It
was then, surrounded by silence, shadows, and the light of the rising
moon, that he heard the priest's words. Like most children of this century, he was little inclined to religious sentiment; nevertheless, something in this sentence struck a chord inside him, and so at once he
turned and set off toward the Rue Chanoinesse, where he had already
resolved never to set foot again.

To their mutual surprise, Godefroid and the priest turned together
into the Rue Massillon, which starts off from the cathedral's small

northern portal, and then, still together, into the Rue Chanoinesse, where it becomes the Rue des Marmousets as it runs on toward the Rue de la Colombe. Seeing Godefroid stop at the vaulted porch of Madame de La Chanterie's house, the priest turned and examined the young man by the light of a lamp that will no doubt be one of the last to disappear from the heart of old Paris.

"Have you come to see Madame de La Chanterie, Monsieur?" asked the priest.

"Yes," Godefroid answered. "Your words to that worker have shown me that this house must be a place salutary to the soul, if this is indeed where you live."

"Then you witnessed my defeat?" asked the priest as he lifted the knocker. "For I did not succeed."

"I would have thought it was the worker who did not succeed. He seemed most desperate for a loan."

"Alas!" the priest answered. "One of the greatest evils of our revolutions in France is that each serves as fresh encouragement to the ambition of the inferior classes. Hoping to improve his circumstances, striving for wealth—all too widely considered the only security to be had nowadays—he spends his days hatching ludicrous schemes, which, should they go awry, will surely bring him up before a court of law. This is what indulgence sometimes leads to."

The porter opened a heavy door, and the priest asked Godefroid: "Monsieur has perhaps come for the small apartment?"

"I have, Monsieur."

The priest and Godefroid then passed through a rather large courtyard, at the far end of which rose the dark form of a tall house flanked with a remarkably ancient square tower, rising even higher than the roof. As anyone who knows the history of Paris will tell you, the level of the pavement has risen to such an extent before and around the cathedral that no trace remains of the twelve steps churchgoers once climbed to enter it. Today the base of the porch columns sits level with the paving stones. Thus, what was once this house's ground floor must today form its cellar. Two or three steps lead to the tower's entrance; inside, an old spiral staircase winds around a central shaft carved to resemble a climbing vine, in a style dating back to the fourteenth century, reminiscent of the Louis XII staircases at the Château of Blois. Impressed by a thousand marks of antiquity, Godefroid could not help but say to the priest, with a smile, "This tower wasn't built yesterday."

"It is said to have survived the assaults of the Normans, and may have been part of the first palace of the kings of Paris; but a more credible tradition holds that it was the abode of the great Canon Fulbert, the uncle of Héloïse."

With this the priest opened the door of an apartment on what seemed the ground floor but was in fact the second; its windows opened onto the courtyard they had just crossed as well as a smaller interior court.

They entered to find a maidservant working by the light of a small lamp, her simple dress enlivened only by a cambric bonnet with embossed flutes. She thrust a needle into her hair, and with her knitting still in her hand she rose to open the door of a drawing room giving onto the interior courtyard. Her dress was not unlike the habit of the Sisters of Charity.

"Madame, I have brought you a tenant," said the priest, ushering Godefroid into the second room, where the young man found three seated figures; in the center of that small circle of armchairs sat Madame de La Chanterie herself.

These three arose, as did the mistress of the house; then the priest pulled up a chair for Godefroid, and Madame de La Chanterie motioned her future tenant to sit down, accompanying this gesture with the dated expression "Pray be seated, Monsieur!" The Parisian could not help but think himself far from Paris, somewhere in lower Brittany perhaps, or in the Canadian hinterland.

No doubt there are degrees of silence, as there are of sound. Already struck by the silence of the Rue Massillon and the Rue Chanoinesse, where scarcely two carriages pass by in a month, then struck again by the silence of the courtyard and the tower, Godefroid must now have thought himself at the very heart of silence in this drawing room protected from the world outside by so many old streets, old courtyards, and old walls.

This area of the island, known as the Cloister, has preserved the quality common to all cloisters: there is a damp, cold feeling to the place, and it maintains its deep monastic stillness even at the height of the daily bustle. It should also be noted that this entire portion of the Île de la Cité, pressed between Notre-Dame and the river, lies to the north of the cathedral and hence in its shadow. The easterly winds sweep through its streets unobstructed, and the mists rising from the Seine are trapped by the dark wall of the old metropolitan church. Thus, we might easily guess Godefroid's state of mind as he made his way into this ancient dwelling, and into the presence of four silent figures as solemn as the very things that surrounded them. He did not look around him, for his curiosity was fixed on Madame de La Chanterie herself, having been intrigued by her name from the moment he first heard it spoken. She was clearly a person of another century or even, we might say, of another world. She had a bland face, with a complexion at once soft and cold, an aquiline nose, a motherly brow, brown eyes, and a double chin, all framed by curls of silvery hair. Her dress fully merited the archaic name of "sheath," so tightly did it enclose her, in the high style of the eighteenth century. It was fashioned of carmelite-gray silk with long, close-set green stripes, seemingly a relic of that same era. The corseted bodice was concealed beneath a mantilla of paduasoy edged in black lace, and closed over her breast by a pin ornamented with a miniature. Her feet, shod in black velvet boots, rested on a small cushion. Like her servant, Madame de La Chanterie was busy knitting stockings, and a needle was thrust into the crimped curls beneath her lace bonnet.

"Have you seen Monsieur Millet?" she asked Godefroid in the falsetto peculiar to dowagers of the Faubourg Saint-Germain, finding the young man virtually speechless and as if to offer him an opening.

"Yes, Madame."

"I fear the apartment might not suit you," she replied, noting the impeccable elegance and newness of her future tenant's clothing: polished boots, yellow gloves, fine shirt studs, and a pretty watch chain running through the buttonhole of a black silk waistcoat adorned with blue flowers. Madame de La Chanterie took a small whistle from one of her pockets and blew into it. The maidservant entered.

"Manon, my girl, show Monsieur the apartment. And would you be so kind, dear vicar, as to accompany Monsieur?" she went on, speaking to the priest. "If by chance you find the rooms acceptable," she said, rising again and looking at Godefroid, "then we shall discuss the terms."

Godefroid bowed and went out. He heard a metallic jangling as Manon took the keys from a drawer, and he watched her light a candle in a large brass holder. Manon walked wordlessly ahead of him. Climbing the stairs, Godefroid began to doubt the reality of his surroundings; this little world was so like that of the fanciful novels he'd once loved to read that he thought himself lost in some waking dream. Any Parisian who like Godefroid had ventured into this place, so far from his up-to-date neighborhood, from the luxury of his house and furnishings, from the bright lights of the restaurants and theaters, from the bustling heart of the city, would surely have thought likewise. The servant's candlestick dimly lit the curve of the old staircase, veiled by spiderwebs generously bedecked with dust. Manon wore a wide-pleated shift of rough homespun, with a neckline cut square both behind and in front; it hung stiffly, straight as a die, merely swaying a little as she walked. On reaching the fourth floor, which passed for the third, Manon stopped, turned her key in an ancient lock, and opened a door crudely painted to resemble figured mahogany.

"Here it is," she said, entering ahead of him.

Who had lived in these rooms? A miser, perhaps, or a painter now dead of starvation, or a cynic who loathed the society of men, or a churchman withdrawn from the world? Such questions sprang immediately to Godefroid's mind, summoned up by the odor of poverty, the greasy spots on the smoke-tinged wallpaper, the soot-blackened ceilings, the tiny, dust-streaked windowpanes, the brown bricks of the floor, the paneling coated with a sort of sticky glaze. A damp cold emanated from the carved, painted stone of the fireplaces, surmounted by mirrors fixed in overmantels of the seventeenth century. The rooms occupied two sides of this square house, framing the inner courtyard, now shrouded in darkness.

"Who lived in this place?" Godefroid asked the priest.

"A former Councillor to Parliament, Madame's great-uncle, a Monsieur de Boisfrelon. Senile since the time of the Revolution, the old man died in 1832, at the age of ninety-six. Madame could not bear the thought of a stranger occupying his rooms immediately after his death, but neither can she abide a vacant apartment."

"Oh! Madame will have the rooms cleaned and furnished to Monsieur's satisfaction," Manon added.

"That will depend on the manner in which you choose to lay out the apartment," said the priest. "Here you could have a fine parlor, a large bedroom, and a dressing room, and the two smaller chambers around the corner, overlooking the courtyard, would make an admirable study. Such are my own rooms, one floor below, as well as those of the apartment above."

"Yes," said Manon, "Monsieur Alain's apartment is exactly like yours, but he has a view of the tower."

"I believe it might be best to see the rooms and the house again by daylight . . ." said Godefroid, meekly.

"As you wish," said Manon.

The priest and Godefroid descended the stairs, with Manon lighting their way after closing the door behind them. Entering the drawing room again, Godefroid found himself in bolder spirits, and he was able to inspect his surroundings—both human and inanimate—as he spoke with Madame de La Chanterie. The drawing room's windows were hung with draperies of old red damask; a pelmet covered the rod, and silk cords held the curtains in place. An old tapestry rug, too small to cover the entire floor, had been spread over the red tiles. The paneling was painted gray. The fine ceiling, divided into two parts by a central beam emerging from above the fireplace, seemed a concession to luxury installed long after the house's beginnings. The white wooden armchairs bore an upholstering of tapestry. A modest clock stood on the mantelpiece between two torches of gilded brass. Madame de la Chanterie kept her knitting close at hand in a wicker basket on an old table with cabriole legs. All of this was lit by the glow of a hydrostatic lamp.

Sitting perfectly still, silent as Buddhist monks, the little group had clearly broken off their conversation as they heard the stranger's approaching footsteps in the hall. Their faces were discreet and impassive, in perfect harmony with the drawing room, the house, and the neighborhood. Madame de La Chanterie concurred with Godefroid's observations on the state of the apartment and replied that she preferred to make no improvements until she was sure of her tenant's intentions—or, more precisely, her boarder's. For such would he be if he complied with the ways of the household, so unlike the ways of Paris! The denizens of the Rue Chanoinesse lived as if in the heart of the provinces: lodgers were generally expected to return home before ten o'clock; noise was not tolerated; women and children were excluded as potentially upsetting to long-standing habits. Only a churchman could tolerate such conditions. Above all else, Madame de La Chanterie desired a tenant well used to a modest existence, and not too demanding, for she could supply only the absolute essentials to furnish the rooms. Monsieur Alain (she gestured toward one of the four men present) was quite content here, in any case, and she would do for her new tenant precisely as she had done for the old.

"I do not believe Monsieur will be inclined to come and join our monastery," said the priest.

"Why! What makes you say that?" said Monsieur Alain. "We're all very happy here, and we have nothing to complain of."

"Madame," replied Godefroid, arising, "I shall have the honor of calling on you again tomorrow."

In spite of the visitor's youth, Madame de La Chanterie and the others rose to their feet along with him, and the vicar accompanied him to the front steps of the tower. A whistle blast was now heard, and on this signal the porter appeared with a lantern. He saw Godefroid into the street, then closed the huge yellow door behind him, heavy as the front gate of a prison, with fittings of indeterminate age in the form of elaborate arabesques.

Once Godefroid had climbed into a cabriolet and begun to roll toward the other Paris—lively, illuminated, and warm—this entire episode began to seem little more than a dream. Already his strong impressions felt as distant as memories, and as he strolled down the Boulevard des Italiens he could not help but muse, "Tomorrow I will return to that house—but will those people still be there?"

Waking the next day in the cozily up-to-date surroundings of his own apartment, duly appointed with the trappings of what the English call "comfort," Godefroid thought back to his visit to the curious neighborhood known as the Cloister of Notre-Dame, reviewing every detail, and considered the meaning of what he had seen. The four strangers' dress, demeanor, and silence had left a particularly strong impression in his mind; he assumed them to be boarders in Madame de La Chanterie's house, like the priest. As for the lady herself, he sensed that her solemnity had its roots in some great unhappiness, borne with stern and quiet dignity. But no matter how his reason strived to explain the nature of these discreet figures, Godefroid could not help but see their existence as enveloped in some great mystery.

He made a quick inventory of his rooms, choosing the furnishings he would keep for use in his new life, those that seemed indispensable; but when he mentally transported them to the grim surroundings of the Rue Chanoinesse, he laughed out loud at the contrast they would make with their new home, and he resolved to sell it all at once and be done with it. He would leave the furnishing of his rooms to Madame de La Chanterie. It was a new life he yearned for, and any object that might remind him of the old one could only be pernicious to behold. In his desire for transformation—for by nature he was the sort of person who embarks on a new project with one mighty, irreversible leap, rather than proceeding step by step as others do—he found himself consumed by a novel idea, which he turned over and over in his mind all through breakfast: he would liquidate his fortune, pay off his debts, and deposit the rest of his capital with the bankers who had once enjoyed his father's custom.

He was thinking of Mongenod and Company, a Parisian banking house established in 1816 or 1817, whose reputation for uprightness had never once been sullied, even as so many of its competitors succumbed, in one fashion or another, to the corruptions of the world of business. Thus, despite their immense wealth, the Houses of de Nucingen and du Tillet, like the Keller Brothers, like Palma and Company, are besmirched by a secret mistrust—or, if not precisely secret, at least expressed only by word of mouth. To be sure, so glittering is the effect that can be procured by dubious dealings, so immaculately can political success or dynastic power cleanse ignoble origins, that by this time no one gave a second thought to the mud that sustained the roots of those majestic trees, those pillars of the State. Nevertheless, every one of the bankers just named suffered the stab of a secret wound whenever he heard the praises of the House of Mongenod being sung. Like the venerable banks of England, the House of Mongenod displays no exterior finery. It does its business in silence, without publicity, but it pursues its affairs with unfailing prudence, wisdom, and loyalty, and this allows it to conduct its operations in perfect security, from one end of the world to the other.

The sister of Frédéric Mongenod, the current director, is the wife of the Viscount de Fontaine. Thus, by way of the Baron de Fontaine, his family is linked to Monsieur Grossetête, the Receiver-General of his province—and brother to the founder of Grossetête and Company of Limoges—as well as to the Vandenesse family, and to Planat de Baudry, another receiver-general. This kinship, which offered the late Mongenod *père* a very advantageous place in the financial world of the Restoration, had also earned him the confidence of the old nobility's most illustrious families, whose immense fortunes naturally gravitated toward his bank. Unlike the Kellers, the de Nucingens, and the du Tillets, the Mongenods have displayed no longing to enter the Peerage; on the contrary, they have always kept their distance from the world of politics, and they know of it only what a serious banking establishment cannot afford not to know.

The House of Mongenod occupies a magnificent mansion on the Rue de la Victoire, with a courtyard in front and a garden in back. This is also the home of the family matriarch, Madame Mongenod, and her two sons, all three of them equal partners in the enterprise. (As for the Viscountess de Fontaine, she had sold back her interest in the company after her father's death in 1827.) Frédéric Mongenod was then a handsome man of about thirty-five, cool and quiet of demeanor, reserved as a Genevan, dapper as an Englishman, who had inherited from his father all the qualities required for his difficult profession. More learned than the common run of bankers, he was possessed of the universal knowledge that comes with a Polytechnic education; but, like many bankers, he had a special predilection, a favorite fancy outside the world of commerce: he loved mechanics and chemistry. Mongenod the younger, Frédéric's junior by ten years, occupied a position in his elder brother's offices rather like that of a head clerk to a *notaire* or solicitor; Frédéric taught him the ways of the business, just as he himself had learned from his father all the knowledge and discernment a true banker needs. For a good banker is to money as a writer is to ideas: both must know everything.

Godefroid introduced himself by his family name. A moment later, he realized the full extent of the esteem in which his father was held, for he was shown through all the outer offices and straight to the anteroom outside Mongenod's private study. The doors to this study were made of glass; thus, despite his desire not to listen, Godefroid distinctly overheard the conversation taking place within.

"Madame, your account stands at sixteen hundred thousand francs both in credit and in debit," Mongenod the younger was saying. "I cannot say what my brother's intentions may be, and he alone can tell you if an advance of one hundred thousand francs is possible . . . You have been most imprudent . . . Imagine committing sixteen hundred thousand francs to the uncertainties of commerce . . ."

"Too loud, Louis," said a woman's voice. "Your brother has told you before, you must speak softly. There might be someone in the antechamber."

It was then that Frédéric Mongenod opened the door between his private rooms and his study. Catching sight of Godefroid, he came forward to meet him, at the same time offering a respectful greeting to the person with whom his brother was speaking.

"Whom do I have the honor of——" he said to Godefroid, hastily ushering him into his study.

Godefroid gave him his name, and immediately Frédéric gestured toward a chair. As the banker was opening his desk, Louis Mongenod and a woman, who was none other than Madame de La Chanterie, arose and approached Frédéric's chair. These three withdrew to a window alcove, where they were joined by Madame Mongenod *mère*, and together they began to converse in low tones. Madame Mongenod was always consulted in matters of business; for thirty years she had advised both her husband and her sons with such unfailing intelligence that she now served as managing associate, her signature required for every transaction. Looking around him, Godefroid spotted a case full of boxes marked "de La Chanterie account," numbered from one to seven. When the conference had concluded with a word from the banker to his brother—"Well then! Go and see the cashier"—Madame de La Chanterie turned around and caught sight of Godefroid. Holding back a gesture of surprise, she whispered a number of questions to Mongenod, who responded with similar discretion.

Madame de La Chanterie wore small slippers of black prunella and gray silk stockings; her gown was the same as the day before, but her shoulders were wrapped in a Venetian *bauta,* a sort of mantelet then coming back into fashion. On her head she wore a green silk bonnet lined with white, in what is known as the dowager style, with cascades of lace framing her features. She stood very straight, and from her posture one could suppose her to be, if not highborn, at least long accustomed to the aristocratic life. Were it not for her excessive affability, one might well have found her haughty. In short, she cut an imposing figure.

"It is not so much chance as the design of Providence that has brought us together here today, Monsieur," she said to Godefroid, "for I had very nearly made up my mind not to take in a prospective lodger whose manner I thought at odds with the spirit of my house; but Monsieur Mongenod has just revealed certain facts about your family, which I—"

"But, Madame! . . ." the banker interjected.

"Monsieur," said Godefroid, addressing Monsieur Mongenod but at the same time speaking to Madame de La Chanterie, "I have lost my family, and I come here to seek financial counsel from those who were once my father's bankers, in hopes of putting my fortune to good use in a new life."

With a few words, Godefroid gave a summary account of his travails and expressed his desire to make a new start. "Once," he said, "a man in my circumstances would have become a monk; but now that the religious orders have been driven from our land . . ."

"Go and live with Madame, if Madame will consent to take you as her boarder," said Frédéric Mongenod after exchanging a glance with Madame de La Chanterie, "and do not sell your securities; leave them to me. Tell me the precise amount of your obligations; I will see to it that your creditors are repaid in regular installments, and you will have some hundred and fifty francs per month for your own needs. It will take two years to settle your affairs. During that time, you will have ample opportunity to consider the question of a career, surrounded by wise souls with much good advice to offer you."

Louis Mongenod reappeared with a hundred thousand-franc notes, which he presented to Madame de La Chanterie. Godefroid offered his future landlady his arm and walked her outside to her fiacre.

"Well! Then we shall see each other again soon, Monsieur," she said warmly.

"When might I find you at home, Madame?" asked Godefroid.

"In two hours."

"And in the meantime, I will see to selling my furniture," he said with a bow.

Walking arm in arm with Madame de La Chanterie, Godefroid could not stop thinking of the glorious glow cast over her by Louis Mongenod's words, "your account stands at sixteen hundred thousand francs." He had imagined her living a quiet life in the obscure confines of the Cloister of Notre-Dame; but now that single thought—"She must be rich!"—showed her in an entirely new light. "How old might she be?" he wondered. And he began to suspect that the house on the Rue Chanoinesse might hold in store something more intriguing than any novel. "She might very well be noble, by the look of her! Perhaps she is a financier herself?"

In our day, out of a thousand young men in Godefroid's situation, nine hundred and ninety-nine would have resolved to marry her then and there.

A furniture merchant who also dabbled in rugs and most particularly in furnished apartments offered Godefroid some three thousand francs for the pieces he had decided to sell and gave him leave to hold on to them for a few days longer, until the grim apartment on the Rue Chanoinesse had been made livable. The troubled young man now returned to his future lodgings. He summoned a painter recommended by Madame de La Chanterie, who for a reasonable price promised to whiten the ceiling, clean the windows, refresh the color of the floor tiles, and repaint the paneling in the fashion of Spa-wood, all within the week. Godefroid measured the rooms, intending to cover the floors with several identical green rugs of the least expensive sort. He wanted his cell simple and uniform. Madame de La Chanterie approved of this notion. With Manon's help, she calculated the quantity of white calico needed to make draperies for the windows and the modest iron bed; she would see to the purchase of the fabric and the sewing herself, for a fee that Godefroid found extraordinarily reasonable. Including the furniture he would provide, the restoration of his apartment would cost him no more than six hundred francs.

"Which means that I shall deposit some thousand francs with Monsieur Mongenod."

Hearing these words, Madame de La Chanterie turned to him and said, "In this house we lead a Christian life, in which superfluous possessions have no place, as you know. I believe you are keeping too much for yourself."

And as she offered him this advice she stared pointedly at a glittering diamond set into the ring that held Godefroid's blue cravat.

"I tell you this," she went on, "only because I understand it is your intention to break with the dissolute life you complained of to Monsieur Mongenod."

Godefroid gazed at Madame de La Chanterie as she spoke, savoring the harmonies of her limpid voice; he examined that pure white face, every bit the equal of those stern, cold Dutchwomen's faces so skillfully rendered by the Flemish masters, on which wrinkles are an impossibility. "Fair and plump!" he said to himself as he went on his way; "but let us not forget her white hair . . ."

Like all those of weak nature, Godefroid had effortlessly envisioned a new life, sure that it would be a happy one, and he was eager to make the move to the Rue Chanoinesse; nevertheless, he had not entirely abandoned his prudence or, if you prefer, his wariness. Two days before he was to move, he returned to see Monsieur Mongenod, hoping to learn more of the place he would soon call his home. He had spent only a few moments in that house, inspecting the improvements being made to his rooms; but he had not failed to notice the continual comings and goings of figures whose appearance and manner, while not exactly mysterious, nevertheless suggested that some secret business, some specific occupation was practiced within those walls. In those days, it was widely suspected that the House of Bourbon's elder branch might at any moment launch an attempt to retake the throne, and Godefroid wondered if some sort of conspiracy might be afoot in that house. But as he sat in the banker's study, facing that steady, penetrating gaze, he was ashamed of himself for this thought. He watched a slightly mocking smile take shape on Frédéric Mongenod's lips. "The Baroness de La Chanterie is one of the most obscure figures in Paris," he answered, "but also one of the most honorable. Do you have some reason for seeking this information?"

Godefroid sought refuge in banalities: he would soon find himself among strangers with whom he would be living for some time, and it was only right that he know the nature of his new companions, et cetera. But the banker's smile grew ever more sardonic, and Godefroid, increasingly abashed, suffered the shame of his stratagem while enjoying none of its fruits, for he dared pose no further questions concerning Madame de La Chanterie or her housemates.

Two days later, at about ten o'clock on a Monday evening, having dined one last time at the Café Anglais and enjoyed the first two short plays at the Théâtre des Variétés, he appeared at the door of the house on the Rue Chanoinesse, ready for his first night in this new abode. He was received by Manon, who promptly led him up to his rooms.

The charms of solitude might be compared with the pleasures of the savage life, which no European has ever fled once he has tasted of them. This might seem an unlikely proposition in our present age, when we have grown so accustomed to living through others that we think nothing of making their business our own, an age that will soon see the end of all private life, so bold and greedy have the eyes of the Press, that modern Argus, become. Nevertheless, the history of Christianity's first six centuries offers ample confirmation of this truth: Never did any holy hermit of that time choose to return to life in society. There are few psychic wounds that solitude cannot heal; and so, from the moment he entered his new home, Godefroid reveled in its perfect tranquillity and silence, just as a weary traveler delights in the first moments of a warm bath.

Thus, on his first morning at Madame de La Chanterie's house, he was forced to look deep into his own soul, cut off as he was from all he once knew, cut off from Paris itself, even here in the very shadow of the cathedral. Here, stripped of all social vanity, his acts would have no other witness than his own conscience and Madame de La Chanterie's circle of friends. He had left the broad highway of the world and entered an unknown lane; but where would this lane take him? To what sort of occupation would he devote himself?

He had sat lost in these reflections for two hours when Manon, the house's only domestic, knocked at his door to tell him that the midday meal was served, and that the others were awaiting him. The bells were ringing noon. The new boarder hurried down the stairs, anxious to deepen his acquaintance of the five souls among whom he would now live his life. He entered the drawing room to find all the house's inhabitants standing before him, dressed exactly as they were on the evening of his first visit.

"Did you sleep well?" asked Madame de La Chanterie.

"I did not wake before ten o'clock," Godefroid answered, bowing to his four fellow-boarders, who gravely returned his greeting.

"We expected as much," said the old man named Alain, with a smile.

"I understand from Manon that I have missed breakfast," Godefroid went on. "It seems I have already failed to observe the rules . . . At what hour do you arise?"

"Not as early as the monks of old, to be sure," Madame de La Chanterie graciously replied. "Rather, we arise when the workers do . . . at six o'clock in winter, and three-thirty in summer; and our retirement, too, is dictated by the sun: we are always abed by nine o'clock in winter, and eleven o'clock in summer. After our morning prayers, we break our fast with a bit of milk from our farm—all of us except Father de Vèze, that is. He can take no food until he has said the First Mass at Notre-Dame, at six o'clock each day in summer, and seven in winter, which these gentlemen attend without fail, as does your humble servant." Madame de La Chanterie finished this explanation at table, with her five boarders around her.

The dining room was painted all in gray, with paneling that clearly betrayed the tastes of the century of Louis XIV. It adjoined a sort of antechamber set aside for Manon and seemed to run parallel to Madame de La Chanterie's bedroom, which no doubt opened onto the drawing room. An old wall clock was the room's only ornament; it was furnished with two sideboards, six chairs—whose oval backrests bore tapestries evidently fashioned by Madame de La Chanterie's hand—and a mahogany table, which Manon did not cover with a cloth for this midday meal. The repast, of monastic frugality, was composed of a small turbot in white sauce, potatoes, a salad, and four plates of fruit (peaches, grapes, strawberries, and fresh almonds), with an accompaniment of buttered radishes, cucumbers, sardines, and honey served in the comb, as the Swiss do. It was presented on porcelain plates decorated with cornflowers and small green leaves, in a style that must have been the epitome of elegance under Louis XVI but which our age's increasingly refined tastes have rendered perfectly common.

"We are abstaining from meat today," said Monsieur Alain. "You know already that we attend Mass every morning; no doubt you have guessed that we comply just as faithfully with every one of the Church's prescriptions, no matter how severe."

"And you will begin your new life by doing as we do," said Madame de La Chanterie glancing sideways at Godefroid, whom she had seated next to her.

Of his five tablemates, Godefroid already knew the names of Madame de La Chanterie, Father de Vèze, and Monsieur Alain; but to the others he had not been formally introduced. These two figures ate their meal in silence, with the sort of grave attention that monks often devote to the food set before them.

"Does this beautiful fruit also come from your farm, Madame?" asked Godefroid.

"Yes, Monsieur," she said. "We have our own little model farm, exactly like the Government, and a country house, near Villeneuve Saint-Georges, some three leagues from here by the Route d'Italie."

"It is our common property, and will be left to whomever of us survives the others," said the aged Alain.

"Oh! but it is not a very large farm," added Madame de La Chanterie, apparently anxious that Godefroid might take these words as an enticement to join their coterie.

"There are thirty *arpents* of cropland and six *arpents* of pastures," interjected one of the two strangers, "and a house behind the farm buildings, with a four-*arpent* yard."

"But a property like that must be worth more than a hundred thousand francs," Godefroid answered.

"Oh! To us it is only a source of fresh food," the stranger replied.

He was a man of stern appearance, lean and tall. His demeanor was that of an old soldier; his white hair placed his age at something over sixty, and in his face could be read a long history of violent anguish, kept in check by religious faith.

The second stranger, in whom the characteristic traits of the rhetoric master and the businessman were united, was a man of average size, portly but nonetheless brisk, with a face that radiated the sort of joviality peculiar to Parisian *notaires* and solicitors.

Their dress had the impeccable tidiness that comes only with monomaniacal care and maintenance; in the smallest details of their clothing one could recognize the work of one single hand, that of Manon. Their garments were perhaps ten years old, and had withstood the passage of time by the same means as a curate's habit: the occult power of the serving woman and of constant use. They wore the uniform of a certain way of life, we might say, for they had all given themselves over to one single notion; the same word could be read in each of their gazes, and their faces radiated a gentle resignation, an inviting serenity.

"Would it be indiscreet, Madame," said Godefroid, "to ask these gentlemen's names? I am prepared to tell them the story of my life; might I not learn something of theirs?"

"This gentleman is named Monsieur Nicolas," answered Madame de La Chanterie, drawing Godefroid's attention to the tall, lean one. "He was once a colonel in the Gendarmerie, and retired with the rank of brigadier. And the other," she added, designating the small stout man, "is a former Councillor to the Royal Court of Paris, who withdrew from the magistracy in August 1830; his name is Monsieur Joseph. Although you have been among us only since yesterday, I will tell you that in society Monsieur Nicolas once bore the name of the Marquis de Montauran, and Monsieur Joseph that of Lecamus, Baron de Tresnes; but for us as for the rest of the world, those names no longer exist. These gentlemen have no heirs, and their family names were thus fated to disappear. They have chosen to hasten that process and have become simply Monsieur Nicolas and Monsieur Joseph, just as you will be Monsieur Godefroid."

Godefroid could not help but start on hearing these two names, one so celebrated among Royalists, who have not forgotten the catastrophic end of the Chouan uprising in the early days of the Consulate, the other so venerated in the annals of the late Parliament of Paris. Nevertheless, gazing on these twin relics of the fallen monarchy's staunchest underpinnings, the Nobility and the Law, he discerned no wavering in their expression, no change in their physiognomy to suggest a resurgence of worldly thoughts. These two men no longer remembered—or no longer wanted to remember—what they had once been. This was a first lesson for Godefroid.

"Gentlemen, your names carry an entire history within them!" he told them respectfully.

"The history of our times," answered Monsieur Joseph. "Nothing but ruins!"

"You are in good company," Monsieur Alain replied with a smile.

A few words will suffice for the portrait of this last gentleman: he was the very figure of the Parisian petit bourgeois, a friendly fellow with a calflike face made more intriguing by a shock of white hair, but made blander by an ever-present smile.

As for the priest, Father de Vèze, his station in life told all there was to know. One glance from or at a priest fully devoted to his mission, and you know him entirely.

From his first encounter with this little society, Godefroid had been struck by the profound and unmistakable respect Madame de La Chanterie inspired in her four boarders. To a man—not excluding the priest, for all the unworldliness of his vocation—they behaved just as they might in the presence of a queen. Nor could Godefroid fail to notice the air of sober moderation that reigned over this meal; his tablemates truly seemed to be eating for nourishment's sake alone. Like the others, Madame de La Chanterie took only a single peach and a half cluster of grapes, but she insisted that her new boarder not imitate their frugality, passing him one dish after another.

His first lunch in his new home had only heightened Godefroid's curiosity. When the meal was over, they all retired to the drawing room; leaving Godefroid to his own devices, Madame de La Chanterie and her four friends withdrew to a window alcove for a private conference. Their discussion lasted nearly a half hour, with no sign of excitement or animation. They spoke in low tones, carefully weighing their words, reflecting on everything that was said. From time to time Monsieur Alain and Monsieur Joseph could be seen paging through a small notebook, as if searching for some piece of information.

"See what you can see outside the city walls," said Madame de La Chanterie to Monsieur Nicolas, who set off at once.

These were the first words that Godefroid was able to make out.

"And you will go to the Saint-Marceau area," she continued, speaking to Monsieur Joseph. "And you, search the Faubourg Saint-Germain high and low, and try to find what we need . . ." she added, looking at Father de Vèze, who now left the room in his turn.

"And as for you, my dear Alain," she added with a smile, "you will go and make your rounds, and inspect our charges . . . And now we have made our plans for the day," she concluded, coming back to Godefroid.

She sat down in her armchair, took up a pile of cut cloth from a nearby table, and began to sew, like the simplest pieceworker.

Lost in conjectures, still suspecting that he had blundered into some sort of Royalist conspiracy, Godefroid took his hostess's words as an opening. He sat down next to her, studying her closely. He was struck by the singular dexterity with which she worked, she whose manner so perfectly bespoke the grande dame. She had the swift, sure touch of an experienced seamstress, the practiced gestures of the professional, so easily distinguished from those of the amateur.

"From the way you go about that," Godefroid said to her, "one might think you had been in the trade for years!"

"Alas!" she answered without lifting her eyes, "indeed I once was, through no choice of my own! . . ."

Two heavy tears overflowed from the old woman's eyes and fell from her cheeks onto the cloth in her lap.

"Forgive me, Madame," cried Godefroid.

Madame de La Chanterie glanced at her new boarder and read in his features such regret that she consoled him at once with a friendly wave of her hand. Hurriedly she dried her eyes, and soon her face had recovered its characteristic stolidity. Not that there was anything hard about this woman's face; but there was nevertheless something hardened.

"You find yourself, Monsieur Godefroid, for as you know we shall call you only by your Christian name, you find yourself here surrounded by the wreckage of a great storm. Each of us has been injured and wronged—in our hearts, our family interests, or our fortunes—by the forty-year tempest that toppled the monarchy and the Church, and scattered to the four winds the most vital elements of what was once France. A word that might seem perfectly innocent to others can cut us to the quick, and that is the reason for the silence that reigns in this house. We rarely speak of ourselves; we have forgotten ourselves, and have found the means to substitute another life for our own. Hearing you bare your soul in Mongenod's offices, I thought I sensed some kinship between your lot and ours, and so I convinced my four friends to welcome you into our midst; and in any case our monastery was in need of another monk. But what will you make of your new life? One cannot simply closet oneself away from mankind without some sort of personal and moral preparation."

"Madame," said Godefroid, "hearing you speak in this way, I believe I would be most delighted to have you as the arbiter of my destiny."

"You speak like a man of the world," she answered. "Imagine trying to flatter me—me, a woman of sixty! . . . My dear child," she continued, "you must know that you are surrounded by people with a powerful faith in God, who have all felt His hand, and who have given themselves over to Him almost as entirely as the Trappists of old. Have you ever observed the profound serenity of the true priest, of one who has devoted himself to the Lord, forever hearing His voice in his ears, tirelessly striving to become an obedient instrument for the hands of Providence? . . . He has lost all vanity, all self-love, everything that causes continual suffering to worldly folk; he feels a tranquillity greater than any fatalist's, and a resignation that allows him to bear every trial. The true priest, like Father de Vèze, is thus as a child with its mother, for the Church, my dear sir, is a very good mother indeed. Well! One can be a priest without a tonsure; not every priest is in the Orders. To devote yourself to good is to imitate the true priest—to obey God! I do not mean to preach. My aim is not to convert you. I am simply trying to explain the nature of our life."

"Teach me, Madame," said Godefroid in a docile tone, "so that I might never again breach your rules."

"That would be too much to undertake all at once; you will learn by degrees. Above all, in this house you must never speak of your misfortunes. They are mere child's play compared with the terrible catastrophes that God has visited on those around you . . ."

As she spoke, Madame de La Chanterie continued to take her stitches with dismaying regularity; but now she raised her eyes to Godefroid and found him entranced by the haunting gentleness of her voice, a voice suffused with what we might rightly call apostolic unction. The young unfortunate gazed with admiration on the truly extraordinary phenomenon incarnated in this woman's person. Her face was aglow; a hint of pink had spread over her cheeks, usually white as church candles. Her eyes were shining, and the youthfulness of her spirit conferred a fresh animation on her delicate wrinkles, imbuing them with a sort of grace. In short, everything about her aroused the affections. Godefroid then realized the full depth of the abyss that separated this woman from all vulgarity of sentiment. He imagined her standing on an inaccessible mountaintop to which Religion had guided her steps, and he was still too much of this world not to feel a surge of passion, not to dream of hurtling into the divide that separated them, climbing the steep slopes of her pinnacle, and taking his place at her side. Lost in rapt contemplation of the woman before him, he told her of his many disappointments, of all that he was unable to say at Mongenod's, where his confession had only skimmed the surface of his sorrows.

"My poor child! . . ."

Every now and then this motherly exclamation fell from Madame de La Chanterie's lips, and each time it came as a balm to the young man's heart.

"How will I fill the emptiness of my life after so many failed dreams and spurned affections?" he finally asked, staring into his landlady's meditative face. "I came here to reflect and to make up my mind," he went on. "I have lost my mother, and now you shall take her place . . ."

"Will you show me," she asked, "all the obedience of a real son? . . ."

"Yes, if you will show me the tenderness that inspires it."

"Well then! We shall try," she answered.

Godefroid reached out to take Madame de La Chanterie's hand; she offered it freely, understanding his intention, and he brought it respectfully to his lips. It was a hand of remarkable beauty, unwrinkled, neither plump nor bony, white enough to arouse a young woman's envy, its graceful forms worthy of the sculptor's art. Godefroid wondered at those hands, seeing in them a harmony with the enchantments of their owner's voice and the celestial blue of her gaze.

"Stay where you are," said Madame de La Chanterie, arising and disappearing into her bedroom.

A flood of emotion coursed through Godefroid's veins as he wondered just what this might mean. His perplexity was of short duration, however, for after a moment she returned with a book in her hand.

"These, my dear child," she said, "are the prescriptions of a great doctor of the soul. When the things of this world have not given us the happiness we hoped for, we must seek that happiness in a higher sort of life, and this is the key to that new world. Read one chapter of this book each morning and evening; but read it with every ounce of your attention, study the words as if you were reading a foreign language . . . After a month, you will be an entirely new man. For twenty years I have read a chapter of this book each day, and so have my friends, Messieurs Nicolas, Alain, and Joseph; they would no more neglect that ritual than they would neglect to sleep and wake every day. You must do as they do, for the love of God, for the love of me," she concluded, with divine serenity and regal confidence.

Turning the book in his hands, Godefroid looked at the spine and found the title *Imitation of Christ* printed in gold. The dandy that he had once been was confounded by this old woman's naïveté, her child-like innocence, her certainty that she was about to save a lost soul. Madame de La Chanterie stood in a joyous attitude, as if she were offering a hundred thousand francs to a merchant on the verge of bankruptcy.

"For twenty-six years," she said, "this volume has been by my side. Dear God, let this book be contagious! Now go at once and buy me another copy, for I am expecting certain persons who must not be seen . . ."

Godefroid bowed to Madame de La Chanterie and climbed the stairs to his room, where he tossed the book onto a table, muttering, "Silly old woman! . . . Ye gods! . . ."

As one might expect of a volume many times read and re-read, the book fell open before him. Godefroid sat down as if to collect his thoughts, for he had felt more emotions in the course of this morning than in all the most agitated months of his life; more than anything, his curiosity had never been so intensely aroused. Letting his gaze wander aimlessly over the room, as is the wont of those lost in deep meditation, he happened to glance at the two pages open before him, and as if in spite of himself he read this title:

CHAPTER XII
THE ROYAL ROAD OF THE HOLY CROSS

And he took up the book! And then, like a sudden burst of flame, these words leapt out from that beautiful chapter, dazzling his eyes:

He Himself opened the way before you in carrying His cross, and upon it He died for you, that you, too, might take up your cross and long to die upon it.

Go where you will, seek what you will, and you will not find a higher way, nor a less exalted but safer way, than the *way of the Holy Cross.* Arrange and order everything to suit your will and judgment, and still you will find that some suffering must always be borne, willingly or unwillingly, and thus you will always find the Cross.

Either you will experience bodily pain or you will undergo tribulation of spirit in your soul. At times you will be forsaken by God, at times troubled by those about you and, what is worse, you will often grow weary of yourself. You cannot escape, you cannot be relieved by any remedy or comfort but must bear with it as long as God wills. For He wishes you to learn to bear trial without consolation, to submit yourself wholly to Him that you may become more humble through suffering.

"What a book!" he said to himself, turning the pages.

And then he came across these words:

When you shall have come to the point where suffering is sweet and acceptable for the sake of Christ, then consider yourself fortunate, for you have found paradise on earth.

Irritated by this simplicity, which is the very soul of force, and furious to find himself beaten by this book, he slammed it shut. But he then discovered this admonition, inscribed in letters of gold on the green Moroccan leather of the cover:

SEEK ONLY THE ETERNAL!

"And is that what these people have found? . . ." he mused.

He resolved to purchase a fine new edition of the *Imitation of Christ* at once, thinking that Madame de La Chanterie would surely want to read her customary chapter that night. He hurried downstairs, through the front door, and into the street; but after a few steps he drew to a halt, not knowing which way to turn, wondering where, in what bookshop, he would find the work he sought. Just then, behind him, he heard the heavy thump of the front door swinging shut a second time.

Two men were emerging from the de La Chanterie *hôtel*—for if the reader has carefully noted the character of this old house, he will have recognized the distinguishing features of the great *hôtels* of yesteryear. (Nevertheless, it was only as a pleasantry that Manon, come to summon Godefroid to the midday meal, had asked him if he had enjoyed his first night in the Hotel de La Chanterie.) It was not Godefroid's intention to spy on these two, but he followed them all the same. Taking him only for another passerby, they spoke loudly enough to be overheard as they walked through the empty streets.

The two strangers set off down the Rue Massillon, walked the length of Notre-Dame's northern flank, then turned to cross the porch.

"Well now, my friend, you see how simple it is to get a few *sous* out of them? . . . You just have to talk like them, that's all."

"But now we're in debt?"

"To whom?"

"That lady . . ."

"I'd like to see that old bat try to take me to court, I'd . . ."

"You'd . . . you'd pay her back, that's what you'd do."

"You're right, because if I paid her back there'd be more loans to come, even bigger than what she gave me today . . ."

"Wouldn't we do better to follow their advice, and see if we can't make a new start in honest trade? . . ."

"Faugh!"

"After all, she said they could find us some backers . . ."

"We'd have to say good-bye to our lives . . ."

"I'm tired of my life . . . It's no life for a man, to be forever in his cups . . ."

"Yes, but don't forget how the priest let down old Marin the other day! He wouldn't give him a *sou*."

"Bah! That swindle of Marin's only works for millionaires."

Just then these two, whose dress showed them to be shop foremen, abruptly turned around and made for the Place Maubert by way of the Hôtel-Dieu bridge; Godefroid stepped aside, but they did not fail to note how closely he had been following them. They shot each other a troubled glance, clearly ruing the words they had spoken so freely.

Godefroid found this conversation all the more interesting for its reference to the little scene he had witnessed the day of his first visit, between Father de Vèze and the worker.

"What on earth goes on at Madame de La Chanterie's?" he wondered anew.

Still reflecting on this question, he continued his stroll until he came to a bookshop on the Rue Saint-Jacques; a moment later, he emerged with a very fine copy of the most elegant French edition of the *Imitation of Christ*. He walked homeward at a leisurely pace, hoping to arrive just as dinner was served. As he walked, he meditated on the sensations he had felt that morning, and sensed a fresh wind blowing through his soul. To be sure, he was racked by an intense curiosity, but above all else he felt an inexplicable desire: he was drawn to Madame de La Chanterie, he longed ardently to be beside her, to devote himself to her, to please her, to earn her praise. In short, he was in the grips of Platonic love. He had glimpsed an unsuspected grandeur in her soul, and now he wanted to know it entirely. He burned to penetrate the secrets of these perfect Catholics' existence. In short, the majesty of that little congregation's religion meshed so harmoniously with all that is majestic in French womanhood that he resolved to earn a place in their midst, at all costs. In a more industrious Parisian, such a conversion might seem unduly hasty; but, as we have seen, Godefroid was as a drowning man, clutching at the frailest branch, thinking it sturdy, and his soul, thoroughly plowed by the events of his life, lay ready to receive any seed.

He found his new friends in the drawing room, and he presented the book to Madame de La Chanterie, saying, "I did not want you to be deprived of it tonight . . ."

"God willing, this will be your last fit of elegance," she answered, eyeing the magnificent tome in her hands.

Noting once again the plainness of his new companions' dress, the rigorous absence of finery, and recalling that this same principle was applied to every detail of the house's decor, Godefroid did not fail to understand the full sense of Madame de La Chanterie's gracious reproach.

"Madame," he said, "the people you aided this morning are monsters. I could not help but overhear their conversation as they were leaving this afternoon, and it betrayed the most appalling ingratitude . . ."

"Those are the two locksmiths from the Rue Mouffetard," said Madame de La Chanterie to Monsieur Nicolas. "That is your affair . . ."

"The fish escapes more than once before it is caught," replied Monsieur Alain with a laugh.

Greatly surprised by Madame de La Chanterie's complacency at this revelation of her beneficiaries' ingratitude, Godefroid fell into a pensive silence.

That evening's dinner was enlivened by the good humor of Monsieur Alain and the former Councillor, but the old soldier remained somber, downcast, and cold; his face bore the ineradicable trace of some bitter sorrow, some unending pain. Madame de La Chanterie was equally attentive to all. Godefroid could not help but sense that he was being observed by his tablemates, who were no doubt as prudent as they were pious. His vanity led him to imitate their reserve, and he was careful to weigh his every word.

This first day proved far more animated than those that followed. Godefroid was still excluded from all discussions of serious matters, and finding himself alone in his rooms for a few hours every morning and evening, he had no choice but to open the *Imitation of Christ*. At length he began to study that book as one does when one is confined with only one volume to hand. Such enforced solitude with a book is much like enforced solitude with a woman: just as one will inevitably come to despise or adore the woman, one will either become lost in the author's thoughts or find it unbearable to read so much as ten lines.

Now, it is impossible to remain unaffected by the *Imitation*, for that book is to dogma as action is to thought. The Catholicism it embodies is a vibrant thing, moving and active; it does not shrink back from real life but confronts it head-on. This book is a true and trusted friend. It deals with every passion, every difficulty—even the most mundane— more eloquently than any preacher, for its voice is your own, arising from within your heart, and you hear it in your soul. It is the Gospels translated, germane to every era, applicable to any situation. It is extraordinary that the Church has not canonized de Gerson, for manifestly it was the Holy Spirit that guided his pen.

But to Godefroid, the de La Chanterie *hôtel* was home not only to this book but also to a woman, and he grew more attached to that woman with each passing day. In her he saw flowers buried beneath the snows of winter; he glimpsed the delights of the holy friendship that only Religion allows, a friendship on which the angels smile, a friendship, indeed, that bound all five members of this household, over which no evil could triumph. There is a sentiment superior to all others, the love of one soul for another, which we might compare to some exquisitely rare flower born on Nature's highest peaks, of which only one or two specimens are brought before the eyes of men in the span of a century. This is the sentiment that makes two lovers one, the source of their unerring fidelity, inexplicable by the ordinary laws of this world. From it grows an attachment without disappointment, without quarrels, without vanity, without struggles, indeed without contrasts, so perfectly does it intermingle two souls. And it was the delights of this sentiment—immense, infinite, born of Catholic Charity—that Godefroid had now glimpsed. At times the phenomenon before him seemed almost too good to be true, and he struggled to find some earthly motivation for the sublime friendship shared by these five, so deep was his surprise at finding true Catholics, Christians from the earliest days of the Church, in the Paris of 1835.

In the first week of his new life in this house, seeing his companions in such concerted cooperation, overhearing so many snatches of earnest conversation dealing with such serious matters, Godefroid finally came to understand what prodigiously active lives they led; indeed, he soon realized that none of them slept more than six hours a night.

The hours before noon constituted a sort of workday in themselves; thus, their midday meal marked the end of what we might call their day's first day. Strangers appeared to bring or take away various sums of money, some of them considerable. Mongenod's cashier often called at the house early in the morning, before the bank opened its doors, as an exceptional favor on the part of his employers.

Monsieur Mongenod himself came one evening, and Godefroid noted a touch of filial affection in his exchanges with Monsieur Alain, an affection mingled with profound respect, as much for him as for Madame de La Chanterie's other three lodgers.

That evening, the banker posed Godefroid only the most banal sort of questions—if he was happy here, if he intended to stay on, and so forth—all the while pressing him to persevere in his resolution.

"My happiness would be complete, save for one thing I lack," said Godefroid.

"Oh? And what is that?" asked the banker.

"An occupation."

"An occupation!" interjected Father de Vèze. "Then you have changed your mind? You came to our cloister in search of repose . . ."

"But without the prayer that animated the monasteries, without the meditation that peopled the solitude of the monks, repose can easily become a disease," said Monsieur Joseph sententiously.

"Learn to keep books," said Monsieur Mongenod with a smile, "and within a few months you will have made yourself most useful to my friends here."

"Oh! With great pleasure," cried Godefroid.

The next day was a Sunday, and Madame de La Chanterie compelled her boarder to offer her his arm and accompany her to High Mass.

"I hope this is the only force I will ever have to exert on you," she said. "Many times in the past week I have wanted to speak to you of your salvation, but I am still not certain that the moment has come. You could have a very fine occupation indeed if you shared our beliefs, for you would also share in our work."

At Mass, Godefroid noted the fervor of Messieurs Nicolas, Joseph, and Alain; and since the previous few days had already convinced him of those gentlemen's superiority, their wisdom, the breadth of their knowledge, the greatness of their spirits, he could not help but conclude that the Catholic religion must have secrets that had so far escaped him, if men such as these so readily humbled themselves for its cause.

"After all," he said to himself, "this is the religion of Bossuet, Pascal, Racine, Saint Louis, Louis XIV, Raphael, Michelangelo, Ximenes, Bayard, du Guesclin, and so many others like them; and who am I, puny creature that I am, to compare myself with such geniuses, such statesmen, such poets, such leaders?"

If no profound teachings were to come from all these details, it would be imprudent to linger over them, given the current climate; but they are indispensable to the interest of this story, which today's public will no doubt already find difficult enough to believe, beginning as it does with an almost preposterous notion: the hold that a woman of sixty years had gained over a gravely disillusioned young man.

"You did not pray," said Madame de La Chanterie to Godefroid on the porch of Notre-Dame, "not for anyone, not even for the repose of your mother's soul."

Godefroid blushed and made no reply.

"I would be most pleased," Madame de La Chanterie went on, "if you would now go upstairs and not return to the drawing room for an hour. If you love me," she added, "you will meditate on a chapter of the *Imitation*, the first chapter of the third book, entitled 'The Inward Conversation.'"

Godefroid bowed coolly and climbed the stairs to his apartment.

"The devil with them," he said to himself, in genuine anger. "What do these people want from me? What are they up to? . . . Bah! Every woman has the same bag of tricks, even the most devout. And if Madame," he went on, referring to his hostess in the same manner as her other lodgers, "if Madame does not want me near, then that must mean some conspiracy against me is afoot."

His mind full of these thoughts, he went to his window and tried to look into the drawing room, but the configuration of the building made this impossible. He started down the stairs but returned immediately to his room upon reaching the floor below his; for, given the rigidity of the principles that governed the house's inhabitants, he felt sure that an act of espionage would result in his banishment. The loss of these five people's esteem struck him as a very serious thing, as terrible as any public disgrace. He waited some three quarters of an hour, then finally resolved to catch Madame de La Chanterie unawares by appearing at the drawing room door before the hour had run out. He invented a lie to serve as his pretext: he would say that there was something amiss with his watch, and as evidence of this he set the hands twenty minutes ahead. Then he made his way downstairs, careful not to make the slightest noise. He strode to the door of the drawing room and threw it open.

Before him he saw a young man of some celebrity, a poet whom he had often met in society, Victor de Vernisset, kneeling before Madame de La Chanterie and kissing the hem of her gown. Godefroid would have been less astonished to see the heavens shatter, like the crystal the ancients believed them to be, than he was by this sight. The most dreadful thoughts flooded into his mind, and he was all the more thunderstruck when, just as an acerbic remark came to his lips, he caught sight of Monsieur Alain counting out a stack of thousand-franc notes in one corner of the room.

In a moment Vernisset was on his feet again as the good Alain looked on in astonished silence. Madame de La Chanterie shot Godefroid a petrifying glance, for the mixed expression on her new lodger's face had not escaped her eye.

"This gentleman," she said to the young poet, gesturing toward Godefroid, "is one of us . . ."

"You're a very lucky man, my dear friend," said Vernisset, "you are saved! But, Madame," he went on, turning to Madame de La Chanterie, "even if all of Paris had seen me, I would be happy, for nothing can repay the debt I owe you! . . . You have won me over forever! I belong entirely to you. Ask of me what you will, I will obey! My gratitude knows no bounds. I owe you my life; it is yours to do with as you please . . ."

"Come, come, young man," said the good Alain, "calm yourself. You need only work, nothing more, and above all you must never attack Religion in your writings . . . In other words, do not forget the debt you owe!"

And he handed him an envelope thick with the banknotes he had just counted out. Victor de Vernisset's eyes were damp with tears; he respectfully kissed Madame de La Chanterie's hand, cordially clasped those of Monsieur Alain and Godefroid, and went out.

"You have disobeyed Madame," the little man said gravely, his features expressing a sadness that Godefroid had not seen before. "That is a grievous misstep; another of the same sort and we shall have to part ways . . . You will find that a very hard thing, now that you have earned our trust . . ."

"My dear Alain," said Madame de La Chanterie, "please do me the great favor of overlooking this foolish mistake . . . We must not ask too much of a newcomer, of one who has never known the true depths of unhappiness, who has no religion, whose only vocation is an irresistible curiosity, and who has not yet come to believe in our ways."

"Forgive me, Madame," answered Godefroid. "Henceforth, my only goal will be to prove myself worthy of you. I will gladly submit to any trial you may find necessary before I am fully allowed into the secret of your endeavors, and if the good Father de Vèze would consent to undertake my education, I will offer him my soul and my mind."

These words left a faint blush of joy coloring Madame de La Chanterie's cheeks. Reaching for Godefroid's hand, she clasped it in hers and said with unusual warmth: "That's fine!"

That evening after dinner, Godefroid witnessed the visit of a vicar-general of the Parisian diocese, two canons, two former mayors of Paris, and a lady who served as parish visitor for the Church. It was an evening free from pretense or insincerity, and the conversation was merry but in no way frivolous.

Among the house's visitors, Godefroid was exceedingly surprised to see the Countess de Cinq-Cygne, that glorious figure of the aristocracy to whose salon no bourgeois or nouveau riche could dare dream of admission. The presence of so grand a lady in Madame de La Chanterie's drawing room was extraordinary enough in itself; but the manner of the two women's greeting and conversation struck Godefroid as simply inexplicable, for it suggested a long-standing intimacy that greatly elevated Madame de La Chanterie in his eyes. Madame de Cinq-Cygne was gracious and affectionate with her friend's four companions, and deeply respectful toward Monsieur Nicolas. As we can see, social vanity had not entirely lost its hold over Godefroid. Thus, whatever doubts and indecisions he may once have felt vanished then and there: vocation or no vocation, he resolved to throw himself into any task Madame de La Chanterie might demand of him, in hopes that he might one day be invited to join their Order, or at least be initiated into their secrets. Only then, he promised himself, would he make up his mind whether to accept this new life or not.

The next day he went to see a bookkeeper whose name Madame de La Chanterie had given him, and arranged to come and work with him at certain hours. His daily routine was thus settled: in the morning he was catechized by Father de Vèze, then he would go to the bookkeeper's for two hours, and finally, from noon to evening, he would devote himself to the imaginary commercial ledgers that his master assigned him to keep.

Several days passed in this manner, and so Godefroid came to understand the pleasures of a day in which every hour has its own purpose. Many a happy existence has its roots in this perfect, unvarying regularity, this continual return of familiar tasks at predictable intervals, which proves how deeply the founders of the religious orders must have meditated on the nature of Man. Resolutely mindful of Father de Vèze's teachings, Godefroid had begun to fear for the future of his soul, realizing how badly he had underestimated the gravity of religious matters. Finally, with each passing day, Madame de La Chanterie, in whose company he spent an hour every afternoon, allowed him to discover yet greater treasures within her. He had never imagined a benevolence so entire, or so unbounded. In a woman of the age Madame de La Chanterie appeared to be, you will find none of the pettiness of her younger sisters. Rather, you will find a true friend, generous with her attentions, her every action marked by the grace and delicacy that nature instills in women for the sake of men; and she no longer sells you these charms but offers them freely. She is either intolerable or perfect, for either her youthful pretensions still throb with life beneath her skin or else they are dead and gone. As for Madame de La Chanterie, she was perfect. She seemed never to have been young, for no trace of her past could be read in her gaze. Each day Godefroid's knowledge of her sublime character grew more intimate; but far from sating his curiosity, these daily discoveries only spurred his desire to know more of this saintly woman's life. Had she ever been in love? Had she married? become a mother? There was nothing of the spinster about her. She had all the finesse of a woman of high birth, and in her robust good health, in the extraordinary phenomenon of her conversation, one could see signs of a perfectly celestial existence, a sort of ignorance of the everyday world. With the exception of the merry Monsieur Alain, all these creatures had suffered; but Monsieur Nicolas himself seemed to confer the laurel wreath of martyrdom on Madame de La Chanterie. Nevertheless, the memory of her sorrows was so well contained by her Catholic resignation, by her secret occupations, that she seemed never to have known an unhappy moment in her life.

"You are," Godefroid told her one day, "the lifeblood of your friends;

you are the bond that unites them; you are, so to speak, the caretaker of a great undertaking; and since we are all of us mortal, I wonder what might become of your circle without you ..."

"That is a matter of great concern to my friends; but Providence, to whom we owe our new bookkeeper," she said smiling, "will not fail us. In any case, I will seek out another to replace me."

"Then your bookkeeper will soon be entering into your service?" Godefroid laughed.

"That depends on him," she replied, still smiling. "He must be sincerely religious, he must be pious, he must rid himself of every trace of self-love, he must think nothing of our wealth, he must strive to elevate himself above all petty social concerns, using the two wings that God gave to each of us ..."

"And what wings are those?"

"Simplicity and purity," answered Madame de La Chanterie. "Your ignorance proves all too clearly that you are neglecting your reading," she added, chuckling at the innocent stratagem she had devised to test Godefroid's knowledge of the *Imitation of Christ*. "Finally, you must fill your soul with the lessons of Saint Paul's Epistle on Charity. It is not you who will be ours," she said, a sublime expression coming over her face, "it is we who will be yours, and with that you might count yourself more wealthy than any sovereign the world has ever known. This newfound fortune will bring you the same joy it has brought us; and allow me to inform you, if you remember the *Thousand and One Nights*, that Aladdin's treasure is nothing compared with ours ... Indeed, for a good year now, we have found ourselves unable to manage it. The task was simply beyond us, and that is why we require a bookkeeper."

She gazed deep into Godefroid's eyes as she spoke. He did not know what to make of this strange confidence; once again, as so many times before, he recalled the conversation between Madame de La Chanterie and Madame Mongenod, and hovered between doubt and belief.

"Oh! You could be so happy," she said.

Tormented by his curiosity, Godefroid resolved at that moment to overcome the four friends' discretion and force them to speak of themselves. Now, of all Madame de La Chanterie's lodgers, the one toward whom Godefroid felt most strongly drawn—who seemed, indeed, likely to enjoy the affectionate esteem of people from all walks of life—was the good, the gay, the simple Monsieur Alain. By what route had Providence brought that artless creature to this monastery without walls, deep in the heart of Paris, whose code the flock observed by choice as faithfully as if they were governed by the sternest superior? What drama, what great event had compelled him to turn away from the world, and to enter onto this painful and treacherous path through a great city's sorrows?

One evening Godefroid resolved to pay a call on his neighbor, hoping to satisfy a curiosity made all the keener by the very unlikelihood of catastrophic events in his new friend's past; for that very reason, Alain's story promised to be more intriguing than any tale of corsairs and their adventures. Hearing the word "Enter!" in response to his two discreet raps on the door, Godefroid turned the key, which was never removed from its lock, and found Monsieur Alain sitting at one corner of his hearth. He had been reading a chapter of the *Imitation of Christ* before retiring, his book lit by two candles topped with the adjustable green shades favored by players of whist.

He sat wrapped in his grayish flannel dressing gown, his legs covered in footed trousers, his feet propped by the hearth on a little petit-point cushion, fashioned, like his slippers, by Madame de La Chanterie's hand. His head was that of an old man, with no other finery than a crown of white hair very like an aged monk's tonsure, its whiteness contrasting with the brown tapestry that padded his enormous armchair.

Monsieur Alain gently set the well-worn volume on a small table whose legs took the form of wreathed columns; removing his spectacles from the end of his nose with his other hand, he gestured toward a second armchair.

"Are you ill, to have left your room at such an hour?" he asked Godefroid.

"Dear Monsieur Alain," Godefroid answered forthrightly, "I am tormented by a curiosity that can be proven either very innocent or very indiscreet by a single word from you. I hope I have made clear in what spirit I ask you this question."

"Oh! oh! and what question is that?" he replied, looking at the young man with an almost mischievous air.

"What was it that led you into the life you lead here? Anyone who embraces the doctrine of this house, who so thoroughly renounces his self-interest, must be a man repelled by the world; he must have been sorely wounded, or have wounded others."

"What! my child," the old man answered, his wide mouth breaking into a characteristic smile, making of his rosy lips the truest picture of affection that a painter's genius might conceive, "can one not be moved to profound pity simply by the sight of the miseries that Paris holds within her walls? Did Saint Vincent de Paul require the goad of remorse or wounded vanity to devote his life to abandoned children?"

"With that there is nothing more to be said, for indeed, if ever a soul resembled the soul of that Christian hero, it is most assuredly yours," answered Godefroid.

Age had hardened the old man's wrinkled, almost yellow face, yet he blushed excessively on hearing these words, fearing that Godefroid might think he had sought to elicit this praise. But no; his obvious modesty made it clear that no such thought had ever entered his mind. Godefroid knew full well that Madame de La Chanterie's companions had no taste for that sort of incense. Nevertheless, this compunction troubled Alain's impeccably simple spirit, leaving him as shaken as a young girl who has conceived an impure thought.

"While I am still far from him spiritually," Monsieur Alain replied, "I am quite sure I resemble him physically . . ."

Godefroid was about to respond, but with a gesture the old man bade him be silent. Alain had spoken truly: he possessed that saint's tubercular nose, and his face, very like that of an aged vine worker, was a true twin to the great common face of the father of the Foundling Hospital.

"In any case, you are quite right," he went on. "My vocation for our work was inspired by a sense of remorse, in the wake of an adventure . . ."

"An adventure! You!" Godefroid gently cried, so surprised at this word that he forgot the reply he was intending to make.

"Oh! To you this will no doubt seem a mere bagatelle, a trifle; but in

the courtroom of my conscience, it was judged otherwise. If y
wish to participate in our endeavor once you have heard my tale, it
will be because you realize that our sentiments are proportionate to
the force of our souls, and that the conscience of a weak Christian can
very well be troubled by a deed that causes no torment to a man of
stronger will."

It would be difficult to express the ardor of the neophyte's curiosity
on hearing this strange little preamble. What crime could this man
have committed, this man whom Madame de La Chanterie called her
"paschal lamb"? A novel entitled *The Crimes of a Sheep* could not have
been more intriguing. Perhaps, to a flower or a blade of grass, a sheep
is a very fierce creature indeed. If we are to believe one of the mildest
Republicans of our day, even the most kindly of creatures might be
cruel toward something. But the good gentleman Alain! A man who,
like Sterne's Uncle Toby, never crushed a fly before it had bitten him
twenty times over! To think that a soul so gentle as his might once
have been racked by repentance!

These reflections filled the pause marked by the old man after the
words "Listen to me!" As Godefroid mused, Alain pushed his cushion
beneath the neophyte's feet so that they might share it.

"I was then a little short of thirty years old," he said. "As best I can
remember, this was back in '98, a time when a young man needed the
experience of a sixty-year-old to survive. One morning at nine o'clock,
just as I was about to sit down to breakfast, my old serving woman announced the visit of one of the few friends I had kept through all the
Revolution's upheavals. Thus my first word to him was an invitation to
breakfast with me. My friend, a boy of twenty-eight by the name of
Mongenod, accepted my offer with a somewhat discomfited air. I had
not seen him since 1793 . . ."

"Mongenod? . . ." cried Godefroid. "The—"

"If you want to know the end before the beginning," the old man interjected with a smile, "how can I tell you my story?"

Godefroid gestured a promise to hold his tongue.

"When Mongenod sat down," the good Alain went on, "I realized
that his shoes were terribly worn. Frequent bleachings had left his
flecked stockings with precious little resemblance to silk. His apri-

cot satinette breeches were badly rumpled and very worn; constant use had altered the color of the fabric in certain troublesome places, and the buckles seemed to be made not of steel but of common iron, like the buckles of his shoes. He wore a white waistcoat with a floral pattern, grown yellow from overuse, betraying a terrible but respectable poverty, like the crumpled frill hanging from the neck of his blouse. Finally, the look of his surcoat (for that is what we used to call a frock coat ornamented with a single cape, in the manner of a Crispin jacket) confirmed my suspicion that my friend had fallen on hard times. It had been brushed with admirable care, but the hazelnut-colored fabric was threadbare, the collar badly stained by pomade or powder, and the shiny metal of the buttons had long since gone rust red. In short, there was in his dress something so shameful that I scarcely dared look at him. His *claque,* a sort of half circle of felt which in those days was carried under the arm rather than worn on the head, must have seen several governments come and go. Nevertheless, my friend had evidently spent a few *sous* on the ministrations of a barber, for he was freshly shaved, and his hair, pulled back and held in place by a comb, was luxuriously powdered and smelled of pomade. Two parallel chains of tarnished steel hung against the front of his breeches, but there was no sign of a watch in either fob. It was winter, and Mongenod had no greatcoat; the cape of his surcoat was spattered with melted snow that must have fallen from the rooftops as he came down the street. He pulled off his rabbit-fur gloves, giving me a glimpse of his right hand, scarred by some arduous sort of manual labor. This struck me as odd, for his father, an attorney to the Grand Conseil, had left him a considerable fortune, earning some five or six thousand francs interest per year. All at once I realized that Mongenod had come in hopes of a loan. I had two hundred gold *louis* hidden away, an enormous sum for the time, worth I no longer know how many hundred thousand francs in *assignats.* Mongenod and I had been students at the same school, Les Grassins, and later found ourselves in the employ of the same prosecutor, a very good man by the name of Monsieur Bordin. When you have shared your youth and the follies of your adolescence with another, an almost sacred sort of bond exists between the two of you; his voice and his gaze have the power to touch certain strings of your heart that can be made to vibrate only by the effect of your shared memories. Even if you have sometimes had reason to complain of him, the rights of friendship never truly expire. Between the two of us, however, there had never been the slightest coolness. On his father's death, in 1787, Mongenod found himself richer than I. Although I never borrowed from him, I did owe him for certain indulgences forbidden me by my father's rigor; thus, were it not for my generous friend, I would never have seen the first performance of *The Marriage of Figaro*. In those days, Mongenod was what people called a very dashing gentleman, with a penchant for gallantry. I used to take him to task for the ease with which he fell in with strangers, and his willingness to accommodate them; his purse opened too easily, he loved the high life, he would have offered himself as your witness after laying eyes on you only twice ... My goodness! You have led me back into the familiar byways of my youth!" cried the good Alain, smiling merrily at Godefroid as he paused in his speech.

"I hope I have not caused you any pain," said Godefroid.

"Oh, no! and I trust you can see, from the great detail of my account, how vital a place this incident occupies in my life ... Mongenod was a man of noble heart and fine spirit, something of a Voltairean, and liked to think of himself as a gentleman," Monsieur Alain went on. "At Les Grassins he had rubbed elbows with the nobility; this, along with his many dalliances, had given him the polished ways of the highborn man, of what was then called an aristocrat. Imagine my surprise, then, as my eyes wandered from his face to his clothes and discovered these unmistakable symptoms of penury. The young, elegant Mongenod of 1787 was no more. Now, in those days of widespread poverty, there were some who affected the dress of the poor, and indeed many of these impostors had excellent reasons for doing so; thus, I was eager for some word of explanation and did all I could to coax it out of him. 'My dear Mongenod, what a state you are in!' I said, accepting a pinch of tobacco from his imitation gold snuffbox. 'A very sad state,' he answered. 'I have but one friend left ... and that friend is you. I have done all I could to forestall this moment, but now I have come to ask you for one hundred *louis*. A considerable sum, I know,' he said, noting my surprise, 'but if you gave me only fifty, I should never be able to repay you; whereas, with one hundred, if my current undertaking fails, I would still have fifty *louis* to try my fortune by other means—for I am quite sure my despair would inspire me to some new plan, which for the moment I cannot predict.' 'You have nothing!' I said. 'I have,' he replied, holding back a tear, 'five *sous* in change from my last coin. Before appearing at your door, I paid a visit to the barber and had my shoes waxed. Everything I own is with me at this very moment. However,' he went on, throwing out his arms, 'I owe my landlady a thousand *écus* in *assignats*, and yesterday I was refused credit at our local cookshop. In other words, I have nothing!' 'And what do you intend to do now?' I said, already caught up in my friend's concerns. 'If you refuse me, I will sign on as a soldier . . . ' 'You, a soldier! You, Mongenod!' 'And if I am not killed, then perhaps I shall become General Mongenod.' 'Well then,' I said, deeply moved, 'trouble yourself no further, and come and sit down to breakfast. I have one hundred *louis* to lend you . . .'

"Here," the old man said to Godefroid, a look of cunning in his eyes, "I thought it best to tell him a little lender's lie.

" 'That is the sum total of my fortune,' I said to Mongenod. 'My intention was to invest it, and I was waiting for the price of government securities to fall to the lowest possible point; but I will gladly entrust it to you. You may consider me your associate. I will leave it up to your conscience to repay me in due course, for there is no finer account book than the conscience of an honest man.' Mongenod gazed into my face as I spoke, as if he were engraving my words upon his heart. He held out his right hand, and I my left, and we clasped hands, I with great tenderness, he with two heavy tears slipping unhindered over his care-ravaged cheeks, a sight that deeply aggrieved my heart. I was all the more touched when, forgetting himself in his emotion, Mongenod pulled from his pocket a wretched calico handkerchief, torn and tattered, to wipe his eyes. 'Stay where you are,' I said to him, hurrying off to my lockbox, as deeply moved as if I had just heard a woman confess her undying love. I returned with two rolls of fifty *louis* each. 'Here, count them . . .' But he wouldn't count them, and he glanced around the room in search of a desk, telling me he wanted to write up a promissory note. This I categorically refused. 'If I were to die,' I told him, 'my heirs would torment you. This shall remain between us.' Having found so true a friend in me, Mongenod lost the air of anxious sorrow with which he had entered; his features relaxed, and soon he was in far better spirits. My housemaid served us oysters, white wine, an omelette, a brochette of kidneys, some leftover Chartres pâté that my old mother had sent me, and then a bit of dessert, coffee, and Island liqueurs. Mongenod eagerly took his fill, having eaten nothing for two days. Lost in reminiscences of our life before the Revolution, we sat at the table until three in the afternoon, like the best friends in the world. Mongenod told me how he had come to lose his fortune. First, the reduction of the city securities dividends had deprived him of two thirds of his annual income, for this was where his father had invested the greater part of his capital; then, having sold his house on the Rue de Savoie, he was obliged to accept his payment in *assignats*. Next he took it into his head to found a newspaper, *The Sentinel*, which he was forced to abandon after six months. Most recently, he had placed all his hopes in the success of a comic opera entitled *The Peruvians*. This last revelation left me trembling. To think of Mongenod, become an author after squandering his fortune on *The Sentinel*, living in the world of the theater, spending his days with musicians, with singers from the Théâtre Feydeau, with all that strange crowd that lurks behind the curtain! This was no longer the Mongenod I knew so well. I could not repress a shudder. But how to take back my hundred *louis*? I could see the two rolls of coins in the pockets of his breeches, like two pistol barrels. Soon Mongenod went on his way; finding myself alone, with the spectacle of his terrible poverty no longer before me, I began reconsidering what had just taken place, and my fine feelings quickly faded. 'Suppose Mongenod has simply fallen into depravity,' I thought; 'suppose this was all nothing more than an act!' Recalling his merry smile as I so casually offered him my fortune, I suddenly imagined some Molière valet grinning with delight as he dupes a foolish, doddering Géronte. These thoughts led me to a decision that should have been my first step: I would seek to learn a bit more of my old friend Mongenod, who had left me his address on the back of a playing card. A certain concern for his sensibilities stopped me from going and seeing him the next day; he might have interpreted my promptness as a sign of mistrust. The day after that, I had urgent business to attend to. A full two weeks went by with no further sign of Mongenod. Finally, one morning, I set out from my lodgings on the Croix-Rouge crossroads and walked to the Rue des Moineaux, where Mongenod had taken furnished rooms in an apartment house of the lowest order. His landlady nevertheless seemed a very worthy woman, the widow of a farmer-general who had fallen victim to the scaffold; virtually penniless after his death, she had used her last few *louis* to enter the perilous trade of the subletter. She has since bought seven houses in the Saint-Roch neighborhood and has made her fortune. 'Citizen Mongenod is not at home, but you'll find someone in,' this woman told me. My curiosity roused by these last few words, I hurried up to the sixth floor, and my knock was answered by a most charming young person! . . . oh! a young person of the greatest beauty, who half-opened the door and stood looking at me with some wariness. 'My name is Alain. I am a friend of Mongenod's,' I said. The door opened at once, and I entered an apartment of appalling shabbiness, but kept impeccably clean by her care. She pulled a chair toward a hearth full of cold ashes, in one corner of which I saw a crude clay stove. The apartment was terribly cold. 'I'm so happy to have this opportunity to express my gratitude, Monsieur,' she said, clasping my hands affectionately, 'for you have saved us. Were it not for you, I might never have seen Mongenod again . . . He might well have . . . have what? . . . have thrown himself into the river. He was in a state of deep despair when he went to see you . . .' Examining this young woman, I was rather surprised to see her head covered with a scarf, beneath which I could discern only a dark shadow. Looking more closely, I realized that her head had been shaved. 'Are you ill?' I said, still gazing at this curious sight. She glanced toward a dim mirror set into a filthy mantelpiece and began to blush; then her eyes filled with tears. 'Yes, Monsieur,' she hurriedly replied. 'I was having the most terrible pains in my head, and I had to let them shave off my beautiful hair, which once fell to my heels.' 'Do I have the honor of addressing Madame Mongenod?' I said. 'Yes, Monsieur,' she answered, casting me a truly celestial glance. I took my leave of this poor little woman and made my way downstairs in hopes of a fruitful talk with the landlady, but she had gone out. I suspected that the young woman had sold her hair to have money for bread. I went at once to a wood merchant and ordered a half cartload of wood, asking the carter to give her a receipt of full payment in the name of Citizen Mongenod.

"There ends the period of what I have long called *my* foolishness," said the good Alain, joining his hands and raising them slightly in a gesture of repentance.

Godefroid could not help but smile, and as we will see, in this he was very wrong.

"Two days later," Alain resumed, "I stumbled into one of those vague figures we all meet up with from time to time, neither friend nor stranger—in short, what people call an *acquaintance:* a certain Monsieur Barillaud, who in the course of our conversation happened to mention his friendship with the author of *The Peruvians.* 'Then you know Citizen Mongenod?' I asked him.

"That was how we were made to refer to each other in those days," he added parenthetically, before returning to his story.

"He looked at me in surprise, then cried out: 'And how I wish I'd never met him! More than once he has come to me in search of a loan, and it seems he thinks too much of our friendship to repay me! He's a very queer fellow: likable enough, but full of illusions! . . . Oh! a most ardent imagination he has! I will say this in his favor: he never sets out to deceive. Nevertheless, since he deceives himself in every possible manner, he often behaves like the most duplicitous rogue.' 'How much does he owe you, then?' 'Bah! Some hundred *écus* . . . He is like a sieve. No one knows where his money goes; I don't suppose he knows himself.' 'Has he any money of his own?' 'Oh! yes indeed,' Barillaud answered with a laugh. 'Just lately, he has been talking of buying land among the savages in the United States.' I stalked off, my goodwill toward Mongenod soured by the splash of vinegar these aspersions had thrown onto my heart. I went to see my former employer, in whom I sometimes confided when I needed advice. I told him of my interview with Mongenod, and of the loan I had offered him. 'What!' he cried. 'What sort of behavior is this for one of my former clerks? You should have told him to return the next day and then come to see me at once. You would have learned that my door is now closed to

Mongenod. In the past year alone I have lent him more than thirty *écus*—an enormous sum! And only three days before sharing your breakfast, he met me in the street and drew so heart-rending a portrait of his destitution that I offered him two *louis* on the spot!' 'Then I have fallen prey to a most talented actor,' I answered. 'The shame is his, not mine. But what am I to do now?' 'At the very least, you will need a formal attestation of debt, for however bad a debtor might be, he can always become honest again, and then you will be repaid.' With this Bordin opened a drawer in his desk and pulled out a folder marked with Mongenod's name. He showed me three promissory notes, each in the amount of one hundred *livres*. 'The next time he comes to see me, I will add to this sum the interest he currently owes me, along with the two *louis* and whatever he may ask of me that day; then he will have to sign a promissory note for the entire amount, acknowledging that the interest accrues from the day of the loan. In that way the matter will at least be in order, and I will have some hope of repayment.' 'Well!' I said to Bordin, 'could you do for me as you have done for yourself? You are an honest man, and you always do what is right.' 'I seek only to retain my mastery over the situation,' the ex-prosecutor replied. 'To behave as you have done is to put yourself at the mercy of a man who might well make you his dupe. And I, for one, have no desire to be a dupe! A former prosecutor at the Châtelet, duped by a debtor? Never! Lend a man a sum such as you have so foolhardily lent to Mongenod, and it will not be long before he sees himself as its rightful owner. It is no longer your money but his, and you become his creditor, and a most disagreeable thorn in his side. Your debtor will then make certain compromises with his conscience in order to be rid of you; out of a hundred men, seventy-five will do all they can to avoid meeting up with you again for the rest of their days ... ' 'Then you believe that only twenty-five percent of your fellows are honorable men?' 'Is that what I said?' he answered with an arch smile. 'That seems a bit high.' Fifteen days later I received a letter from Bordin summoning me to his offices to collect my attestation of debt. I went at once. 'I tried to rescue fifty of your hundred *louis*,' he told me. (I had informed him of all the details of my conversation with

Mongenod.) 'But the flock has already flown. Say farewell to your gold! Your canaries have flown off to warmer climes. This man is nothing short of a swindler. He stood right here before me and told me that his wife and father-in-law have left for the United States with sixty of your hundred *louis,* for the purpose of buying land. And soon he will be off to join them, intending to earn his fortune, he claims, and then to return and repay all his debts. He entrusted me with his account book, which seemed perfectly in order, and requested that I remain informed of his creditors' whereabouts. And here is what I learned from his accounts,' Bordin said, pulling out a file and reading the sum total of Mongenod's debts: 'Seventeen thousand francs, enough to buy a house worth two thousand *écus* in interest!' He returned the file to its place and handed me a bill of exchange for one hundred golden *louis,* reckoned in *assignats,* along with a letter written in Mongenod's hand, acknowledging receipt of the hundred *louis* and pledging to repay me with interest. 'Then everything is in order,' I said to Bordin. 'He cannot deny his debt, at least,' my former employer answered me; 'but over those who have nothing, the King, I mean the Directorate, holds no power.' I left with these final words ringing in my ears. Sure that I had been swindled by a ploy against which the law could do nothing, I renounced whatever esteem I once had for Mongenod, and in the best philosophical manner I resigned myself to my loss.

"Forgive me for dwelling on these vulgar and seemingly insignificant details, but I have reasons for doing so," the old man said, looking at Godefroid. "I am trying to explain how I was led to behave as most other men do, blindly, with nary a thought for the rules that the savages observe in even the most trivial matters. Many people would see the example of a serious man like Bordin as justification for such behavior; but today I find my actions inexcusable. If you condemn your fellow man, and refuse him your esteem forever, you alone must bear the responsibility for your decision. And even then, is it right to make of your heart a courtroom in which to try your fellow? Where would you find the law? On what would you base your judgment? What constitutes a weakness in your soul might very well be a strength in another's! So many lives, so many varied circumstances behind every deed, for in human existence no two events are ever identical. Only society has the right to repress us, for I contest its right to punish: to repress is sufficient, and in that there is cruelty enough.

"Thus, under the effect of a Parisian's empty words, and of my admiration for my former employer's wisdom, I condemned Mongenod in my mind," the old man went on, returning to his story after drawing this divine lesson. "The premiere of *The Peruvians* was announced. I was expecting Mongenod to invite me to the first performance, sure that I had earned a certain authority over him. That simple loan had led me to see my friend as my vassal, who owed me far more than the interest on my money. Such is the way of men! . . . But the invitation never came. Worse yet, I caught sight of him coming toward me one day in the dark passageway under the Théâtre Feydeau, well dressed, almost elegant; he walked straight past me, as if he had not caught sight of me. Once he was behind me, I turned to run after him, only to find that my debtor had escaped by a side passage. I was gravely offended, and this vexation did not subside over the following days but only grew more acute. Here is why. Not long after this encounter I wrote Mongenod in these terms:

My friend, I trust you do not think me indifferent to the events of your life, whether they be happy ones or not. Are you pleased with *The Peruvians*? You neglected to invite me to the first performance, which was of course your right. Had I been present, I would have applauded with great enthusiasm. In any case, I hope that you will find in this endeavor a real Peru, for my funds have been put to fine use, and I am counting on you for repayment.

YOUR FRIEND, ALAIN.

"After two weeks had passed with no response to my letter, I returned to the Rue des Moineaux. The landlady informed me that the young woman had indeed gone away with her father, just as Mongenod told Bordin. Mongenod usually left his rooms early in the morning and returned late at night. Another two weeks went by, and I wrote another letter, conceived as follows:

My dear Mongenod, I no longer see you, you no longer answer my letters; I cannot understand your behavior. What would you think of me were I to treat you in such a way?

"This letter I signed not with the words 'your friend,' but rather 'very cordially yours.' Another month passed, with no news of Mongenod. *The Peruvians* did not meet with the great success that Mongenod was hoping for. I purchased a ticket for the twentieth performance and found it sparsely attended, although Madame Scio sang wonderfully. In the lobby I was told that the play would run only a few nights more. On seven different occasions I went to see Mongenod but never found him in; each time I left my name with the landlady. I then wrote him again:

Monsieur, already you have lost my friendship; if you do not wish to lose my esteem, you will now treat me as you would a stranger, which is to say politely, and tell me if you will be able to repay me when your debt comes due. My future actions toward you will be determined by the nature of your response.

YOUR SERVANT, ALAIN.

"No answer came. It was then 1799; two months later a year would have passed since Mongenod's visit. Soon the debt came due, and I went to see Bordin. Armed with my attestation of debt, he filed a complaint and petitioned for redress. Now, this was a disastrous time for France's military ambitions, and with one debacle following on another, the price of government securities had fallen enormously: a single investment of seven francs could purchase an annual return of five francs. Thus, my hundred golden *louis* would have provided me with a yearly revenue of fifteen hundred francs. Morning after morning I sat with my cup of coffee, brooding over the daily newspaper, grumbling, 'Cursed Mongenod! If it weren't for him, I could be earning a thousand *écus* per year!' Mongenod had become my bête noire, I sometimes railed at him aloud even as I was out walking in the street. 'But there is always Bordin,' I used to tell myself; 'he will catch up with him one day, and that will be a very fine day indeed!' I poured out my hatred in endless imprecations; I cursed the man, pronouncing him guilty of every sort of wickedness. Ah! Monsieur Barillaud could not have spoken more truly. Finally, one morning, my debtor was shown into my rooms, as serene as if he didn't owe me a *centime*. Seeing him here before me, I found myself burning with a shame that rightly should have been his. I felt profoundly culpable, like a criminal caught in the act. This was after the coup of the *dix-huit brumaire*; France's fortunes had greatly improved, the price of securities was beginning to rise, and Bonaparte had set off for the battle of Marengo. 'It is unfortunate, Monsieur,' I said, standing to receive Mongenod, 'that I owe your visit only to the good offices of a bailiff.' Mongenod pulled up a chair and sat down. 'I have come to tell you,' he answered, 'that I find myself unable to repay you.' 'You robbed me of the chance to invest my money before the rise of the First Consul, when I would have made a small fortune . . . ' 'I know, Alain,' he said, 'I know. But what good will it do you to take me to court and ruin me with legal fees? I have had news from my wife and father-in-law; they have bought some land and sent me the bill for the various necessities of their new life, which cost me my entire fortune. I have had my few personal effects sent to Vlissingen. I intend to board a Dutch ship bound for America, and nothing shall hold me back. Bonaparte has won the battle of Marengo, and the treaty will soon be signed; I can thus travel without fear, and soon I shall be reunited at last with my family—for my dear little wife was with child when she left.' 'Then you have sacrificed me to your own interests?' I said. 'Yes,' he answered, 'I believed you were my friend.' At that moment I felt a lesser man than Mongenod, so sublime did he seem as he spoke those words, so simple and yet so great. 'Did I not tell you of my intentions, here in this very room?' he went on. 'Was I not perfectly open with you? I came to you, Alain, as the only person who might still have some faith in me. Fifty *louis* would be lost forever, I told you; but a hundred I will return to you. I named no date, for how can I predict the end of my long battle with poverty? You were the only friend I had left. All the others, even our old overseer Bordin, had come to despise me, precisely because I owed them money. Oh! You do not know, Alain, how cruel is the pain that grips the heart of an honest man fallen into penury when he comes to ask a friend for assistance! . . . And everything that follows! I dearly hope you never learn of these things; they are more horrible than the torments of death. You wrote me letters that you would have found odious indeed had I written them to you in similar circumstances. What you expected of me was not in my power. You are the only one to whom I shall seek to justify myself. For all the rigor with which you have treated me, and although you were transformed from a friend to a creditor the day you sent Bordin for an attestation of debt, thereby renouncing the sublime contract we made in this room with a simple handshake and a mutual flow of tears, I have kept in my mind only the memory of that happy morning. For that reason, I have come here to say: "You who know nothing of poverty, do not condemn poverty's ways!" I had not an hour to write you my response, not even a second! Perhaps you would have preferred that I come and ply you with sweet words? . . . You might as well ask a hare fleeing a pack of dogs and huntsmen to rest in a clearing and nibble at the grass! I did not send you an invitation, it is true; I did not have tickets enough to meet the demands of all those on whom my fate depended. I was a mere novice to the theater, and I fell prey to the musicians, the actors, the singers, the orchestra. To finance my journey and my family's needs, I have sold *The Peruvians* to the director, along with two other plays I had been keeping in the drawer of my desk. I leave for Holland without a *sou* to my name. I shall have to live on bread until I have reached Vlissingen. My voyage is paid for, and nothing more. Were it not for the pity of my landlady, who has not lost her faith in me, I would have been obliged to travel on foot, carrying my bag on my shoulders. Thus, in spite of your mistrust, my gratitude to you remains entire, for without you I could never have sent my wife and her father to New York. No, *Monsieur* Alain, I will not forget that the hundred *louis* you lent me could have bought you a fifteen-hundred-franc annuity today.' 'I would like to believe you, Mongenod,' I said, almost struck dumb by his tone. 'Ah! So you no longer call me *Monsieur*,' he exclaimed, gazing tenderly into my eyes. 'By God! I would be far less sorry to leave France if I knew I still had one friend here, in whose eyes I am not a swindler, or a wastrel, or an idle dreamer. Even in the depths of my misery, I loved an angel, and a man who loves well, Alain, is never entirely detestable . . . ' On these words I held out my hand, and he pressed it warmly. 'May Heaven protect you,' I said to him. 'Then we are still friends?' he asked. 'Yes,' I replied. 'Let it not be said that the playmate of my childhood and the boon companion of my youth set out for America with the weight of my anger on his shoulders!' With tears in his eyes, Mongenod gave me a final embrace and hurried to the door. A few days later I met Bordin. I told him the story of our last interview, and with a smile he answered, 'Let us hope this was something more than an act! He asked nothing of you?' 'No,' I answered. 'He came to see me as well,' he replied. 'I was very nearly as weak as you, and he asked me for something to sustain him on the road. Ah well, we shall see what we shall see!' Bordin's remark left me shaken once again; had I stupidly allowed myself to be swayed by my own sensitivity? 'But he did just as I did—him, a prosecutor!' I often reminded myself.

"It would serve no purpose to tell you of what followed; suffice it to say that I lost my entire fortune, with the exception of my remaining hundred *louis*. These I invested in government securities, but the price had grown so high that at age thirty-four I found myself struggling to survive on an income of five hundred francs. On Bordin's recommendation, I was given a position in a branch of the state pawnshop on the Rue des Petits-Augustins, which offered a salary of eight hundred francs. I adopted a very modest way of life. I lived on the Rue des Marais, in a small fourth-floor apartment composed of two rooms and a closet, which cost me two hundred fifty francs. I took my meals in a boardinghouse for forty francs a month. Evenings, I kept ledgers. Ugly as I am, and poor to boot, I was forced to abandon all hope of marriage."

Hearing Alain's harsh judgment of himself expressed with such endearing resignation, Godefroid made a gesture that conveyed the likeness of their two destinies more eloquently than any confession. The little man paused, as if awaiting some word from his listener.

"You have never been loved? . . ." asked Godefroid.

"Never!" he replied, "except by Madame, who returns to all of us the love that we feel for her, a love that I might well call divine ... You have seen it for yourself: we live through her life, just as she lives through ours. We share one single soul among us, and although they are not *physical*, our pleasures are nonetheless intense, for we exist only by our hearts ... What more can I tell you, my child? When a woman has learned to appreciate our spiritual qualities, she cares little for the externals, and then she is old ... In short, I have suffered terribly ..."

"Ah! As do I ..." said Godefroid.

"Under the Empire," Alain went on, his eyes downcast, "the securities dividends were not distributed regularly, and we had to expect an occasional suspension of payment. From 1802 to 1814, not a week went by that I did not curse Mongenod for all my travails. 'Were it not for Mongenod,' I used to tell myself, 'I could have married. Were it not for him, I would never have had to endure these privations.' But sometimes, too, I said to myself, 'Perhaps the wretch's sad destiny pursues him yet, in that foreign land!' In 1806, one day when life seemed particularly difficult to bear, I wrote him a long letter, which I forwarded to him by way of Holland. I received no reply, and for three years I waited, investing all my frustrated hopes in that response. Finally I resigned myself to my lot. I had my five-hundred-franc annuity and my twelve hundred francs from the pawnbrokers, for I had been given an increase in wages; to supplement my income, I kept books for Monsieur Birotteau, the perfumer, who paid me a modest salary of five hundred francs. Thus, I kept body and soul together; indeed, I was able to put aside eight hundred francs each year. At the beginning of 1814, I invested nine thousand francs of my savings in government securities, at forty francs per share; this assured me an annuity of sixteen hundred francs for my old age. Soon I was earning fifteen hundred francs from the pawnbroker and six hundred for my bookkeeping services; together with my sixteen hundred from the State, I enjoyed a total income of three thousand seven hundred francs. I took an apartment on the Rue de Seine and began to lead a more comfortable life. Nevertheless, my work kept me in contact with this city's many unfortunates. My twelve years at the pawnshop had given me a close acquaintance with the misery that still exists in our society.

Now and then I offered my personal assistance to those in particularly difficult straits. It gave me great pleasure to find that, of the ten households to which I lent my assistance, one or two did in fact succeed in finding a way out of poverty. I now came to realize that there is no true beneficence in simply showering our money on the poor. What people call charity, it seemed to me, is often nothing more than a sort of subsidy for criminal behavior. I began to study this question. I was then fifty years old, and for all practical purposes my life was over. 'What am I good for?' I asked myself. 'To whom will I leave my fortune? Suppose I filled my apartment with fine furniture, suppose I hired an excellent cook, suppose I could be assured of a comfortable existence for the rest of my days—what would I do with myself? How would I occupy my time?' Thus, eleven years of revolutions and fifteen years of poverty had devoured what should have been the happiest days of my existence! Slowly but implacably, my life had been eroded away, dissipated in days of fruitless labor—or, at best, in the mere struggle to survive. At the age of fifty, one can no longer simply free oneself from the obscurity of one's destiny, from a life stunted by want, and catapult oneself toward a more brilliant future; nevertheless, one can always make oneself useful. My reflections on charity had convinced me that the value of monetary aid is increased tenfold when it is accompanied by a close supervision of the recipient, for the poor require guidance above all else; if they can be taught to profit by the work they do for others, they will at least enjoy the benefits of the speculator's intelligence. I obtained some fine results with this system, of which I was very proud. I had found both a goal and an occupation, not to mention the exquisite delights of playing the role of Providence, on however small a scale."

"And today you play that same role on a larger scale?" Godefroid asked, excitedly.

"Oh! So you want to know the entire story?" the old man said. "Not yet." He paused, then went on: "Would you believe it? The meagerness of my income often brought me back to thoughts of Mongenod. 'But for Mongenod, I could be doing so much more,' I sometimes said to myself. 'If a scoundrel had not deprived me of my fifteen-hundred-franc annuity,' I often thought, 'I could easily rescue that family from their misery.' And so I excused my own impotence by accusing another; and those to whom I could offer only consoling words cursed Mongenod along with me. Their maledictions greatly soothed my embittered heart. One morning, in January 1816, my housekeeper announced a visitor. Who was it? . . . Mongenod! Monsieur Mongenod! And who did I then see before me? That beautiful young woman, now aged thirty-six, accompanied by three children; then Mongenod, looking younger than when he had set off, for wealth and happiness always cast a sort of glow over their favorites. I had last seen him thin, pale, yellow, and haggard; he returned hale, portly, jolly as a prebendary, and quite elegantly dressed. He gave me a hearty embrace. Finding himself rather coolly received, he said: 'Could I have come earlier, my friend? Only since 1815 have the seas been reopened to travelers, and I needed a further eighteen months to liquidate my holdings, close my accounts, and collect my outstanding debts. I have succeeded, my friend! I received your letter in 1806, and left at once on a Dutch ship to bring you a small fortune, but the unification of Holland with the French Empire offered the English a motive to seize the vessel. I was captured and taken to Jamaica; by a fortuitous stroke of luck, I managed to make my escape. I returned at once to New York, only to find that I was ruined; for, in my absence, poor Charlotte had become the defenseless prey of a whole horde of swindlers. I was thus forced to rebuild the edifice of my fortune from the ground up. Nevertheless, here we are home again at last. I can see with what interest you are studying these children; perhaps you can guess how often we have told them of our family's benefactor!' 'Oh! yes, Monsieur,' said lovely Madame Mongenod, 'never did a day go by that we did not remember your kindness. With every transaction we made, we thought of you. For so long we have worked in joyful anticipation of this moment, knowing full well that this tribute can never acquit our debt of gratitude.' With this Madame Mongenod held out the magnificent coffer you see before you, in which I found one hundred and fifty thousand-franc notes. 'My poor Alain, you have suffered terribly, I know; from afar we imagined your torments, and exhausted ourselves in fruitless attempts to send you this money,' Mongenod went on. 'You were unable to marry, you told me so yourself; but here is our eldest daughter, raised with the notion of becoming your wife, with a dowry of five hundred thousand francs...' 'No, I will not be the cause of her sorrows! May God protect me from that!' I quickly cried, my eyes fixed on a girl as beautiful as her mother had been at that age. I drew her toward me and kissed her on the forehead. 'Have no fear, my beautiful child!' I said to her. 'A man of fifty years and a girl of seventeen! And a man as ugly as I!' I cried. 'Never!' 'Monsieur,' she answered me, 'my father's benefactor will never be ugly in my eyes.' These words, spoken spontaneously and with perfect sincerity, showed me that everything in Mongenod's story was true; I then extended my hand toward my old friend, and we embraced a second time. 'Dear Mongenod,' I told him, 'I have wronged you; so often I have accused you, cursed you . . .' 'You had no choice, Alain,' he answered, his cheeks reddening. 'You were suffering, and I was the cause...' I pulled the Mongenod dossier from a folder and signed his promissory note to acknowledge repayment. 'And now you must all take lunch with me,' I told them. 'Only on the understanding that you will come and dine with us as soon as we have settled into our new home,' Mongenod answered, 'for we arrived only yesterday. First we must find a house, and then I intend to open a bank for North American trade here in Paris. One day, when I am gone, I will leave it all to this fine lad,' he concluded, showing me his elder son, a boy of fifteen. We spent the rest of the day together, and that evening we went to the theater, as Mongenod and his family were starved for entertainment. The next day I invested my new fortune in government securities, bringing my annuity to fifteen thousand francs. With this I was able to abandon the bookkeeping that had once occupied my evenings and to tender my resignation from the pawnshop, much to the delight of the ill-paid part-time workers below me. My friend went on to found the banking house of Mongenod and Company, which reaped enormous profits in the early days of the Restoration; he died in 1827, at the age of sixty-three. His daughter, whose dowry later grew to a million francs, married the Viscount de Fontaine. The son, whom you know, is not yet married; he lives with his mother and younger brother. Their bank offers us all we might possibly require. Frédéric—for in that distant land his father had christened him with my name—Frédéric Mongenod is, at thirty-seven years, one of the most competent and trustworthy bankers of Paris. Not long ago, Madame Mongenod finally confessed to me that she had indeed sold her hair for two *écus*, so that they might have bread to eat. Every year she offers me twenty-four cartloads of wood for the poor, in repayment for the half cartload I sent her so long ago."

"And now I understand your relationship with the House of Mongenod," said Godefroid, "and the source of your fortune . . ."

The little man looked at Godefroid, still smiling that same gentle, sly smile.

"Go on . . ." Godefroid then said, sensing from Monsieur Alain's air that he had not yet told him all.

"The resolution of this affair, my dear Godefroid, made the most profound impression on my heart. Despite all he had endured, my friend forgave my injustice; but I could not forgive myself."

"Oh!" said Godefroid.

"My annual income then exceeded my requirements by some ten thousand francs; I resolved to devote this sum to acts of carefully considered beneficence," Monsieur Alain quietly continued. "It was at about that time that I met a judge of the lower court of the Seine precinct, a man by the name of Popinot, whose passing we mourned three years ago. For fifteen years, he had been practicing charity of the most active sort in the Saint-Marcel neighborhood; it was he, along with Madame and our venerable vicar of Notre-Dame, who conceived the association to which we have devoted our lives. And so, since 1825, we have struggled to do good for our fellow men, always in secret, and not without success. Our association has found its soul in Madame de La Chanterie, for she is truly at the heart of all we do here. The vicar worked to deepen our faith, showing us that our acts must be unfailingly virtuous if we are to inspire virtue in others—in short, that we must lead by example. The further we advanced down that path, the happier we found ourselves, in perfect measure. Thus, from my regret at having misjudged my childhood friend grew the idea of devoting my life to the poor, offering both my own labors and the fortune Mongenod had brought me, which I had accepted so readily, never questioning the enormity of that sum in comparison to the modest loan I had offered him—but the destination of my new fortune made up for that."

This story alone, recounted without false eloquence and with a touching bonhomie in the speaker's voice, gesture, and gaze, would have been enough to inspire Godefroid to join this noble, holy circle, had he not already resolved to do just that.

"You know little of the ways of the world," said Godefroid. "Most men would never give a second thought to the error that so tormented your conscience."

"I know only the unfortunates of this world,"Alain answered. "I have little desire to know a world where people can think so little of misjudging their fellow men. But soon it will be midnight, and I have my chapter of the *Imitation of Christ* to meditate on. Good night."

Godefroid took the old man's hand and clasped it in fervent admiration. "Can you tell me the story of Madame de La Chanterie?" he asked.

"I cannot, without her consent," the little man answered, "for it involves one of the most terrible events in the history of the Empire. I met Madame through my friend Bordin; he knew all the secrets of her noble life, and it was he who led me into this house, so to speak."

"In any case," Godefroid answered, "I thank you for having told me your story. It holds lessons I would do well to learn."

"Do you know the moral of that story?"

"Tell me," Godefroid replied, "for I might see in it something other than you!"

"Well!" said the old man, "here it is: Pleasure is nothing more than an accident in a Christian's life. It is not the goal. So often we realize this too late."

"And what happens when one becomes a Christian?" asked Godefroid.

"Look!" said Alain.

With one finger he directed Godefroid's attention to a plaque that the new boarder might have failed to see, since this was his first visit to the old man's rooms. Godefroid turned around and read these words, inscribed in letters of gold on a black background: *Transire benefaciendo.*

"That, my child, is the true meaning of life for a Christian. This is our device. If you become one of us, this will be the whole of your charge. When we arise, when we retire, as we dress, we have this injunction ever before our eyes, and we repeat it to ourselves at every hour of the day ... Ah! If you only knew what immense pleasures are to be found in that task! ..."

"As for instance? ..." said Godefroid, hoping for some sort of revelation.

"To begin with, we are as rich as the Baron de Nucingen ... But the *Imitation of Christ* forbids us to possess anything solely for ourselves; we are merely distributors, and were we to allow ourselves the slightest surge of pride, we would cease to be worthy of that role. No longer could we aspire to *Transire benefaciendo,* for pride is the emptiest of all the pleasures of the mind. The moment you tell yourself, your chest swelling, 'I am playing the role of Providence,' as you might have done this morning had you been in my place, offering a poor family a new lease on life, the moment you come to believe such a thing, you become a Sardanapalus! You are corrupted! The other gentlemen in this house have learned never to think of themselves as they perform their good deeds; you must strip away all vanity, all pride, all self-love—and that, I assure you, is no easy thing! ..."

Godefroid wished Monsieur Alain a good night and returned to his rooms, deeply moved by what he had heard; but his curiosity was more irritated than satisfied, for the central figure of this house's *tableau vivant* remained Madame de La Chanterie. This woman's life had come to mean so much to him that he vowed not to leave these lodgings until he had uncovered her secret. He had at least learned that these five companions constituted an ambitious enterprise devoted solely to charity, but this interested him far less than his new heroine.

For the next few days the neophyte observed this elite little society with redoubled attention and came to feel the effects of a spiritual phenomenon neglected by our modern-day philanthropists, no doubt out of mere ignorance: he was changed for the better by those around him. The law that governs the influence of a given milieu over the physical nature of its inhabitants also holds true for their moral and spiritual sides, whence it follows that the housing of convicts together under one roof is among the greatest of all crimes against society, and their isolation an experiment extraordinarily unlikely to bear fruit. Rather, convicts should be placed in the hands of religious institutions, and surrounded by the wonders of Saintliness rather than the miracles of Evil. We may expect that the Church would embrace this task with unbounded devotion. It has long sent missionaries into the heart of the most savage or barbaric lands; with what joy, then, would it charge its servants with the mission of taking in civilization's savages, and of teaching them the catechism—for every criminal is an atheist, though often he does not know it.

Godefroid saw in his five housemates the very qualities they demanded of him. They seemed to know nothing of pride, or of vanity. Their humility was sincere, their piety genuine, with none of the ignoble pretensions of *religiosity*, in the most debased sense of that word. These virtues were contagious; he was gripped by a desire to imitate these five anonymous heroes, and finally he fell into an impassioned study of the book that he had at first dismissed. Within two weeks he had reduced life to its essentials, to what it truly is when viewed from the heights of religious faith. Finally, his sense of curiosity, once so worldly, so easily aroused by vulgar concerns, became purified. To be sure, he did not lose it entirely, for still he could not quell his fascination with Madame de La Chanterie; nevertheless, without exactly trying to do so, he displayed a discretion that his fellow boarders did not fail to notice, for the divine spirit had rendered their faculties of observation astonishingly keen—as is true, moreover, of all deeply devout souls. Any concentration of the soul's moral forces, through any system, increases their power tenfold.

"Our friend is not yet converted," the good Father de Vèze often said, "but he is asking to be . . ."

Godefroid's inexhaustible interest in Madame de La Chanterie's story would not go unsatisfied much longer, for its revelation was soon made unavoidable by an unexpected circumstance.

Paris was then abuzz with the execution of two criminals at the Barrière Saint-Jacques after a particularly sensational trial, worthy of a special place in the annals of French justice. The great fascination of this trial stemmed from the prisoners themselves, men of great audacity, superior in intellect to the common run of criminals, who horrified Parisian society with the cynicism of their replies on the stand. We should note that no newspaper ever found its way into Madame de La Chanterie's home; it was only thanks to Godefroid's bookkeeping master that he learned of the rejection of their appeal, for the trial itself had ended well before he came to this house.

"Do you ever encounter anyone akin to these terrible scoundrels?" he asked his new companions. "And if you do, how do you go about dealing with them? . . ."

"First of all," said Monsieur Nicolas, "there are no terrible scoundrels. To be sure, there are certain diseased temperaments that can be treated only at the Charenton asylum; these few medical exceptions aside, we encounter only people without religion, or people who reason poorly, and it is the mission of the charitable to pick such lost souls up off the ground and to set them back onto the proper path."

"And all things are possible for the apostle," said Father de Vèze, "for he has God beside him . . ."

"But suppose you were sent to minister to these two convicts," said Godefroid. "Surely you could have no effect on them."

"We would not have enough time," the good Alain observed.

"As a general rule," said Monsieur Nicolas, "the souls that religion is called upon to treat are hardened nearly beyond repentance; it is asked to work wonders but never given the time to do so. In our hands, these two could have become very distinguished men, as they possess an immense energy; but they have committed a murder, and we will never have that chance. Human justice has claimed them for itself . . ."

"Then," said Godefroid, "you oppose the death penalty? . . ."

Monsieur Nicolas abruptly rose and left the room.

"Never speak of the death penalty in Monsieur Nicolas's presence. He was once assigned to oversee the execution of a criminal whom he recognized as his own illegitimate son . . ."

"And he was innocent, too!" Monsieur Joseph concluded.

Just then Madame de La Chanterie returned to join the little gathering after a few moments' absence.

"But in the end, you must admit," said Godefroid to Monsieur

Joseph, "that Society cannot long exist without the death penalty, and that, tomorrow morning, when these men climb the steps to the guillo——"

All at once Godefroid felt his mouth clapped shut by a forceful hand, and Father de Vèze led Madame de La Chanterie out of the room again. Her face had gone white, and she seemed about to faint.

"What have you done?" said Monsieur Joseph to Godefroid. "Take him away, Alain!" he said, removing his hand from Godefroid's lips, then rising to follow Father de Vèze into Madame de La Chanterie's rooms.

"Come with me," said Monsieur Alain to Godefroid. "You leave us no choice but to reveal the secrets of Madame's life."

And so, a few moments later, the two friends found themselves once more in Alain's bedroom, where the old man had earlier recounted his own story.

"Well?" said Godefroid, visibly distraught to find himself the cause of what, in this saintly house, could rightly be called a catastrophe.

"I am waiting for Manon to come and assure us that all is well," the little man answered, hearing the domestic's footsteps on the stairs.

"Monsieur, Madame will be fine; the Father convinced her she'd misunderstood your conversation!" said Manon, casting Godefroid an almost furious glance.

"My God!" cried the poor young man, his eyes filling with tears.

"Come now, sit down," said Monsieur Alain to Godefroid, taking a seat as he spoke.

And he fell silent for a moment, collecting his thoughts.

"I do not know," said the kindly old man, "if I have the talent required to give a proper account of a life so cruelly tested; I am a very poor orator, and you must excuse me if you find my words inadequate to the events and calamities of my tale. Remember that I left school long ago, and that I am the child of a century in which thought was valued more highly than effect, a prosaic time, before men had learned to call things by any name other than their own."

Godefroid gestured as if to say, "I am listening," and in this expression of confidence and support the good Alain glimpsed a very real admiration.

"As you have just seen, my young friend," the old man went on, "you can remain among us no longer without some knowledge of the horrifying events of that sainted woman's life. There are certain cursed ideas, allusions, and words that are strictly forbidden in this house, lest they reopen Madame's wounds; for her pain, once or twice reborn, might well be enough to kill her . . ."

"Oh! My God!" cried Godefroid. "What have I done?"

"Were it not for the timely intervention of Monsieur Joseph, who sensed that you were about to name the dreaded instrument of death and so stifled your words at once, you would have destroyed poor Madame . . . It is time that you knew all, for you will become one of us, of that we are all now convinced.

"Madame de La Chanterie," he went on after a pause, "is a descendant of one of the first families of lower Normandy. She was born Barbe-Philiberte de Champignelles, into a family from the younger branch of that house. She was thus destined to take the veil if she could not find a husband willing to forgo any inheritance; this was common practice among the less well-to-do. Now, there was a local gentleman by the name of de La Chanterie, the scion of a family dating back to the crusade of Philippe Auguste but since fallen into obscurity, who was most eager to regain the standing to which his high birth entitled him. Indeed, he had doubly fallen from grace, for as a Royal tax collector at the time of our war with the principality of Hanover, he had appropriated some three hundred thousand *écus* destined for the King's armies. This old man had a son residing in Paris, where, overly confident in his family's considerable fortune—further inflated by the rumors of his province—he was leading a life that deeply troubled his father. Mademoiselle de Champignelles's merit gained some celebrity in the Bessin region, and soon the old man, whose small fiefdom lay between Caen and Saint-Lô, heard it deplored that so perfect a young lady, so likely to bring a man happiness, should be obliged to live out her days in a convent. Inquiring further into the young person's situation, he learned that the de Champignelles family might be persuaded to offer young Philiberte's hand to his son, so long as no dowry was expected. He traveled to Bayeux, where he succeeded in procuring a number of interviews with the de Champig-

nelles family and found himself charmed by the girl's evident qualities. At sixteen, Mademoiselle de Champignelles foretokened the fine
woman she would later become, displaying a firm piety, unfaltering
good sense, and inflexible uprightness; she was not the type to stray
from a husband, even one she had not chosen for herself. The old nobleman saw in this charming girl the woman who could rein in his son,
through the authority of her virtue and the force of a character he
found steady but never severe; for—have you noticed?—no woman is
milder than Madame de La Chanterie, or more trusting. Even now, in
the twilight of her life, she has retained all the openness of innocent
youth. In her younger days, she refused even to believe in the possibility of evil; the slight guardedness you have seen in her was born
solely of her later misfortunes. Flush with his ill-gotten gains, the old
man pledged to renounce Mademoiselle Philiberte's inheritance; in
exchange, the de Champignelles, who were allied with some very important houses, promised to have the de La Chanterie fiefdom promoted to a barony, and they were true to their word. The young man's
aunt, Madame de Boisfrelon—the wife of the Councillor to Parliament who died in what is now your apartment—agreed to leave her
entire fortune to her nephew. With these matters arranged, the father
sent for his son. A Counsel of the Grand Conseil, aged twenty-five at
the time of his marriage, the son had committed many follies with the
young lords of his time and lived the sort of life they led; thus, the old
embezzler had several times been obligated to pay off his considerable
debts. In anticipation of further such lapses to come, the unhappy father amiably ceded a part of his fortune to his future daughter-in-law;
but as a precaution, he ensured that the de La Chanterie fiefdom
could be passed on only to the male offspring of this union . . . a measure made quite useless by the Revolution," Monsieur Alain added
parenthetically. "The young Counsel had a face like an angel, and a
bearing both graceful and athletic; he thus enjoyed the power to
charm any woman he pleased. As you might well expect, Mademoiselle de Champignelles was soon quite smitten with her new husband.
Delighted with this promising start, and thinking his son on the road
to redemption, the old man sent the newlyweds to Paris at his own expense. This was in early 1788; there followed nearly a full year of con-

jugal bliss, in which Madame de La Chanterie tasted of all the little favors, all the delicate attentions that a man in love can lavish on his only beloved. The honeymoon was to be a brief one, but while it lasted it brought a flood of joy to the heart of that noble and unhappy woman. As you know, women in those days raised their children themselves, and Madame now had a daughter. At such a time, a woman should be the object of redoubled tenderness, but it was precisely then that Madame's torments began. The young Counsel was forced to sell all his available assets to pay off some old debts he had hidden from his father, as well as some new losses incurred at the gaming table. Then the National Assembly announced the dissolution of the Grand Conseil, of the Parliament, of all the judicial posts acquired at so high a cost by their occupants. The young household, now augmented by a daughter, thus found itself with no other assets than the properties promised them in the old man's will and the dowry he had granted Madame de La Chanterie. Within twenty months of her marriage, that charming woman, aged seventeen and a half, had no choice but to move with her daughter to a small apartment in a squalid neighborhood of Paris, and to work with her hands for her living. Her husband had now entirely abandoned her, and step by step he descended into the society of the lowest sort of creatures. Never did Madame rebuke her husband, never did she accuse him of any wrongdoing. All through those dark days, she told us, she prayed to God for her dear Henri, for such was the scoundrel's name—and that name must never be spoken in this house, nor Henriette. But let me return to my story. Leaving her little room on the Rue de la Corderie-du-Temple only to collect payment or to seek out new work, Madame de La Chanterie was able to eke out a living, thanks largely to the hundred *livres* sent her each month by her father-in-law, moved as he was by her exceeding virtue. Nevertheless, foreseeing the day when this source would run dry, the unhappy young woman had taken up the arduous profession of the corset maker, and went to work for a famous *couturière*. Soon the old tax collector did indeed die, and his legacy was quickly devoured by his son, thanks to the overturning of the laws observed under the vanished monarchy. The former Counsel had now become one of the most bloodthirsty members of the revolutionary tribunal, and made himself the terror of Normandy; all his passions were thus satisfied at once. With the fall of Robespierre he was imprisoned in turn, and his execution seemed a virtual certainty, given the loathing he had earned in his home province. In a letter of farewell, Madame de La Chanterie's husband informed her of the fate that awaited him. Wasting no time, she left her little girl in the care of a neighbor and set off for the city where the wretch was being held, bringing with her the few *louis* that constituted her entire fortune; that sum bought her entrance into the prison, and she succeeded in saving her husband's life through a ruse that would later serve Madame de Lavalette so well: exchanging clothes with him, she stayed behind in the cell while he left the prison undetected. She was sentenced to death for her treachery, but even her accusers found this an overly vindictive punishment, and the tribunal once presided over by her husband discreetly undertook to gain her release. She returned to Paris on foot with no one to help her, sleeping in barns and often relying on the charity of strangers for her food."

"Dear Lord!" cried Godefroid.

"Wait!" resumed the little man, "this is nothing. Over the next eight years, the poor woman saw her husband on three occasions. On the first, the gentleman spent twice twenty-four hours in his wife's modest lodgings, taking all her money even as he heaped tendernesses upon her, swearing that he had undergone a complete conversion. 'I was,' she told us, 'powerless against a man for whom I prayed every day, and who occupied my every thought.' The second time, Monsieur de La Chanterie arrived deathly ill, and with what a disease! . . . She tended to him, and saved him; then she tried to lead him back into more honest sentiments and a more upright way of life. Promising to do everything that this angel asked of him, the revolutionary nevertheless plunged once more into the most horrible dissolution, and escaped the long arm of the Public Ministry only by again taking refuge in his wife's home, where he died a peaceful death.

"Oh! But this is still nothing," cried the good man, observing Godefroid's astonishment. "No one in the society he had adopted as his own was aware that he had a wife. Two years after the wretch's death, Madame de La Chanterie learned of the existence of a second

Madame de La Chanterie, a widow like herself, and like herself penniless. The bigamist had found two angels, equally incapable of betraying him.

"Sometime around 1803," Monsieur Alain continued after a pause, "Madame de La Chanterie's uncle, Monsieur de Boisfrelon, who had fled the country during the Revolution, returned to Paris and offered her a fortune of two hundred thousand francs. The old tax collector had entrusted him with this sum for safekeeping, asking that it be used for the maintenance of Madame's offspring. Monsieur de Boisfrelon convinced the widow to return to Normandy, where she completed her daughter's education and, on the advice of the former magistrate, bought a part of her father-in-law's domain for a very reasonable price."

"Ah!" cried Godefroid.

"This is still nothing," said the good Alain, "the hardest times are still ahead. To continue: In 1807, after four years of tranquillity, Madame de La Chanterie married her only daughter to a gentleman whose piety, background, and fortune she found most promising: the fair-haired boy, as they say, of the high society of the provincial capital where she and her daughter spent their winters. That society was composed of seven or eight families, from the highest ranks of the nobility: the d'Esgrignon family, the Troisvilles, the Casterans, the Nouâtres, and so on. After eighteen months, this man left his wife, changed his name, and vanished somewhere in Paris. Only later, by the illumination of lightning bolts in the midst of a great tempest, did Madame de La Chanterie learn the cause of that separation, for her daughter, whom she had raised with devoted attention and educated in the purest religious sentiment, had told her nothing. Madame de La Chanterie was deeply hurt by this lack of trust. Several times already her daughter had displayed traits reminiscent of her father's wild temperament, exacerbated by an almost masculine willfulness. The husband had chosen to run off without warning, leaving his affairs in a lamentable state. To this day Madame de La Chanterie remains dismayed by this catastrophe, which no human power could have prevented. Those she had prudently consulted before the marriage had assured her that the fiancé's fortune was unencumbered, his lands owned outright; but the fact was that for ten years the estate had been mortgaged for more than its value. The property was thus sold, and the poor bride, with only her own small fortune to her name, returned to live with her mother. Madame de La Chanterie later learned that it was only in hopes of collecting their debts that the local worthies had vouched for the wretch, as he owed them all, to one degree or another. Thus, from the moment of her arrival in the province, Madame de La Chanterie had been seen as a potentially useful dupe. Nevertheless, there were other reasons for this catastrophe, as you will soon see from a confidential document placed in the hands of the Emperor. For it was through his devotion to the King's cause in the stormiest days of the Revolution that this man had garnered the benevolence of his province's leading monarchists. He was once one of Louis XVIII's most active agents, intimately involved in every Royalist plot after 1793, escaping detection so consistently and with such dexterity that in the end he began to arouse suspicions among his masters. Thanked for his services by Louis XVIII and excluded from all further affairs, he had returned to his properties, now encumbered with mortgages and liens. Little of this was known at the time (those privy to the secrets of the Royal cabinet were loath to acknowledge so dangerous a collaborator), but his background made him the object of a sort of cult in a city devoted to the Bourbons, where the cruelest tactics of the Chouans were considered justifiable acts of warfare. The d'Esgrignons, the Casterans, the Chevalier de Valois, in a word the whole of the Aristocracy and the Church opened their arms to the Royalist diplomat and nestled him safely in their lap, their protective embrace made all the tighter by his creditors' desire for repayment. For three years this scoundrel—a perfect counterpart of the late Monsieur de La Chanterie—forced himself to lead what appeared an upright existence, displaying the most profound devotion and quelling his penchant for vice. In the first months of the marriage, he established a sort of influence over his wife; he attempted to corrupt her with his doctrines, if indeed atheism can be called a doctrine, and with his flippant treatment of the most sacred principles. Now, on first returning to his native province, this second-rate diplomat had formed a close friendship with a young man, also saddled with debts but of an air as courageous and forthright as he himself was dissembling and cowardly. This houseguest's adventurous life, fine features, and good character had much to move a young girl's heart; thus, the husband was able to use him as a sort of tool to underscore his own loathsome ideas. Never did the girl breathe a word to her mother of the abyss into which she had been thrown. Nor could the mother have suspected, given the pains she had taken to assure her only daughter a good marriage; mere *prudence* would be far too weak a word to describe the energy she had devoted to that task. When it did finally come, this revelation was a terrible blow for a woman so pure, so devout, and so grievously tested by life. Its effect was to destroy Madame de La Chanterie's faith in herself, isolating her from her daughter all the more in that, as a recompense for her sufferings, the young woman virtually demanded her freedom, dominated her mother, even mistreated her on occasion. Thus, wounded in all her affections, deceived by a beloved husband for whom she had willingly sacrificed her happiness, her fortune, and her life, deceived by the exclusively religious education she had given her daughter, deceived by Society itself in the matter of this marriage, and finding only ingratitude in a heart she had sown with the finest sentiments, she drew all the nearer to God, whose hand had struck her so brutally. She transformed herself into something very like a nun; she went to church every morning, she embraced the ascetic ways of the monastic life, and she began to set aside her money for the needs of the poor ...

"Has there ever been a life holier and more sorely tried than this noble woman's? Has there ever been a woman more stoical in misfortune, more courageous in danger, more perfectly Christian?" said the little man, looking into Godefroid's wondering eyes. "You have come to know Madame; no doubt you have admired her good sense, judgment, and thoughtfulness, for she possesses each of these in the highest degree. Now, these misfortunes alone would suffice to define any life as unsurpassed in adversities; and yet they are nothing in comparison with what God still held in store for her.

"But let us now speak of Madame de La Chanterie's daughter," said the old man, returning to his tale.

"Mademoiselle de La Chanterie was a girl of eighteen at the time of her marriage, dark-eyed and thin, of delicate complexion, with a fine-hued and remarkably pretty face. Above her elegant forehead, she displayed a mane of the most beautiful black hair, in perfect harmony with her brown, gaily twinkling eyes. There was a sort of daintiness in her appearance that belied her true nature and the manly force of her will. She had small hands and small feet; there was something slender and frail about her entire person, perfectly antithetical to any notion of force and energy. Having lived all her life at her mother's side, she was a girl of perfect innocence and remarkable piety. Like Madame de La Chanterie herself, she felt a fanatical attachment to the Bourbons; she was the sworn enemy of the Revolution and viewed Napoleon's reign as nothing other than a plague visited upon France in punishment for the wrongs of 1793. Such was of course her husband's thinking as well; indeed, the similarity of his opinions to his mother-in-law's had been a persuasive argument for that marriage—and one seconded by all the aristocrats of the province. Now, the husband's friend had commanded a band of Chouans in the hostilities of 1799, and it seems that the Baron (for Madame de La Chanterie's son-in-law was a baron) had no other plan, in bringing together his wife and his friend, than to use their mutual affection to procure the Chouans' aid and assistance. Although deep in debt and unable to support himself, that young adventurer lived a rich and sociable life, and was a most useful contact with other Royalist conspirators.

"Here I am obliged to say a few words on an association that caused a great stir in its day," said Monsieur Alain, interrupting his account. "I am referring to the Chauffeurs. These villains victimized every department of the west to one degree or another, although their goal was not so much simple pillage as a revival of the Royalist uprisings. The west was full of young men resisting the law of conscription, which was then, as you know, applied with a rigor that bordered on the tyrannical; among their ranks the Chauffeurs no doubt found an ample supply of recruits. From Mortagne to Rennes, and even beyond, to the very banks of the Loire, they launched one nocturnal raid after another; in this part of Normandy, their principal targets were the holders of private and Church properties seized and sold off after the Revolution. They thus spread terror through the entire province, and it would be no lie to say that in certain regions the law was powerless to combat them. These last, lingering echoes of the civil war did not cause as great a scandal as you might suppose, accustomed as we are nowadays to the clamorous publicity given by the popular press to the most insignificant political or civil trial. The government of the Empire was no different from any other absolutist power: the censors allowed nothing to be published on political matters, apart from faits accomplis, and even then only in grossly distorted form. If you were to take the trouble of looking through *Le Moniteur* or any other newspaper from that time, even those of the west, you would not find a single word on the four or five criminal trials that cost sixty or eighty of these brigands their heads. The name Chauffeurs was used in the Revolution to refer to the people of the Vendée, to the Chouans, to all who took up arms to defend the House of Bourbon; but it remained in judicial use under the Empire to refer to the Royalists still engaged in smaller, more isolated conspiracies. For these remaining fanatics, the Emperor and his Government were the enemy, and anything that could be taken from them was a thing rightly taken. I am merely telling you of these opinions; I do not seek to justify them in any way. And now I will go on with my story."

After a pause of the sort required in such a long account, the old man continued: "Now think of the Royalists ruined by the civil war of 1793, still gripped by their obsession; think of the effect of this penury on certain exceptional temperaments, such as Madame de La Chanterie's son-in-law and the onetime Chouan leader, and you will understand how an act of piracy directed against the Imperial Government—an act permitted by their political beliefs and considered helpful to the cause of justice—might also serve their own private interests. Thus, the young rebel leader set out to reignite the embers of the Chouan spirit in the surrounding countryside, in preparation for further attacks. Then came a terrible crisis for the Emperor: his armies were immobilized on Lobau Island by the English and Austrian forces, and likely to be defeated by a combined attack; but his subsequent victory at Wagram left little hope for the conspiracies then forming within France's borders. Nevertheless, these attempts to revive the civil war in Brittany, in the Vendée, and in a part of Normandy coincided opportunely with a crisis in the Baron's personal affairs, and he conceived the idea of committing a robbery to save his properties from his creditors. His plan was to attack a coach transporting the State's tax receipts, ostensibly to finance the arms and munitions needed by the Chouans and the resisters; but his real intention was to divert a large part of the money—some hundred thousand francs—for his own private use. His wife and his friend, more noble of sentiment than he, refused to allow this; a series of venomous arguments ensued, but his wife and the young rebel leader remained adamant that their takings must go entirely to the Royalist forces. Faced with this refusal, the Baron chose to disappear, thereby saving himself from debtors' prison. His creditors hoped to repay themselves from his wife's assets, but the wretch had exhausted the source of goodwill that leads a woman to sacrifice herself for her husband. As I have told you, poor Madame de La Chanterie knew nothing of all this. But that is only the beginning of an explanation; there is much yet to be said of the complex web that underlies these events.

"But the hour is late," said Alain, looking at his little clock, "and we would be here a good deal longer if I were to tell you the rest of this story. My friend Bordin, celebrated by the Royalists for his handling of the Simeuse trial, undertook the defense in this case, which has come to be known as the Affair of the Chauffeurs of Mortagne. When I first moved into this house, he entrusted me with two documents, which are still in my possession, for he died shortly thereafter. You will find that they lay out the facts much more succinctly than I ever could. This is a most complicated case. I would soon lose myself in the details, and you would have to listen to me speak for another two hours at least, whereas these pages will give you an excellent summary of the entire story. Tomorrow morning I will give you some final clarifications concerning the role of Madame de La Chanterie, for you will have learned enough from your reading to allow me to conclude in a few words."

He handed Godefroid a sheaf of yellowed papers. Wishing his neighbor a good night, the young man retired to his room. Before he fell asleep, he read the following two documents:

BILL OF INDICTMENT
Special Criminal Court of the Department of the Orne

The Prosecutor-General to the Imperial Court of Caen, appointed to the Special Criminal Court established by the Imperial decree of September 1809 and convening in Alençon, hereby submits to the court these findings of his investigation.

A conspiracy to commit armed robbery, carefully planned over many months and linked to a plot to foment unrest in the western provinces, has manifested itself in a number of attacks on citizens and their property, but most notably in the pillaging, on the——th of May 180——, of a coach carrying the tax receipts from the Caen Tax Bureau to the National Treasury. This attack recalls the most deplorable memories of a civil war now happily extinguished, replicating all the criminality of that conflict's combatants, but without the justification of their deeply held beliefs.

From its origin to its final moments, this plot is a tangled web, labyrinthine in its details; for this reason, the investigation required more than a year. Nevertheless, in every step of the crime's progress we shall find a wealth of evidence to reveal its preparation, its execution, and its consequences.

The guiding force behind this conspiracy is one Charles-Amédée-Louis-Joseph Rifoël, a former leader of the Chouans who calls himself the Chevalier du Vissard, born at Le Vissard, in the community of Saint-Mexme, near Ernée.

This culprit, to whom H.M. the Emperor and King granted clemency when peace returned to our land, and who rewarded his sovereign's magnanimity by falling back into his criminal ways, has already paid the ultimate price for his many misdeeds; but we must recall certain of his actions in these pages, for he enjoyed a considerable influence over the prisoners now before the court, and he is intimately involved in every aspect of this case.

Taking a false name to disguise his identity, as was the rebels' common practice, this dangerous agitator traveled through the western provinces under the alias Pierrot, searching out recruits for a new uprising; but his surest harbor was the Château de Saint-Savin, the residence of one Madame Lechantre and her daughter, Madame Bryond. This château lies in the community of Saint-Savin, near Mortagne, a locale intimately connected with the most terrible memories of the uprising of 1799. It was here that a band of brigands, led by a woman and aided by the infamous Marche-à-Terre, assassinated a courier and ransacked his coach. Indeed, criminality seems little short of endemic in this area.

For more than a year, Madame Bryond had been linked with this Rifoël by an intimacy that we will not attempt to define.

In April 1808, a meeting took place in Mortagne between Rifoël and a certain Boislaurier, a ringleader of the bloody uprisings in the west, who often went by the name of Auguste. It was he who devised the plot now brought before the court, and who provided all the direction necessary for its execution.

The nature of the relationship between the two leaders, previously unclear, has now been successfully established through the testimony of many independent witnesses, and further confirmed by the trial that followed Rifoël's arrest.

In the course of this meeting, Boislaurier agreed to ally himself with Rifoël for the purpose of future crimes.

Together, and without other accessories for the moment, they made their felonious plans, inspired by the absence of His Imperial and Royal Majesty, then commanding his armies in Spain. It was likely at this meeting that they resolved to make the seizing of State tax receipts their principal goal.

Some time later, a certain Dubut, from Caen, sent an emissary to the Château de Saint-Savin: one Hiley, alias the Plowman, famed for his skill in armed robbery. His mission was to offer the two men the instruction they would require to carry out this scheme.

Through Hiley, the conspirators soon gained the cooperation of a certain Herbomez, nicknamed General Intrepid, a former rebel like Rifoël, and similarly contemptuous of the Emperor's amnesty.

Herbomez and Hiley then recruited seven bandits from the surrounding communities, whom we may now identify as follows:

1. Jean Cibot, known as the Bread Thief, one of the most brazen members of the band formed by Montauran in the year VII, and an active participant in the earlier assassination of the courier in Mortagne.
2. François Lisieux, nicknamed the Grandson, a resister from the department of Mayenne.
3. Charles Grenier, alias Broom Flower, a deserter from the sixty-ninth half brigade.

4. Gabriel Bruce, alias Big John, one of the fiercest Chouans of the Fontaine division.

5. Jacques Horeau, alias the Stuart, ex-lieutenant of the same half brigade, a henchman of Tinténiac, who attained a certain notoriety in the Quiberon Expedition.

6. Marie-Anne Cabot, alias the Youth, a former groom to Monsieur Carol d'Alençon.

7. Louis Minard, a resister.

These conspirators were lodged in three nearby towns by three innkeepers loyal to Rifoël: Binet, Mélin, and Larivinière.

The necessary weapons were furnished by the *notaire* Jean-François Léveillé, an unrepentant rebel sympathizer and an intermediary with other rebel leaders still in hiding, and by one Félix Courceuil, alias the Confessor, a former surgeon of the rebel armies of the Vendée, both of them from Alençon.

Eleven rifles were concealed in Monsieur Bryond's house outside of Alençon without his knowledge, as he was then residing at his country house between Alençon and Mortagne.

After Monsieur Bryond abandoned his wife, leaving her to the fateful path she would follow, these rifles were mysteriously removed from the house and transported to the Château de Saint-Savin by Madame Bryond herself, in her personal coach.

The Orne and surrounding departments now fell prey to numerous acts of armed robbery, surprising both the authorities and the citizenry after so many years of unbroken calm. The timing of the attacks proves that these despicable enemies of the Government and Empire of France had learned from their contacts abroad of the coalition of 1809.

The *notaire* Léveillé, Madame Bryond, Dubut of Caen, Herbomez of Mayenne, Boislaurier of Le Mans, and Rifoël were the ringleaders of this felonious band, whose numbers include those arrested with Rifoël and duly punished, those named in the present indictment, and a number of others who have eluded the forces of justice, either through flight or through their accomplices' refusal to cooperate with the law.

Dubut resided in the community of Caen, and was thus able to alert Léveillé when the tax receipts were due to be sent off. In preparation for that event, Dubut made several journeys from Caen to Mortagne; Léveillé, too, was frequently seen on the public highways.

Let us note here that Léveillé came to Mélin's inn to see Bruce, Grenier, and Cibot as the rifles were being transported; finding his companions unloading these weapons for storage in a shed, he personally assisted in the operation.

A general meeting was arranged at the Hôtel de l'Écu-de-France in Mortagne. All of the accused assembled there, in various disguises. It was then that Léveillé, Madame Bryond, Dubut, Herbomez, Boislaurier, and Hiley—this last the most cunning of the secondary accomplices, just as Cibot is the boldest—obtained the cooperation of a certain Vauthier, alias Old Oak, a former domestic of the famous Longuy, and now a stableboy at the inn. Vauthier agreed to warn Madame Bryond when the tax coach made its customary stop at the hotel.

Until now, the brigands have been lodged separately, sometimes in one town, sometimes in another, through the careful planning of Courceuil and Léveillé. The time has now come to bring them together. This reunion is made possible by Madame Bryond, who offers the brigands a repair in an uninhabited wing of the Château de Saint-Savin, a few leagues from Mortagne, where she has been living with her mother since her husband's disappearance. Overseen by Hiley, the brigands settle into these new lodgings and stay for several days. Aided by her chambermaid, a girl by the name of Godard, Madame Bryond supplies everything required for the lodging and feeding of her guests; she provides straw to serve as their bedding, and in the company of Léveillé, she comes several times to visit the conspirators in the hiding place she has offered them. Provisions and foodstuffs are brought in under the direction of Courceuil, by order of Rifoël and Boislaurier.

The primary raid is now fully planned out, and the bandits have been issued their weapons. Leaving their lair at Saint-Savin, the brigands launch a series of smaller nocturnal sorties as they wait for the tax receipts to be sent off; the entire province is thus terrorized by their repeated assaults.

It was unquestionably this band of brigands that carried out the attacks on La Sartinière, Vonay, and the Château de Saint-Seny. As bold as they were felonious, the criminals left their victims so terrified that none offered any useful information to the forces of justice; our investigators were thus obliged to work by supposition alone.

But even as the brigands are exacting this toll from the holders of the nationalized assets, they are all the while carefully exploring the Woods of Le Chesnay, which they have chosen as the site of their crime.

The Chaussard brothers, former gamekeepers on the Troisville estate, operate an inn in the village of Louvigny, not far from those woods. This inn was to serve as the brigands' final meeting place. The two brothers know full well the role they will play; Courceuil and Boislaurier had made overtures to them long before, attempting to revive their loathing for the government of our august Emperor, and informing them that among their guests they would soon find the redoubtable Hiley and the equally redoubtable Cibot.

And so, on the sixth, Hiley leads the seven bandits to the Chaussard brothers' inn, where they stay for two days. On the eighth he leads them off again, to a destination three leagues away, ordering the brothers to assemble some provisions and bring them to a crossroads some small distance from town. Hiley then returns to the inn and spends the night alone.

Two figures on horseback—no doubt Madame Bryond and Rifoël, for it has been asserted that this woman often accompanied Rifoël in his travels, disguised as a man—arrive during the evening and enter into conversation with Hiley.

The next day, Hiley writes a letter to Léveillé and has it delivered by one of the Chaussard brothers, who returns at once with a reply.

Two hours later Madame Bryond and Rifoël arrive on horseback to confer with Hiley.

At some point in the course of these many conferences, it becomes clear that an ax will be needed to break open the crates. The *notaire* thus accompanies Madame Bryond to Saint-Savin, where a fruitless search for an ax is conducted. He then sets out for the inn again; halfway to his destination, he meets up with Hiley and informs him that they are in need of an ax.

Hiley returns to the inn and orders dinner for ten; he is then joined by the seven brigands, now fully armed. Hiley orders them to stow their weapons in military fashion, and they all sit down and sup hastily. Hiley asks that an abundant supply of provisions be prepared, to be taken away later; pulling the elder Chaussard aside, he asks him for the loan of an ax. The astonished innkeeper, if we are to believe him, refuses to comply. Courceuil and Boislaurier then arrive, and these three spend the next few hours pacing through Hiley's room, discussing their plans. Courceuil, alias the Confessor, the craftiest of all these brigands, finally gets hold of an ax; toward two o'clock in the morning, they all leave the hotel by different exits.

Every moment is now precious, for the attack on the coach has been fixed for later this fateful night. Hiley, Courceuil, and Boislaurier bring their cohorts into the woods and position them. Hiley will lie in wait with Minard, Cabot, and Bruce, on the right-hand side of the road. Boislaurier, Grenier, and Horeau take up their place on the opposite side, with Courceuil, Herbomez, and Lisieux lined up on the edge of the woods. Their respective positions are shown on the attached scale map, drawn up by the engineer of the surveyor's office.

The coach leaves Mortagne at around one o'clock in the morning, driven by a certain Rousseau, whose role in these events is sufficiently suspicious as to compel his arrest. Traveling at a walk, it will arrive in the Woods of Le Chesnay at around three o'clock.

Only one gendarme has been sent to escort the coach; he and the driver are planning to take their breakfast in Donnery. This gendarme is accompanied by three travelers who happen to be heading in the same direction.

For some time, the driver walks very slowly beside his horses; but upon reaching the bridge of Le Chesnay, at the entrance to the woods of the same name, he suddenly whips up the horses with a force and an urgency that would not go unnoticed, veering off the main highway into a smaller, more circuitous route known as the Senzey road. With this the coach disappears from sight, its direction indicated only by the sound of the horses' bells. The gendarme and the young travelers break into a gallop in hopes of catching up. A shout rings out: "Stop where you are, boys!" Four rifle shots are fired.

The gendarme has not been hit; he draws his sword and sets off in the direction he believes the coach to have taken. He is stopped by four armed men, who fire upon him. He is saved by his own determination and alacrity, bolting away to tell one of the young men to hurry to Le Chesnay and have the tocsin bell sounded; but two of the brigands rush forward to block his passage, their rifles raised. He is thus forced to take several steps backward. Just as he is turning to look into the woods, a bullet strikes him under the shoulder, breaking his arm. He falls to the ground, incapacitated.

The shouts and rifle fire have been heard at Donnery. The watchman and one of the guards of that residence come running; a volley of shots keeps them well away from the coach. The gendarme tries to intimidate the brigands with a series of loud shouts simulating the approach of imaginary reinforcements. He cries: "Forward! First platoon, this way! We have them! Second platoon, this way!"

In response, the brigands cry out: "Take up your weapons! This way, brothers! Hurry, boys!"

Deafened by the gunfire, the watchman cannot hear the wounded gendarme's cries, nor those of the guard, who has adopted a similar ruse, and is for the moment keeping the brigands at bay. Nevertheless, the watchman hears the sound of wooden crates being smashed open nearby. He hurries toward the source of this sound, only to find his way blocked by four armed bandits. He shouts: "Give yourselves up, villains!"

The culprits reply: "Come no closer, or you're a dead man!" He hurtles forward; two gunshots are fired, and he is hit: the bullet passes through his left leg and pierces his horse's flank. Drenched in his own blood, the brave soldier has no choice but to abandon this hopeless combat, and he vainly cries out, "Help! The brigands are in Le Chesnay!"

Thus, greatly outnumbering their adversaries, the bandits emerge victorious from this skirmish. They ransack the coach, which has deliberately been driven into a ravine. As a feint, a piece of cloth has been tied over the driver's head. The crates are smashed open, the bags of money thrown onto the ground. The horses are unhitched from the coach, and the currency loaded onto their backs. Scorning some 3,000 francs in copper, the bandits make off with a total of 103,000 francs, which they carry away on four horses. They make for the hamlet of Menneville, on the outskirts of Saint-Savin, where an isolated house is owned by the Chaussard brothers. This house is occupied by their uncle, a Monsieur Bourget, who has been kept informed of this plot from the beginning. With his wife at his side, the old man bids the bandits welcome, urges them to keep quiet, unloads the money, and draws drinks for all. The wife serves as a sort of sentinel for the château. The old man unsaddles the horses and leads them back to the abandoned coach. The robbers have bound the two young travelers with ropes, along with the dissembling coachman; Bourget frees them all, entrusts the four horses to the coachman, and returns home. After a necessarily brief rest, the bandits now prepare to take to the road again. Courceuil, Hiley, and Boislaurier call out their accomplices' names one by one, offering each a modest reward, and with this the band sets out one last time.

They arrive at a spot known as Champ-Landry, where, obeying the voice that leads all miscreants into the contradictions and miscalculations of crime, they throw their rifles into a wheat field. This marks the end of their cooperation. Terrified by the audacity of their attack, and by its very success, they scatter in all directions.

A robbery has thus been committed, aggravated by armed assault. Now begins a second sequence of events, with a new set of agents, whose role is to receive the stolen funds and send them on to their final destination.

From his hideout in Paris, Rifoël has kept a close eye on the conspiracy's progress; he now writes Léveillé to bring him fifty thousand francs posthaste.

Courceuil, ever the efficient collaborator, has already sent Hiley to inform Léveillé of the crime's success and of his arrival in Mortagne. Léveillé comes to meet him.

Vauthier, their trusted accomplice, volunteers to collect the money from the Chaussard brothers' uncle Bourget; but when he arrives at the house, the old man tells him he must first speak to his nephews, who have entrusted a large sum to Madame Bryond. In the meantime, he tells Vauthier to wait for him in the road, some distance away. There he brings him a sack containing twelve hundred francs, which Vauthier is to deliver to Madame Lechantre's, for her daughter.

At Léveillé's insistence, Courceuil returns to see Bourget, who now sends him directly to his nephews. The elder Chaussard leads Vauthier into the woods and points out a tree beneath which a sack lies buried, containing one thousand francs. Over the following days, Léveillé, Hiley, and Vauthier make repeated visits to the brothers' home, each time recovering a small sum—indeed, a very minimal sum compared with the total plundered from the coach.

These monies are delivered to Madame Lechantre in Mortagne; at her daughter's written request, she transports them to Saint-Savin, where Madame Bryond is now staying.

This is not the place to consider what prior knowledge Madame Lechantre might have had of this conspiracy. For the moment, let it suffice to note that she left Mortagne for Saint-Savin on the eve of the crime's execution, to take her daughter away; that the two women met midway and returned together to Mortagne; that the next day the *notaire* was sent by Hiley to convince the two women to transport the funds so arduously recovered from Bourget and the Chaussards to a house in Alençon, owned by a merchant named Pannier. We will refer to this house again in a moment.

Madame Lechantre writes the watchman of Saint-Savin, requesting that he join her and her daughter at Mortagne and escort them to Alençon.

Under cover of darkness, and with Mademoiselle Godard assisting, some twenty thousand francs are loaded into the coach.

The *notaire* has drawn up their itinerary. In the village of Littray, they stop at an inn run by one of their confederates, a certain Louis Chargegrain. The *notaire* comes to meet the coach; despite his precautions, a number of witnesses observe the unloading of the valises and portmanteaus in which the money has been concealed.

But even as Courceuil and Hiley, disguised as women, stand in an Alençon square with Pannier—a sworn ally to Rifoël and treasurer to the rebels since 1794—debating how best to deliver the money to Paris, news of the first arrests and searches has begun to spread. Terrified, Madame Lechantre abandons Léveillé and flees the inn by night; she and her daughter travel on back roads to the Château de Saint-Savin, where they take cover in a secret room. A similar terror soon overtakes the other conspirators. Courceuil, Boislaurier, and his relative Dubut exchange two thousand francs in *écus* for gold in a merchant's shop and flee through Brittany to England.

Arriving at Saint-Savin, Mesdames Lechantre and Bryond learn of the arrest of Bourget, the coach driver, and the resisters.

The police and the magistrates are pursuing their investigations with such success that the miscreants now urgently set about finding some way to protect Madame Bryond from judicial inquiries, for her charms have made her the object of their deepest devotion. She leaves Saint-Savin for Alençon, where, after some deliberation, her acolytes arrange to conceal her in Pannier's cellars.

With this begins a new chain of events.

After the arrest of Bourget and his wife, the Chaussards refuse to turn over any further funds, claiming that they have been betrayed. This unexpected defection comes just when the accomplices find themselves most urgently in need of money, if only to help them procure a safe hiding place. To be sure, this is not Rifoël's case; he simply has a voracious appetite for gold. Hiley, Cibot, and Léveillé begin to doubt the Chaussard brothers' loyalty.

Here we must cite yet another incident requiring the court's attention. Two gendarmes assigned to determine Madame Bryond's whereabouts gain entrance to Pannier's home and witness a meeting of the conspirators; but these men, unworthy of their superiors' confidence, soon succumb to her charms. These ignoble soldiers are named Ratel and Mallet. They lavish their most assiduous attentions on Madame Bryond and offer to escort her to the Chaussards' house so that the brothers might be forced to make restitution.

Madame Bryond sets out on horseback under cover of darkness, disguised as a man and accompanied by Ratel, Mallet, and the Godard girl. On her arrival, she takes one of the Chaussard brothers aside, and an animated discussion ensues. She is armed with a pistol and has vowed to blow her accomplice's brains out if he refuses her demands; but he escorts her into the woods, and she returns with a heavy handbag. Regaining the safety of her hiding place, she opens the bag and finds only fifteen hundred francs in copper and twelve-*sou* coins.

Plans are then made to assemble as many accomplices as can be found for a raid on the Chaussard brothers' home, so that the secret of the money's whereabouts might be tortured out of them.

But Pannier flies into a fury on learning of Madame Bryond's failure. He screams vilifications and threats, to which she responds with warnings of Rifoël's wrath. In the end, however, she has no choice but to flee.

All of this comes to us from Ratel's confession.

Moved by her plight, Mallet tells Madame Bryond of a hiding place he knows. Together they all make for the Woods of Troisville, where they take some rest; then Mallet and Ratel return by night to the Chaussard home, accompanied by Hiley and Cibot, only to find that the brothers have vanished, no doubt taking the remaining funds with them.

This was the conspirators' last attempt to recover their loot.

The time has thus come to establish the specific role played by each of the participants in this crime.

Dubut, Boislaurier, Gentil, Herbomez, Courceuil, and Hiley are the leaders, some conceiving the plan, others carrying it out.

Boislaurier, Dubut, and Courceuil, fugitives from justice, to be tried in absentia, are habitual rebels and troublemakers, implacable enemies of Napoleon the Great, of his victories, of his dynasty, of his government, of our new laws, of the Constitution of the Empire.

Herbomez and Hiley were the muscles of the association, boldly executing the plan conceived by the other three, who served as its brains.

The guilt of their seven auxiliaries, Cibot, Lisieux, Grenier, Bruce, Horeau, Cabot, and Minard, is evident; it emerges clearly from the confessions of those presently in custody, for Lisieux died during the inquiries, and Bruce was never found.

The conduct of the coachman Rousseau strongly suggests his complicity. The slow pace at which he led the coach, the suddenness with which he whipped up the horses as the coach was entering the woods, his insistence that he was blindfolded throughout the incident—whereas, according to the young men, the chief brigand told him to take off the handkerchief and acknowledge them—each of these curious facts distinctly implies his involvement.

As for Madame Bryond and the *notaire* Léveillé, what complicity could be closer and more constant than theirs? Again and again they provided the material needs of the crime; they knew every detail of the plan, and did all they could to ensure its success. Léveillé traveled whenever and wherever the plot required it. Madame Bryond devised one stratagem after another, risking everything, even her life, to assure that the funds reached their final destination. She offered her château and her coach for the criminals' use; she was informed of the plot from the beginning and did nothing to dissuade the bandits' leader from his intentions, although she could easily have employed her sinful influence to convince him to change his ways. She brought her chambermaid, Mademoiselle Godard, into the affair. As for Léveillé, his involvement in the crime's execution is clearly shown by his attempt to procure the ax.

Madame Bourget, Vauthier, the Chaussards, Pannier, Madame Lechantre, Mallet, and Ratel all participated in the crime to one degree or another, as did the innkeepers Mélin, Binet, Laravinière, and Chargegrain.

Bourget died in the course of the investigation, after making a confession that removed all doubt concerning the role of Vauthier and Madame Bryond; it is true that he attempted to minimize the involvement of his wife and his nephew Chaussard, but his motive in this is easily understood.

Nevertheless, the Chaussards lodged and fed the brigands with full knowledge of their intentions; they saw them armed, they witnessed all the preparations for the crime, and they permitted the use of their ax, knowing that it would serve to smash open the crates. Finally, they received the stolen funds and watched as large sums of money were passed from one hand to another; they concealed and consumed the greater part of the take for themselves.

Pannier, the former treasurer of the rebel factions, concealed Madame Bryond in his house; he is among the most dangerous of all the accomplices and was involved in the crime from its inception. He is the hub of a network of unknown relations that remain obscure to this day; but the law will not fail to discover them. He is Rifoël's faithful ally, the protector of the secrets of the counterrevolutionary movement in the west; he regretted that Rifoël had brought women into the plot, and that he confided in them; he sent money to Rifoël, and received a share of the stolen funds.

The conduct of the two gendarmes Ratel and Mallet calls for the most rigorous punishment justice can mete out, for they have betrayed their solemn duty. One of these two, foreseeing his fate, has committed suicide, but not before providing a number of important revelations. The other, Mallet, denies nothing; his confessions remove all doubt of their involvement.

Notwithstanding her continual denials, Madame Lechantre was fully informed of this plot. She attempts to support her allegation of innocence with a feigned religious devotion, but her hypocrisy has antecedents that clearly establish her cool resolve in even the most extreme circumstances. She claims she was deceived by her daughter and believed the money to be the rightful possession of Monsieur Bryond—an obvious fabrication. If Monsieur Bryond had possessed such a fortune, he would never have fled the country to avoid the spectacle of his own ruination. Any qualms Madame Lechantre might once have felt concerning this theft were assuaged when she saw it approved by her ally Boislaurier. And how does she explain Rifoël's presence at Saint-Savin, his many comings and goings to and from her home, his relationship with her daughter, the brigands' sojourn in her château, where they were served by the Godard girl and Madame Bryond? She claims to have slept through it all; she protests that she is in the habit of retiring at seven o'clock in the evening, but she is unable to respond when the investigating magistrate observes that she must then have arisen at dawn and discovered some trace of the night's activities and of the presence of a large crowd, and must have felt some concern at her daughter's nocturnal travels. To this she objects that she was at prayer. This woman is a model of hypocrisy. Finally, her journey on the day of the crime, her precaution of bringing her daughter back to Mortagne, her role in the transport of the money, her sudden flight when all was discovered, the urgency with which she went into hiding, the very circumstances of her arrest, all this points to a long-standing collusion with the bandits. Her behavior was not that of a mother striving to enlighten her daughter and wrest her from the dangers she faced but rather that of a terror-stricken accomplice, and the motivation for this complicity is no mere excess of maternal indulgence. It is the effect of an intensely partisan turn of mind, inspired by her notorious hatred for the Government of His Royal and Imperial Majesty. In any case, maternal indulgence is no excuse for her actions, and we must see her long-standing and therefore premeditated consent to her daughter's actions as the most obvious indication of her guilt.

Like the elements of the crime, its artisans are here exposed for all to see. We have before us a monstrous convergence of factional depravity and larcenous intent; we see assassination as a tool of the partisan spirit, in which some find justification for the most ignoble excesses. The leaders' voice calls for the theft of public moneys to fund future crimes; vile, savage mercenaries commit the robbery in exchange for a handful of gold, and do not quail at the thought of murder; and then a second circle of dangerous rebels, every bit as guilty as the first, helps to conceal the loot and to divide it up. What society could tolerate such depredations? These bandits deserve to be punished with a rigor far greater than our judicial system allows.

The Special Criminal Court must thus determine whether the indictees Herbomez, Hiley, Cibot, Grenier, Horeau, Cabot, Minard, Mélin, Binet, Laravinière, Rousseau, Madame Bryond, Léveillé, Madame Bourget, Vauthier, the elder Chaussard, Pannier, the widow Lechantre, and Mallet, named and identified above, accused and held in governmental custody, and the indictees Boislaurier, Dubut, Courceuil, Bruce, the younger Chaussard, Chargegrain, and Mademoiselle Godard, these latter missing and on the run from justice, are or are not guilty of the deeds detailed in the present bill of indictment.

Written in Caen, Office of the Public Prosecutor,
this 1st of December 180——
Signed: Baron Bourlac

This document, far briefer and more peremptory than the indictments of today—so minute, so exhaustive in their analysis of the most minor circumstances, and especially of the accused's life prior to the crime itself—left Godefroid profoundly shaken. The very dryness of the account, in which only the principal events of the affair were laid out in the red ink of the official pen, spurred his imagination into action. For those of a certain turn of mind, such spare, concise narratives hold a particular fascination: the pleasure of immersing themselves in the text, and of exploring all the mysterious depths beneath the words themselves.

Deep in the night, aided by the silence, the darkness, and Alain's suggestion of some terrible connection with Madame de La Chanterie, Godefroid devoted all the energies of his intelligence to the elucidation of this grim tale.

The name Lechantre was surely the patronymic of the de La Chanterie family, stripped of its aristocratic component under the Republic and the Empire.

In his mind's eye he saw the landscapes where this drama was set. The faces of the secondary accomplices paraded past. In his fantasy, he conjured up not the criminal named Rifoël but rather the Chevalier du Vissard, a young man in the mold of Walter Scott's Fergus—in short, the French equivalent of the Jacobite. In his imagination he composed the novel of a young girl heartlessly deceived by a wicked husband (the sort of novel then in fashion), in love with a young rebel leader in open revolt against the Emperor, throwing herself heart and soul into a conspiracy like Diana Vernon, exulting in her new life, and once entered onto this dangerous slope, unable to stop! Had she tumbled all the way to the scaffold?

A whole world lay before Godefroid's eyes. He wandered through the groves of Normandy; he spied the Breton chevalier and Madame Bryond through the hedges; he lived in the old Château of Saint-Savin; he witnessed all the machinations of the tale's characters, glimpsing by turns the *notaire*, the merchant, and the brazen leaders of the Chouans. He sensed the almost universal eagerness for conspiracy in a region where the forays of the great Marche-à-Terre still burn bright in the common memory, like the Counts of Bauvan and Longuy, and the massacre at La Vivetière, and the death of the Marquis de Montauran, with whose exploits Madame de La Chanterie had already regaled him.

This vision of the story's settings, characters, and properties thus came to Godefroid in a sudden flash. Recalling that this affair involved the imposing, noble, and pious old woman whose virtues had so affected him that he thought himself changed forever, he now shuddered with dread as he took up the second document the good Alain had given him. This one bore the title

Brief for Madame Henriette Bryond des Tours-Minières,
née Lechantre de La Chanterie

"No doubt about it now!" Godefroid said to himself.
This document read as follows:

The sentence has been pronounced, and the prisoner's guilt established; but if ever our sovereign had good reason to exercise his power of clemency, can it not be found in the circumstances of this case?

At issue here is a young woman condemned to death who has declared herself with child.

On the threshold of a prison, in the presence of the waiting scaffold, this woman will speak the Truth.

The Truth will speak in her favor; it is the Truth that will bring her her pardon.

As with every case involving a large number of conspirators in a plot of a partisan nature, the trial judged by the Criminal Court at Alençon left many questions unposed and unanswered.

The Chancellory of His Royal and Imperial Majesty now knows what to expect of the mysterious figure known as the Merchant, whose presence in the department of the Orne the Public Ministry made no attempt to deny in the course of the debates. Nevertheless, the Prosecution did not think it suitable to call him to the stand, and the Defense had neither the power to bring him into court nor the ability to discover his whereabouts.

As the prosecutor, the Prefecture, the Police of Paris, and the Chancellory of H.R. and I. M. know, the figure who goes by this name is none other than Monsieur Bernard-Polydore Bryond des Tours-Minières, an agent of the Count de Lille since 1794, known abroad as the Baron des Tours-Minières, and in the annals of the Parisian Police as Contenson.

He is a most exceptional man, whose youth and nobility have been dishonored by vices so consuming, by an immorality so profound, by misdeeds so criminal, that his wretched life would surely have ended on the scaffold were it not for his skill in making himself useful to those in power by playing the double role implied in his two names. Nevertheless, increasingly ruled by his passions, by the indomitable force of his wicked desires, he finally fell well below wretchedness, and into the last ranks of humanity, despite his incontestable talents and remarkable mind.

When the vigilance of the Count de Lille cut off Bryond's flow of external funds, he attempted to extricate himself from the bloody arena into which his needs had driven him.

Had his career grown insufficiently remunerative? Was it remorse, perhaps, or shame that brought this man back to a province where his heavily mortgaged properties would offer so few resources for his genius? This we cannot believe. It seems far more likely that he had some mission to carry out in that region, where a few embers of our recent civil strife still continued to smolder.

Traveling through this province, where his perfidious collaboration in the intrigues of the English and of the Count de Lille had earned him the unquestioning faith of those loyal to the movement defeated by the genius of our immortal Emperor, he encountered a former rebel leader with whom he had had dealings as an envoy from abroad in the Quiberon Expedition and the last rebel uprising of the year VII. This agitator has since paid the ultimate price for his attacks on the State; but it was Bryond who encouraged him in this vein, thereby gaining access to all the secrets of a rebel movement that has remained incorrigibly oblivious both to the glory of H. M. the Emperor Napoleon I and to the true interests of the country incarnated in his sacred person.

At the age of thirty-five, this man Bryond, affecting the deepest piety, professing unbounded devotion to the Count de Lille and heartfelt veneration for the memory of the rebels fallen in uprisings past, carefully concealing the debilitating effects of a misspent youth, still able to inspire confidence through a certain personal charm, lovingly protected by his creditors, the object of an exceptional indulgence from the *cream* of that province, this man Bryond, a true whited sepulcher, was introduced with the most glowing recommendations into the society of Madame Lechantre, who was thought to possess a great fortune.

Plans had been laid to marry Madame Lechantre's only daughter, young Henriette, to this protégé of the local high society.

Priests, onetime aristocrats, creditors, each for their own reasons, honorable in some cases, grasping in others, unthinking in most—in short, the whole of this little world—colluded to bring about the union of Bernard Bryond and Henriette Lechantre.

The good sense—and no doubt certain misgivings—of the *notaire* overseeing Madame Lechantre's affairs was the unwitting cause of the young girl's undoing. Monsieur Chesnel, a *notaire* of Alençon, designated the lands of Saint-Savin, the bride's sole asset, as the only joint property she would bring to the marriage, reserving the house and a modest annuity for the mother.

. From Madame Lechantre's cautious and frugal turn of mind, Bryond's creditors had believed her to possess some considerable capital, but they soon saw these hopes dashed; realizing that they would have nothing from her, they filed complaints against Bryond, thereby revealing the precarious state of his finances.

The newlyweds' union was now increasingly troubled by violent arguments, in which the young woman glimpsed the moral depravity, the religious and political atheism, and—dare it be said?—the infamy of the man with whom her destiny had been so cruelly joined. Initiating his wife into the secrets of the odious conspiracies then working toward the overthrow of the imperial government, Bryond offered his house as a safe haven for Rifoël du Vissard.

Rifoël's character, bold, good-hearted, and generous, exerted a considerable charm on all those around him, as has been abundantly demonstrated in three separate trials judged by three Special Criminal Courts.

The irresistibility of his influence over a desperate young woman is all too plain to see from the horrific events that have brought her to beg for mercy at the foot of the throne. But as the Chancellory of His Royal and Imperial Majesty might easily verify for itself, the fault lies primarily with Bryond's base machinations in the early days of this marriage; for far from serving as a guide and counselor for a young girl placed in his care by a deceived mother, he chose rather to foster the growing intimacy between young Henriette and his friend the rebel leader.

Their attachment was thus planned out from the start by the detestable Bryond, who prides himself on his contempt for the world around him, whose only concern is the satisfaction of his own passions, who sees the virtues of civil and religious morality as mere insignificant obstacles to his own pleasure.

Let us note the predictability of such cunning in one who has served as a double agent since 1794, and who, for eight years, was able to deceive the Count de Lille, his adherents, and perhaps even the Imperial Police: do such men not belong to whomever will pay them most generously?

It was thus Bryond who urged Rifoël into crime, and into the plunder of State funds and the pillaging of nationalized assets through a series of armed assaults that terrorized the populace of five departments. He demanded a tribute of three hundred thousand francs from these ill-gotten gains as a remedy for his own financial distress.

In case of resistance from his wife or from Rifoël, he had devised a plan to avenge the disgust he inspired in their honest hearts: to deliver them both into the implacable hands of the law the moment they had committed some capital offense.

Realizing that these two were more devoted to partisan philosophy than to his own interests, he abandoned them and returned to Paris, armed with a wealth of information on rebel activities in the western departments.

As the Chancellory knows, Vauthier and the Chaussard brothers served as his informants.

He now secretly returned to his own province, in disguise. After the theft of the tax receipts, Bryond discreetly contacted the prefect and his men, using the alias of the Merchant. And what was the result of this meeting? Never was a more extensive conspiracy, with so many confederates from such varied rungs of the social ladder, more promptly and completely uncovered by the Judiciary than the plot to attack the tax coach from Caen. Six days after the robbery, every last conspirator had been placed under surveillance, with a vigilance that proved the most exhaustive knowledge of the plan and its participants. It is only as grounds for our own conclusions that we cite the arrest, trial, and execution of Rifoël and his accomplices; the Chancellory, we repeat, knows more of this matter than we do.

If ever a prisoner were justified in seeking the sovereign's clemency, is it not Henriette Lechantre?

Caught up in this affair by her passions, by dreams of rebellion that she suckled with her mother's milk, she is certainly unpardonable in the eyes of the Law; but in the eyes of the most magnanimous of all Emperors, do the most infamous of all betrayals and the most consuming of all convictions not eloquently plead her case?

Could so great a commander, could the immortal genius who bestowed his grace on the Prince de Hatzfeld, could the Emperor, who like God Himself is able to look into the human heart and read the indomitable influence of destiny's voice, refuse to recognize the force, invincible for so young a woman, that would justify his leniency, notwithstanding the gravity of the prisoner's crime?

Already twenty-two heads have been culled by the sword of Justice, at the behest of three Criminal Courts. There remains only the head of a young woman of twenty, a minor; will the Emperor Napoleon the Great not leave her to her own repentance? Is her punishment not best left to God?

For Henriette Lechantre, Madame Bryond des Tours-Minières,

Her defender,

BORDIN

Attorney to the Lower Court
of the Department of the Seine

This horrifying story haunted what little sleep Godefroid found that night. He dreamt of the ultimate sanction as devised by the philanthropic mind of the good Doctor Guillotin. Through the warm mists of a nightmare, he glimpsed a young woman, beautiful, strong-willed, defiant, undergoing the final preparations, then rolling through the streets in a tumbrel, then climbing the steps of the scaffold and crying out: "Long live the King!"

Curiosity gnawed at Godefroid's soul. At dawn he arose, dressed, paced this way and that in his room. Finally he stood motionless at the window, mechanically gazing at the heavens as he reconstructed this drama in several volumes, much as a modern author might do. And against a dim background of Chouans, country folk, provincial gentlemen, rebel leaders, policemen, lawyers, and spies, he saw the radiant figures of the mother and daughter standing out from the rest; the mother perfectly ignorant of her daughter's plight, the daughter placed in the hands of a monster, falling victim to her attraction for a valiant man of the sort that would later be considered heroic, and whom Godefroid saw as a brother to Charrette, or to Georges Cadoudal, or to any of a thousand other giants of the great battle between the Republic and the Monarchy.

Now Godefroid heard Alain stirring in his room. He hurried to his door but soon returned to his own apartment, for he had found the old man kneeling at his prie-dieu, saying his morning prayers. The sight of the venerable figure in that pious attitude reminded Godefroid of his own neglected duties, and he knelt down in fervent prayer.

"I was waiting for you," the little man said as Godefroid entered a quarter of an hour later. "I knew how impatient you would be to hear more, and so rose earlier than usual."

"Madame Henriette? . . ." asked Godefroid, trembling visibly.

"Is Madame's daughter," the old man concluded. "Madame's full family name is Lechantre de La Chanterie. The Empire recognized neither noble titles nor extensions to the patronymic or original names. Thus, the Baroness des Tours-Minières was called Madame Bryond. The Marquis d'Esgrignon went back to his family name of Carol; they called him Citizen Carol, and later Monsieur Carol. The Troisvilles became Messieurs Guibelin."

"But what happened? Did the Emperor grant her clemency?"

"Alas! no," answered Alain. "The poor girl perished on the scaffold at the age of twenty-one. After reading Bordin's letter, the Emperor responded to his Minister of Justice more or less as follows:

'Why condemn the spy so severely? A spy is no longer a man, and he must abandon the sentiments of men; he is a cog in a machine. Bryond was only doing his duty. If tools of his type were not what they are—bars of steel, incapable of any thought save the good of the power they serve—then government itself would be impossible. The Judiciary's decrees must be carried out, lest my magistrates lose all confidence in themselves and in me. Furthermore, this outfit's foot soldiers have already been put to death, and their guilt is lesser than that of their leaders. Finally, we must teach the women of the west not to dally in conspiracies. It is precisely because this case involves a woman that justice must be done. The spirit of forgiveness must never outweigh the interests of power.' That was the substance of his reply, which the Minister kindly conveyed to Bordin after his interview with the Emperor. Learning that France and Russia would soon be engaged in battle, and that the Emperor would be forced to travel seven hundred leagues from Paris to attack a vast and empty land, Bordin realized the true reason for his intransigence. In order to ensure the tranquillity of the western provinces, already swarming with dissidents, Napoleon thought it necessary to instill a profound terror in the populace. Thus the Minister advised the attorney to trouble himself no further for his clients and their fate . . ."

"For his client and her fate," said Godefroid.

"Madame de La Chanterie was sentenced to twenty-two years in prison," Alain said. "She had already begun serving her sentence in Bicêtre Prison, near Rouen, and refused to allow any appeal of her case until Henriette had been saved, for her daughter had grown so precious to her since those dark days that, were it not for Bordin's promise to procure the Emperor's clemency, she might never have survived the reading of her sentence. Thus, a plan was laid to deceive the despondent mother. She was allowed to see her daughter once, after all the other conspirators had been put to death; what she did not know was that her daughter had been granted a reprieve thanks only to a false declaration of pregnancy.

"Ah! Now I understand! . . ." cried Godefroid.

"No, my dear child, there is still much that you cannot guess. Long after that final meeting, Madame still believed her daughter to be alive . . ."

"But how?"

"When Bordin told Madame des Tours-Minières of the rejection of her appeal, that sublime little woman found the courage to write some twenty letters, all dated after the day of her execution, each a month after the last, in hopes of convincing her mother of her continued existence. She invented an illness, and with each letter her symptoms grew more severe, until finally, after two years, she succumbed. In this way Madame de La Chanterie was prepared for her daughter's death, albeit from natural causes; it was not until 1814 that she finally learned the dreadful truth. For two full years Madame remained in prison, thrown in with the vilest creatures of her sex and dressed in convict garb; but at the beginning of the second year, thanks to the insistent efforts of the de Champignelles and the de Beauséants, she was at least given a private cell, where she lived like a cloistered nun."

"And the others?"

"Léveillé, Herbomez, Hiley, Cibot, Grenier, Horeau, Cabot, Minard, and Mallet were sentenced to death and executed at once. Pannier, Chaussard, and Vauthier were branded and sent to the penal colony for twenty years' hard labor; but the Emperor pardoned Chaussard and Vauthier. Mélin, Larivinière, and Binet were condemned to five years in prison, Madame Bourget to twenty-two. Chargegrain and Rousseau were acquitted. Those tried in absentia were all condemned to death, with the exception of Mademoiselle Godard, who you have no doubt guessed, is none other than our poor Manon . . ."

"Manon? . . ." cried Godefroid, dumbfounded.

"Oh! There is so much you do not know of Manon!" the good Alain replied. "Sentenced to twenty-two years, that devoted girl turned herself in so that she might serve Madame de La Chanterie in her prison. Our dear vicar is the priest of Mortagne. It was he who gave the last rites to the Baroness des Tours-Minières; it was he who accompanied her to the scaffold, and to whom she gave her final farewell kiss. That good, that sublime priest had already assisted the Chevalier du Vissard in his last moments. Our dear Father de Vèze thus learned all the conspirators' secrets . . ."

"Now I understand why his hair is so white!" said Godefroid.

"Alas!" Alain continued. "From Amédée du Vissard he received a miniature of Madame des Tours-Minières, the only remaining likeness of her; thus, the father became sacred for Madame de La Chanterie, when at last she made her glorious return to civilized society . . ."

"And how did that come about?" asked Godefroid.

"With the accession of Louis XVIII, in 1814. Boislaurier, Monsieur de Boisfrelon's younger brother, had been ordered by the King to encourage revolt in the west, first in 1809 and again in 1812. These brothers' family name is Dubut; the Dubut from Caen is a relative of theirs. There were three sons in that family: Dubut de Boisfranc, President at the Cour des Aides, Dubut de Boisfrelon, the Councillor to Parliament, and Dubut-Boislaurier, a captain of the dragoons. The father had given his three sons the names of three different properties, hoping to cleanse them of their humble origins, for their grandfather was a simple cloth seller. The Dubut from Caen, who succeeded in eluding the clutches of the law, belonged to the branch of the family that remained in commerce; he hoped that his devotion to the Royal cause would earn him right of succession to the title of Monsieur de Boisfranc, and Louis XVIII granted his faithful servant's wish. He was made grand provost in 1815, and later prosecutor-general under the name of de Boisfranc; at the time of his death, he was the First President of a Royal Court. The Marquis du Vissard, the older brother of the unfortunate chevalier, was made Peer of the French Realm and lavished with honors by the King, who made him a Lieutenant in the Maison Rouge company of his Household Guard; after the Maison Rouge was dissolved, he was promoted to prefect. Monsieur d'Herbomez's brother was made a count and a receiver-general. The poor banker Pannier died of sorrow in the penal colony. Boislaurier died childless, as a lieutenant general and governor of a Royal château. As for Madame de La Chanterie, she was brought before the King by Messieurs de Champignelles, de Beauséant, the Duke de Verneuil, and the Keeper of the Seals. 'You have suffered greatly for me, Madame Baroness; you have earned my heartfelt gratitude and full favor,' he told her. 'Sire,' she answered, 'Your Majesty has many wrongs to consider, and I do not wish to add the weight of an inconsolable grief to your burden. I have learned to live my life in the shadows, weeping for my daughter and doing good for my fellow man. If anything could ease my sorrow, it would be the kindness of my King, and the pleasure of knowing that Providence will not allow a devotion such as mine to go to waste.' "

"And how did Louis XVIII answer her?" asked Godefroid.

"The King offered Madame de La Chanterie two hundred thousand francs in restitution, for her lands at Saint-Savin had been sold to satisfy the tax bureau," the old fellow answered. "The letters of pardon sent to the Baroness and her servant express the King's regret at the sufferings they endured for his sake, recognizing that *the zeal of his servants had led them into regrettable acts;* but—and this is a horrible thing, which you will find the most curious trait of that monarch's character—he employed Bryond in his private police force until the end of his reign."

"Oh! Kings! Kings!" cried Godefroid. "And is the wretch still alive?"

"No. The wretch, who at least had the discretion to conceal his true identity under the name of Contenson, died toward the end of 1829 or the beginning of 1830. He fell into the street as he was pursuing a criminal over the rooftops. Louis XVIII thought much as Napoleon did where the police are concerned. Madame de La Chanterie is a saint; she prays for that monster's soul, and has two Masses said for him each year. Let me assure you that she learned of her daughter's peril only when it came time to transport the stolen funds, and even then thanks only to her relative Boislaurier. In spite of this, and although she was defended by one of the best-known lawyers of his day—the father, furthermore, of a renowned orator—she did not succeed in establishing her innocence. President du Ronceret and Vice President Blondet of the Tribunal of Alençon did all they could to save our poor mistress from prison, but in vain. The Special Criminal Court was headed by the celebrated Mergi, a Councillor to the Imperial Court and later a prosecutor-general famous for his fanatical devotion to the altar and the throne, who sent more than a few Bonapartist heads rolling into the basket. He enjoyed some considerable influence over his colleagues and convinced them to vote for Madame de La Chanterie's guilt. Messieurs Bourlac and Mergi argued their case with exceptional vehemence. The Presiding Judge referred to the Baroness des Tours-Minières as Madame Bryond, and to Madame as Madame Lechantre. The names of the accused were all recast in the Republican style, and almost all of them denatured. The trial had its share of extraordinary moments, more than I can recall; but one has remained in my memory, an act of audacity that might show you what manner of men were these Chouans. The proceedings attracted an audience greater than you might possibly imagine: the corridors were packed, and the throng in the square outside surpassed the crowds on a market day. One morning, at the start of the session, before the judges had entered the courtroom, the famous Chouan known as the Bread Thief leapt over the barrier and into the audience; elbowing his way through, he disappeared into the crowd and fled on the tide of the terrified mob, *butting like a wild boar*, as Bordin later told me. The gendarmes and bailiffs set after him at once and captured him on the stairs just as he was about to gain the square outside. The number of bailiffs was doubled after this brazen act, and a squadron of gendarmes was posted to keep watch in the square, for it was feared that there might be other Chouans lurking in the crowd, waiting to come to the prisoners' aid. Three people were trampled to death as a result of the Bread Thief's attempted escape. We have since learned that Contenson (like my old friend Bordin, I can call him neither the Baron des Tours-Minières nor Bryond, which is a name from a time now past), we have learned, I say, that the wretch had extracted some sixty thousand francs from the stolen funds and spent it for his own purposes; he gave ten thousand to young Chaussard, whom he introduced into the police force, infecting him with his own tastes and vices; but none of his accomplices came to a happy end. The fugitive Chaussard was thrown into the sea by Monsieur de Boislaurier on learning from Pannier of his treachery, for Contenson had advised him to rejoin the fugitive conspirators to keep watch over them. Vauthier was killed in Paris, no doubt by one of the shadowy companions of the Chevalier du Vissard. Finally, the younger Chaussard was assassinated in one of those nocturnal affairs that so often involve the police; presumably Contenson had sought to deliver himself of Chaussard's demands or remorse by throwing him on the mercy of his fellows, as they say. Madame de La Chanterie invested her compensation in state securities and acquired this house, at the urging of her uncle, the former Councillor de Boisfrelon, who financed the purchase himself. The neighborhood was tranquil and close to the Archepiscopal's Palace, where our dear father had been posted to serve the Cardinal; it was primarily for this reason that Madame accepted the offer of that kindly old man, whose yearly revenue, after twenty-five years of revolutions, had fallen to six thousand francs. Furthermore, Madame had conceived the desire to embark on a new life, in hopes that a cloistered existence might still the fearsome torments she had endured over the previous twenty-six years. I trust you now realize the full majesty and grandeur of that august martyr of a woman we call Madame ..."

"Yes," said Godefroid. "There is indeed a sort of grandeur and majesty about her, conferred by all these many cruel blows."

"Each wound, each new blow only redoubled her patience and resignation," Alain went on; "but if you knew her as we do, if you knew the depth of her compassion for others, if you knew how active is the inexhaustible tenderness that flows from her heart, you would be endlessly dismayed at the many tears she has shed, the many desperate prayers she has offered up to God. One would have to have caught only the briefest glimpse of happiness, as she did, to endure such turmoil! She is a tender heart and a gentle soul in a body of steel, hardened by privation, toil, and austerity."

"Her life might explain why solitary folk live longer than others," said Godefroid.

"Some days I wonder: What could be the meaning of such an existence, so sorely tried by the cruelest torments the imagination can conceive? ... Does God reserve such trials for those who will sit beside Him the day after their death?" the good Alain mused, unaware that his ingenuous meditation formed a perfect summary of Swedenborg's doctrine on angels.

"But can it really be," cried Godefroid, "that Madame de La Chanterie was forced to mingle with ..."

"Madame was sublime in her imprisonment," Alain replied. "For three years she brought to life the fiction of the Vicar of Wakefield, and made more than one convert among the fallen women around her. Observing her fellow prisoners, she was overcome with great pity for the sorrows of the poor; that sense of pity weighs on her to this day, and has made her the queen of Parisian charity. Deep in the horrors of Bicêtre Prison, she conceived the plan to which we have devoted our lives. She describes it as a wonderful dream, an angelic inspiration in the depths of Hell; but she never dared hope that it might one day become a reality. By 1819, it seemed that tranquillity had once more settled over Paris; it was then, and it was here in this house, that her thoughts returned to that dream. A number of pious souls—the Duchesse d'Angoulême, later the Dauphine; the Duchesse de Berry; the Archbishop, later the Chancellor—generously offered the sums necessary to found this undertaking. To their donations was added the available portion of our incomes, from which each of us takes only what we absolutely require."

Tears came to Godefroid's eyes.

"We are the faithful servants of a Christian Idea, and we belong body and soul to that great Project, whose spirit, whose founder, is the

Baroness de La Chanterie, whom you hear us so respectfully call Madame."

"Ah! And I will belong to you all, completely," said Godefroid, extending his hand toward the good Alain.

"Do you now understand that certain subjects of conversation are strictly forbidden here, even by the vaguest allusion?" the old man continued. "Do you understand the vow of discretion and delicacy that each of us has taken, for the sake of one who seems to us a saint? Do you understand the charm exerted by a woman made holy by sorrow, a woman who has seen so much of life, to whom every sort of misfortune has spoken its final word, who draws a lesson from every adversity, whose every virtue bears the double endorsement of cruel tribulation and constant practice, a woman of unsullied soul, who of motherhood knew only the pains, of conjugal love only the heartbreak, on whom Life smiled for no more than a few months, for whom Heaven has surely reserved some sort of laurel wreath as a reward for such resignation, for such goodness in the face of so many sorrows? Does she not compare favorably with Job, she who never once made a murmur of complaint? Little wonder that you find her words so powerful, her age so youthful, her soul so infectious, her gaze so convincing; she is the perfect confessor for all sorrows, for she has known every sort of sorrow there is. All suffering falls silent in her presence."

"She is a living icon of Charity!" cried Godefroid, overcome with enthusiasm. "Am I to be allowed into your number, then?"

"You must first agree to our tests, and above all you must *believe!*" the old man gently cried. "So long as you lack the necessary faith, so long as your heart and mind have not absorbed the divine sense of Saint Paul's Epistle on Charity, you cannot take part in our works."

SECOND EPISODE

THE INITIATE

Sublime good can be every bit as contagious as evil. Thus, after Madame de La Chanterie's boarder had spent several months in that silent old house, after the good Alain had told him every last secret detail of its history, inspiring a profound respect for the almost monastic existence lived within its walls, he found himself enjoying the sort of spiritual well-being that comes with an orderly life, quiet habits, and a harmony of character with one's companions. In all those four months, Godefroid had never once heard a voice raised in anger, never a single argument, and at last he admitted to himself that, since he had attained the age of reason, he could not remember ever having felt so completely—not *happy*, but—*at peace*. Seeing the world from a distance, he was able to judge it with lucidity. At length the desire he had harbored for three months, the longing to take part in these mysterious figures' work, became a passion; and one need not be a great philosopher to imagine the force that a passion can acquire when it is experienced in solitude.

One day, then, a day made solemn by the omnipotence of the spirit, having looked deep into his heart, having carefully considered the state of his forces, Godefroid climbed the stairs to see the aged Alain, the one whom Madame de La Chanterie called her "lamb," the one whom, of all his housemates, he found the least intimidating and the most approachable. He was hoping to expand his acquaintance with this quasi-sacred Order, to learn more of their calling and their activities. From certain allusions made in his presence, he supposed that he would soon be put to some sort of test; it was this initiation that he now eagerly awaited. His curiosity had not been sated by Alain's explanation of his entrance into Madame de La Chanterie's circle. He wanted to know more.

Thus, at ten-thirty one evening, Godefroid stood before this little man for the third time, just as he was about to begin his nightly reading of the *Imitation*. Seeing the Initiate at his door, the gentle adviser could not repress a smile, and before Godefroid could speak a word, Alain asked him: "Why should you come to me, my dear boy, and not to Madame? I am the most ignorant, the least spiritual, the most imperfect member of this household. Madame and my friends have spent the past three days looking into your heart," he added with a knowing air.

"And what have they found? ..." asked Godefroid.

"Ah!" the little man answered directly, "they have found a rather naïve desire to belong to our flock. A desire, but not yet an ardent vocation. It is true," he quickly continued as Godefroid began a gesture of protest, "you have more curiosity than fervor. In short, you remain too attached to your former way of thinking not to see something adventurous in the incidents of our life—something romantic, as they say ..."

Godefroid could not prevent a blush from flooding his cheeks.

"You see us as something akin to the caliphs in the *Thousand and One Nights*, and you feel a sort of anticipatory satisfaction at the thought of playing the kindly spirit in the tales of beneficence you so love to imagine! ... Well now, my son, your embarrassed laughter tells me we were not mistaken. Do you truly believe you can conceal your sentiments from us? Do not forget, we have made it our trade to decipher all the most secret workings of the soul, all the ruses of poverty, all the schemes of the indigent. We have made ourselves spies for the cause of virtue, working for the police of the Lord; we are a circle of experienced judges, whose code consists solely of absolutions; we are doctors trained in the treatment of every sort of suffering, offering only one remedy: money, carefully put to the proper use! Nevertheless, my child, we do not scorn the motivations that bring us a neophyte, so long as he remains among us and becomes a brother in our Order. We will judge you only by your work. There are two sorts of curiosity: one directed toward good, the other toward evil. You are now gripped by a curiosity for good. If you are to be a worker in our vineyard, the juice of the grapes will give you an unquenchable thirst for the divine fruit. As with any natural science, initiation into our life will be easy in appearance and difficult in reality. Beneficence is no different from poetry: the external airs are so very easy to put on. But here, as on Parnassus, we do not content ourselves with perfection. In order to become one of us, you must acquire a vast knowledge of life, and of what sort of life, good God! The life of Paris, which defies even the wisdom of the Prefect of Police and his men. Is it not our task to undermine the endless conspiracies of evil? To seize it in all its ever-changing forms, so varied as to seem nothing short of infinite? In Paris, Charity must be as knowing as vice, just as the policeman must be as cunning as the thief. Each of us must be innocent and untrusting; our judgment must be as sure and speedy as our eye. Thus it is, my child, that we are all old and aged by life; but we are so pleased with the results we have obtained that we have each vowed not to die without leaving a successor—and you are all the more dear to us in that, if you persist, you will be our first pupil. To us, there is no such thing as chance; it was God who brought you to our door! You are a good soul gone bitter, but the devil's ferment has grown weaker within you since you came into our household. Madame's divine nature has had its effect. Yesterday we held council; and since you have seen fit to grant me your confidence, my good brothers decided to make of me your guardian and your tutor . . . Does that please you?"

"Ah! My dear Monsieur Alain! Your eloquence has awakened a—"

"It is not I, my child, it is the world that is eloquent . . . Grandeur is assured us so long as we obey the word of God, so long as we imitate Jesus Christ, insofar as we are able, with the assistance of faith . . ."

"This moment has decided the course of my existence. I can feel the fervor within me!" cried Godefroid. "I too want to spend my life doing good . . ."

"That is the secret to remaining with God," the little man replied. "Have you studied that device: *Transire benefaciendo*? *Transire* means to go beyond this world, leaving behind a long string of good deeds."

"I understand full well, and of my own volition I have hung the Order's device directly facing my bed."

"Capital! In itself, this is an act of little consequence, but in my eyes it means a great deal! And so, my child, I intend to place your foot in the stirrup and offer you your first order of business, your first duel with misery . . . We will shortly be parting ways . . . For I too will soon be leaving my monastery, to take my place in the heart of a volcano. I am to become a foreman in a great factory whose workers have become infected with communist doctrine; they dream of social upheavals, of cutting their masters' throats, not knowing that this would mean the death of industry, of business, of factories . . . I shall be there for, who knows? perhaps a year, overseeing the receipts and accounts, and attempting to find my way into some hundred or hundred and twenty poor families no doubt led astray by poverty long before they were led astray by wicked books. Nevertheless, we shall see each other here every Sunday and feast day . . . We shall be living in the same neighborhood; we may thus meet at the church of Saint-Jacques-du-Haut-Pas, where you will find me every morning at seven-thirty Mass. Now, should we ever meet elsewhere, you must not greet me in any way, unless you see me rubbing my hands together as people do to express satisfaction. That is one of our signs. Like deaf-mutes, we have our own language of gestures, whose necessity will soon become abundantly clear to you."

Godefroid made a gesture that the good Alain interpreted without effort, for he smiled and immediately went on:

"Now, here is the nature of your task. We exercise neither beneficence nor philanthropy as you know them, which can be divided into several branches, each of them exploited by this world's defrauders as if they were merely some other sort of commerce. Rather, we practice Charity as it is defined by the great and sublime Saint Paul; for, my child, we believe that only Charity can treat the wounds of Paris. Thus, unhappiness, poverty, suffering, sorrow, and evil, no matter what cause they proceed from, all have the same rights in our eyes. Whatever his beliefs or opinions may be, an unhappy man is first and foremost an unhappy man; and we must turn his face toward our holy mother the Church only after we have saved him from hunger or despair. And even then, we must convert him more by example and goodness than by any other means; for in that way we believe God will assist us. Thus, any sort of coercion is to be avoided. Of all the miseries of Paris, the most difficult to unearth, and the bitterest, are those of the upright, those of the higher ranks of the bourgeoisie whose families have fallen into indigence, for they make it a matter of honor to conceal their misfortunes. Sorrows of this sort, my dear Godefroid, are the object of our special attention. Indeed, so many of those we rescue are people of intelligence and heart; they return everything we have lent them, with interest, and in the end their restitutions cover any losses we might incur in aiding the infirm, or the shameless, or those stripped of all virtue by their misfortunes. We sometimes obtain useful information from those we have helped; but our project has become so vast, its workings so complex, that we can no longer deal with all our affairs ourselves. Thus, seven or eight months ago, we resolved to retain the services of a doctor in every arrondissement of Paris. Each of us is responsible for four arrondissements. To each doctor we pay an indemnity of three thousand francs; he must devote his time and attentions to our patients first of all, but we do not prevent him from caring for others. Do you know that in eight months we have not been able to find twelve such precious men, twelve upstanding assistants, despite all the resources offered to us by our benefactors and our personal acquaintances? Did we not require men of perfect discretion, men of unblemished morality and well-honed knowledge, active men, eager to do good? But, although there are ten thousand souls in Paris who might be more or less able to serve us, one is unlikely to meet twelve such good men in the course of a year."

"Our Savior found it very difficult to bring together his twelve apostles, and even then, a traitor and an unbeliever found their way into their midst!" said Godefroid.

"In any case, as of two weeks ago, all our districts have been supplied with a Visitor," the little man continued with a smile, "for such is the name we give to our doctors; and so, for the past fortnight, our task has remained great, but our efficiency has doubled. Now, I am telling you this little secret of our nascent Order because you must make the acquaintance of the doctor assigned to the district where you will be living, not least because you will find him a precious source of information. This Visitor is named Berton, Doctor Berton, and he lives in the Rue d'Enfer. And now, here is the matter itself. Doctor Berton has been treating a woman whose illness could be said to defy all human science. But that is the concern of the College of Medicine; our task is to uncover the poverty of the patient's family, which the doctor believes to be horrific and, most important, concealed with an energy and a pride that cry out for our care. In the past, my child, I could have dealt with this matter myself; today, my new task compels me to take on an assistant, and that will be you. This family lives in the Rue Notre-Dame-des-Champs, in a house overlooking the Boulevard du Mont-Parnasse. You will take rooms in that house, and you will attempt to discover the truth. You must practice the grimmest parsimony where your own needs are concerned; as to expenditures on this family's behalf, do not fear: I will give you whatever sums we may find necessary, once we have carefully considered the circumstances. But you must closely study the nature of these poor people's souls. Good hearts and noble sentiments, these are our only collateral! Miserly for ourselves, generous toward the suffering, we must be cautious and even calculating, for we draw our funds from the treasury of the poor. Thus, tomorrow morning, you will leave this house; but never forget the great power you will have at your disposal. The Brothers are with you! ..."

"Oh!" cried Godefroid. "I'm quite sure I won't sleep tonight! You have awakened in me such a delight in good works, and such a longing to prove myself worthy of joining your Brotherhood! ..."

"Ah! My child! One last word of advice! The prohibition against acknowledging me in the street also applies to the other gentlemen, to Madame, and even to our domestics. Our work requires a perfect incognito, which we have so often been forced to protect that we have made of it an absolute law. We must remain an anonymous force among the great crowds of Paris ... You must also remember the guiding principle of our Order, dear Godefroid, which tells us that we must never be seen as Good Samaritans, that we must keep to the very minor role of the intermediary. We always introduce ourselves as agents of a pious person, and a holy one (do we not work for God?), so that no one might feel they owe us their gratitude, or take us for wealthy men. Real, sincere humility must inspire you and govern your every thought, and not the false humility of those who shun publicity only to better gain the spotlight ... You may certainly feel joy when you succeed, but so long as you have vanity and pride working within you, you will not be worthy of entrance into the Order. We have known two perfect men: the first was one of our founders, Judge Popinot; the other, whose name we came to know solely by his works, is a country doctor celebrated in a distant canton. This latter, my dear Godefroid, is one of the greatest men of our time; he brought an entire province from savagery to prosperity, from irreligion to Catholicism, from barbarity to civilization. The names of those two men are etched into our hearts, and we continually look to them as our models. We would be very happy indeed if one day we could enjoy the kind of influence in Paris that that country doctor exerted over his canton. But here the wounds are far graver, and for the moment they exceed our abilities. If God will consent to keep Madame among us for some years longer, and to send us a few more aides such as you, then perhaps we will leave behind us an institution able to inspire reverence for its holy religion. Adieu, then, my friend . . . Now begins your initiation . . . Ah! Here I have been prattling on like a schoolmaster, and I have forgotten the most important part. This is the family's address," he said, handing Godefroid a square of paper, "and Monsieur Berton's, on the Rue d'Enfer . . . Now, go and pray to God that He might come to your aid."

Godefroid clasped the kindly old man's hands and pressed them tenderly, wishing him a good evening and assuring him he would not fail to observe his every recommendation. "All that you have told me," he added, "is engraved in my memory for the rest of my life . . ."

The old man smiled, expressing no doubt in Godefroid's sincerity. He stood up from his chair and walked toward his prie-dieu. Godefroid returned to his room, overjoyed to be participating at last in the mysterious workings of this house, and to have before him a new task, which, in the current state of his soul, promised to be nothing other than a pleasure.

Alain was not present at breakfast the next morning, but Godefroid made no allusion to the cause of his absence; nor was he questioned about the mission entrusted him by the old man. This was his first lesson in discretion. Nevertheless, when the meal was over, he took Madame de La Chanterie aside and told her that he would be away for a few days.

"That's fine, my child!" answered Madame de La Chanterie. "Try to do your godfather proud, for Monsieur Alain has staked his good name on your success."

Godefroid now took his leave of the three others, who bade him a warm farewell, as if blessing his first steps in this arduous new career.

The idea of association, one of the greatest of all social forces, the source of Europe's rise in the Middle Ages, is rooted in sentiments that have withered in France since 1792, when the Individual finally triumphed over the State. Association requires, first, a sense of devotion that is no longer understood in our land; second, an artless faith that runs counter to the new spirit of our nation; and finally, a discipline against which we now inevitably rebel, and which is to be found only in the Catholic faith. We French may well try to form associations, yet no sooner have our countrymen left an assembly marked by an outpouring of the finest sentiments than they begin searching for some way to milk that common cow for their own benefit, making a mockery of that collective devotion, of that union of strengths. But the beast's bounty is not sufficient for the needs of all these separate strategists, and it dies withered and gaunt.

We will never know how many generous sentiments have been eroded, how many ardent sparks have been snuffed out, lost forever to our country, by the base chicanery of the French Charbonnerie, by the false subscription drive for the colony of Champ d'Asile, by any of a hundred political shams that should have been great and noble dramas but ended up as mere farces, directed by the correctional police. And our industrial associations have gone much the same way: the love of Self has replaced the love of the collective Body. No doubt we will one day return to the guilds and Hansas of the Middle Ages, but for the moment they seem an impossible dream. The only *societies* left to us are our religious institutions, and these have now become the target of brutal and concerted attacks, for the natural tendency of the unwell is to despise the remedies and even the doctors who might bring them a cure. France understands nothing of self-abnegation. Thus, an association can survive only if it is imbued with the religious spirit, for none other can quell the rebellions of the human mind, the cunning of ambition, the seductions of cupidity in all its varied forms.

Those who long for a new world do not realize that association offers us new worlds by the score.

Godefroid felt a changed man as he walked through the streets. Had some passerby been able to enter his soul at this moment, he would have been awed by the remarkable communicability of collective power. Godefroid was no longer one man alone but a being made multiple, for he represented five others, who walked beside him with every step, and whose united strength supported his every action. Knowing this power to be lodged in his heart, he felt a surge of vitality, a noble strength that he found wonderfully exhilarating. He later called this one of the finest moments of his existence; for all at once he enjoyed a new sensation, that of an omnipotence more certain and unshakable than any despot's. The power of the soul is like the power of the mind: it is limitless.

"What a life it is to live for others!" he said to himself. "Together, we act in concert, as if we were all one man; separately, each of us acts as if we were acting together! And all this guided only by Charity, the most beautiful, the most living of all the figures of Catholic virtue! So this is what life can be! But come, we must repress this puerile joy; I can almost hear Father Alain laughing at me now. Still, is it not strange? Just when I was prepared to discard my own existence, I found the very power I had sought for so long! The world of the suffering will be mine!"

He strode from the Cloister of Notre-Dame to the Avenue de l'Observatoire in a state of such exaltation that he could not say how long he had walked.

Arriving at the intersection of the Rue Notre-Dame-des-Champs and the Rue de l'Ouest, neither of which was paved at that time, he was surprised to find so much mud and muck in a spot offering such magnificent prospects. Pedestrians were forced to walk close by the houses or wooden fences that walled off the marshy gardens, and even there the footpath was often flooded with stagnant water, and so transformed into a small, flowing stream.

After a brief search he discovered the house in question and approached it with some difficulty. This building had clearly served as a factory, long since closed down. Tall and narrow, and entirely devoid of ornament, it seemed little more than a high wall pierced with square windows, except on the ground floor, where there was only a shabby little door.

Godefroid assumed that the landlord had divided the former factory into a number of small apartments, in hopes of deriving some revenue from it, for above the door he spied a small placard hand-painted with the words SEVERAL ROOMS TO LET. Godefroid rang, but no one came; as he stood waiting, a passerby informed him that the house had another entrance on the boulevard, where he would find someone to welcome him.

Godefroid followed the stranger's advice. Turning onto the boulevard, he found himself before a small garden, parallel to the street, beyond which stood the house's façade, half-hidden by trees. The garden was somewhat unkempt, and since the boulevard lies at a higher elevation than the Rue Notre-Dame-des-Champs, it sloped downward, forming a sort of moat. Godefroid followed a pathway into the garden, where he spied an old woman whose shabby clothing seemed to harmonize perfectly with the house.

"Was that you ringing from the Rue Notre-Dame?" she asked.

"Yes, Madame . . . Are you the one I must speak to if I wish to see the rooms?"

Receiving an affirmative response from the caretaker, a woman of uncertain age, Godefroid asked if the house's lodgers were orderly and quiet, as he spent his days in occupations that required silence and tranquillity; he was unmarried, and he was hoping to arrange for a regular housekeeping service.

Hearing these well-chosen words, she adopted a gracious air and said, "Monsieur has come to the right place; for, excepting the days of the Chaumière ball, the boulevard is as deserted as the Pontine Marshes . . ."

"You know the Pontine Marshes?" asked Godefroid.

"No, Monsieur; but I have an old man upstairs whose daughter's lot in life is to be forever on death's doorstep, and that's something she often says; I'm only repeating it. That poor old man will be very happy to learn that Monsieur is hoping for quiet; it wouldn't do his daughter much good to have a regular tempest for a neighbor . . . And then on the third floor we have two writers, of a sort; but they come home every day at midnight, and every night they go off at eight in the morning. They call themselves authors, but I don't know where they work, or when."

As she spoke, the caretaker led Godefroid up one of those dreadful staircases of brick and wood, so badly put together that one never knows if it is the wood that is trying to escape from the bricks or the bricks that have grown weary of the embrace of the wood, brick and wood alike reinforced with an impregnable barrier of dust in the summer and mud in the winter. The cracked plaster walls displayed more inscriptions than the Académie des Belles-Lettres ever dreamt of. The caretaker stopped at the first landing.

"Here, Monsieur, are two adjoining rooms, very clean, just across from Monsieur Bernard's. That's the old gentleman I was telling you of, a very proper man indeed. He's been decorated, but he must have fallen on hard times, because I never see him wearing his decor . . . When they were first here, they had a domestic from the provinces, but they let him go three years ago . . . The lady's young son has taken over for him; now it's him who sees to the housekeeping . . ."

Godefroid made a gesture.

"Oh!" cried the caretaker, "don't you worry, they won't bother you a bit, they never talk to anyone. That gentleman has been here since the July Revolution; he moved in in 1831 . . . They're up from the provinces, and I'm supposing they lost their fortune when the Government changed; they're very proud, and taciturn as fish . . . In these four years, Monsieur, they've never accepted the least little favor from me, for fear it might cost them . . . A hundred *sous* on New Year's Day, that's all I ever get from them . . . Now, those authors, on the other hand! I get ten francs a month just for telling anyone who comes looking for them that they moved out at the end of the month before."

The caretaker's penchant for chatter led Godefroid to hope that she might prove a useful ally. As she vaunted the fine condition of the two rooms and two closets, she informed him that she was not precisely a caretaker but the trustee of the building's owner, for whom she managed the house, so to speak.

"You may place your trust in me, Monsieur, indeed you can! Madame Vauthier would sooner have nothing at all than have a *sou* that belongs to someone else!"

Madame Vauthier soon reached an agreement with Godefroid, who wished to rent these lodgings by the month, and furnished—for these dreary little rooms, meant for students or struggling authors, could be rented furnished or not. The house's uppermost floor was a vast attic, full of furniture. As for Monsieur Bernard, he had furnished his lodgings himself.

Encouraging Madame Vauthier's loquacity, Godefroid learned that her ambition was to run a proper boardinghouse but that, in five years, she had never found a single lodger willing to sign on for room and board. She lived on the ground floor, on the boulevard side, and thus watched over the house herself, assisted by a large dog, a large serving girl, and a little domestic, who saw to the boots, the rooms, and the errands—both of them poor like her, in keeping with the wretchedness of the house and its lodgers, and the wild, desolate air of the garden before it.

These servants were mere children, abandoned by their families; the widow Vauthier paid them solely in food, and what food! Godefroid had caught a brief glimpse of the boy. As a sort of livery, he wore a tattered blouse, slippers rather than shoes, and wooden clogs when he ventured outside. Tousled as a sparrow after a bath, his hands black with dirt, he went off to measure lumber in one of the work sites on the boulevard as soon as he had finished his morning duties at the house. Then, at day's end—which, for lumber merchants, comes at four-thirty—he resumed his domestic occupations, such as fetching water from the fountain on the Place de l'Observatoire and delivering it to the widow's lodgers, along with small armloads of wood that he sawed and bundled himself.

Every evening Népomucène, for such was the name of the widow Vauthier's young slave, placed his day's earnings in the hands of his mistress. Every Sunday and Monday in summer, the unhappy foundling became a serving boy for the wine merchants near the city gates. For these occasions the widow always took care to dress him in presentable clothes.

As for the fat girl, she saw to the cooking under the widow Vauthier's watchful eye. Once this was done, she helped the caretaker with her work, for the widow had a profession of her own: she made felt slippers for itinerant vendors.

It took Godefroid no more than an hour to learn all this, for the widow showed him the entire establishment, explaining its transformation from factory to rooming house. Until 1828 the building had been used for breeding silkworms, not so much to make silk as to harvest what are known as the seeds. This silkworm nursery had been fed by an eleven-*arpent* orchard of mulberry trees in the Montrouge plain, and another three *arpents* on the Rue de l'Ouest, now replaced by houses. The widow went on to explain that Monsieur Barbet had funded this factory through a loan to its founder, an Italian named Fresconi, and it was thanks only to the sale of those three *arpents* that he had recovered his investment. Just as she was pointing out the plot of land in question, across the Rue Notre-Dame-des-Champs, a tall, withered old man with perfectly white hair appeared at the end of the street, near the intersection with the Rue de l'Ouest.

"Ah! Well! He couldn't have picked a better time!" cried Madame Vauthier. "See there, this is your neighbor, Monsieur Bernard . . ."

"Monsieur Bernard," she called out as soon as the old man was within range of her voice, "your solitude is at an end, this gentleman has come to rent the rooms across from yours . . ."

Monsieur Bernard raised his eyes and examined Godefroid with unconcealed apprehension, as if saying to himself, "So my fears have been realized at last . . ."

"Monsieur," he said aloud, "you intend to take rooms in this house?"

"Yes, Monsieur," Godefroid answered candidly. "This is not a place for the fortunates of this world, and I could find no cheaper lodgings in the neighborhood. Fortunately, Madame Vauthier does not aspire to rent to millionaires . . . Good-bye, my good Madame Vauthier. Please see to it that my rooms are ready at six o'clock this evening; I shall return at that hour precisely."

And Godefroid strode off toward the Rue de l'Ouest at a leisurely pace, for the anxiety visible on the old man's face led him to believe that their conversation was not yet at an end. And indeed, after a brief hesitation, Monsieur Bernard turned on his heel and set out after Godefroid, evidently hoping to catch up with him.

"That old meddler! He's going to convince him not to come back . . ." the widow Vauthier said to herself. "That's twice he's cost me a new lodger! . . . But patience! In five days his rent comes due, and if he doesn't settle it *recta*, I'll toss him into the street. Monsieur Barbet is a real tiger, and it doesn't take much to excite him . . . Oh! How I wish I knew what they were saying . . . Félicité! . . . Félicité! You great cow! Will you come here at once? . . ." cried the widow in her true voice, rather more formidable than the fluting tones she had adopted for her conversation with Godefroid.

The servant, a fat, redheaded, walleyed girl, came running.

"Keep an eye on things here for a few moments, you hear me? . . . I'll be back in five minutes."

And the widow Vauthier, onetime cook to the publisher Barbet— one of the most merciless of all Paris's moneylenders—set out after her two lodgers, intending to eavesdrop from a distance, then rejoin Godefroid at the conclusion of his conversation with Monsieur Bernard.

Monsieur Bernard walked with a rather halting gait, like a man un- certain of his next move, or a debtor trying to invent some excuse to give a creditor who has stalked off in a very bad humor. Still walking ahead of the stranger, Godefroid turned around from time to time to cast a glance in his direction, all the while pretending to study his new neighborhood. Thus, it was only in the middle of the great allée of the Luxembourg Gardens that Monsieur Bernard finally accosted Gode- froid.

"Excuse me, Monsieur," said Monsieur Bernard with a bow imme- diately returned by the young man. "A thousand pardons for detaining you without having the honor of your acquaintance, but is it quite cer- tain that you will be taking up lodgings in that awful house?"

"But, Monsieur . . ."

"Yes," the old man resumed, silencing Godefroid with an unyield- ing gesture, "you may well ask what right I have to involve myself in your affairs, by what right I pose such a question . . . Listen to me, Monsieur, you are young, and I am old, so much older than my years—and I am no less than sixty-seven, though I could easily pass for eighty . . . Age and misfortune permit many things; indeed, does the law not exempt septuagenarians from certain public duties? But I do not wish to speak to you of the rights enjoyed by the elderly; I wish to speak to you of yourself. Do you know that the neighborhood you have chosen is deserted after eight o'clock in the evening, and that it is a place not without its dangers, of which robbery is the least? . . . Have you not noticed the many empty lots, the orchards, the gardens? And yet I live there myself, you might answer; but I, Monsieur, never leave my rooms after six o'clock in the evening. You will no doubt observe that there are two young men living on the third floor, above the apartment you intend to make yours . . . But, Monsieur, those two poor men of letters are saddled with debts and on the run from their creditors; they have come here to hide, and they spend their days away from the house, returning only at midnight. They have precious little to fear from robbers or cutthroats! And of course, they are always together, and always armed . . . It was I who obtained their weapons permits from the Prefecture of Police . . ."

"Oh! Monsieur," said Godefroid, "I do not fear robbers, for reasons very like those that make your two young gentlemen invulnerable, and I value my life so little that, should some misguided soul make the mistake of assassinating me, I would bless the murderer with my dying breath . . ."

The old man looked Godefroid up and down. "You don't seem such a very poor young man," he replied.

"I have at most enough to live on, to buy bread to eat, and I have come to this neighborhood, Monsieur, in search of the very silence you have warned me of. But may I inquire into your reasons for seeking to drive me away?"

Here the tall stranger fell silent, for he spied Madame Vauthier drawing near. Godefroid examined him closely and was surprised at his exceptional thinness, no doubt caused by sorrow, and perhaps hunger, and very likely hard work. Each of these debilitating forces had left its mark on that face, whose withered skin clung tightly to the bones, as if baked by the fires of Africa. His high, looming forehead sheltered two steel blue eyes beneath its cupola, eyes as cold, hard, wise, and penetrating as the eyes of the savages but marred by two deep and very wrinkled dark circles. His long, slender nose and proudly raised chin gave the old man a certain resemblance to the popular image of Don Quixote; but this was the face of a cruel Don Quixote, a Don Quixote without illusions, Don Quixote as a formidable figure.

In spite of this severity, the old man could not entirely conceal the fear and frailty that indigence confers on all its victims. These two afflictions had created something like cracks in a face that seemed so sturdy as to defy even the devastating pickax of misery. His mouth was eloquent and serious. Don Quixote was complicated by the President de Montesquieu.

He was dressed entirely in black wool, long since become threadbare. His coat, of an old-fashioned cut like his trousers, had been patched and stitched several times over, with no great skill. The buttons had recently been replaced. His coat was buttoned up to the chin to conceal the color of his linens, and his reddish black cravat hid the trumpery of a false collar. No doubt worn for many years, this black suit exuded poverty from every fiber. But the mysterious old man's grand air, his unbent posture, the lucidity that inhabited his brow and revealed itself in his eyes, all this belied any notion of indigence. A passerby would have been hard put indeed to classify this Parisian.

With his thoughtful gaze, Monsieur Bernard might easily have passed for some sort of local scholar, a professor lost in single-minded and demanding meditations. Godefroid examined him with an interest and curiosity heightened by the knowledge of the mission of mercy on which he had been sent.

"Monsieur, if I could be certain that it was silence and repose you seek, I would say to you: 'Take rooms as near me as you can,'" he answered. "By all means, rent the apartment," he said, raising his voice in such a way as to be heard by the Vauthier woman, who was then walking by, straining to hear his words. "I am a father, Monsieur; in all the world I have only my daughter and her son to help me withstand the miseries of life, and my daughter requires silence and absolute tranquillity . . . To this day, all who have come to find lodgings in the apartment you wish to take have bowed to the reasoning and prayers of a despairing father; it little mattered to them whether they lived on one street or another of a truly deserted neighborhood, where lodgings of little cost are as plentiful as modest boardinghouses. But I sense that your mind is made up, and I beg you, Monsieur, do not deceive me, for otherwise I should be forced to leave, and move outside the city walls . . . This move itself might cost me my daughter's life," he said, his voice choked with emotion. "And even if she survived it, oh, who knows if the doctors would be willing to travel beyond the walls? . . . Even now, they come to see my daughter only out of devotion to God."

If this man had been able to weep, his cheeks would have been streaming with tears as he spoke these last words; but to cite an expression that today has become commonplace, he had tears in his voice, and he covered his brow with his hand, which seemed to be nothing but muscle and bone.

"And what is your daughter's illness?" asked Godefroid in an amicable and sympathetic tone.

"A terrible malady to which the doctors have given all manner of names or, more precisely, a malady that has no name . . . My fortune is gone . . ." Here he paused, gesturing his defeat in a manner peculiar to the poor. Then he went on: "What little money I had left—for I was ruined in 1830, fallen from a great height—in short, everything I once possessed was soon devoured by my daughter, Monsieur, who had already ruined her mother and her husband's family . . . Today, my small pension is scarcely sufficient to buy the barest essentials required by my poor, good daughter's condition . . . She has exhausted my capacity for tears . . . I have lived through a thousand torments. Monsieur, I must be a man of granite not to have died; or rather, God has chosen not to deprive the child of her father, knowing that she needs a guardian, a protector, for her mother died trying to care for her . . . Ah! Young man, you have come to this place just when the old tree that has never bent suddenly feels the ax of poverty, sharpened by grief, plunging deep into its heart . . . And I, who have never once uttered a murmur of complaint, I will tell you of her illness, in hopes of convincing you not to come to this house or, if you insist, to show you the vital importance of respecting our repose . . . At present, Monsieur, my daughter howls like a dog, day and night—"

"She is mad!" said Godefroid.

"She has full use of her reason, and she is a saint," the old man answered. "In a moment, when I have told you all, you will conclude that it is I who am mad. Monsieur, my only daughter was born to a mother who enjoyed the most excellent health. In all my life I have loved only one single woman, and it was she. I chose her for my bride; for love alone, I married the daughter of one of the finest colonels in the Imperial Guard, a Pole who was once the Emperor's aide-de-camp, the distinguished General Tarlowski. My own occupation required great moral purity, to be sure, but above all else I was born with a heart unable to lodge more than one sentiment at a time; and so I loved my wife faithfully, and she truly deserved all my devotion. And as a father I am just what I was as a husband. That single sentence will tell you all you need to know. My daughter never left her mother's side, and never did a child live more chastely, in a more Christian manner, than that dear girl. She was born more than pretty, she was born beautiful; and her husband, a young man whose morals I have never doubted—for he was the son of a close friend of mine, a President of the Royal Court—could certainly not have contributed to her illness in any way."

Godefroid and Monsieur Bernard observed an involuntary pause, each looking into the other's eyes.

"As you know, marriage sometimes brings about a great change in a young woman," the old man went on. "The first pregnancy went smoothly and produced a son, my grandson, who lives with me today, the only offspring of two conjoined families. With her second pregnancy came the onset of the most extraordinary symptoms; her baffled doctors attributed her sufferings to the peculiar phenomena that sometimes accompany that state, and to which they can respond only with a note in the annals of medicine. My daughter gave birth to a stillborn child, its body literally twisted, its life crushed out by some internal force. Her illness had begun, and the pregnancy had nothing to do with it . . . Perhaps you are a medical student?"

Godefroid made a gesture that might have meant either yes or no.

"That terrible, wrenching delivery," Monsieur Bernard went on, "made a violent impression on my son-in-law, and he fell into a deep melancholy that eventually cost him his life. Two or three months later, my daughter began to complain of a generalized weakness, affecting most particularly her feet, which, as she put it, felt as though they were made of cotton. That numbness soon became paralysis; but what a paralysis, Monsieur! You may bend my daughter's feet beneath her, you may twist them this way and that; she feels nothing. The limb simply lies there before you, seemingly without blood, muscle, or bone. This affliction, which bears no resemblance to any known syndrome, soon spread to her arms, and then her hands; we believed it might be caused by some disorder of the spinal column. Each new doctor, each new remedy only aggravated her condition, and my poor daughter could no longer move without dislocating her hips, or her shoulders, or her arms. For some time we had an excellent surgeon— very nearly our house surgeon, you might say—who together with the usual doctor or doctors (for they often came to call purely out of curiosity) put her limbs back into place . . . would you believe it, Monsieur? three or four times a day! Ah! . . . Her illness takes so many forms that I have forgotten this one: when her weakness was first coming over her, before the paralysis of her limbs, my daughter was overtaken by the strangest attacks of catalepsy . . . You must know what catalepsy is. For days at a time, she lay just as she was lying at the time of the attack, her eyes open, perfectly still. She experienced the most monstrous effects of that affliction, even bouts of lockjaw. In this phase of her illness, seeing her so curiously paralyzed, I thought of turning to magnetism for her treatment. My daughter, Monsieur, was a remarkably lucid and intelligent girl; but her mind was invaded by all the phenomena of somnambulism, even as her body was afflicted by so many varied disorders . . ."

Godefroid could not help but wonder if the old man's reason was entirely sound.

"I was raised on Voltaire, on Diderot, on Helvétius; I am a true child of the eighteenth century," he continued, paying no mind to the expression in Godefroid's eyes. "I am a son of the Revolution, and once I mocked everything that Antiquity and the Middle Ages tell us of possession; but, Monsieur, possession is the only possible explanation for the state in which my child now finds herself. Cursed with somnambulism, she has never been able to explain the cause of her sufferings; she could not understand them herself, and every method of treatment she demanded of us proved equally ineffective, even though we were careful to follow her instructions to the letter. Once she wanted to be enveloped in the carcass of a freshly slaughtered pig; then she ordered us to poke her legs with iron darts that had been heavily magnetized and heated red-hot in the fire, or to pour molten sealing wax the length of her back ...

"And, oh, Monsieur, what disasters ensued! Her teeth fell out! She became deaf, and then mute; and then, after six months of absolute silence and complete deafness, her speech and hearing suddenly returned. She regained the use of her hands, as abruptly as she had lost it; but for seven years now her feet have remained useless to her. She experienced sudden attacks of hydrophobia, with symptoms of great severity, entirely characteristic of that disease. Not only did the sight of water—or the sound, or simply the presence of a glass or a cup— send her into a fit of rage, but she also developed a howl precisely like that of a dog, a melancholy howl as such a beast might make on hearing the sound of an organ. Several times she lay on the point of death. She was given the last rites, and then all at once she returned to life, still suffering with all her reason intact, all her clarity of mind; for the faculties of her soul and her heart have for the moment remained untouched ... But while she lived on, Monsieur, she caused the death of her husband, and of her mother, who could not bear this endless succession of crises ... Alas, Monsieur! ... What I have told you here is nothing! Every one of her natural functions has been perverted, and only medicine could tell you of the strange aberrations of her organs ... And it was in this state that I had to bring her from the provinces to Paris in 1829; for the two or three celebrated Parisian doctors to whom I had written for help—Desplein, Bianchon, and Haudry—refused to believe such an illness could be real. Magnetism was then strenuously discounted by the medical academies; and though never questioning the good faith of the provincial doctors, or my own, they attributed her symptoms to a sort of carelessness of observation or, if you like, to a sort of exaggeration commonly displayed by patients and their families. But they were soon forced to change their opinion, and it is thanks to her symptoms that so much research has recently been conducted in the area of nervous diseases, for they classified her bizarre condition as a neurosis. At their last consultation, they resolved to withdraw all her medications; they felt that her illness must be allowed to run its course, so that they might study its effects. Since that time, only one doctor has continued to see her, the doctor who tends to the poor of this neighborhood. We must content ourselves with easing her pain, and soothe it as best we can, since we understand nothing of its cause."

Here the old man fell silent, as if overcome with dismay at his own words.

"For the past five years," he went on, "my daughter has lived in a continuous cycle of remissions and relapses; but at least no new phenomenon has appeared. She suffers to a greater or lesser extent from the various nervous attacks I have described, but her legs and the perturbations of her natural functions have remained utterly unchanged. Meanwhile, our financial difficulties have become graver with each passing year. Thus, we were soon driven from our apartment near the Beaujon Hospital in the Faubourg du Roule, where we had lived since 1829. But my daughter cannot tolerate change; twice already it has nearly cost us her life, first in the course of our voyage to Paris, then again as we wandered the streets of this neighborhood in search of a new home. Desperate to find lodgings for my daughter, I accepted Madame Vauthier's terms on the spot. But I strongly sensed that our difficulties were not at an end, and indeed they were not; for I was made to wait until 1833 for the settlement of my pension—after thirty years' service to my country! It was just six months ago that I began to receive my payments, and the new government has compounded my many hardships by according me only the absolute minimum."

Godefroid could not hold back a gesture of astonishment that called out for a fuller explanation, and the old man clearly understood its meaning, answering at once, with an accusing glance toward the heavens: "I am one of a thousand victims of the political upheavals of our times. I keep my family name a secret, for it has inspired many dreams of vengeance; and if the lessons of one generation's experience can be of any use to the next, then I advise you, young man, to avoid all involvement in the workings of any political regime ... Not that I regret having done my duty; on that point my conscience is perfectly clear. But the powers of the present day no longer feel the sort of solidarity that binds one Government to the next, no matter how different the two may be; and if zealous service is rewarded, it is only thanks to the new Government's short-lived concern for its own security. No matter how faithful, the tool that once served it is sooner or later cast aside and forgotten. You see in me one of the staunchest supporters of the elder branch of the Bourbon family, just as I once was of the Emperor and his allies, and yet today I find myself in the most abject poverty! I am too proud to put out my hand and beg; I must thus accept that no one will ever take note of my sufferings. Five days ago, Monsieur, the neighborhood doctor, who is treating my daughter—or I should perhaps say observing her—told me that he was not up to the challenge of curing an illness that takes on a new form every two weeks. Neuroses are the despair of medicine, he told me, for their roots lie in a system that cannot be explored. He told me of a certain Jewish doctor, widely considered a charlatan, it seems; but he observed that the man is a foreigner, a Polish refugee, and that he has earned the bitter jealousy of his fellows through his patients' extraordinary recoveries, which have caused a great stir. He assured me that some consider him very wise, and very skillful. But he is a temperamental, untrusting man, who chooses his patients with great care, for fear of wasting his time; and moreover he is a ... communist ... His name is Halpersohn. My grandson has gone to see him twice, but to no avail; he has never called at our house, and I fully understand why! ..."

"Why?" said Godefroid.

"Oh! My grandson is a boy of sixteen, and even more shabbily clothed than I; and would you believe it, Monsieur, I do not dare present myself at the doctor's office. My dress is too unlike what one expects of a man of my age, and one as sober as I. If he discovered the grandfather to be penniless, after the grandson has already shown himself to such ill effect, how could the doctor be expected to give my daughter the care she needs? He will do as they always do with the poor . . . And just think, my dear Monsieur: I love my daughter for all the sorrows she has caused me, just as I once loved her for all the joy she brought me. She has become a veritable angel. Alas! Today, she is nothing more than a soul, casting its light over her son and myself; her body no longer exists, for she has lost even the sensation of pain . . . Think what it must be like for a father to look on such suffering every day! My daughter's bedroom has become her entire world! I decorate it with all her favorite flowers; she spends most of her time reading, but when she has the use of her hands she sews, with fingers as deft as a fairy's . . . She knows nothing of the deep poverty into which we have been plunged . . . Imagine the strangeness of our existence and you will have some idea why we admit no visitors to our home . . . Do you understand me fully, Monsieur? Do you begin to see why a neighbor is out of the question? I would ask so much of him as to be infinitely in his debt, and I could never hope to repay that obligation. For one thing, my every waking hour is accounted for: I oversee my grandson's education, and my own work is so demanding, so very demanding, Monsieur, that I sleep no more than three or four hours each night."

"Monsieur," said Godefroid after patiently hearing the old man out to the end, all the while observing him with pained attention, "I will be your neighbor, and I will help you . . ."

The old man could not conceal a surge of wounded pride, and even irritation, for he believed no good could come from his fellow men.

"I will help you," Godefroid continued, taking the old man's hands and pressing them with pious affection, "but only as I am able . . . Listen to me. What do you intend to make of your grandson?"

"He is destined for a career in the Palais de Justice, and will soon begin the study of law."

"Then your grandson will cost you six hundred francs a year . . ."

The old man stood silent.

"I myself have nothing," Godefroid continued after a pause, "but I can do much. I will bring the Jewish doctor to your door! And if your daughter is curable, she will be cured. We will find some way to repay this Halpersohn."

"Oh! If my daughter were to be cured, I would make a sacrifice that can only be made once in a lifetime!" the old man cried. "I would give up my last crust of bread!"

"You will keep your bread . . ."

"Oh! youth! youth! . . ." cried the old man, shaking his head . . . "Adieu, Monsieur, or rather good-bye. The library will be opening shortly, and I must go there every day for my work, since I have sold all my books . . . I am most grateful for the kindness you have shown me, but we shall see if you can truly grant all the favors I must ask of my neighbor. I expect nothing more of you than that . . ."

"Yes, Monsieur, please allow me to be your neighbor. Barbet is not the sort to allow an apartment to sit empty, and you might easily find yourself faced with a far worse companion in misery than I . . . I do not ask you to believe in me; I only ask that you let me be of use to you . . ."

"And why should you want that?" the old man cried, descending the steps of the Carthusian cloister that then separated the Rue d'Enfer from the central allée of the Luxembourg Gardens.

"Did you never do a good turn for another in the course of your life?"

The old man looked at Godefroid with a furrowed brow, his eyes full of memories, as if paging through the book of his life in search of an act worthy of such uncommon kindness. Dubiously bidding the stranger farewell, he turned away coolly.

"Well, for our first meeting, he did not seem overly alarmed," the Initiate told himself.

Godefroid then made for the Rue d'Enfer and the address given him by Monsieur Alain. There he found Doctor Berton, a cold, severe man, who to his great surprise confirmed every detail of Monsieur Bernard's account and offered him Halpersohn's address.

That Polish doctor, now so justly famous, was then living in a small, isolated two-story house on the Rue Marbeuf in Chaillot. Halpersohn lived on the second floor; the ground floor was occupied by General Roman Tarnowicki, and the two refugees' domestics roomed in the attic. For the moment, Godefroid could not see the doctor, who had been summoned to a distant province by a wealthy patient; but at this he was almost relieved, for in his eagerness he had neglected to consider the question of the doctor's fee, and he had no money to offer him. He was thus forced to make a brief call at Madame de La Chanterie's, to collect the funds he would require for his task.

These errands, along with dinner in a restaurant on the Rue de l'Odéon, brought Godefroid to the hour appointed for his return to the Boulevard du Mont-Parnasse. In preparation for his arrival, Madame Vauthier had brought several pieces of incomparably shabby furniture down from the attic. She seemed almost unused to letting rooms for the purpose of being lived in. The bed, chairs, tables, chest of drawers, desk, and curtains had clearly been bought at an auction held to reimburse a pauper's creditors, since, as is often the case in such circumstances, they had no real value of their own.

Madame Vauthier stood with her hands on her hips, awaiting the thanks she was owed. She thus took Godefroid's smile as a smile of delight.

"Ah! My dear Monsieur Godefroid, for you I have chosen the finest furnishings in our storerooms!" she said with a triumphant air. "Look at these pretty silk curtains, and this mahogany bed—*not a single wormhole*! It once belonged to Prince de Wissembourg and sat in his private mansion. I was working as a kitchen maid in his service when he left the Rue Louis-le-Grand, in 1809 . . . From there I went straight to work for my landlord."

Godefroid stemmed this flow of confidences by paying his month in advance, adding a further six francs for Madame Vauthier's housekeeping services. Just then he heard a bark. Were it not for Monsieur Bernard's warnings, he would have thought that his neighbor kept a dog in his rooms.

"Does that dog bark at night? . . ."

"Oh! Don't you worry, Monsieur, just be patient; in a week's time he'll be gone for good. Monsieur Bernard won't be able to pay his rent, and out the door he'll go . . . My word, what very singular people they are! I've never seen their dog. The beast goes months—months! what am I saying? it can go half a year—without making a sound! You'd think they didn't have a dog at all! It never leaves the lady's bedroom . . . There's a very sick lady lives there, you know. She hasn't left her room since she first came through the door . . . Old Monsieur Bernard works very hard, and so does his grandson, who's a day pupil at the Louis-le-Grand school, in his last year—and him only sixteen! There's gumption for you! But it's true, the lad works like a madman ... You'll hear them bringing flowers in and out of the lady's room, because they're forever buying her flowers and treats, and all the while the grandfather and grandson eat nothing but bread ... The lady must be in frightful shape, not ever to have gone out since she came in. And to hear Monsieur Berton tell it—that's the doctor who comes to see her—the only way she'll leave is feet first."

"And what does this Monsieur Bernard do?"

"He's a scholar, by the look of it; because he writes, and he's always going off to work in some library. Whatever it is he's composing, Monsieur treats it as collateral and regularly lends him money on it."

"Monsieur? Whom do you mean?"

"My landlord, Monsieur Barbet, the bookseller and publisher, now retired after sixteen years in business. He came here from Normandy; he started out selling lettuce in the streets, and then in 1818 he went into books, first on the quays and then in his own little shop, and today he's a rich man ... He's a sort of Jew, who can do thirty-six jobs at once; he was more or less an associate of the Italian who built this place for his silkworms ..."

"So this house is a refuge for struggling writers?" said Godefroid.

"Is Monsieur so unfortunate as to be one himself?" asked the widow Vauthier.

"I'm only starting out," Godefroid answered.

"Oh, my dear Monsieur, for the little misery I wish on you, I'd advise you to stop where you are ... Now a journalist, for example, that's different ..."

Godefroid could not help but laugh. He bade good night to his landlady the onetime cook, a perfect, unwitting exemplar of the true bourgeois spirit. Preparing for bed in that horrible room, its floor paved in red bricks without a trace of color, its walls covered with paper that cost seven *sous* a roll, Godefroid missed not only his little apartment on the Rue Chanoinesse but also, and above all, the society of Madame de La Chanterie. He felt a great emptiness inside him. His mind had already fallen into new habits, and he could not recall having felt such longing at any moment of the life he once led. This very brief comparison had a prodigious effect on his soul; he understood that no life could equal the one he intended to embrace, and his resolve to become a follower of the good Father Alain grew all the more unshakable. He did not yet have the vocation, but he had the desire.

The next morning he rose early, as had become his custom. Looking out the window, he spied a boy of about seventeen, dressed in a smock. No doubt he was returning from a public fountain, for he carried a jug full of water in each hand. This young man could not have known that he was being observed; his face thus expressed his sentiments undisguised, and Godefroid had never seen anything so naïve, or so sad. The boy's youthful grace seemed hobbled by poverty, study, and great physical fatigue. Monsieur Bernard's grandson's skin was excessively white, its pallor further emphasized by his dark brown hair. He made three trips; returning for the last time, he observed the arrival of a load of fresh wood that Godefroid had ordered the day before, for the late winter of 1838 was setting in at last, and a light snow had fallen in the night.

The widow Vauthier's servant Népomucène had gone off at sunrise to order that wood, from which Madame would subtract a healthy tax for her own use. He and the other boy now stood talking in the courtyard while he waited for the sawyer to finish unloading the wood so that he could carry it upstairs. It was easy to deduce that the sudden change in the weather had begun to worry Monsieur Bernard's grandson and that the sight of this wood, as much as the leaden sky, had reminded him that he would soon require a supply of his own. But suddenly, as if abruptly reproaching himself for wasting so much precious time, the young man picked up his two jugs and hurried into the house, for the bells of the Convent of the Visitation were ringing seven-thirty, and he was to be at the Louis-le-Grand school before half past eight.

Just as the young man was entering the house, Madame Vauthier came to bring some hot coals for her new lodger's fire; opening his door to her, Godefroid was able to witness a small scene on the landing. A gardener from the neighborhood had rung several times at Monsieur Bernard's door but received no response, as the bell was wrapped in paper; he rather roughly hailed the young man when he appeared on the landing, demanding payment for the rental of his flowers. Hearing the creditor's raised voice, Monsieur Bernard emerged from his rooms.

"Auguste," he said to his grandson, "go and get dressed; it is time you were off to school."

He took the two jugs and carried them into his rooms, where several jardinieres full of flowers could be seen; then he closed the door and returned to speak with the gardener. Godefroid's door remained open, since Népomucène had now begun bringing in the wood, a task that would require many trips. The gardener fell silent upon the appearance of Monsieur Bernard, who had an imposing air in his violet silk dressing gown buttoned up to the chin.

"Surely you can state your business without shouting," said Monsieur Bernard.

"Be fair, my dear Monsieur," said the gardener. "You promised to pay me every week, but I haven't had a *sou* from you for three months, or ten weeks. You owe me one hundred twenty francs. We're accustomed to renting our flowers to rich people, who always give us our money as soon as we ask for it; but this is the fifth time I've been forced to come and see you. We have our own rent to pay, and our workers, and I'm scarcely better off than you are. My wife won't be bringing you your milk and eggs this morning either; you owe her thirty francs, and she'd rather not come than come only to torment you, because she's a very kindly woman, my wife is! If we all did things her way, business would be impossible. That's why I don't see this as she does, you understand . . ."

Just then Auguste emerged from the apartment. He wore a shabby green coat and woolen trousers of the same color, with a black tie and well-worn boots. His clothes had been carefully brushed, but they bore witness to financial distress of the gravest sort, for they were both too short and too tight; they seemed likely to split open with every move the youth made. In spite of many repairs, his suit's whitened seams, ripped buttonholes, and shapeless appearance displayed all the ignoble stigmata of indigence, evident to even the most unpracticed eye, and contrasted starkly with Auguste's youthful demeanor. Sinking his fine, strong teeth into a piece of stale bread, he set off down the Boulevard du Mont-Parnasse toward the Rue Saint-Jacques, eating his breakfast as he walked, his books and papers clasped under one arm, his magnificent dark locks erupting from beneath a small cap perched on his large head.

He had exchanged a brief glance of unbearable sadness with his grandfather as he passed by, for he knew the old man was facing an almost insurmountable difficulty, whose consequences could be terrible indeed. In order to make room for the young scholar, the gardener had stepped back into Godefroid's doorway. Just as he reached the threshold, Népomucène appeared on the landing with a fresh armload of wood; for lack of room, the creditor was forced into Godefroid's apartment, and he retreated as far as the window.

"Monsieur Bernard," cried the widow Vauthier, "do you think Monsieur Godefroid rented these rooms as your meeting place?"

"Excuse me, Madame," the gardener answered, "the landing was full . . ."

"I meant no criticism of you, Monsieur Cartier," the widow said.

"Stay!" Godefroid cried to the gardener. "And you, my dear neighbor," he added, looking at Monsieur Bernard, who appeared humiliated beyond words, "if you find it more convenient to use this room to speak with your gardener, then please come in."

Still mute with shame, the grand old man cast Godefroid a glance that contained a thousand thanks.

"As for you, my dear Madame Vauthier, I will thank you to treat Monsieur Bernard with a bit more respect. For one thing, he is an old man; for another, it is to him that you owe my decision to take rooms in your house."

"Well, I never!" cried the widow.

"And furthermore, if the unfortunates of this world do not help each other, who will help them? Leave us, Madame Vauthier, I can blow on the coals myself. Have the rest of my wood stored in your cellar; I have no doubt you'll take excellent care of it."

Madame Vauthier disappeared, her cupidity roused by these last few words.

"Please make yourselves at home, gentlemen," said Godefroid, gesturing to the gardener and pulling up two chairs for the debtor and the creditor.

The old man remained standing, but the gardener sat down at once.

"Come now, my dear fellow, I am sure the rich do not pay quite so regularly as you say, and in any case you mustn't torment a worthy man for the sake of a few *louis*. Monsieur receives his pension only once every six months, and he cannot possibly give you a voucher for such a small sum. If you absolutely must have the money, I will advance it to you myself."

"Monsieur Bernard received his payment some twenty days ago, and he's given me nothing . . . It's not my intention to cause him any grief . . ."

"And you have been supplying him with flowers for . . ."

"Yes, Monsieur, for six years, and he's always paid me properly."

Monsieur Bernard was not listening. His ear was trained on the sounds coming from his own rooms; hearing a series of cries through the wall, he hurried out without a word, in evident distress.

"Now, my good man! Bring Monsieur Bernard some beautiful flowers, the finest you have, this very morning, and have your wife bring him some good eggs and some milk; I will pay you this evening."

Cartier stared at Godefroid, uncomprehending.

"No doubt you know more about all this than Madame Vauthier. She warned me to come at once if I ever wanted to be paid," he said. "Neither she nor I, Monsieur, can understand why people who eat little more than bread, who haunt the back doorways of restaurants searching for vegetable peels or stray bits of carrot, or turnip, or potato—yes, Monsieur, I once saw the boy filling an old sack with such things— why such people should spend nearly a hundred francs a month for flowers . . . I've heard the old man's pension amounts to no more than three thousand francs."

"In any case," Godefroid replied, "it is not your place to judge them. If they wish to ruin themselves for the sake of flowers, that is entirely their concern."

"Very true, Monsieur, so long as I have my money."

"Bring me your invoice."

"As you like, Monsieur . . ." said the gardener with a faint note of respect in his voice. "No doubt Monsieur is hoping to meet the lady no one ever sees . . ."

"See here, my dear friend, you're forgetting yourself!" Godefroid coolly answered. "Go home and choose your finest flowers to replace the ones you have come to take away. And if you can bring me some good cream and fresh eggs for my own use, then you will have my regular custom. I shall come and visit your establishment this morning."

"It's one of the finest in Paris, Monsieur! My flowers are displayed in the Luxembourg Gardens. You'll find my garden on the boulevard; it covers three *arpents*, just behind the garden of the Grande-Chaumière."

"Very well, Monsieur Cartier. It would appear you are a wealthier man than I . . . Treat us kindly, for who can say? We might well have need of each other someday."

The puzzled gardener withdrew, wondering what manner of man Godefroid might be.

"And yet I was once much as he is!" Godefroid told himself as he blew on the coals to start his fire. "What a perfect representative of today's bourgeoisie: eager for gossip, consumed by egalitarian notions, jealous of his clientele, enraged at not understanding why a poor sick woman might stay in her room and never show herself . . . And how jealously he guards the secret of his own fortune, and how readily he reveals it if it means he can place himself above his fellow man! He must be at least a lieutenant in the Garde Nationale. Even today, so long after Molière, Monsieur Dimanche still walks the streets! A moment longer and the good gentleman Cartier would have been proclaiming himself my loyal friend."

This soliloquy, so expressive of the many changes in Godefroid's thinking over the previous four months, was now interrupted by the return of the old man.

"Forgive me for disturbing you, my good neighbor," he said in an anxious voice, "but I have just met the gardener on his way out. He greeted me politely; does this mean that his grievance has been resolved? Truly, young man, it would seem that Providence sent you to rescue us in our most desperate hour. Alas! I fear that he might have told you a great many things about us. It is true that I received my six-month pension payment two weeks ago, but I had other debts more pressing than his, and I had no choice but to reserve the sum required for our rent, lest we be driven into the streets. I have told you of my daughter's condition, and you must have heard her . . ."

He looked questioningly at Godefroid, who nodded.

"Well! You must see that an eviction would be a fatal blow for her . . . We would have to place her in a public hospital . . . My grandson and I have long dreaded this day, and it was not Cartier that we feared the most, but rather the cold of winter . . ."

"My dear Monsieur Bernard, I have a fresh supply of wood; please take some," Godefroid replied.

"How can I ever repay such kindness?" cried the old man.

"By accepting it without a second thought," Godefroid warmly answered, "and by granting me your full confidence."

"But what right do I have to such generosity?" asked Monsieur Bernard, his wariness returning. "Oh, my pride has long since been defeated, and my grandson's with it, after so many humiliating discussions with the two or three creditors we have left—for the truly poor have no creditors; to have creditors, one needs a certain exterior splendor, which we have lost . . . But I have not yet abdicated my good sense, or my reason . . ." he added, as if speaking only to himself.

"Monsieur," Godefroid earnestly replied, "the tale you told me yesterday would wring tears from a moneylender."

"On the contrary . . . our landlord Barbet is hoping to profit from my poverty, and he keeps a close watch on it through the prying eyes of his former servant, the Vauthier woman."

"But what profit can he hope to make from you?" asked Godefroid.

"That I will tell you another time," the old man answered. "My daughter must be cold, and since you have offered . . . In my present circumstances, I would welcome charity from my bitterest enemy . . ."

"I will bring you some wood," said Godefroid. He gathered up a dozen logs and carried them across the landing, into the first room of the old man's apartment.

Monsieur Bernard had taken as many himself, and seeing this little supply of fuel sitting in his apartment, he broke into the feeble, almost imbecilic smile by which those saved from a mortal and seemingly inescapable danger express their joy, a joy troubled by a certain lingering terror.

"Accept everything I offer you without misgivings, my dear Monsieur Bernard. When your daughter is saved, when you are happy again, I will gladly explain all this to you; but until then, let me do as I wish . . . I have been to see the Jewish doctor, and unfortunately Halpersohn is away; he will not return for two days . . ."

Just then a voice that Godefroid found fresh and melodious in timbre—and he was not wrong—cried out: "Papa! Papa!" on two expressive tones.

As he stood speaking with the old man, Godefroid had noted the impeccable white woodwork of the door facing the entryway, suggesting a vast difference between the sick woman's bedroom and the rest of the apartment. His curiosity, already aroused, now reached fever pitch; his mission of mercy had become a mere pretext, for his real goal was to see the ailing woman. He refused to believe that any creature endowed with such a voice could be an object of revulsion.

"You trouble yourself too much, Papa! . . ." the voice was saying. "You really should have more servants . . . At your age! . . . My goodness! . . ."

"My dear Vanda, you know very well I want no one serving you but myself and your son."

Godefroid heard this exchange through the closed sickroom door, but only faintly, for a thick curtain had been hung over the doorway to muffle all sound. Nevertheless, these words offered him an insight into the true nature of the family's situation. Surrounded by luxury, the patient clearly knew nothing of her father's and son's real circumstances. Certain suspicions had already been planted in Godefroid's mind by Monsieur Bernard's quilted silk robe, by the flowers, by his conversation with Cartier. Godefroid stood lost in contemplation, virtually dumbstruck by this prodigious feat of paternal love. The contrast between the apartment proper and the patient's room, such as he imagined it, was dizzying enough. Judge for yourself!

Through the door to the third room, which the old man had left half open, Godefroid glimpsed two matching bunks of painted wood, as one might find in the humblest boardinghouse, each bearing a straw mattress topped with a thin layer of padding and a single blanket. A little cast-iron stove of the sort doormen use for their cooking, fueled with a few meager lumps of coal, would have sufficed to illustrate Monsieur Bernard's penury even without the other elements of the room's decor, which nevertheless harmonized perfectly with that horrible stove.

Taking a step forward, Godefroid saw the sort of pottery found only in the humblest households: basins of glazed clay, with potatoes soaking in dirty water. Before the window over the Rue Notre-Dame-des-Champs sat two tables of blackened wood, both of them strewn with papers and books, indicating the nocturnal occupations of the old man and the youth alike. Each table bore a wrought-iron candlestick such as one finds in the homes of the poor; Godefroid noted that they held only the very meanest sort of candles, of the variety that comes eight to a pound. A third served as their kitchen table; here Godefroid saw two gleaming place settings and a little vermeil spoon, along with plates, a bowl, Sèvres porcelain cups, a sheathed, double-edged knife of vermeil and steel, and finally the sick woman's dishes.

The stove was lit, and a faint wisp of steam rose from the basin. A painted wooden armoire no doubt held the linens and effects of Monsieur Bernard's daughter, for on the father's bed Godefroid saw the suit of clothes the old man had worn the day before, now laid crosswise over the mattress to serve as a foot warmer.

Other articles of clothing similarly positioned on the grandson's bed suggested that this formed the entirety of their wardrobe, for under the beds Godefroid saw only shoes. The floor tiles, no doubt rarely swept, recalled a classroom in a boarding school. A six-pound loaf of bread, partially eaten, sat on a wooden shelf over the table. In short, this was financial misery in its ultimate phase, poverty become a scrupulously organized way of life, exuding the cold respectability of a resolve to endure its miseries; a poverty that leaves its victims not a moment's rest, for they seek to, and must, and yet cannot perform all their domestic chores themselves, and they sadly overuse whatever possessions they have left. Not surprisingly, a dense, nauseating odor filled the air of this rarely cleaned room.

The antechamber in which Godefroid now stood was at least moderately decent, and he supposed that it served to hide the horrors of the grandson's and grandfather's room. This antechamber, hung with squared wallpaper in the Scottish style, was graced with four walnut chairs and a little table, and ornamented with colored engravings of the Emperor as portrayed by Horace Vernet, of Louis XVIII, of Charles X, and of Prince Poniatowski—this last no doubt a friend of Monsieur Bernard's father-in-law. The window was hung with calico curtains edged in red ribbon and fringe.

Godefroid had been watching for Népomucène; hearing him on the landing with another armload of wood, he waved him into Monsieur Bernard's antechamber. With a thoughtfulness that demonstrated the Initiate's progress, he closed the bedroom door so that the widow Vauthier's serving boy would not see the old man's desperate poverty.

Much of the space in the antechamber was taken up by three jardinieres full of the most magnificent flowers, two of them oblong and one round, all made of rosewood, and quite elegant; thus, after laying the wood on the floor, Népomucène could not help but exclaim: "Aren't they pretty! . . . What a lot they must cost!"

"Jean! Don't make so much noise! . . ." shouted Monsieur Bernard.

"You hear that?" said Népomucène to Godefroid. "The old codger's batty for sure . . ."

"And do you know how you will be at his age? . . ."

"Oh! Indeed I do," answered Népomucène. "I'll be in a sugar bowl."

"In a sugar bowl? . . ."

"Yes, they'll have used my bones to make bone black. I've seen the refiners' carts often enough at the Catacombs, coming to fetch bone black for their factories. I hear they use it to make sugar."

And with this philosophical response he went off for another load of wood.

Godefroid now discreetly closed Monsieur Bernard's front door behind him, leaving the old man alone with his daughter. In the meantime, Madame Vauthier had prepared her new lodger's breakfast and had climbed to his rooms with Félicité to serve it. Godefroid sat staring at the fire in his hearth, lost in meditations on the misery he had just beheld, a misery that contained so many different miseries within it, but in which he also glimpsed the ineffable joys of the thousand triumphs attained by filial and paternal love, like a handful of pearls scattered over a sheet of coarse fustian.

"Even among the most celebrated works of our time, what novel could rival this reality?" he asked himself. "What a beautiful thing it is to embrace such existences! . . . To uncover the causes and effects of such misery, righting the wrongs, soothing the pains, lending a hand to the goodness of men! . . . To be reborn in the guise of the wretched, to find one's way into such rooms! To be a real actor in an unending drama—the very sort of drama that holds us spellbound when we read of it in the works of a famous author . . . I never thought Virtue could be more enticing than Vice."

"Is Monsieur satisfied? . . ." asked Madame Vauthier, who with Félicité's help had brought the table near Godefroid's chair.

Before him Godefroid found an excellent cup of café au lait accompanied by a steaming omelette, fresh butter, and little pink radishes.

"Where the devil did you dig up these radishes? . . ." Godefroid asked.

"They were given to me by Monsieur Cartier," she answered, "and I'm offering them to Monsieur as a mark of my esteem."

"And how much would you ask to bring me such a breakfast every day?" said Godefroid.

"Well now! Monsieur, be fair; it would be difficult to do for less than thirty *sous*."

"Thirty *sous* it is, then!" said Godefroid. "But tell me, how is it that just a short distance from here, at Madame Machillot's, they ask only forty-five francs per month—precisely thirty *sous* a day—for dinner? . . ."

"Oh! But, Monsieur, there's such a great difference between making dinner for fifteen people and going to fetch all the things you need for breakfast! Think of it! A roll, eggs, butter, sugar, milk, coffee, and then there's the fire to be lit . . . Remember, you'll pay sixteen *sous* for a simple cup of café au lait on the Place de l'Odéon, and you still have to leave one or two *sous* for the waiter! . . . No such worries here! Here you have all the comforts of home, and you can take your breakfast in your slippers."

"Very well," Godefroid answered.

"Were it not for Madame Cartier, who supplies me with milk, eggs, and herbs, I'd never manage. You really should go and see their business, Monsieur. Oh! What a beautiful sight! They have five workers in their gardens, and Népomucène brings them water all summer; they rent him from me to water the plots . . . They make armloads of money from their melons and strawberries . . . It seems Monsieur has taken a great interest in Monsieur Bernard? . . ." the widow Vauthier asked quietly. "Answering for their debts and all . . . Perhaps Monsieur doesn't know just how much they owe . . . They owe thirty francs to the lady from the lending library on the Place Saint-Michel, who comes every three or four days—and she needs it, too. Dear Lord in Heaven! How that poor sick woman reads! She reads and reads! At two *sous* a book, thirty francs in three months . . ."

"That means one hundred books a month!" said Godefroid.

"Ah! There's the old man going off to buy Madame's cream and rolls! . . ." the widow Vauthier went on. "That's for her tea. I swear, the lady lives on nothing but tea! She takes tea twice a day, and twice a week he brings her a special treat . . . She's got a great liking for sweetmeats, that's for sure! The old man brings her cakes or pâtés from the pastry shop on the Rue de Bussy. Oh! If it's for her, he never asks the price . . . She's his daughter, he says! . . . It's not often that a man his age does so much for his daughter! . . . He runs himself ragged for her, him and his Auguste . . . Is Monsieur like me? I'd gladly give twenty francs for a look at her. Monsieur Berton says she's a monster, the sort of thing you show for money. They did the right thing, coming to a neighborhood like this, where there's never anyone about . . . So, Monsieur intends to take his dinners at Madame Machillot's? . . ."

"Yes, I must go and arrange that soon . . ."

"Monsieur, I don't mean to dissuade you, but cookshop for cookshop, you'd be better off on the Rue de Tournon; you wouldn't have to commit yourself for the entire month, and the food's a good sight better . . ."

"Where on the Rue de Tournon?"

"Madame Girard's old place, though it's changed hands since her time . . . That's where the two gentlemen who live upstairs like to go, and they're happy, happier than you can imagine . . ."

"Well then, Mother Vauthier, I shall gladly take your advice . . ."

"My dear Monsieur," she said, emboldened by the friendly and familiar air that Godefroid had deliberately assumed, "tell me now, in all seriousness, are you really such an *easy mark*? Because your idea of paying off Monsieur Bernard's debts . . . I'd be very sorry to see you do that; remember, my fine Monsieur Godefroid, he's nearly seventy years old, and when he's gone, whoops! no more pension! And then how can you ever hope to be repaid? . . . Young folk are so imprudent! Do you realize he owes more than a thousand *écus*?"

"To whom?" asked Godefroid.

"Oh! That's none of my affair," the Vauthier woman answered mysteriously. "All I know is he owes them, and just between us, things are looking none too rosy for him at the moment . . . With debts like that, he won't find a *liard* of credit around here . . ."

"A thousand *écus*!" repeated Godefroid. "Well, have no fear, Madame Vauthier: if I had a thousand *écus*, I would certainly not be living here. My problem, you see, is that I cannot bear the sight of other people's suffering, and for a few hundred francs, I can at least know that my venerable neighbor has the bread and wood he needs . . . What does a few hundred francs matter! People are often happy to lose that much at cards . . . But three thousand francs . . . Good Lord, surely you don't think . . ."

Taken in by Godefroid's feigned candor, Madame Vauthier let a satisfied smile take shape on her sickly countenance, confirming the lodger's suspicions. Godefroid felt sure that the old woman was an accomplice in some machination aimed against poor Monsieur Bernard.

"It's very odd, Monsieur, the ideas that sometimes come into a person's head! You're going to think me quite a busybody, but when I saw you chatting with Monsieur Bernard yesterday, I was sure you were a publisher's agent; there are a lot of them about in the neighborhood. I once lodged a shop foreman who worked for a printer on the Rue de Vaugirard, and he had the same name as you . . ."

"What does it matter to you how I earn my living?" asked Godefroid.

"Bah! You may tell me, or you may not," the Vauthier woman replied, "but I'll find it out all right in the end . . . Now take Monsieur Bernard, for example: Well! For eighteen months I had no idea what he was, but come the nineteenth month I finally discovered he'd once been a magistrate, or a judge, or some such thing, something to do with the law, and he's writing a book on the subject . . . What's in it for him? That's what I'd like to know! And if he told me, I'd say no more about it. So there we are!"

"I am not yet a publisher's agent, but perhaps I will be soon."

"You see! I thought so," the widow Vauthier said excitedly, turning around and abandoning the bed she was making as a pretext to stay in her lodger's rooms. "You've come to put one over on . . . Well! Forewarned is forearmed . . ."

"One minute!" cried Godefroid, blocking Madame Vauthier's path toward the door. "See here, what is your interest in all this?"

"Well, well!" the old woman replied, leering at Godefroid. "Aren't you the clever one!"

She went and latched the front door to his rooms, then returned and sat down on a chair before the fire. "Word of honor, sure as my name is Vauthier, I took you for a student, until I saw you giving your wood to old man Bernard. Oh! you're crafty, all right! Goodness gracious, you must be an actor! And here I took you for a *mark*! Well, then: will you promise me a thousand francs? Cross my heart, old Barbet and Monsieur Métivier promised me five hundred francs to keep an eye on Monsieur Bernard's progress."

"Five hundred francs! Those two! . . . Come now!" cried Godefroid. "Two hundred at most, woman, and even then, *promised* seems a bit much . . . and of course you're not likely to file a complaint against them if they refuse to pay you! . . . Now, if you were to help me close a deal with Monsieur Bernard like the one they are hoping for, then I would gladly give you four hundred francs! But tell me: How far have they got with him?"

"Well, they gave him an advance of fifteen hundred francs, after he told them of his thousand *écus* in debt ... They doled it out to him a hundred francs at a time ... just to be sure he stayed needy ... They're the ones setting the creditors on him. I'm sure it was them who sent Cartier today ..."

Here Godefroid shot Madame Vauthier a knowing, ironic glance, revealing his awareness of her role in this affair. Indeed, her words had brought him two revelations at once, for he now also understood his rather singular conversation with the gardener that morning.

"Oh!" she went on, "they've got him in their clutches, no doubt about that. Where can he ever hope to find a thousand *écus*! They're planning to pay him five hundred francs the day he gives them the manuscript and five hundred francs for each volume put up for sale ... It'll come out under the name of a publisher those two gentlemen have set up on the Quai des Augustins ..."

"Oh! You must mean little what's-his-name?"

"Yes, that's right, Morand, Monsieur's former agent ... I understand this is going to make someone a great deal of money?"

"Oh! I only know that it is going to cost someone a great deal of money," answered Godefroid with an expressive grimace.

Now came a quiet knock at the door; grateful for this interruption, Godefroid arose to open it.

"What's said is said, Madame Vauthier," he whispered intently to his landlady, seeing Monsieur Bernard on the threshold.

"Monsieur Bernard," she cried, "I have a letter for you ..."

The old man followed her into the stairway.

"I'm sorry, Monsieur Bernard, the fact is I have no letter. I only wanted to tell you to beware of that young fellow. He's in publishing."

"Ah! It's all clear to me now," the old man said to himself.

And he returned to his neighbor's rooms with a very different expression than before.

The quiet coolness on Monsieur Bernard's face so contrasted with the openness and affability of his earlier effusions of gratitude that Godefroid could not help but wonder what had happened.

"Monsieur, forgive me for troubling your repose, but you have done so much for me since yesterday, and the benefactor creates certain expectations in the mind of the indebted."

Godefroid bowed slightly.

"I who have suffered the Passion of Jesus Christ every two weeks for the past five years! I who represented Society and the Government for thirty-six years, I who served as the instrument of public Vengeance, and have long since lost all my illusions, as you might easily understand . . . Indeed, I have lost everything but my sorrows . . . But, Monsieur, your thoughtfulness in closing the door to the pigsty where my grandson and I sleep—that small act was like Bossuet's glass of water . . . Yes, I have rediscovered in my heart . . . in my depleted heart, bled dry of its tears as my body of its sweat, I have rediscovered one last lingering drop of the elixir that, in our youth, allows us to see the best in every human action. Thus, I came here to give you my hand, which I now give only to my daughter; I came to offer you the heavenly rose of a renewed belief in human kindness . . ."

"Monsieur Bernard," said Godefroid, recalling the lessons of the good Alain, "it was never my goal to earn your gratitude . . . You have misunderstood my intentions . . ."

"Ah! Very frank indeed!" replied the former magistrate. "Well! That pleases me. I had nearly resolved to thwart your plans . . . Forgive me! I have only esteem for you. So you are in the publishing trade, and you have come to snatch my work away from Barbet, Métivier, and Morand . . . This explains everything. You are simply making an opening to me, just as they did; but in yours there is goodness."

"Is that what the Vauthier woman was telling you just now?" Godefroid asked the old man.

"Yes," he answered.

"Well, Monsieur Bernard, in order to determine what I can *give* you beyond what these gentlemen are *offering* you, you must tell me of your arrangements with them."

"That seems fair," the former magistrate replied, apparently pleased to find himself the object of such competition, which could only be to his profit. "Do you know the nature of my work?"

"No, I know only that there is a good bargain to be struck here."

"It is only nine-thirty; my daughter has had her breakfast, my grandson, Auguste, will not be back until quarter till eleven, and it will be an hour before Cartier comes by with the flowers. We are thus at leisure to talk, Monsieur ... Monsieur ... ?"

"Godefroid."

"Monsieur Godefroid, the idea for this work came to me in 1825, at a time when, faced with the continual squandering of inherited properties, the Ministry proposed a new law on the rights of primogeniture, only to see it voted down. I had already noted certain flaws in our nation's legal codes and institutions. Considerable labor had been devoted to the drafting of our codes, but this was simple jurisprudence; no one had dared to consider the deeds of the Revolution—or of Napoleon, if you prefer—in their entirety, to study the spirit of these new laws, to judge their effects in actual practice. That is the general goal of my work; it is provisionally entitled *The Spirit of the New Laws* and considers our organic laws as well as the codes—*all* the codes, I mean, for we have far more than five. Thus, my book comprises five volumes, with another volume of citations, notes, and references. In three months it will be finished. The owner of this house was once a publisher himself; on the basis of certain questions I had put to him, he sensed—perhaps I should say smelled—the possibility of money to be made. As for me, from the beginning, my only thought was the good of my country. And now old Barbet has swindled me ... No doubt you are wondering how a mere publisher could have rooked an old magistrate; but, Monsieur, you know the desperate straits I am in, and then Barbet is a practiced moneylender, with the sharp eye and perfect cunning of all such men ... His money always followed hard on the heels of my needs, inevitably coming to me just when I most desperately required it, just when I found myself most defenseless ..."

"Oh! No mystery in that, my dear Monsieur," said Godefroid. "He simply had old woman Vauthier as his spy. But come now, what are the conditions? ... Tell me clearly."

"They lent me fifteen hundred francs, currently represented by three promissory notes of one thousand francs apiece; but those three thousand francs are mortgaged to the rights to my work, which can be mine only if I pay off the notes, which have now been pronounced delinquent . . . These, Monsieur, are the complications that come with poverty . . . By the most conservative estimate, the first edition of my immense work, the product of ten years' labor and thirty-six years' experience, will easily make ten thousand francs. And five days ago, Morand offered me a thousand *écus* and forgiveness for my promissory notes in exchange for sole ownership of the rights . . . Since I have not the slightest hope of finding three thousand two hundred and forty francs, I will have no choice but to accept, unless you intercede . . . My honor was not enough for them; as a further guarantee, they had the promissory notes declared delinquent in court, making me liable for debtors' prison. If I pay them back, the usurers will have doubled their money; if I agree to the settlement, they will earn a fortune, for one of them used to deal in paper, and God knows what tricks they might have to bring down the costs of production. And with my name on the book, they know they may rely on an initial order of a thousand copies at least."

"What, Monsieur, you, a former magistrate, in such a predicament! . . ."

"What can I tell you? Not a single friend to come to my rescue! Not a single remembrance! . . . And yet I saved so many heads from the guillotine, even if I caused many others to fall! . . . But of course there is my daughter, my daughter, to whom I have become a nurse! At whose side I sit, day after day, for I work only at night . . . Oh! Young man, only the wretched can know what true poverty is . . . Looking back, I realize that I was too severe in my younger days."

"Monsieur, I will not ask you your family name. I do not have a thousand *écus* at my disposal, and I will have far less after I have paid Halpersohn and your other debts. Nevertheless, I will save you, if you will swear to do nothing with your work without my approval; for we cannot proceed in this matter until we have consulted someone who knows the trade. I work for powerful people, and I can assure you of success if you will promise to say nothing of this to anyone, not even your children, and if you faithfully keep that promise . . ."

"The only success I wish for is the return of my poor Vanda's health; for, Monsieur, in the heart of a father, such suffering extinguishes every other sentiment, and the love of glory is nothing to one who sees the grave half open before him."

"I shall call on you tonight; Halpersohn is expected back at any moment, and I have made a vow to go each day and see if he has returned . . . I will devote this entire day to your cause."

"Oh! If you were to bring about my daughter's recovery, Monsieur . . . Monsieur, I would gladly let you have my work for nothing! . . ."

"Monsieur," said Godefroid, "I am not in the publishing trade! . . ."

The old man threw out his arms in surprise.

"I speak the truth; I allowed old Madame Vauthier to labor under that impression so as to gain a better idea of the traps that had been set for you . . ."

"Who are you, then? . . ."

"Godefroid!" replied the Initiate. "And since you have allowed me to help you put food on your table," he added with a smile, "you may call me Godefroid de Bouillon."

The former magistrate was too moved to laugh at this little joke. He held out his hand to Godefroid and squeezed the hand that met his.

"You insist on concealing your identity? . . ." said the former magistrate, looking at Godefroid with regret and a certain disquiet.

"If you will allow me . . ."

"As you wish, then! And come to my rooms this evening; you will see my daughter, if her state permits it . . ."

This was clearly the greatest concession the unhappy father could make, and the old man was pleased to see from Godefroid's thankful gaze that he did not fail to realize it.

An hour later, Cartier appeared with a wonderful array of flowers. He placed a fresh layer of moss in the jardinieres and lovingly arranged the blooms; Godefroid paid the bill, just as he paid the invoice from the lending library that arrived a few moments later. These books and flowers were the daily bread of the patient—or, more precisely, the martyr—in the next room, and she was perfectly content with this meager nourishment.

Reflecting on this family's inextricable entanglement in sorrow,

Godefroid could not help but remember the Laocoöns (the sublime image of so many lives!) as he set off toward the Rue Marbeuf on foot. There was still more curiosity than beneficence in his heart; the idea of that poor woman surrounded by luxury in the midst of appalling poverty interested him far more than the horrific details of this strangest of nervous afflictions—fortunately a rare exception in the annals of medicine but by no means unknown to historians: Tallemant des Réaux, one of our most garrulous chroniclers, cites just such a case. We like to imagine women as elegant even in their cruelest sufferings; thus, it was with a certain pleasure that Godefroid dreamt of entering her bedroom, to which only the doctor, the father, and the son had been admitted for six years. Soon, however, he rebuked himself for his curiosity. Indeed, the neophyte was beginning to realize that this very natural sentiment would inevitably fade as he pursued his beneficent ministry, through the continual sight of ever new interiors and new wounds.

For indeed, it is possible to attain a state of divine mansuetude that nothing dismays and nothing surprises, just as one in love might, after many years, arrive at a sublime tranquillity of the sentiments, sure of their force and durability, through constant experience of their pleasures and pains.

Godefroid learned that Halpersohn had arrived home during the night but had been obliged to climb into his coach and visit his patients early that morning, as they were eagerly awaiting his return. The porter told Godefroid to come back the next morning before nine.

Recalling Monsieur Alain's admonition to observe the greatest parsimony in his personal expenditures, Godefroid now went to the Rue de Tournon and dined for twenty-five *sous;* as a sort of reward for this act of self-denial, he found himself surrounded by printers' boys, typesetters, and correctors. Overhearing a discussion of the costs of producing a book, he eagerly joined in and learned that an in-octavo volume, composed of forty sheets and printed in a thousand copies, need in ideal circumstances cost no more than thirty *sous* per copy. He then thought of visiting several dealers in legal books to give himself an idea of the customary sales prices, the better to pursue his discussions with the publishers who now held Monsieur Bernard in their grasp, should he ever meet up with them.

At around seven o'clock that evening, he returned to the Boulevard du Mont-Parnasse by the Rue de Vaugirard, the Rue Madame, and the Rue de l'Ouest, realizing just how deserted his new neighborhood was, for he saw no one in the streets as he walked. To be sure, the cold weather was setting in; great flakes of snow were falling, and the coaches rolled soundlessly over the cobblestones.

"Ah! There you are, Monsieur!" said the widow Vauthier as she caught sight of Godefroid. "If I'd known you'd be back so early, I would have made you a fire."

"No need," answered Godefroid, as Madame Vauthier followed him up the stairs. "I shall be spending the evening with Monsieur Bernard . . ."

"Well! You're not by any chance his cousin, are you? Two days you've been here, and already you're like peas in a pod . . . I was thinking Monsieur might like to finish the conversation we started earlier."

"Ah! The four hundred francs!" answered Godefroid quietly. "Well, Mother Vauthier, you would have had them this evening if you had said nothing to Monsieur Bernard . . . Do you remember the dog in the fable? He was carrying a bone in his mouth when he saw its reflection in a stream; trying to pick up the second bone, he dropped the first, and he ended up with neither. This may well be your fate, Madame Vauthier. As far as I am concerned, at least, my prospects are dashed, for you have given away my game . . ."

"Oh, no, my dear Monsieur, don't think that . . . Tomorrow, while you're having your breakfast . . ."

"Oh! Tomorrow I shall be off first thing in the morning, like your authors . . ."

Here Godefroid was well served by his previous life, by his days as a dandy and a journalist: he knew just what words would prevent her running to her employer and warning him of this threat to his plans. Should she do so, he knew, Barbet would immediately set legal proceedings in motion, placing Monsieur Bernard's liberty at risk; only by allowing the three businessmen to go on thinking their scheme unendangered could he ensure their inaction. What Godefroid did not yet know, however, was just what the Parisian character can be when it takes the form of the widow Vauthier, for her goal was to have Godefroid's money along with her landlord's. Thus, she hurried straight to her Monsieur Barbet, while Godefroid changed clothes for his visit to Monsieur Bernard's daughter.

The bells at the Convent of the Visitation, the neighborhood time-keeper, were ringing eight o'clock when the curious Godefroid rapped quietly at his neighbor's door. Auguste appeared and showed him in. As this was a Saturday, the young man's evening was his own; Godefroid found him dressed in a little black velvet frock coat, a blue silk cravat, and a relatively clean pair of black trousers. But his astonishment at seeing the young man so unlike himself vanished the moment he entered the sick woman's room. He now fully understood the reasons for her father's and son's elegant dress.

For the contrast between the lavishness of this room and the squalor he had observed that morning was too great not to dazzle Godefroid's eyes, so to speak, for all his long familiarity with luxury's elegant and whimsical ways.

The walls were hung in yellow silk, with decorative twists of bright green silk cord that conferred a sort of gaiety on the room, whose cold floor tiles were concealed beneath a velvet pile rug showing a scattering of flowers against a white background. The two window recesses were like two pretty little groves so abundantly full of flowers were the jardinieres nestled inside them. Fine, silk-lined white curtains and stout shutters shielded this opulence from prying eyes, for it was a rare sight indeed in this neighborhood. All around the room, the woodwork was painted with pure white glue paint, highlighted with thin lines of gold.

A heavy tapestry curtain, with an extravagant spray of leafy branches embroidered in petit point against a yellow background, was hung over the doorway to muffle all sound from outside. This magnificent arras was the handiwork of the patient herself, who worked with wondrous dexterity when she had the use of her hands.

Across the room, facing the door, the hearth's green-velvet-draped mantel displayed the last relics of the lavish existence these two families once enjoyed: Godefroid's eye lit first on a curious clock in the form of an elephant bearing a porcelain tower, from which emerged a profusion of flowers, then on two candelabras of a similar style, and finally on a set of precious chinoiseries. The fireguard, the andirons, the shovels, the tongs, everything was of the finest quality and the highest price.

The largest of the jardinieres sat in the center of the room beneath a porcelain lamp, painted with flowers, that hung from a rosette on the ceiling.

The magistrate's daughter lay on a bed of sculpted wood painted white and gold, as in the days of Louis XV. Beside the sickbed stood a pretty marquetry table, holding everything necessary to the life that was lived in that bed. A double-branched lamp was affixed to the wall, easily folded away or pulled forward with the most delicate touch of the hand. A cunning little table sat before the patient, convenient for all her needs. The bed was covered with a superb counterpane and hung with curtains held back by metal clasps; its surface was densely strewn with books, with a small sewing basket among them. Were it not for the two candles of the movable lamp, Godefroid might easily have failed to descry the ailing woman beneath all this paraphernalia.

He saw only a face, very white but darkened around the eyes by long suffering. Her eyes were as bright as fire, and her face was ornamented by magnificent black locks artfully arranged into large, looping curls, suggesting that the patient spent a certain portion of her days combing and styling her hair—a supposition confirmed by the portable mirror at the foot of her bed.

This room lacked none of the little necessities dictated by modern tastes. A small collection of curios, meant for poor Vanda's amusement, proved that her father's affection was not immune to excess.

Arising from a magnificent tapestry-upholstered Louis XV *bergère*, also painted gold and white, the old man came forward to greet Godefroid, who would most certainly never have recognized him otherwise, for his cold, severe face now exuded the gaiety of the aged courtier, noble and seemingly carefree. His puce-colored robe harmonized perfectly with the opulence around him, and he took snuff from a golden snuffbox studded with diamonds! . . .

"This, my dear child," said Monsieur Bernard to his daughter, clasping Godefroid's hand, "this is the neighbor of whom I told you."

With a gesture, he bade his grandson draw up one of the two armchairs that sat on either side of the fireplace, their design matching that of the *bergère*.

"The gentleman's name is Monsieur Godefroid, and he has shown us much kindness . . ."

Vanda nodded in response to Godefroid's deep bow. By the manner in which her neck tensed and relaxed, Godefroid saw that her life was now lodged entirely within her head. Her wasted arms and limp hands lay flat on the fine, white sheet like two things alien to her body, which seemed to occupy no physical space in her bed. The patient's various necessities were stowed away on shelves behind the headboard, shielded from view by a silk curtain.

"Monsieur, you are the first person that I have seen for six years, excepting the doctors, whom I no longer think of as men; you have no idea what passions you have excited in me ever since my father first told me of your visit . . . A curiosity very like that of our mother Eve . . . My father, who is always so good to me, and my son, whom I love so dearly, are certainly more than enough to fill the desert of a soul now robbed of its body; but that soul has remained a woman's soul, after all, and perhaps you will not be surprised at the interest I have taken in you . . . I hope you will do me the pleasure of taking a cup of tea with us . . ."

"Monsieur has promised us his entire evening," the old man answered with the courtly elegance of a millionaire receiving guests in his home.

Auguste sat reading by the light of the candelabras on the mantelpiece; near his tapestry chair stood a table ornamented with inlays and a collection of copperware.

"Auguste, my child, tell Jean to come and serve us tea in an hour."

Auguste gestured his acknowledgment of this request, and of the affectionate gaze with which his mother made it.

"Would you believe, Monsieur, that for six years I have had no servants around me but my father and my son? And now I do not think I could bear to have any other. Without them, I am sure I would die . . . There is Jean, of course—he is a poor Norman who has served us for thirty years—but my father will not allow him into my room."

"I should say not," the old man smoothly replied. "You have seen him for yourself, Monsieur: he is the one who saws our wood and stacks it inside; he does our cooking and runs our errands; his smock is always filthy; were he to come in, he would surely soil all this elegance, so necessary for the eyes of a poor girl for whom all of Nature has been reduced to one room . . ."

"Oh! Madame, I must agree with your father . . ."

"But why?" she said. "If Jean spoiled my room, my father would simply have it redecorated."

"To be sure, my child, but for this one thing: you cannot leave your room! And then, you don't know how decorators are in Paris! . . . It would take them three months to finish their work. Think of all the dust that would come from taking up your carpet. Allow Jean into your room? How can you think of such a thing? . . . A father and son are capable of the most fastidious and loving attentions, thanks to which we have spared you the discomforts of sweeping and dust . . . If we had Jean in to clean, all our precautions would be made useless within a month . . ."

"It is not a question of thrift," said Godefroid, "but of your own health. Your father is quite right."

"I'm not complaining, mind you," Vanda answered in a teasing voice.

The sound of that voice was very like music. Her soul, her mobility, and her very life had become concentrated in her gaze and her voice; and through diligent practice—for which she certainly did not lack the time—Vanda had succeeded in overcoming the difficulties caused by the loss of her teeth.

"I remain happy in the midst of my sorrows, Monsieur, and thankful, at least, for our fortune, which has greatly helped me to endure my sufferings . . . If we were poor, I would have ceased to exist eighteen years ago, and yet here I am, still living! . . . I have my joys, and they are all the sweeter in that each is a victory over death . . . You must think me very talkative . . ." she concluded with a smile.

"Madame," answered Godefroid, "I pray you, do not stop speaking, for I have never heard a voice such as yours... It is music: Rubini himself is not more enchanting..."

"Do not speak of Rubini, nor of the Théâtre des Italiens," said the old man with a touch of sadness in his voice. "My daughter was once a fine musician, and she remains much enamored of that art; but for all our wealth, that is a pleasure I cannot hope to offer her."

"Forgive me," said Godefroid.

"In time you shall become used to our ways," said the old man.

"Let me tell you how," the patient said with a smile. "Once we've cried out 'Danger ahead' several times, you will learn how to play the game of blindman's bluff that is our conversation..."

Godefroid exchanged a rapid glance with Monsieur Bernard, who, seeing tears in his neighbor's eyes, raised a finger to his lips, beseeching him not to undo the heroic efforts to which he and her son had devoted themselves for the past seven years.

Reflecting on this sublime, endless imposture, whose success was proven by the patient's perfect obliviousness, Godefroid briefly imagined himself peering over a sheer precipice, with two chamois hunters clambering unconcerned over the rocks below. That magnificent diamond-studded golden snuffbox, which the old man casually fingered as he sat at the foot of the bed, was like the ineffable mark of genius that draws a cry of wonderment from the admirer of a great artist's work. Godefroid gazed at the little box, wondering why it had not been sold, or pawned at the Mont-de-Piété, but he refrained from questioning the old man on this point.

"This evening, Monsieur Godefroid, the promise of your visit so excited my daughter that all the manifestations of her strange illness, over which we have despaired for the past twelve days, have entirely vanished... I trust you can conceive of my gratitude."

"And mine?..." the patient tenderly cried, leaning her head to one side in a most coquettish manner. "To me Monsieur is an envoy from the world of society... Since the age of twenty, Monsieur, I have forgotten everything I once knew of drawing rooms, and parties, and balls... I who so love to dance, who so adore the theater, and music above all. I try to picture it all in my mind! I read a great deal. And of course my father tells me of the world outside..."

Hearing these words, Godefroid felt an urge to kneel down before the unhappy old man.

"Yes, when he goes to the Théâtre des Italiens, and he goes often, he paints me a portrait of the ladies' gowns, and describes the effect of the songs. Oh! I would so like to be cured, first for the sake of my father—who lives only for me, as I live through him and for him—and for my son's sake as well ... I so wish he could have a different sort of mother! Oh! Monsieur, what excellent creatures are my old father ... and my wonderful son .... But also, I would so love to hear Lablache, Rubini, Tamburini, la Grisi, and *I Puritani* ... Yet ..."

"Come now, my child, calm yourself! ... If we begin to speak of music, all will be lost!" said the old man, smiling.

Yes, he was smiling, and clearly this smile, and the youthful glow that it brought to his face, never failed to deceive his daughter.

"Very well, I'll be good," said Vanda with a defiant air. "But if only I could have a harmonium ..."

This instrument was a recent invention, sufficiently small and portable as to be placed at the sick woman's bedside and requiring only the pressure of a foot to produce sounds much like an organ. A well-crafted harmonium could be as good as a piano but cost three hundred francs. She had been coveting such an instrument for two months, having read of it in the newspapers and reviews.

"You shall have one, Madame," Godefroid replied, noting the glance the old man cast his way. "I have a friend who is soon to leave for Algiers; as it happens, he owns a superb harmonium, and I will gladly borrow it from him, for you would do well to try out the instrument before buying one. It may be that sounds so vibrant and powerful will disturb you ..."

"May I have it tomorrow? ..." she said, with the eager vivacity of a Creole.

"Tomorrow is very soon," Monsieur Bernard answered, "and besides, tomorrow is Sunday."

"Ah! ..." she said, looking at Godefroid, who thought he could see a soul fluttering before him in Vanda's darting glances.

Until this moment, Godefroid had not realized how powerful the voice and the eyes can be when they have become the sole repositories of an existence. Her gaze was no longer a gaze but a flame or, better yet, a divine glow, a radiance communicating life and intelligence, thought made visible! Her voice, with its thousand distinct intonations, left no need for movement, or gestures, or nods of the head. The variations of her face's tint, which changed like the fabled chameleon, completed this illusion—or if you will, this mirage. That suffering head, sunk into its lace-fringed muslin pillow, was an entire person unto itself.

Never in his life had Godefroid seen so awesome a sight; he could scarcely contain his emotions. No less sublime (for everything about this moment was strange, full of poetry and horror), the scene's witnesses, too, seemed to exist only through their souls. This atmosphere of pure sentiment exerted a celestial influence on all present; like the patient herself, her visitors had lost all sensation of their bodies' existence. To sit in that room was to be nothing more than a spirit. Contemplating the wreckage of what was once a lovely woman, Godefroid forgot the thousand elegant details of the decor and felt himself transported into the very heavens. Only after a half hour did his eye land on a shelf of curiosities beneath a portrait of Madame Bernard. The patient urged him to go and inspect this canvas at closer range, for it was painted by Géricault.

"Géricault was raised in Rouen," she said. "His family contracted certain obligations to my father who was then First President, and he offered his thanks in the form of this masterpiece, which shows me at the age of sixteen."

"This is a very fine painting," said Godefroid, "and entirely unknown to the scholars of that genius's exceedingly rare works."

"To me it has become a simple object of affection," she said, "for I see only with my heart—and that is the most beautiful sort of life you can imagine," she added, looking at her father and offering him her entire soul in her gaze. "Ah! Monsieur, if you knew what a man my father is! Who would ever believe that such a grand, severe magistrate, to whom the Emperor felt so indebted that he presented him with that snuffbox, and whom Charles X rewarded with the Sèvres tea service you see there," she said, nodding toward the console table, "who could ever believe that this unyielding pillar of power and justice, this wise scholar of political affairs, conceals within a heart of stone all the delicacy of a mother's love? Oh! Papa! Papa! Kiss me . . . Come here, I beg of you, if you love me."

The old man stood up, bent over the bed, and kissed the broad, white, poetic brow proffered to him by his daughter, whose fits did not always resemble this affectionate outburst.

The old man returned soundlessly to his chair, his feet shod in slippers embroidered by his daughter's hand.

"And in what occupation do you spend your days?" she asked Godefroid after a pause.

"Madame, I am in the employ of a pious organization, whose calling is to give aid to the indigent."

"Ah! What a wonderful mission, Monsieur!" she said. "Would you believe that I have sometimes thought of devoting myself to that same task? . . . But then what have I not thought of, at one time or another?" she continued, with a small toss of her head. "Pain is like a torch whose light shows us what life can be . . . If only I could recover my health! . . ."

"What fine times you would have, my child," said the old man.

"I would certainly like to," she answered, "but would I be able? My son will become a magistrate worthy of his two grandfathers, I hope, and so he will leave me. What will I do then? If God sees fit to give me back my life, I will devote it solely to Him! Oh! But only after I have given you everything you desire!" she cried, looking at her father and her son. "There are moments, dear father, when the ideas of Monsieur Maistre fill my mind, and I believe my suffering must be some sort of punishment."

"This is what comes of too much reading," the old man cried, clearly distressed by his daughter's notion.

"After all, however innocent his actions were, my grandfather, that brave Polish general, played some part in the division of Poland."

"Ah, so now it's Poland, is it!" Monsieur Bernard shot back.

"What can I do, Papa? I suffer so infernally that I find myself filled with a horror for life, and disgust for myself. And so I wonder: What have I done to deserve this? An illness such as mine is not simply an absence of health; it is a disturbance of the entire system, and—"

"Sing that old song from your homeland, the one your poor mother used to sing. Monsieur would like that; I've told him of your fine voice," said the old man, obviously hoping to distract his daughter from this train of thought.

In a low, gentle voice, Vanda began to sing a song in Polish that left Godefroid stupefied with admiration and an overwhelming sadness. The melody recalled the keening, melancholy airs of Brittany; it was like a poem that resonates in the heart long after one has heard it. Godefroid looked into her face as he listened, but he could not endure the ecstatic gaze of this half-mad ruin of a woman, and his eyes wandered to the tasseled cords hanging from either side of the bed's canopy.

"Ha! Ha!" said Vanda, laughing at Godefroid's fixed scrutiny of the tassels, "you must be wondering what those are for."

"Vanda!" said the father, "come now, calm yourself, my girl! Look, it's time for our tea. This, Monsieur, is a very costly device," he told Godefroid. "My daughter cannot arise from her bed, but neither can she remain in it for long without the covers needing to be straightened or the sheets changed. These cords run over two pulleys. By laying her on a leather sling tied at the four corners, we can pull her from her bed without exhausting her or ourselves."

"Pulled from my bed!" Vanda madly repeated.

Fortunately Auguste now reappeared, carrying a teapot. He set it down on a small table, then brought out the Sèvres tea service and a plateful of pastries and sandwiches, along with cream and butter. This sight caused an immediate transformation in the sick woman's state of mind, which was then on the verge of a crisis.

"Look, Vanda, here is Nathan's newest novel. If you awaken during the night, you will have something to read."

"*The Pearl of Dol!* Ah! It must be a love story. Auguste! Did you hear? I'm going to have a harmonium."

Auguste looked up in surprise and shot his grandfather a curious glance.

"See! How he loves his mother!" Vanda went on. "Come and kiss me, my little cat. No, it is not your grandfather, it is this gentleman you should be thanking. Our neighbor is going to lend me a harmonium tomorrow morning... What is it like, Monsieur?"

In response to the old man's encouraging gesture, Godefroid described the instrument in detail, all the while savoring Auguste's tea, which was of excellent quality and exquisite flavor.

At about ten-thirty the Initiate withdrew, wearied by the spectacle of the two caretakers' hopeless battle, admiring the heroism and patience with which they played two very different roles, each as exhausting as the other, day in and day out.

"Well!" said Monsieur Bernard, following him to his door. "Now, Monsieur, you understand what sort of life I lead! All day long I live like a thief, racked with fears and alarms, forever on my guard. A single word, a single gesture might well mean my daughter's death! One missing trinket would reveal everything to her keen mind; sometimes I think she can almost see through the walls."

"Monsieur," answered Godefroid, "on Monday Halpersohn will pronounce your daughter's diagnosis, for he has returned from his journey. I doubt that science has the power to restore her body . . ."

"Oh! I dare not hope for that," the former magistrate replied, "but at least let her life be made bearable . . . I knew I could count on your intelligence, Monsieur, and I wanted to thank you before you retired, for you have understood everything . . . Ah! She's going to have one of her fits!" he suddenly said, hearing a cry through the wall. "This was all too much for her!"

And, quickly pressing Godefroid's hand, the old man hurried back into his rooms.

At eight o'clock the next morning, Godefroid knocked at the celebrated Polish doctor's door. The doorman hurried off to find the valet and tell him of the visitor's arrival; left alone, Godefroid looked over his surroundings with great curiosity. But soon the valet appeared and led him to the second floor of the little house.

As he was hoping, Godefroid's promptness had spared him a tedious wait; no doubt he was the morning's first visitor. From the doctor's very simple anteroom, he entered a large office to find an old man in a dressing gown, smoking a long pipe. The gown, of black bombazine, had grown shiny from years of use; no doubt it dated back to the Polish emigration.

"And how may I be of service to you?" the Jewish medico asked him. "You're not a sick man, I can see that!" And he skewered Godefroid with the curious and penetrating gaze peculiar to Polish Jews, whose eyes seem almost to have ears.

To Godefroid's surprise, Halpersohn turned out to be a man of fifty-six, with short Turkish legs and a robust, powerful torso. There was something Oriental about him, and his face must have been exceedingly handsome in his youth; of that former magnificence there remained only a long, Hebraic nose, curved like a scimitar. His forehead was truly Polish, broad and noble, but wrinkled like crumpled paper, recalling the face of Saint Joseph as he is portrayed by the Italian Masters. His eyes were as green as seawater and ringed with darkened, grayish membranes, like the eyes of a parrot; in their depths could be read an expression of profound cunning and avarice. His mouth, like a deep, slashing wound, added a note of finely honed cynicism to that sinister countenance.

This face, pale and thin—for Halpersohn was a remarkably slender man—was topped with an ill-combed shock of gray hair and ornamented by a long, very full beard of deep black mingled with white, concealing all but his forehead, eyes, nose, cheekbones, and mouth.

This friend of the revolutionary Lelewel wore a black velvet skullcap that tapered to a small point on his forehead, bringing out the honeyed color of his skin, worthy of Rembrandt's brush.

The question put to him by this doctor—now so famous, as much for his talents as for his avarice—took Godefroid by surprise, and he could not help but wonder: "Does he think me a thief?"

A closer look around the office gave Godefroid his answer. He had thought himself the first to arrive; he was in fact the last, and the patients before him had left some rather sizable offerings on the doctor's table and mantelpiece. Twenty- and forty-franc coins stood in impressive stacks, accompanied by two one-thousand-franc notes. Was this the fruit of a single morning's work? Godefroid thought it unlikely, concluding rather that this display was an invention of the doctor's ingenious mind: no doubt he hoped to increase his receipts by showing his clients—carefully chosen from among the upper classes—that he was customarily paid not in pinches but in handfuls.

And indeed, Moses Halpersohn must have been paid quite generously, for he cured his patients' diseases, and had a special gift for the sort of desperate case that leaves other doctors scratching their heads. We in Europe know nothing of the many secrets of the Slavic peoples; they possess a whole array of powerful remedies, the fruits of their relations with the Chinese, Persians, Cossacks, Turks, and Tartars. There are peasant women in Poland, often thought to be witches, who use the sap of certain herbs to concoct an infallible remedy for rabies, an illness widespread in that land. Indeed, Poland is home to a vast corpus of unwritten observations on the effects of certain plants, or the barks of certain trees ground into powder, a knowledge passed from family to family and able to effect the most miraculous cures.

For five or six years Halpersohn was considered a charlatan, with his mysterious powders and elixirs, but in fact he possessed the innate wisdom of the finest doctors. He was a true scholar and had closely studied the science of medicine; but also, with his father, an itinerant merchant, he had traveled widely through Germany, Russia, Persia, and Turkey, collecting a wealth of folk remedies from what we French call the "little old women." With his fine knowledge of chemistry, he thus became the living repository of medicinal secrets from every country where he had set foot.

The cure that Saladin works on the King of England in Walter Scott's *The Talisman* is no mere product of an author's brilliant imagination. Halpersohn owns just such a silk purse; when dipped into water, it slightly alters the liquid's color, and the resulting infusion can indeed quell certain fevers. He believes the healing power of plants to be unbounded and able to cure the most horrific afflictions. Nevertheless, like his colleagues, he sometimes finds himself faced with the incomprehensible. Halpersohn admires the invention of homeopathy, more for its therapeutic effects than for its medical theory; at the time of these events, he corresponded frequently with Hédénius of Dresden, Chelius of Heidelberg, and other celebrated German doctors—but he always kept his hand closed, even though it was full of discoveries. He had no desire for disciples.

As we have said, Halpersohn might have come straight from a canvas by Rembrandt, and the decor that framed him in no way undermined this illusion. His office was hung with a paper imitating green velvet and frugally furnished with a green divan. The multihued green rug was threadbare and worn. His visitors sat in a large black leather armchair before the green-curtained window; he himself occupied a mahogany desk chair of Roman form, covered with a green maroquin.

A plain iron safe sat against the opposite wall, facing the fireplace. Atop it stood a Viennese granite clock with bronze figures representing Love at play with Death, the gift of a great German sculptor no doubt cured by Halpersohn's ministrations. The mantelpiece held only a silver cup flanked by two torches. On either side of the divan stood two ebony corner cupboards, in which Godefroid saw silver trays, basins, and carafes, as well as piles of hand towels.

Taking in this room's every detail with a single glance, Godefroid was struck by the simplicity, and even the starkness, of Halpersohn's office. Quickly recovering from his surprise at the doctor's question, he now answered: "Monsieur, I am in perfect health; I have not come on my own account but for one you should have visited long ago, a lady who lives on the Boulevard du Mont-Parnasse . . ."

"Ah! Yes, she's already sent her son to see me several times . . . Well, Monsieur, let her come to my office."

"Come to your office!" repeated Godefroid indignantly. "But, Monsieur, she cannot even be moved from her bed to a chair; she has to be raised up with straps."

"You are not a doctor, Monsieur?" asked the Jewish medico with a singular grimace, rendering even crueler than usual the mask that was his face.

"If the Baron de Nucingen sent a messenger to say he was ailing and wanted to see you, would you answer 'Let him come to my office!'?"

"I would go to him," the Jew coldly answered, launching a spurt of saliva into a Dutch mahogany spittoon filled with sand.

"You would go," Godefroid softly replied, "because the Baron de Nucingen has an annual income of two million francs and—"

"The rest is of no account. I would go."

"Well, Monsieur, you will come and see the sick woman on the Boulevard du Mont-Parnasse for the same reason. To be sure, my fortune cannot rival the Baron de Nucingen's; nevertheless, I invite you to name your own price for her cure, or for your time, should you prove unable to heal her ... I am prepared to pay you in advance; but really now, Monsieur, you who are a Polish immigrant, and a communist, I believe, would you not make one small sacrifice for Poland? This woman is the granddaughter of General Tarlowski, the sworn ally of Prince Poniatowski."

"Monsieur, you have come here in hopes of a cure for this woman and not to give me advice. In Poland, I am Polish; in Paris, I am a Parisian. Each does what good he can in his own way, and believe me, there is a reason for my avarice. The fortune that I am amassing has a purpose, and a sacred one. I sell good health; the rich are willing to pay for it, and I make them buy it. The poor have doctors of their own. If I did not have a goal, I would not be practicing medicine. I live modestly, and spend my time in endless labor; and yet I am a lazy man, and once lived purely for pleasure ... Do you see, young man? You are far too young to judge one as aged as I ...."

Godefroid kept silent.

"You live with the granddaughter of that idiot whose cowardice delivered his country into the hands of Catherine the Second?"

"Yes, Monsieur."

"Be at home on Monday, at three o'clock," he said, setting down his pipe and writing a few words in an appointment book. "You will give me two hundred francs on my arrival; if I promise you a cure, you will give me a further thousand *écus* ... I am told," he went on, "that this woman is as shrunken and shriveled as if she had fallen into the fire."

"Monsieur, you may take the word of the most celebrated doctors in Paris, she suffers from a neurosis so grave that they refused to believe in her symptoms until they saw them with their own eyes."

"Ah, yes! I am beginning to recall the young gentleman's account ... Until tomorrow, Monsieur."

Godefroid now took his leave of this odd and extraordinary gentleman. Nothing about him suggested that he was a doctor, not even his stark office, of which the only notable piece of furniture was that enormous safe, no doubt manufactured by Huret or Fichet.

Godefroid was able to arrive at the Passage Vivienne in time to buy a magnificent harmonium before the shop closed; he gave the shopkeeper Monsieur Bernard's address, asking him to deliver the instrument at once. From there he proceeded toward the Rue Chanoinesse by way of the Quai des Augustins, where he hoped to find a publishers' agent still open for business. His wish was granted: finding just such a young man in his offices, he engaged him in a long talk on the publication of legal studies.

He arrived in the Rue Chanoinesse just as Madame de La Chanterie and her friends were returning from Mass. She cast him a glance of recognition, and he responded with an expressive nod.

"Well!" he said to her. "Dear Father Alain is not with you?"

"He will not be here this Sunday," Madame de La Chanterie answered. "You will not see him for a week . . . unless you await him at your usual meeting place."

"Madame," Godefroid said quietly, "you know that he does not intimidate me as these other gentlemen do, and I was hoping he might hear my confession."

"Why not me?"

"Oh! Of course, to you I will tell all; for I have much to tell. My first mission has shown me the most extraordinary of all sorrows, a brutal conjunction of wretchedness and luxury, and a family so sublime as to surpass all the inventions of our most fashionable writers."

"Nature, and particularly the nature of the soul, always stands above art, just as God stands above His creatures. But come now," said Madame de La Chanterie, "tell me of your expeditions into the terra incognita where you have made your first landfall."

Monsieur Nicolas and Monsieur Joseph—for Father de Vèze had stayed behind at Notre-Dame—now withdrew, leaving Madame de La Chanterie alone with Godefroid. Still reeling from the emotions of the day before, the Initiate told her his story in great detail, with all the force, liveliness, and brilliance conferred by the first impression of such a spectacle, its setting, and its actors. Clearly he told his tale well, for the calm, gentle Madame de La Chanterie wept in sympathy, despite her long acquaintance with these descents into the abyss of misery.

"You did well to send the harmonium," she told him.

"There is so much more I hope to do," Godefroid answered, "for this family has offered me my first glimpse of the joys of charity. I would like the old man to enjoy all the possible benefits he might derive from his work. I do not know if you have sufficient confidence in my abilities to entrust me with this matter. According to the information I have just obtained, we would need some nine thousand francs to print fifteen hundred copies of his book; once put on the market, those fifteen hundred volumes would earn twenty-four thousand francs at least. But first we would have to pay the debt of three thousand and some hundred francs that currently acts as a lien on the manuscript. We would thus be risking a total of twelve thousand francs. Oh! Madame, if you knew how bitterly I regretted squandering my little fortune, as I made my way here from the Quai des Augustins! For the spirit of Charity has revealed itself to me. I am overcome with an initiate's ardor; I long to embrace the life those other gentlemen lead, and I am determined to prove myself worthy. More than once in the past two days I have blessed the stroke of fortune that brought me to this house. I will obey your every command, until you judge me ready to become one of your number."

"Well!" Madame de La Chanterie gravely answered after a moment's reflection. "Listen to me, for I have some very important things to tell you. My child, you have been seduced by the poetry of misfortune. Yes, misfortune often has a sort of poetry about it; for, to my mind, poetry is simply a certain excess in the sentiments, and pain is nothing other than a sentiment. So many lives are lived through pain alone! . . ."

"Yes, Madame, the demon of curiosity has got hold of me . . . What can you expect? I have not yet acquired the habit of looking into the heart of misery, and cannot do so as dispassionately as your three pious soldiers of the Lord. But remember, it was because I had wearied of curiosity's spur that I first resolved to devote myself to your works! . . ."

"Listen, my dear angel," said Madame de La Chanterie, pronouncing these last three words with a gentle saintliness that Godefroid found singularly touching, "we have forbidden ourselves—and forbidden absolutely, for we do not take words lightly here, and when a thing is forbidden we never so much as think of it again—we have forbidden ourselves, then, to enter into any sort of speculation. To print a book for the commercial market, to expect financial rewards from its sale, that is business, and it would lead us inexorably into the intrigues and complexities of commerce. To be sure, your project seems quite feasible, perhaps even necessary. But do you believe this is the first such case to come before us? Twenty times, one hundred times we have seen such a plan as our best hope to rescue a family, and even a houseful of families! But what would we have become had we taken that course? Businessmen! . . . If you wish to vanquish indigence, the secret is not to set to work yourself but rather to enable the indigent to work on their own behalf. In days to come you will encounter sufferings far more bitter than this; will you do the same thing for them? You would soon find yourself undone! Remember, my child, that it has been a year since the Messieurs Mongenod ceased to serve as our accountants. You will soon be devoting half of your time to the maintenance of our books. We now have nearly two thousand debtors scattered throughout Paris, and we must at least know the amount owed by those who might one day repay us . . . We never ask for our money; we only wait. We calculate that half of what we distribute is lost forever. The other half sometimes comes back to us doubled . . . Thus, suppose that your magistrate were to die: what good would our twelve thousand francs have done? But now suppose his daughter were cured, suppose his grandson were to succeed in his studies, and one day become a magistrate himself . . . Well! If he is an honorable man, he will not forget that debt, and he will return to us the money of the poor, with interest. Do you know that more than one family whom we have lifted out of poverty and set on the path to prosperity has stepped in for those less fortunate than they, and repaid double the sum we lent them, and sometimes even triple? . . . These are our only speculations! First of all, remember, as for what is currently preoccupying you (and you are right to be preoccupied by it), that the sale of the magistrate's book depends on the quality of his work; have you read it? And even if it turns out to be excellent, how many excellent books have gone one, two, three years without finding the success they deserve! How often is the laurel wreath laid only on the tomb! And I happen to know that publishers have their own ways of conducting their affairs; of all the businessmen in Paris, there is none riskier to bargain with! Monsieur Nicolas will tell you more of these intricacies, which seem inherent to the nature of that trade. Thus, you see, our reasons are not unfounded. We have experience in all sorts of miseries, and all manners of commerce, for we have been studying Paris for a long, long time . . . and of course we have the Mongenod brothers to help us. They have proven a real guiding light; thanks to them, we know that the Banque de France looks upon the publishing industry with deep suspicion. It is the noblest of all trades, to be sure, but sadly corrupt in its present form . . . Now, as for the other four thousand francs required to rescue this good family from the horrors of indigence—for the poor child and his grandfather must be allowed to buy decent food and clothing—that sum I will give you directly . . . There are certain sufferings, certain miseries, certain wounds that we can dress immediately and without hesitation, little caring whom we are saving: religion, creed, character, none of that matters to us one whit. But when it comes to using the money of the poor to aid an unfortunate in the workings of industry or commerce . . . Oh! then we require guarantees, we become as inflexible as any moneylender. Thus, I ask that you confine your enthusiasm to finding this old man the most honest publisher you can. This is a matter to bring up with Monsieur Nicolas. He knows many lawyers, professors, and authors of books on jurisprudence, and he will certainly have some useful advice for you next Sunday . . . Do not be concerned, if such a thing is possible; this matter will be resolved. In the meantime, perhaps it would be a good idea to have Monsieur Nicolas read the magistrate's work . . . Have it sent to him, if you can . . ."

Godefroid was stunned by the exceptional practicality of a woman he thought animated solely by the spirit of Charity. The Initiate knelt down, kissed one of Madame de La Chanterie's beautiful hands, and said to her, "So you are the soul of reason as well?"

"In our profession we must be all things," she replied with the gentle gaiety peculiar to the truly saintly.

"But did you really say two thousand accounts?" he cried. "That's enormous!"

"Oh! Two thousand accounts from which we might expect restitution," she answered, "trusting solely in the nobility of our debtors' sentiments, as I have said. Then there are another three thousand families who will repay us only with prayers of gratitude. This is why we so desperately need a well-kept set of books. And if you are capable of the most complete discretion, you will be our financial oracle. We will require a daily log, a ledger of current accounts, and a reckoning of our present assets. We all keep notes on our activities, but we can no longer afford to waste our time searching for records . . . Ah, the gentlemen are back," she concluded.

Godefroid sat grave and pensive, paying little heed to the conversation that ensued, still wondering at the revelation that Madame de La Chanterie had offered him, spoken in a tone that showed a sincere desire to reward him for his zeal.

"Two thousand families in our debt!" he said to himself. "And if they all cost as much as Monsieur Bernard will cost us, then we must have millions of francs scattered all over Paris!"

This thought was to be one of the last resurgences of Godefroid's worldly spirit; even then, such considerations were quietly fading from his mind. Pursuing his meditation, he calculated the combined fortunes of Madame de La Chanterie and Messieurs Alain, Nicolas, and Joseph, and Judge Popinot, to which he added the donations collected by Father de Vèze and the funds lent by the House of Mongenod; the sum thus obtained constituted a truly impressive capital, which, increased by those beneficiaries who had expressed their gratitude in concrete form, must have grown exponentially over the past twelve or fifteen years, since his charitable new friends never drew upon it for their own needs. Little by little, he was acquiring a clearer idea of the immense undertaking pursued in this house, and his desire to cooperate in it grew all the stronger.

He arose from his chair as nine o'clock was sounding, preparing to return to the Boulevard du Mont-Parnasse on foot; but Madame de La Chanterie, anxious at the isolation and solitude of the neighborhood, pressed him to take a cabriolet. Alighting from the carriage, Godefroid heard the sounds of the instrument he had purchased that afternoon, even with the shutters in Monsieur Bernard's apartment closed so tightly that no ray of light could be seen. No sooner had he set foot on the landing than Auguste, evidently posted to watch for Godefroid's arrival, opened the door a crack, and said, "Mother would be very happy to see you, and my grandfather would gladly offer you a cup of tea."

Entering the patient's room, Godefroid found her transfigured by the pleasures of music; her face was aglow, and her eyes sparkled like twin diamonds.

"I should have waited for you, so that you could hear the instrument's first chords; but no, I attacked that little organ as one dying of hunger would attack a banquet. You have the sort of soul that understands such things, and so I am forgiven."

With this, Vanda nodded to her son, who approached the bed to work the pedal that operated the instrument's internal bellows. Her fingers had temporarily recovered their strength and agility; thus, gazing heavenward like Saint Cecile, she played a set of variations on the "Prayer of Moses," composed in the few hours since she had sent her son to buy her the score. In her music Godefroid glimpsed a talent to rival Chopin's. Her soul emerged through this procession of divine tones, dominated by a sense of gentle melancholy. Monsieur Bernard had greeted Godefroid with a look the like of which had not been seen in his eyes for many long years. Had the source of this old man's tears not run dry, withered as he was by so many harrowing sorrows, those eyes would plainly have been glistening. Now he sat toying with his snuffbox, contemplating his daughter in indescribable ecstasy.

"Tomorrow, Madame," said Godefroid once the music had stopped, "tomorrow your fate will be decided, for I bring you excellent news. The celebrated Halpersohn will be here at three o'clock. And he has promised to tell me the truth," he added in an aside to Monsieur Bernard.

The old man stood up and seized Godefroid's hand; trembling, he drew him into one corner of the bedroom, next to the hearth. "Oh! What a night I have before me! Tomorrow her fate will be sealed!" he whispered in Godefroid's ear. "Either my daughter will be cured or she will be condemned to die!"

"Take courage," answered Godefroid, "and come and see me after your tea."

"Stop, stop, my daughter," said the old man, "you will give yourself a fit. You mustn't overtax your forces: it will only lead to exhaustion."

Asking Auguste to take the instrument away, he presented his daughter with her cup of tea, coaxing her like a nurse struggling to overcome the impatience of a little child.

"What is this doctor like?" she asked, already distracted by the prospect of a new visitor. Like all prisoners, Vanda was haunted by an unbounded curiosity. When the physical phenomena of her illness subsided, they seemed to flood into her soul, and then she conceived the strangest caprices, and the most violent whims. She wanted to see Rossini; she wept when her father, whom she thought to be omnipotent, refused to allow it.

Godefroid gave her a detailed description of the Jewish doctor and of his office, for she had no idea of the steps her father had taken. Monsieur Bernard had urged his grandson to say nothing of his visits to Halpersohn's, to prevent fruitless hopes taking root in his daughter's mind. Vanda lay as if lost in the words emerging from Godefroid's mouth, thoroughly entranced, and drawn into a sort of delirium by her ardent desire to see this strange Pole.

"Poland has produced such singular and mysterious creatures," said the former magistrate. "Today, for example, apart from this physician, we have Hoëné Wronski, the visionary mathematician, the poet Mickiewicz, the inspired Towianski, and the supernaturally talented Chopin. Great national upheavals always seem to produce truncated giants."

"Oh! dear Papa! What a man you are! If you would only write down all the things you say purely for the sake of my entertainment, you would make a fortune . . . Do you know, Monsieur, my dear, good father invents the most wonderful stories for me when I find myself without novels to read. That's how he puts me to sleep. His voice gently lulls me, and I forget my pain as I wonder at his imaginative mind . . . Who will ever repay him for all his goodness! . . . Auguste, my child, you should kiss your grandfather's footprints for me."

The young man raised his glistening eyes to his mother's face; his gaze, overflowing with long-contained compassion, was a poem in itself. Godefroid stood up, took Auguste's hand, and pressed it warmly. "Madame, God has placed two angels at your side! . . ." he cried.

"Yes, I know, and how often I reproach myself for causing them such trouble! Come, dear Augustin, give your mother a kiss. He is a child of whom any mother would be proud, Monsieur. He is as pure as gold, and free from guile; his soul is sinless, if perhaps a bit too excitable, like his mother's. Perhaps God has confined me to this bed to protect me from the foolish acts committed by women . . . who have too much heart . . ." she added, smiling.

Godefroid answered with a smile and a bow.

"Good-bye, Monsieur, and please remember to thank your friend, for he has made a poor invalid very happy."

"Monsieur," said Godefroid to Monsieur Bernard, who had followed him across the landing and into the solitude of his own rooms, "I believe I can assure you that you will not be despoiled by those three good gentlemen of yours. I will soon have the sum you require to pay off your debts, but you must show me the right of repurchase clause in your contract . . . And I would ask that you give me your book to read as well, so that I might assist you further . . . Not that I intend to read it myself, for I lack the knowledge to judge of its merits; I shall give it to a former magistrate of my acquaintance, a man of unquestioned integrity. If he considers your work deserving, he will place it with an honorable publisher, who will offer you an equitable contract . . . But enough of that for the moment. In the meanwhile, please accept these five hundred francs," he added, handing a banknote to the stunned former magistrate, "to help you with your most pressing needs. I will not ask you for a receipt; you are obliged to me only by your conscience, and your conscience must speak only when you have regained your financial security. . . . I will see to Halpersohn's fee myself . . ."

"Who the devil are you?" said the old man, collapsing into a chair.

"I myself am nothing," answered Godefroid, "but I serve powerful people, who now know of your distress, and have taken an interest in you . . . I can tell you no more than that."

"And what motivates these people? . . ." asked the old man.

"Religion, Monsieur," Godefroid replied.

"Can it be! . . . Religion! . . ."

"Yes, the Catholic religion, Roman and apostolic."

"What! You belong to the Society of Jesus?"

"No, Monsieur," Godefroid answered. "Do not fear: these people have no plans for you, apart from lending you their assistance and restoring your family's happiness."

"Can this be true? Can philanthropy be something other than mere vanity? . . ."

"Ah! Monsieur," said Godefroid curtly, "do not cast aspersions on holy Catholic Charity—what Saint Paul calls the greatest of all virtues! . . ."

Hearing these words, Monsieur Bernard began to pace this way and that in deep agitation. "I accept," he said all at once, "and I will thank you in the only way I can: I will entrust you with my work. The notes and references will be of no use to a former magistrate; and, as I told you, I will require another two months to copy out my citations . . . Until tomorrow, then," he added, shaking Godefroid's hand.

"Might I have made a conversion? . . ." the Initiate asked himself, struck by the change in the grand old man's face on hearing his last response.

Two days later, at three o'clock, a cabriolet drew up before the house; Godefroid watched as Halpersohn emerged, bundled in an enormous bearskin cape. The cold had turned bitter during the night, and the thermometer showed a mere ten degrees.

Curiously but discreetly, the Jewish doctor examined the room in which his recent visitor received him, and in his eyes Godefroid saw a kind of wariness, gleaming like the point of a dagger. This sudden surge of suspicion caused Godefroid a brief inward chill, for he realized that this man must be merciless where business was concerned; and it is so natural to assume that genius goes hand in hand with goodness that he felt a fresh wave of disgust wash over him.

"Monsieur," he said, "I can see that the simplicity of my apartment disturbs you; thus, you will not be surprised if I proceed directly to the essential. Here are your one hundred francs, and here are three thousand-franc notes," he added, taking from his wallet the banknotes Madame de La Chanterie had given him to disencumber Monsieur

Bernard's work. "This should settle your mind on the question of my solvency; but should you require further guarantees, you may make inquiries with Messieurs Mongenod, bankers, on the Rue de la Victoire."

"I know them," answered Halpersohn, thrusting the ten pieces of gold into his pocket.

"And he will go and see them," thought Godefroid.

"Now, where will I find the patient?" asked the doctor, briskly arising, like a man who knows the value of time.

"Come this way, Monsieur," said Godefroid, proceeding him across the landing.

Entering Monsieur Bernard's rooms, the Jew examined his surroundings with a practiced, vigilant eye, for he had powers of observation to rival any spy's. Thus, he immediately recognized the horrors of indigence as he glanced into the room where the magistrate and his grandson slept. Monsieur Bernard had gone in to put on the suit he always wore for his daughter, and unfortunately, in his haste to return and receive his visitor, he had not fully closed the door behind him.

He greeted Halpersohn with dignity and gingerly opened the door to his daughter's room. "Vanda, my child, the doctor is here," he said.

And he stepped aside to let Halpersohn pass by, still wrapped in his cape. The Jew's eyes widened in astonishment as he beheld this room, which in this neighborhood, and most especially in this house, seemed little short of bizarre; but his surprise was short-lived, for among the Jews of Germany and Russia, he had often seen such contrasts between apparent penury and hidden wealth. He strode from the door to the sickbed, never taking his eyes from the patient, and as he arrived at her side, he said to her in Polish, "You are Polish?"

"No, not I, but my mother."

"I believe your grandfather was General Tarlowski? Who was his wife?"

"A Polish woman."

"From what province?"

"She was a Sobolewska, from Pinsk."

"Good. This gentleman is your father?"

"Yes, Monsieur."

"Monsieur," he asked, "your wife—"

"She is dead," Monsieur Bernard answered.

"Did she have very fair skin?" said Halpersohn, slightly put out at this interruption.

"Here is her portrait," Monsieur Bernard replied, walking to the wall and taking down a magnificent frame holding several fine miniatures.

Halpersohn palpated the patient's head and fingered her hair, all the while gazing at the portrait of Vanda Tarlowska, née Countess Sobolewska.

"And what symptoms has the illness caused?"

He sat down in the *bergère*, keeping his eyes fixed on Vanda as the father and daughter gave him a twenty-minute account of her miseries.

"What age is Madame?"

"Thirty-eight years."

"Ah! Very well, then," he cried, rising to his feet. "You may leave it to me, I shall cure her. I cannot promise to give her back the use of her legs, but cured she will be. There remains only to transport her to a convalescent home in my neighborhood."

"But, Monsieur, my daughter cannot be moved."

"I will answer for her life," Halpersohn said grandly, "but only in the circumstances I have just named ... Do you not realize that she is about to exchange her current ailment for another terrible disease, which might well last a year, or six months at the very least? ... You will of course be allowed to come and visit Madame, since you are her father."

"Do you promise me that?" asked Monsieur Bernard.

"I do!" answered the Jew. "Madame has in her body a certain agent peculiar to those of her ancestry. It is of this that she must be delivered. You will first have her brought to Doctor Halpersohn's clinic, on the Rue Basse-Saint-Pierre, in Chaillot."

"But how?"

"On a litter, like any other patient bound for the hospital."

"But the trip will kill her."

"No, it will not."

Halpersohn was already at the apartment's door when he made this curt response. Godefroid hurried to join him on the stairs. So warm in his fur cape that he could scarcely breathe, the Jew whispered to him, "In addition to the thousand *écus,* her treatment will cost you fifteen francs per day, with three months paid in advance."

"Very well, Monsieur. And you do assure me," Godefroid insisted, stepping onto the running board of the doctor's cabriolet, "you do assure me that she will be cured?"

"I assure it," the doctor repeated. "Are you in love with this lady?"

"No," said Godefroid.

"You must not repeat what I am about to tell you. I say it only to prove that I have no doubt of her recovery. Any indiscretion on your part would surely kill her . . ."

A gesture was Godefroid's only response.

"For seventeen years her body has harbored the agent of the Polish *plique;* this is the source of her sufferings, though I have seen cases more terrible than hers. Even with treatment, the victims of this illness do not always recover; I am the only doctor living today who knows how to drive out the *plique* and leave her in perfect health. As you see, Monsieur, I am not entirely ruled by a desire for gain. If the lady were a grande dame—a Baroness de Nucingen, perhaps, or some other modern Croesus's wife or daughter—I could easily ask one hundred, two hundred thousand francs, whatever I pleased! . . . But there we are, it's no great loss."

"But that long trip through the streets! . . ."

"Bah! She may very well seem to be dying, but she will not die! . . . She has the life in her to live a hundred years, once she's cured. Off, Jacques! . . . Rue de Monsieur, and hurry! . . . Hurry! . . ." he said to the coachman.

And he left Godefroid standing on the boulevard, silently watching as the cabriolet disappeared down the street.

"Who on earth was that strange man in the bearskin? . . ." asked old Madame Vauthier, whose watchful eye nothing escaped. "Is it true what the coach driver told me, that he's the greatest doctor in Paris?"

"And what is that to you, Mother Vauthier?"

"Why, nothing at all!" she replied with a scowl.

"You made a great mistake when you chose not to cooperate with me," said Godefroid as they strolled back to the house. "You could have had so much more than you will ever have from Messieurs Barbet and Métivier—for from them, Madame Vauthier, you shall have nothing."

"What makes you think I'm on their side?" she replied with a shrug. "Monsieur Barbet is my landlord, that's all!"

It took two days to convince Monsieur Bernard to part with his daughter and allow her transport to Chaillot. A litter was brought, covered in blue-and-white-striped ticking; fearing nervous convulsions, the father insisted that the precious patient be virtually lashed to the mattress. The convoy set out at three o'clock, with Godefroid and the former magistrate walking on either side of the litter; they finally arrived at the convalescent home at around five, in the glow of the setting sun. Godefroid paid the required four hundred and fifty francs in advance, then returned to the litter to offer the two bearers a tip. He found Monsieur Bernard taking a large, wax-sealed parcel from beneath the mattress.

"One of these fellows will go and find you a cabriolet," said the old man, "for I daresay you will not want to carry these four volumes very far in your arms. Here is my book; you may leave it with my critic for the coming week. I shall be staying on in this neighborhood for at least that long, for I cannot bring myself to abandon my daughter here. I know my grandson, and he can easily look after the apartment himself, particularly with your assistance; indeed, I would ask you to watch over him in my absence. If I were still what I once was, I would ask you my reader's name, for there are few magistrates from those days that I would not know—"

"Oh! There is no secret about it," Godefroid interrupted. "You have given me your complete confidence, and so I do not hesitate to tell you that your critic is the former President Lecamus, Baron de Tresnes."

"Oh! Of the Royal Court of Paris! By all means, let him read it! . . . Why, he is one of the finest figures of our age . . . Men such as he and the late Popinot, the judge of the Lower Court, were magistrates worthy of our long-lost Parliaments at their most glorious. Any fears that might have lingered in my mind are now dispelled . . . And where does he live? I would very much like to go and thank him for his trouble."

"You will find him on the Rue Chanoinesse, under the name of Monsieur Nicolas ... I am off to see him this very moment. Now, what about your agreement with the swindlers? ..."

"Auguste will give you a copy of our contract," said the old man, turning back toward the courtyard of the home.

One of the errand boys ventured off to the Quai de Billy and returned with a cabriolet. Godefroid climbed in and promised the driver a generous tip if he could take him to the Rue Chanoinesse in time for dinner.

Now, thirty minutes after Vanda had set off on her litter, three men dressed in black had knocked at Madame Vauthier's door on the Rue Notre-Dame-des-Champs. No doubt they had been lurking in the street for some time, awaiting a propitious moment for their appearance. The female Judas accompanied them up the stairs, where they knocked discreetly at Monsieur Bernard's door. As this was a Thursday, the schoolboy happened to be at home. He opened the door, and the three men slipped inside, like shadows.

"What do you wish, Messieurs?" asked the young man.

"Are we indeed in the lodgings of Monsieur Bernard ... that is, of Monsieur le Baron? ..."

"But what do you wish?"

"Ah! You know perfectly well what we wish, young man. We were told that your grandfather has just left with a covered litter ... No surprise to us! But of course he has every right. I am a bailiff; I have come to inventory his property, in preparation for seizure. Last Monday you were given notice to pay three thousand francs plus charges to Monsieur Métivier, on pain of imprisonment; and now the debtor has decided he'd rather take to his heels than be taken to Clichy. Might as well be hung for a sheep as a lamb, I suppose! Well! If we can't lay our hands on him, we'll simply have to make do with his fine furniture, for we know all, my young friend ... and we intend to bring the old man to justice ..."

"Here, these are some official papers that your old granddad refused to take from me," said the widow Vauthier, shoving three writs into Auguste's hand.

"Don't leave, Madame; we intend to appoint you legal custodian of the property. The law grants you a stipend of forty *sous* per day, and that's nothing to sneeze at!"

"Ah! And I'll finally see the beautiful bedroom!" cried Madame Vauthier.

"You shall not enter my mother's room!" the young man shot back in a formidable voice, throwing himself between the door and the three men in black.

On a sign from the bailiff, Auguste was seized by his two escorts and his assistant, who had just appeared.

"Give us no trouble, young man! You are not the master here; we have only to make a complaint and you'll be spending the night in police headquarters . . ."

Hearing these fearsome words, Auguste dissolved into tears. "Ah! What a blessing that Mama is away!" he said. "This would have killed her!"

The bailiff, his escorts, and the Vauthier woman were now engaged in a sort of conference, their voices muted to a whisper; nevertheless, Auguste gleaned that they were particularly eager to seize his grandfather's manuscripts. He threw open the door to his mother's room.

"Come in, Messieurs, and please take care not to damage our things," he said. "We will pay you tomorrow morning."

And, still sobbing, he disappeared into the other bedroom. Quickly he took up his grandfather's notes and hid them away inside the stove, which he knew to be unlit.

This bailiff was a shrewd, keen-eyed fellow, worthy of his clients Barbet and Métivier; nevertheless, Auguste had acted with such speed that, by the time the intruder entered the boy's squalid bedroom after a fruitless search of the antechamber, he found him slumped in a chair, sobbing loudly. By law, neither books nor manuscripts may be seized, but the former magistrate had signed away the rights to his work, making such a seizure perfectly legal. Certain steps could be taken to delay this action, however, and Monsieur Bernard would not have failed to take them. The creditors knew that they would have to proceed with cunning, and so the widow Vauthier had done her landlord the great favor of not delivering the warnings of seizure to her tenants. She had planned to throw them into the apartment as she entered with the authorities, or if need be, to tell Monsieur Bernard she had assumed they were addressed to the two writers, who had been absent for the past several days.

It took about an hour to draw up the inventory of items to be seized, for the bailiff was careful to omit nothing, and he found the value of the property sufficient to repay the debt. After the bailiff had gone, poor Auguste took the notices and ran off to find his grandfather at the convalescent home. The bailiff had assured him that Madame Vauthier would be held responsible for the security of his grandfather's belongings, and would be punished severely if anything were found missing; he could thus leave his lodgings without fear.

The idea that his grandfather might be dragged off to prison for his debts threw the poor child into a kind of madness peculiar to the young: a dangerous, destructive frenzy, a ferment of all the many forces of youth, as likely to inspire a criminal act as a heroic one. When poor Auguste arrived at the Rue Basse-Saint-Pierre, the doorman told him that he did not know what had become of the father of the patient brought in at four-thirty, but that Monsieur Halpersohn's orders were to allow no one to see the lady for a full week, not even her father, as one single visit might well endanger her life.

This response brought Auguste's frustration to the boiling point. He set off once more for the Boulevard du Mont-Parnasse, deep in despair, and concocting the most extravagant schemes as he walked. He arrived home at around eight-thirty that evening, having eaten virtually nothing all day, and so exhausted by hunger and grief that he leapt at Madame Vauthier's invitation to share her dinner of potato-and-mutton stew. Once inside that monstrous woman's rooms, he collapsed half dead into a chair. She now set about trying to ingratiate herself with the poor child; encouraged by her honeyed words, he answered a number of artful questions on the new lodger, revealing all that Godefroid had done to improve their lot over the previous week, and even that he was intending to pay off their debts the next day. The widow listened in disbelief, repeatedly refilling Auguste's glass with wine.

At around ten o'clock they heard the sound of coach wheels rolling to a stop in the street, and the widow cried: "Oh! That must be Monsieur Godefroid."

Immediately Auguste took the key to the apartment and hurried upstairs to meet his family's protector; but he found Godefroid's face so changed that he hesitated to speak to him. Nevertheless, the threat that hung over his grandfather compelled the good child to seek Godefroid's aid.

But here is what had happened on the Rue Chanoinesse, and what lay behind Godefroid's grim expression.

Arriving for dinner, the neophyte found Madame de La Chanterie and her flock in the drawing room, and he took Monsieur Nicolas aside to give him the four volumes of *The Spirit of the Modern Laws*. Monsieur Nicolas immediately carried the manuscript up to his room and rejoined the others for dinner; then, after a few hours of conversation, he returned to his room to begin reading the old man's work.

To Godefroid's surprise, Manon came to find him a few minutes later. The former President wished to speak with him at once. Manon led him upstairs to Monsieur Nicolas's rooms; Godefroid did not so much as glance around these unfamiliar lodgings as he entered, so struck was he by the stunned expression on the face of this usually stolid and placid man.

"Do you know," asked Monsieur Nicolas, in the manner of a President of the Court, "do you know the name of the author of this work?"

"Monsieur Bernard," answered Godefroid. "I know him by no other name than that. I never opened the parcel . . ."

"Ah! That is true," said Monsieur Nicolas to himself. "I broke the seal myself. Then," he resumed aloud, "you have made no attempt to inquire into his past?"

"No. I know that he made a marriage of love with the daughter of General Tarlowski; that his own daughter is named Vanda, like her mother; that he has a grandson, Auguste; and I have seen a portrait of Monsieur Bernard as a President of the Royal Court, I believe, dressed in a red gown."

"Here, read this!" said Monsieur Nicolas, showing him the title of this work, written in Auguste's most elegant hand:

The Spirit of the Modern Laws
by
Monsieur Bernard-Jean-Baptiste-Maclod, Baron Bourlac,
Former Prosecutor-General
To the Royal Court of Rouen,
Grand Officer of the Legion of Honor

"Bourlac! Madame's nemesis—and her daughter's, and the Chevalier du Vissard's!" said Godefroid in a weak voice.

And, with his legs about to fail him, the neophyte slumped into an armchair. "A nice beginning I've made!" he murmured.

"This, my dear Godefroid, is a matter that concerns us all," Monsieur Nicolas replied. "You have done your part, now the rest is up to us! I beseech you, you must break off all involvement in this matter at once. Go back to your rooms and collect your affairs, and say nothing to anyone! Or, if you must, at least take great care what you say! And tell Baron Bourlac to come and see me directly. In the meantime, we will consider how best to proceed."

Godefroid raced down the stairs and into the street. He hailed a cabriolet and sped toward the Boulevard du Mont-Parnasse, recalling with horror the indictment presented to the criminal court of Caen, the grisly drama that brought so many to the scaffold, Madame de La Chanterie's long incarceration in Bicêtre . . . He now realized why this former prosecutor, this virtual twin to Fouquier-Tinville, should be living out what remained of his life in such utter isolation, and why he so carefully concealed his family name.

"May Monsieur Nicolas wreak a terrible vengeance on behalf of poor Madame de La Chanterie!" He spoke the last words of this unchristian wish to himself, for he saw Auguste climbing the stairs to his rooms.

"What do you want of me?" asked Godefroid.

"My good Monsieur, a terrible misfortune has befallen us, and I fear I will go mad! Three scoundrels have come and seized everything in my mother's home, and they are searching for my grandfather to put him in prison. But that is not what I have come for," said the boy, with a Roman sense of pride. "I want only to ask you a favor. I believe that is the custom, for those condemned to die . . ."

"Speak," said Godefroid.

"They came for my grandfather's manuscripts; and since I believe he has placed his work in your hands, I beseech you to take the notes away as well, for Madame Vauthier will not allow me to remove anything from our rooms . . . Put them together with the other volumes, and—"

"Very well, very well," answered Godefroid. "Go and fetch them at once."

The young man vanished into his family's rooms, returning a moment later. In the meantime, Godefroid reminded himself that this youth was guilty of no crime, that he must not torment the boy with the truth of his grandfather's career, and of the abandonment visited on him in his sad old age as penance for the frenzies of politics. Without ill will, then, he graciously accepted the parcel he was handed.

"What is your mother's name?" he asked him.

"My mother, Monsieur, is the Baroness de Mergi; my father was the son of the First President of the Royal Court at Rouen."

"Ah!" said Godefroid. "Your grandfather married his daughter to the son of the famous President Mergi."

"Yes, Monsieur."

"My young friend, you must leave me now," said Godefroid. He led the young Baron de Mergi to the landing and called out for the Vauthier woman.

"Mother Vauthier," he said to her, "my apartment is yours; I shall not return."

And he set off down the stairs and into a cabriolet.

"Did you give that gentleman something before he left?" Madame Vauthier asked Auguste.

"I did," said the young man.

"Well, aren't you the clever one! That man is working for your enemies! He had this all planned out from the start, that's for sure. He's swindled you, my boy; if you want proof, he's just told me he'll never be back here again . . . He said I could put his rooms up for rent."

Auguste sprinted downstairs to the boulevard, ran after the cabriolet, and finally managed to bring it to a halt with his shouts.

"What do you want?" asked Godefroid.

"My grandfather's manuscripts! . . ."

"Tell him to apply to Monsieur Nicolas for their return."

The young man took this for the cruel jape of a shameless thief, and he sat down in the snow as the cabriolet vanished into the distance. After a moment he leapt to his feet in a surge of wild energy, then trudged upstairs and fell into bed, exhausted by the day's exertions, his heart broken.

The next morning, Auguste de Mergi awoke alone in the family apartment. Recalling that his mother and grandfather had been present in these rooms only the day before, he felt all the unbearable horror of his plight come flooding into his mind afresh, and a new wave of sorrow washed over him. The profound solitude of an apartment that was once so full of life, where every moment brought some new activity, some new occupation for his hands and mind, proved so painful that he went down to ask old woman Vauthier if his grandfather might have come by the night before or early that morning; for he had awoken quite late, and he supposed that the caretaker would have informed Baron Bourlac of the legal proceedings against him if he had returned.

With a snicker, she replied that he knew full well where his grandfather must be: if he hadn't come back this morning, it could only be because he had taken up residence in the Château de Clichy. Coming from a woman who had treated him with such wheedling solicitude the night before, this taunt only heightened the young man's turmoil, and he ran off to the convalescent home on the Rue Basse-Saint-Pierre, distraught to think that his grandfather might at that moment be locked away in a prison cell.

That night Baron Bourlac had knocked at the door of the convalescent home and found himself denied entrance; he then went to Doctor Halpersohn's house, in hopes of some explanation for this refusal. The doctor did not return home until two o'clock in the morning. The old man had first come to his door at one-thirty, then gone off to wait in the Grande Allée of the Champs-Élysées; returning to the doctor's house at two-thirty, he learned from the doorman that Doctor Halpersohn had retired and could not be awakened on any account.

Finding himself adrift in this neighborhood at two-thirty in the morning, the wretched father wandered in despair along the quays and beneath the frost-covered trees of the Cours-la-Reine, waiting for day to come. At nine o'clock in the morning, he knocked at the doctor's door and asked why he was keeping his daughter under lock and key.

"Monsieur," the doctor answered, "yesterday I took your daughter's health into my hands; but at this moment it is her life that is in my hands, and you must understand that under such circumstances my decrees must be obeyed without fail. I have given your daughter a remedy that will activate the agent of the *plique* within her; and until that terrible illness has been driven out, she cannot be seen. Any strong emotion, any lapse in her treatment could well rob me of my patient and you of your daughter. If you absolutely must see her, I would ask that three doctors be consulted beforehand, so as to absolve me of all responsibility, for it could easily cost her her life."

Greatly diminished by his fatigue, the old man sank into a chair, then promptly stood up again, saying: "Forgive me, Monsieur. I have spent the night awaiting you in a state of the most terrible anxiety, for you do not know how dearly I love my daughter, whom I have tended for fifteen years as she hovered between life and death. I assure you, these eight days of waiting are a veritable torment!"

The Baron left Halpersohn's offices staggering like a drunkard. About an hour after the Jew had accompanied the old man to the staircase, his hand under his arm, Auguste de Mergi appeared at his door. The poor youth had questioned the porter at the convalescent home and learned that the father of the woman brought in yesterday had returned during the night asking to see her, and had spoken of calling on Doctor Halpersohn the next morning; it was thus at his offices that the young man might find some news of him. When Auguste de Mergi appeared in Halpersohn's office, the doctor was taking a cup of hot chocolate and a glass of water from a small round table beside him. He did not interrupt his little repast as the young man entered, but continued to dip his pieces of bread into his chocolate; for the only solid food before him was a slender loaf of bread, cut into four pieces with surgical precision—a skill that Halpersohn had practiced at length through his many travels.

"Well, young man," he said as Vanda's son crossed the threshold, "I suppose you too have come for news of your mother . . ."

"I have, Monsieur," replied Auguste de Mergi.

Auguste was then standing beside the doctor's table, and at once his eye was caught by a small stack of banknotes surrounded by piles of gold coins. In the unhappy child's present circumstances, this temptation proved stronger than his most sacred principles. On that table he glimpsed a means of saving his grandfather and the fruit of his twenty-year labor, now threatened by a conspiracy of money-hungry speculators. He could not resist. A sudden impulse overtook him, quick as a thought, an impulse justified by a sense of devotion that the child could not resist. He said to himself: "This will be my downfall, but I will be saving my mother and grandfather! . . ."

Even as his intellect struggled to rationalize the crime he was about to commit, he found himself possessed of a madman's remarkable coolness and cunning; rather than press the doctor for news of his grandfather, he continued their conversation in its current vein. As one would expect of a keen observer of the ways of men, Halpersohn had not been slow to understand what sort of life these people must live. His conversations with the Baroness de Mergi had revealed the truth, or at least a suspicion of the truth, and as a result he had come to view his new clients with a sort of benevolence, for respect and admiration were beyond his capacities.

"Well, my dear boy," he answered the young Baron familiarly, "I am keeping your mother with me for the moment, and when I give her back to you she will be young, beautiful, and in perfect health. She is one of those rare patients who offer something of real interest to a doctor; furthermore, she is my compatriot, on her mother's side. You and your grandfather shall have to find the courage to go two weeks without seeing Madame . . ."

"Madame Baroness de Mergi . . ."

"If she is a baroness, then you are a baron?" asked Halpersohn.

The theft had now been committed. The doctor had glanced down at his chocolate-soaked bread; at that same moment, Auguste had seized four folded bills and, with the casual gesture of one thrusting his hand into his trouser pocket, secreted them away.

"Yes, Monsieur, I am a baron, like my grandfather; he was Prosecutor General under the Restoration."

"You're blushing, young man . . . Come now, there's nothing to be embarrassed about; it is a perfectly common thing to be both a baron and a poor man."

"But, Monsieur, how do you know we are poor?"

"Why, through your grandfather: he tells me he spent last night in the Champs-Élysées; and although I know of no palace with a vaulted ceiling as lovely as the glimmering dome overhead at two o'clock in the morning, I assure you that the palace where your grandfather was taking his little stroll was a cold and drafty one indeed. No one stays in Château Open-Air of his own volition . . ."

"My grandfather has been here?" Auguste replied, seizing this opportunity to make his retreat. "I thank you, Monsieur. With your permission, I will return soon for news of my mother."

Leaving the doctor's office, the young Baron leapt into a cabriolet and hurried to the bailiff's, where he paid his grandfather's debt in full. The bailiff returned the promissory notes with a receipt, then told the young man to accompany one of his clerks back to the Boulevard du Mont-Parnasse, so that he might relieve the legal custodian of her duties.

"In fact, since Messieurs Barbet and Métivier live in your neighborhood," he added, "I will have my young assistant bring them their money and see that they return the repurchase agreement to you . . ."

Understanding nothing of these terms and formalities, Auguste readily assented. He took the seven hundred francs in change owed him from his four thousand francs and left at once with a clerk. He climbed into the cabriolet in a daze; now that he had achieved his aim, remorse had begun to set in. He foresaw himself dishonored, and cursed by his grandfather, whose inflexibility he knew well; he imagined his dear mother dying of grief at the news of his crime. The entire world around him seemed to take on a new appearance. All at once he felt terribly hot. He stared blindly at the snow; the houses seemed a gathering of specters. Arriving home, the Baron made a decision that only a truly honorable young man could make. He went into his mother's room in search of the diamond-studded snuffbox that the Emperor had given his grandfather, intending to send it to Doctor Halpersohn with the remaining seven hundred francs and the following letter, whose composition required several drafts:

MONSIEUR,

The fruit of my grandfather's twenty-year labor was in danger of being stolen away by usurers, and his liberty with it. Three thousand three hundred francs would spare him this fate; seeing so much gold piled up on your table, I could not resist the joy of assuring my progenitor's freedom, and of rewarding him for his many sleepless nights. I have borrowed four thousand francs from you without your consent; but since I needed only three thousand three hundred, I now send you the remaining seven hundred francs, to which I add a diamond-studded snuffbox presented to my grandfather by the Emperor, of sufficient value to make up the remainder of my debt.

Perhaps you will find it difficult to believe in the honorable intentions of one who will consider you his benefactor for the rest of his days; but if at least you will deign to say no more of an act that would be unjustifiable in any other circumstances, you will save my grandfather's life along with my mother's, and I will be your devoted slave for as long as I live.

AUGUSTE DE MERGI

Auguste sealed this letter away in a parcel with ten *louis,* a five-hundred-franc note, and the snuffbox. Carrying the package in his arms, he set off on foot; by two-thirty he had reached the Champs-Élysées, where he hired an errand boy to deliver it to Halpersohn's door. Then, placing all his hopes in the generosity of Doctor Halpersohn's spirit, he slowly returned home again by the Iéna Bridge, the Invalides, and the boulevards.

The physician had not been slow to discover the theft, or to conceive a very different opinion of his new clients. He concluded that the old man had come to his offices with robbery in mind, and that, his plan having been thwarted, he had then sent the boy. He began to doubt everything they had told him of their life, and he went directly to the offices of the Royal Prosecutor, demanding that proceedings be initiated at once.

Now, Justice proceeds with caution, and rarely does it move as swiftly as the injured party might wish; nevertheless, at around three o'clock, a police superintendent came knocking at Madame Vauthier's door, with several more agents in plainclothes loitering in the street nearby. The superintendent asked her several questions concerning her lodgers, and the widow unwittingly aggravated his suspicions.

Sensing the presence of the policemen, Népomucène concluded that the old man was about to be arrested; and since he was very fond of Monsieur Auguste, he ran to meet Monsieur Bernard the moment he saw him coming down the Avenue de l'Observatoire.

"Get away, Monsieur!" he cried. "They've come to arrest you. The bailiffs came to your rooms yesterday; they're planning to seize all your things. Mother Vauthier kept the papers from you, and I heard her say you'd be sleeping in Clichy tonight or tomorrow. Look, don't you see the bluecoats?"

With one glance the former Prosecutor-General recognized the policemen as bailiff's escorts, and he understood all.

"What about Monsieur Godefroid?"

"He's gone away, never to return. Mother Vauthier said he was a spy for your enemies . . ."

Baron Bourlac resolved to pay a call on Barbet at once; a quarter of an hour later, he was in the Rue Sainte-Catherine-d'Enfer, knocking at the old publisher's door.

"Ah! You've come for the repurchase agreement?" said Barbet in response to his victim's greeting. "Very well, here you are."

And to Baron Bourlac's great astonishment, he placed the document in his hand.

"I don't understand . . ." the old man said.

"But did you not repay your debt?" replied the publisher.

"The debt has been paid?"

"Your grandson gave the bailiff the money this morning."

"Is it true that you had a lien of seizure placed on my property yesterday?"

"Then you haven't been home for two days?" asked Barbet. "But surely a prosecutor-general knows the meaning of a warrant for civil imprisonment . . ."

Hearing these words, the Baron coolly took his leave of Barbet and returned home, assuming that the bailiff had come that day for the mysterious authors on the third floor. He walked slowly, lost in vague apprehensions, finding Népomucène's words increasingly obscure, even inexplicable. Could Godefroid really have betrayed him? He turned mechanically onto the Rue Notre-Dame-des-Champs and entered the building by the smaller door, which by chance he found open. Inside, he ran into Népomucène.

"Oh, Monsieur, come quickly! They're taking Monsieur Auguste off to prison! They collared him on the boulevard. It was him they were looking for all along! They've been interrogating him . . ."

The old man bounded forward like a tiger, ran swift as an arrow through the house and the little garden, and emerged onto the boulevard just in time to see his grandson climbing into a fiacre, flanked by three men.

"Auguste," he cried, "what is the meaning of this?"

The young man dissolved into tears and fainted dead away.

"Monsieur, I am Baron Bourlac, former Prosecutor-General," he said to the superintendent, recognizing him by his sash. "For pity's sake, tell me what is happening . . ."

"Monsieur, if you are Baron Bourlac, two words will tell you everything you wish to know: I have interrogated this young man, and unhappily he has confessed . . ."

"To what?"

"To the theft of four thousand francs from the home of Doctor Halpersohn."

"Auguste! Can this be true?"

"Grandpapa, I sent him your diamond snuffbox as security. I wanted to spare you the shame of imprisonment."

"Ah! You wretch, what have you done!" cried the Baron. "Those diamonds are false! I sold the real ones three years ago!"

The superintendent of police and his clerk cast each other a singular glance. Baron Bourlac did not fail to note that glance, so rich in meaning, and he went numb with terror.

"Monsieur Superintendent," the former Prosecutor-General resumed, "do not fear, I shall go and see the Royal Prosecutor; but I ask you to note that I was maintaining this illusion for the sake of my grandson and daughter. You must do your duty, of course; but in the name of humanity, please put my grandson in a private cell . . . I will come to the prison . . . Where are you taking him?"

"You are indeed Baron Bourlac?"

"Oh, Monsieur! . . ."

"Forgive me, but the Royal Prosecutor, the examining judge, and I find it difficult to believe that people such as you and your grandson could be involved in these doings, and, like the Doctor, we were thinking that some scoundrels might perhaps have taken your names."

He took Baron Bourlac aside and asked him, "You went to see Doctor Halpersohn this morning? . . ."

"Yes, Monsieur."

"And your grandson appeared at his door a half hour later?"

"I know nothing of that, Monsieur. I am only now returning home, and I have not seen my grandson since yesterday."

"He has shown us the notices of seizure; those and your file told me everything I needed to know," the superintendent replied. "The motivation for this crime is clear. Monsieur, I ought to arrest you as your grandson's accomplice, for your responses confirm the allegations made in the complaint; but these notices that were served on you"— and here he held out the documents—"prove beyond question that you are Baron Bourlac. Nevertheless, you must be prepared to appear before Monsieur Marest, the examining judge to whom this case has been assigned. I believe that I may waive the customary rigors, in view of your former title. As for your grandson, I will speak to Monsieur the Royal Prosecutor on my return; given that he is the grandson of a former First President, and his crime a youthful misstep, we will treat him with all possible lenience. But a complaint has been made, the delinquent has confessed, I have written up the charges, a warrant has been issued for his arrest; there is nothing I can do about that! As for his imprisonment, we will put your grandson in the Conciergerie."

"Thank you, Monsieur!" said Bourlac, deeply distraught. And he collapsed in the snow, tumbling down a slope and into a trench between the trees and the boulevard.

The superintendent of police called out for help, and Népomucène came running with the widow Vauthier. They carried the old man into the house, and Madame Vauthier asked the superintendent to send urgently for Doctor Berton as he passed by the Rue d'Enfer.

"What has happened to my grandfather?" asked poor Auguste.

"He's lost his reason, Monsieur! . . . This is what comes of thievery! . . ."

Auguste tried to leap from the fiacre and dash his head against the paving stones, but the two agents held him back.

"Come now, young man, get hold of yourself!" said the superintendent. "You have done wrong, but it is not irreparable! . . ."

"Then please, Monsieur, please tell that woman that my grandfather very likely has not eaten for twenty-four hours! . . ."

"Oh! These poor people! . . ." said the superintendent very quietly, to himself.

He stopped the fiacre and whispered a quick word into the ear of his secretary, who ran off to speak to Madame Vauthier and returned a moment later.

Doctor Berton examined Monsieur Bernard—for he knew him solely by that name—and diagnosed a particularly intense attack of fever, but once the widow Vauthier, in her own unique manner, had told him of the events preceding the attack, he thought he had better find Monsieur Alain at Saint-Jacques-du-Haut-Pas and inform him of these events. Monsieur Alain hailed an errand boy and gave him a penciled message addressed to Monsieur Nicolas, on the Rue Chanoinesse.

On his arrival at the de La Chanterie house, Godefroid had given the bundle of notes and references to Monsieur Nicolas, who spent the greater part of the night reading the first volume of Baron Bourlac's work.

The next morning Madame de La Chanterie informed the neophyte that it was time he set to work on the account books, if his resolution to join their society was still firm. After an initiation into the financial secrets of her little circle, Godefroid threw himself into this task, laboring seven or eight hours a day for several months, closely overseen by Frédéric Mongenod, who came every Sunday to inspect his work and praised his accomplishments to the heavens.

"You are a precious asset indeed for the saints among whom you live," he said, once all the accounts had been updated and clearly laid out. "From now on you will require only two or three hours each day to keep the accounts current; and in your spare time, you might assist the others in their work, if you have not lost the vocation you showed six months ago . . ."

It was then July 1838. In all the time that had passed since his adventures on the Boulevard du Mont-Parnasse, Godefroid had never once raised the subject of Baron Bourlac, eager as he was to prove himself worthy of his new friends; for, hearing no further news of his case, and finding no mention of this matter in the record of expenses, he interpreted his companions' silence on the family of Madame de La Chanterie's two tormentors as either a test of his discretion or evidence that the sublime woman's friends had avenged her at last.

Nevertheless, two months after these events, he had taken a stroll to the Boulevard du Mont-Parnasse, where he found the widow Vauthier and asked her for news of the Bernard family.

"Don't ask me where those people might have gone, my dear Monsieur Godefroid! . . . Two days after you walked off with the parcel—because it was you who snatched this deal away from my landlord, you sly rogue—some people came and took the old blowhard away. They moved everything out in twenty-four hours—just like that! None of them would say a word to me. I think he might have left for Algiers with his brigand of a grandson; because Népomucène, who always had a soft spot for that thief—and he's no better, anyhow—went looking for him in the Conciergerie and didn't find him there. He's the only one who knows where they might be, and now the good-for-nothing's run off and left me here . . . Just you try raising an abandoned child sometime! . . . That's how they repay you—they make your life a misery. I still haven't managed to replace him; every room in the house is rented, what with all these people moving into the neighborhood, and here I am all by myself, working my fingers to the bone."

Godefroid would never have obtained any further news of Baron Bourlac were it not for a chance meeting of the sort that often happens in Paris, which brought this affair to a close.

One day in September, Godefroid was walking down the great Avenue des Champs-Élysées and found himself thinking of Doctor Halpersohn as he passed by the Rue Marbeuf. "I really should go and see him, and find out if he ever cured Bourlac's daughter! . . ." he thought. "What a voice! What talent she had! . . . And she dreamt of devoting her life to God!"

Arriving at the roundabout, Godefroid crossed the street at a run to avoid the carriages bearing down upon him; reaching the opposite side, he collided with a young man walking arm in arm with a woman.

"Ho! Take care!" cried the young man. "Are you blind?"

"It's you!" answered Godefroid, recognizing the young man as Auguste de Mergi.

So well dressed was Auguste, so handsome, so dapper, so proud of the woman on his arm, that Godefroid would never have recognized him were it not for the memories then coursing through his mind.

"Why, it's dear Monsieur Godefroid!" said the lady.

Hearing the celestial tones of Vanda's enchanting voice, and seeing her upright and walking, Godefroid stood riven to the spot, as if his feet had been glued to the ground.

"Cured! . . ." he said.

"Ten days ago, he gave me permission to walk!"

"Halpersohn?"

"Yes!" she said. "But tell me, why did you never come and see us?" she went on. "Oh! But you were quite right not to. It was just a week ago that they cut off all my hair! I must wear a wig for the moment, but the doctor assured me it would grow back! . . . But what a lot of things we have to say to each other! . . . You must come and dine with us! . . . Oh! Your harmonium! . . . Oh! Monsieur . . ."

And she raised her handkerchief to her eyes.

"I will keep it as long as I live! My son will preserve it like a relic! My father searched for you all over Paris; even now, he is trying to locate his unknown benefactors, and he will die of sorrow if you do not help him to find them . . . A dark melancholy has taken root in his soul, and there are days when I can do nothing to defeat it."

Entranced by the voice of this delightful woman, so recently rescued from the tomb, and no less entranced by the voice of his own irresistible curiosity, Godefroid took the Baroness de Mergi's outstretched arm in his. Her son walked on ahead, sent off on some errand with a nod from his mother, whose meaning the young man had instantly understood.

"I will not take you very far; only to the Allée d'Antin, where we have a pretty house in the English style, all to ourselves, each with a floor of our own. Oh! We are so happy there. My father is convinced you are behind all the wonderful changes we have seen in our lives, these past few months! . . ."

"Me! . . ."

"Do you not know that a chaired professorship in comparative law has been created for my father at the Sorbonne, by recommendation of the Minister for Public Education? His first class begins in November. His great book will appear in a month, published by Cavalier and Company; they've promised him an equal share of the profits, and already they've given him an advance of thirty thousand francs, with which he is buying the house we now live in. The Ministry of Justice has granted me a pension of twelve hundred francs, as the daughter of a former magistrate; my father has his own pension, of one thousand *écus*, and as a professor he will earn another five thousand francs. With our frugal habits, we will be almost rich before long! Auguste is to begin his study of law in two months; for the moment, he is employed in the Prosecutor-General's office and earns twelve hundred francs . . . Ah! Monsieur Godefroid, you must take care not to mention Auguste's unhappy adventure in my father's presence. Every morning I bless my dear son for what he did, but to this day his grandfather has not forgiven him! His mother blesses him, Halpersohn dotes on him, but the old prosecutor will not bend."

"What adventure do you mean?"

"Ah! You have lost none of your old nobility!" cried Vanda. "What a good heart you have! . . . Your mother must be so proud of you! . . ." She stopped, as if feeling a sudden pang in her breast.

"I swear to you that I know nothing of this matter," said Godefroid.

"Ah! You really don't know!"

And, beaming with admiration for her son, she artlessly told him of the unauthorized loan Auguste had taken from the doctor's desk.

"If it is true that we can say nothing of this before Baron Bourlac," Godefroid remarked, "then you must tell me now how your son avoided imprisonment..."

"But," answered Vanda, "I believe I have already told you that he works for the Prosecutor-General, who has shown him the most perfect benevolence. He spent no more than forty-eight hours in the Conciergerie, where he was placed in the director's immediate care. Finding Auguste's beautiful, sublime letter that evening, the good doctor withdrew his complaint; and by the intervention of a former President of the Royal Court whom my father has never been able to find, the prosecutor voided the superintendent's report and the warrant for Auguste's arrest. In short, of this entire affair there remains no trace, except in my heart, and my son's conscience, and the mind of his grandfather, who now addresses Auguste as *vous*, and treats him just as he would a stranger. Only yesterday, Halpersohn came to plead my son's case; but my father, who refuses my own entreaties as well—and yet he loves me so dearly!—only answered: 'You are the injured party; you may pardon him, and you must; but I am responsible for the thief ... and in my days as a prosecutor, I never forgave!...' 'But you will kill your daughter!' answered Halpersohn, right there before me. My father made no reply."

"And who was it that rescued your family, then?"

"A gentleman whom we believe to be responsible for discharging the Queen's favors."

"And what does this gentleman look like?" asked Godefroid.

"He's a lean, solemn man, sad, much like my father ... It was he who had my father brought to the new house during his attack of fever. Would you believe it? As soon as my father had recovered, they took me from the convalescent home and moved me into that house with him. I awoke to find myself in my own room again, just as if I had never been away! Halpersohn—who seems quite charmed by our benefactor, I know not how—then told me of all the sufferings my father had endured! Imagine him selling the diamonds from his snuffbox! Imagine my son and my father going without bread, and putting on such a show for my sake!... Oh! Monsieur Godefroid!... They are martyrs, both of them ... What words can I find to thank my father?...

And my son? . . . Only by suffering for them as they did for me can I ever hope to repay them."

"And does that grand gentleman have something of a military bearing? . . ."

"Ah! You know him! . . ." cried Vanda as they approached the front steps of their house.

She seized Godefroid's hand with the force of one in the throes of a nervous fit; opening the door to the drawing room, she pulled him inside and cried out: "Father! Monsieur Godefroid knows our benefactor."

Baron Bourlac, now dressed in a manner befitting an eminent former magistrate, rose and held his hand out to Godefroid, saying, "I knew it all along!"

With a gesture, Godefroid attempted to deny his involvement in the righting of this family's wrongs, but the old Prosecutor-General left him no chance to speak.

"Ah! Monsieur," he said at once, "only Providence can be more powerful, only Love can be more ingenious, only Motherhood can be more clairvoyant than your friends—they embody the spirit of those three great divinities at once! . . . I bless the chance to which we owe this meeting; for Monsieur Joseph has vanished into thin air, avoiding all the traps that I set in my quest to discover his true name and address. I was beginning to fear he had eluded me forever, and I thought I might die of frustration . . . Here, read his letter. But is it really true? You know him?"

Godefroid took the letter and read the following words:

Monsieur Baron Bourlac, by the order of a charitable woman, we have expended a total of fifteen thousand francs to remedy your misfortunes. Make note of this figure, so that this sum might be repaid, by you or your descendants, when your family's prosperity permits it; for it is the money of the poor. When such restitution becomes possible, you may deposit the money with the brothers Mongenod, bankers. May God forgive your errors!

Five crosses formed the mysterious signature at the bottom of the page, which Godefroid now handed back to the Baron.

"The five crosses, . . ." he said to himself.

"Ah! Monsieur," said the old man, "you who know all, you who were the envoy of that mysterious lady . . . tell me her name!"

"Her name!" cried Godefroid. "Her name! That you must never ask, you fool! You must never seek to meet her! Ah! Madame," he went on, taking Madame de Mergi's hand in his own trembling hands, "if you value your father's reason, see that he remains ignorant, see that he does nothing more to uncover this secret!"

The father, the daughter, and the son stood frozen in deepest astonishment.

"Who is this woman?" asked Vanda.

"She is the one who saved your daughter's life," Godefroid went on, looking at the old man, "who returned her to you young, beautiful, fresh, reanimated, who pulled her from her grave; the one who spared you your grandson's shame! who offered you a happy old age, wreathed in honors and respect, the one who saved you all . . ."

Here he paused.

"She is an innocent woman, imprisoned for twenty years by your hand!" Godefroid cried, speaking to Baron Bourlac. "A woman on whom you inflicted the most cruel suffering, whose saintliness you insulted, from whose arms you ripped a beautiful daughter to send her to the most horrible of all deaths, beneath the blade of the guillotine! . . ."

With this Vanda collapsed insensible into an armchair. Godefroid bounded into the hallway and ran down the Allée d'Antin as fast as his legs could carry him.

"If you hope ever to be forgiven," said Baron Bourlac to his grandson, "follow that man and find out where he lives! . . ."

Auguste disappeared like a shot.

At eight-thirty the next morning, Baron Bourlac came knocking at the venerable door on the Rue Chanoinesse and asked the porter if Madame de La Chanterie was at home. The porter directed him toward the tower.

Happily, the brothers were then assembling for breakfast, and Godefroid spied the Baron in the courtyard through one of the small windows that illuminated the staircase. He scarcely had time to run down the stairs, burst into the drawing room, where the others had gathered, and cry out: "Baron de Bourlac!"

Hearing this name, Madame de La Chanterie fled into her room on the arm of Father de Vèze.

"You will not enter, hellhound!" cried Manon, recognizing the prosecutor and blocking his way into the drawing room. "Have you come to kill Madame?"

"Come now, Manon, let Monsieur through..." said Monsieur Alain.

Manon fell into a chair as if both legs had failed her at once.

"Gentlemen," said the Baron in a tone of deep emotion, nodding to Godefroid and Monsieur Joseph and bowing cordially to the two others, "the beneficiary of a good deed can expect certain rights!"

"You owe us nothing, Monsieur," said the good Alain, "your debt is to God alone..."

"You are saints, and you have the serenity of saints," said the former magistrate. "Listen to me, I beg you!... I know that the acts of superhuman kindness that have rained down on me over these past eighteen months are the work of a person I gravely injured in the exercise of my duty; it took me fifteen years to realize her innocence, and that, Messieurs, is the only remorse I have ever felt in all my long career. Listen to me! I have so little time left to live, but I will lose what life remains to me—a life so dear to my daughter and grandson, whom Madame de La Chanterie has saved—if I cannot obtain her forgiveness. Gentlemen, I shall kneel at the entrance to Notre-Dame until she consents to speak just one word to me... I will be awaiting her there... I will kiss the ground beneath her feet, I will find tears to melt her heart, I whose tears have gone dry as dust as I watched my daughter suffer year after year..."

Slowly the door to Madame de La Chanterie's bedroom opened; Father de Vèze slipped out, silent as a shadow, and said to Monsieur Joseph, "The sound of that man's voice is killing Madame."

"Ah! Then she is there! She passes this way to enter her room!" said Baron Bourlac.

He fell to his knees and kissed the floor, dissolving into tears. In a heart-wrenching voice, he cried out: "In the name of Jesus, who died on the cross, forgive me! Forgive me! For my daughter has suffered a thousand deaths!"

The old man slumped to the floor, so still that the witnesses to this scene feared he was dead. At that moment, Madame de La Chanterie appeared at her door like a specter, leaning against the jamb as if unable to stand on her own.

"In the name of Louis XVI and Marie-Antoinette, whom I can see even now on the scaffold, in the name of Madame Élisabeth, and my daughter, and yours, in the name of Jesus, I forgive you . . ."

Hearing these last few words, the former prosecutor raised his eyes and said, "So does an angel find vengeance."

Monsieur Joseph and Monsieur Nicolas helped the Baron Bourlac to his feet and led him into the courtyard; Godefroid went off in search of a carriage. When the sound of rolling wheels could be heard in the street, Monsieur Nicolas led the old man outside.

"Do not return, Monsieur," he said, "lest you kill the mother as well. The power of God is infinite, but human nature has its limits."

That day Godefroid was won over heart and soul to the Order of the Brothers of Consolation.

NOTES

The Wrong Side of Paris is the translation for the French title *L'Envers de l'histoire contemporaine,* literally "The Underside of Contemporary History." Rather more elegant in French than in English, the title also contains some important clues about Balzac's vision of this novel, of his *Comédie humaine,* and of fiction in the larger sense. "L'envers," the *underside,* suggests that this novel will portray a different aspect of life from the usual Balzacian scenes of love and betrayal, greed and ambition in the high society and politics of Paris, the familiar subject matter of the nearly one hundred novels and short stories that Balzac published prior to this, the final installment of his massive fictional cycle *La Comédie humaine (The Human Comedy).* The second part of the title indicates Balzac's belief that the novelist, himself especially, should function as the chronicler of the world he lived in. In the foreword he wrote for *La Comédie humaine,* Balzac famously described himself as the secretary, or scribe, of society.

The two episodes in which the novel is presented appeared in serial version some three years apart. *Madame de La Chanterie* appeared in the literary monthly *Le Musée des familles* in 1845; the second episode, *The Initiate,* appeared in 1848, in the daily newspaper *Le Spectateur républicain,* precisely as the July Revolution was taking place.

—James Madden

FIRST EPISODE. MADAME DE LA CHANTERIE

P. 3. The title Balzac gave to the first installment of this episode was *Les Frères de la consolation,* or *The Brothers of Consolation.* This is the name that Balzacians give to the group that Madame de La Chanterie has gathered around herself.

P. 5, LL. 8–11. *the Paris of the Romans . . . and Louis-Philippe:* Balzac's historical overview of Paris runs from the *Roman* city called Lutetia or Lutèce, through the Germanic *Franks* who gave their name to the country (the Frankish kings—especially Clovis [ca. 465–511], who first converted to Christianity—are by tradition counted among the kings of France); the *Normans,* who took their name from the Norsemen and other Vikings who raided up the Seine in the eighth, ninth, and early tenth centuries; the *Burgundians,* referring here to the armies of the rebellious Dukes of Burgundy of the fourteenth and fifteenth centuries, who rivaled their royal cousins the Kings of France in political and military power; the *Valois* dynasty, which ruled France from the ascension of Philippe VI in 1389 until the death of Henri III in 1589 and was succeeded by the Bourbons in the person of *Henri IV* (born 1553, reigned 1589–1610), the grandfather of the legendary *Louis XIV* (born 1638, reigned 1643–1715); through *Napoleon* Bonaparte (1769–1821), who took power as First Consul in 1799, proclaimed himself Emperor in 1804, and reigned until 1814, followed by his brief return to power, known as the Hundred Days, before meeting final defeat and exile after the battle of Waterloo in 1815; and through the increasing authoritarianism of the restored Bourbons, which led to the coup d'état known as the July Revolution of 1830, which brought to the throne the Bourbons' cousin *Louis-Philippe* (born 1773, reigned 1830–48, died in exile 1850), former Duc d'Orléans and head of the younger branch of the Bourbon family. Throughout Louis-Philippe's eighteen-year reign, conspiracies of varying degrees of seriousness sought to restore the elder, or "legitimate," branch of the royal family. Louis-Philippe was to be the only monarch of the Orléans dynasty, as a republican revolution drove him and his family into exile in 1848, almost exactly as Balzac was completing this novel.

L. 13. *Sainte Geneviève:* a patron saint of Paris, along with the martyred third-century Saint Denis. Geneviève was a fifth-century abbess who oversaw construction of the first church in honor of Saint Denis and who gave Parisians spiritual comfort and encouragement in the face of the assault by Attila and the army of the Huns. The domed building

Balzac refers to, built as a church dedicated to Sainte Geneviève in the late eighteenth century, was designated the "Panthéon" by the Revolution, destined to receive the remains of national heroes such as Voltaire and Mirabeau. Throughout the nineteenth century, the building changed functions with the changing governments before finally being designated once again the Panthéon in 1885, at the death of Victor Hugo, whose remains were entombed there. At the time Balzac wrote, the church of Sainte Geneviève was designated a panthéon.

LL. 15–16. *the Hôtel de Ville and the Hôtel-Dieu:* The Hôtel de Ville (or town hall), the seat of the Parisian municipal government, was located on the Right Bank on the Place de Grève; the Hôtel-Dieu, on the Île de la Cité, was a charity hospital maintained by the Church, the oldest such institution in Paris.

L. 18. *the wretched huddle of houses:* In the early nineteenth century, central Paris still contained many pockets of dilapidated housing that were cleared out over the course of the century, most aggressively by Haussmann under the Second Empire. Balzac was fascinated by the contrast between these hovels and the grandeur of buildings like the Louvre and Notre-Dame.

L. 24. *the ruins of The archbishop's palace:* The Archepiscopal Palace of Paris, which once stood just south of Notre-Dame, was destroyed in a liberal-led political riot in 1831. It was never rebuilt, and in 1845 the "Terrain" Balzac describes was made into a public park, today known as the Square Jean XXIII.

L. 29. *the faubourgs Saint-Antoine and Saint-Marceau:* These working-class districts were located on the eastern and southeast ends of Paris, respectively.

P. 6, L. 24. *a sou:* According to the old monetary system, this coin was worth five *centîmes,* twenty *sous* equaling one franc.

L. 32. *Panurge's sheep:* from the comic epic *Pantagruel,* by François Rabelais (1494–1553), a writer Balzac greatly admired. Panurge, the companion of the giant Pantagruel, watches as his sheep are all killed when they blindly follow one of their number to their deaths. Like lemmings in English, *Panurge's sheep* have become proverbial in French to describe those who are unable or unwilling to think for themselves.

L. 33. *what France calls Equality:* Balzac was a political conservative, regarding the Revolution of 1789 as a monumental catastrophe and the July Revolution as a mistake. He believed that France must return to the traditional values exemplified by "Throne and Altar," the Bourbon monarchy and the Catholic Church. In the famous 1842 preface Balzac wrote for an edition of *La Comédie humaine,* he declared: *"J'écris à la lueur de deux Vérités éternelles: la Religion, la Monarchie."* ("I write by the light of two eternal Truths: Religion [and] Monarchy.")

P. 7, L. 6. *Werner:* Zacharias Werner (1768–1823), a Protestant-born Prussian poet who converted to Catholicism late in life.

L. 20. *the Chaussée d'Antin:* a fashionable neighborhood on the Right Bank, suggesting affluence and elegance.

L. 24. notaire: A *notaire* was a legal professional who supervised contracts, including wills and marriage contracts. Balzac himself studied briefly to be a lawyer, and the business of *notaires* figures prominently in his realistic fiction. The opening scene of *Le Colonel Chabert* (1831) famously depicts a contemporary law office.

L. 25. *Father Liautard's academy:* a school founded in 1804 in the Rue Notre-Dame-des-Champs, as an alternative to the secularism of the state schools.

P. 8, L. 5. *purchase a situation for their son:* At the time, it was necessary to purchase licenses and patents in order to practice law.

P. 9, L. 19. *The Revolution of 1830:* also known as the July Revolution. The increasing authoritarianism of the government of Charles X provoked an uprising in Paris that led to the exile of the elder branch of the Bourbon family and the advent of Louis-Philippe d'Orléans to the throne under a more moderate constitutional monarchy *(see note for p. 5, ll. 8–11, p. 210).*

LL. 29–30. *the Party of Movement and the Party of Resistance:* The Party of Movement, under the nominal leadership of the Marquis de Lafayette, hoped that the July Revolution would be merely a beginning, that liberalism would grow stronger under the new government. The more conservative Party of Resistance, which triumphed in 1832, wanted the reforms incorporated in the 1830 constitution to be a new status quo.

P. 10, L. 7. *Auteuil:* This then-suburban village west of Paris was incorporated into the capital in the late nineteenth century.

P. 11, L. 17. *the Bois de Boulogne:* The paths and avenues of this large forest on the western edge of Paris were a place for fashionable Parisians to see and be seen.

L. 18. *decoration on his breast:* probably a reference to the Cross of the Legion of Honor, an order founded by Napoleon in 1803 and adopted by the Bourbons and later the July Monarchy. Critics said that the decoration was devalued as it was awarded to ever-increasing numbers throughout the first half of the century, essentially as a bribe to ambitious bourgeois.

P. 12, L. 8. *La Fontaine:* One of the most enduringly popular writers in France, Jean de La Fontaine (1621–95) is best known for composing the verse *Fables,* largely based on Aesop.

LL. 31–32. *the private boarding houses of the Latin Quarter:* Balzac depicted life in these *pensions* in his masterwork *Le Père Goriot (Old Goriot).*

P. 13, LL. 1, 34. *Rue Chanoinesse . . . Rue Massillon:* Although the neighborhood has been almost entirely rebuilt over the course of the last two centuries, many of the streets on the north side of Notre-Dame, including these two, are still to be found.

P. 15, LL. 1–2. *the Louis XII staircases at the Château of Blois:* Louis XII reigned from 1489 to 1515. The Château of Blois is a royal château in a town in the Loire valley which shows the influence of many different eras. The ornate open staircases are often referred to as the François I staircases, after Louis's successor.

L. 5. *"the assaults of the Normans":* The Norse raiders of the eighth, ninth, and early tenth centuries invaded towns up the Seine as far as Paris and even beyond.

L. 6. *"first palace of the kings of Paris":* The Île de la Cité was the site of the earliest royal residences in Paris. The still-extant Conciergerie was a royal palace until the construction of the Louvre in the fourteenth century, when it became a prison.

LL. 7–8. *"the great Canon Fulbert, the uncle of Héloïse":* The Héloïse (1101–64) in question was the wife of Pierre Abélard (1079–1142), one of the most brilliant theologians of his time. The wealthy canon Fulbert (ca. 1080–1142), who made his fortune selling relics of dubious provenance, hired the young scholar as a tutor to his bright niece, Héloïse. The two were secretly married, and when Héloïse was subsequently found to be pregnant, the enraged Fulbert had Abélard abducted and castrated. The two lovers were then sent to distant abbeys, but they maintained a correspondence that is one of the touchstones of French literature.

L. 18. *the Sisters of Charity:* also known as the *Soeurs Grises,* the "Gray Sisters." The order was founded by Saint Vincent de Paul (1581–1660) *(see note for p. 48, l. 11, p. 217).*

P. 16, L. 19. *carmelite-gray:* another reference to a religious order. The Carmelites were a mendicant order of nuns; their most famous member was Saint Theresa of Avila.

L. 27. *the Faubourg Saint-Germain:* Roughly corresponding to the modern seventh *arrondissement* on the Left Bank, the Faubourg Saint-Germain was the most aristocratic neighborhood in Paris, and a symbol of the most reactionary factions of royalist politics.

L. 32. *yellow gloves:* Like the rest of Godefroid's outfit, yellow gloves were emblematic of dandyism.

P. 17, L. 35. *"Councillor to Parliament":* The *parlements* of the *Ancien Régime* were not legislative bodies but judicial courts; Monsieur de Boisfrelon would have served as a magistrate.

P. 19, L. 36–P. 20, L. 1. *what the English call* comfort: Although the French now use the word *confort,* in Balzac's time "comfort" was associated with the prosperous English; this is another sign of Godefroid's dandyism.

P. 20, LL. 30–32. *the Houses of Nucingen . . . Palma and Company:* all members of Balzac's cast of recurring characters. The ruthless Baron de *Nucingen* is one of the most frequently reappearing characters, notably in *La Maison Nucingen (The House of Nucingen)*; the ambitious *du Tillet* first appears in *La Grandeur et la décadence de César Birotteau (The Rise and Fall of César Birotteau)*; the politically ambitious *Keller Brothers* are minor characters, based on such banker-politicians as Casimir Perier and Jacques Laffitte; *Palma* is a minor character who hovers between the worlds of high finance and low usury.

P. 21, L. 10. *Fontaine:* The story of the aristocratic Fontaine family, including their profitable marriages to such rich bourgeois as the Mongenods and the Grossetêtes, is told in *Le Bal de Sceaux (The Sceaux Ball)*.

L. 13. *the Vandenesse family:* One of the most aristocratic families of Balzac's fictional world, the Vandenesses appear most prominently in *Le Lys dans la vallée (The Lily of the Valley)*.

L. 20. *the Peerage:* This refers not just to the aristocracy as a class, but to the Chamber of Peers, the upper house of the French legislature under both the Restoration and the July Monarchy. Peers were named by the King, and the chamber was heavily weighted with nobles. Membership denoted undisputed social and political success for politically ambitious bourgeois, called *parvenus* and *arrivistes* by their better-born detractors.

L. 24. *. . . and a garden in back:* These great townhouses, *hôtels particuliers,* were symbolic of wealth and social status.

L. 33. *a Polytechnic education:* Founded by the Revolutionary government in 1794, the *École Polytechnique* teaches military engineering and the sciences; the school was and is known for its academic rigor.

P. 23, L. 32. *"the religious orders . . . our land":* a consequence of the Revolution. The National Assembly outlawed religious orders in 1792. Although the restrictions were eased by laws of the Empire and Restoration governments, the orders found it difficult to re-establish themselves.

P. 24, L. 8. *fiacre:* a public carriage; a hackney cab.

P. 26, LL. 2–3. *the House of Bourbon's elder branch: See note for p. 5, ll. 8–11, p. 210.*

LL. 19–20. *the Café Anglais and Théâtre des Variétés:* The former, in the Boulevard des Italiens, and the latter, in the Rue Montmartre, were both haunts of the elegant *beau monde* under the July Monarchy and in Balzac's fiction.

P. 28, L. 29. *model farm:* Model farms, sponsored by the government or by private parties seeking to improve agriculture, were popular in the early nineteenth century.

P. 29, L. 1. *arpents:* The arpent was equal to about .85 acre.

L. 30. *the Gendarmerie:* the military forces in charge of preserving domestic order under the Ancien Régime.

L. 32. *"the Royal Court of Paris":* not the entourage of the King, but one of the high judicial courts of the *parlement (see note for p. 17, l. 35, p. 214).*

L. 33. *August 1830:* The implication is that Monsieur Joseph refused to serve the July government, that he is a good royalist.

L. 36. *Marquis de Montauran:* The name Montauran comes from the novel *Les Chouans, ou la Bretagne en 1800 (The Chouans, or Brittany in 1800),* Balzac's first success as a writer and the first novel incorporated into what would become *La Comédie humaine.* The *Chouans* (from the word in Breton dialect for "owl") were counterrevolutionary insurgents, spurred on by priests and nobles, who rose up against the republican governments in 1792–93 and again in 1799–1800. Balzac's novel tells the story of Monsieur Nicolas's elder brother, who becomes ensnared in a political conspiracy while attempting to take command of a group of *Chouan* fighters. As the reader will see, Balzac used this first novel of his cycle as an intertext for *L'Envers,* which would prove to be the final novel of *La Comédie humaine.*

P. 30, LL. 8–9. *the Consulate:* The first government headed by Napoleon Bonaparte, the Consulate lasted from 1799 until the declaration of the Empire in 1804.

P. 32, L. 33. *"the Trappists of old"*: The monasteries of the Trappist order were perhaps the most austere in Europe, remarkable especially for their strict maintenance of a vow of silence.

P. 34, L. 17. *the celestial blue of her gaze*: Madame de La Chanterie is described as having brown eyes on page 16 (line 16); such inconsistencies with regard to details—ages, dates, physical characteristics—are not uncommon in *La Comédie humaine*, usually, if not in this case, owing to the interconnecting nature of individual texts. This particular discrepancy is probably the result of Balzac's haste in composition.

L. 36. Imitation of Christ: or the *Imitatio Cristi*, a fifteenth-century devotional work. The authorship of the *Imitation* was for centuries disputed; scholars now generally agree that it is the work of Thomas à Kempis (ca. 1380–1471). In *La Cousine Bette*, also written in the late 1840s, the unhappy Adeline Hulot also turns to the *Imitation* for spiritual comfort.

P. 36, L. 28. *hôtel*: the French word for a great Parisian townhouse.

P. 38, L. 29. *the Rue Mouffetard*: the main artery of the Faubourg Saint-Marceau, the poorest district in Paris *(see note for p. 5, l. 29, p. 211)*. The street was called the "Boulevard des Italiens du faubourg" for the cheap cafés and taverns found there, and it is now popular with Parisian students and tourists for the same reason.

P. 39, L. 25. *Gerson*: Jean de Gerson (1363–1429), a prominent fifteenth-century theologian and Chancellor of the University of Paris, widely believed by French partisans to be the author of the *Imitation of Christ*.

P. 41, LL. 22–24. *"Bossuet . . . du Guesclin"*: Jacques-Bénigne *Bossuet* (1627–1702), Bishop of Meaux and a celebrated orator and writer, was a great defender of the authority and orthodoxy of the Catholic Church and the absolute monarchy of Louis XIV. Blaise *Pascal* (1623–62), scientist, mathematician, and writer, was heavily influenced by the pious and austere Jansenist movement. He wrote the famous *Provincial Letters* to advance the Jansenist cause against their Jesuit adversaries. In literature, Pascal is best remembered for his *Pensées*, haunting fragments of notes that he left for a planned *Defense of the Christian Religion*, which he left incomplete when he died. Jean *Racine* (1639–99) was, with Pierre Corneille, the greatest tragedian of the Golden Age of Louis XIV; his plays, especially the later ones based on Old Testament stories, reflect his Jansenist upbringing and his late-in-life return to his faith. *Saint Louis* or King Louis IX (born 1214, reigned 1226–70) was canonized for his virtuous rule and the two crusades he led. *Louis XIV* (born 1638, reigned 1643–1715) became increasingly pious as he grew older. *Raphaël,* or Raffaello Sanzio (1483–1520), studied with Michelangelo and was patronized by several popes; his religious works include *The Marriage of the Virgin* and *The Seated Virgin. Michelangelo* Buonarroti (1475–1564) sculpted the *Pietà* and painted the Sistine Chapel ceiling. Cardinal *Ximenes* (1436–1517), a powerful prelate and politician, counselor and confessor to Isabella of Castile, later Grand Inquisitor of Spain, played a vital role in the unification of Spain. Pierre Terrail, Lord of *Bayard* (1476–1524), was a great soldier in the service of Louis XII and François I, known as much for his virtue as for his courage on the battlefield. Bertrand *du Guesclin* (ca. 1315–1380) was the Constable of France under Kings Charles V and VI of France; his fierce courage made him one of the greatest heroes of the Middle Ages.

P. 42, L. 31. *Vernisset.* This minor character appears in several of Balzac's later works. He was to have played a major role in the unfinished *Femme auteur (The Woman Author),* which Balzac left unfinished. The dishonorable behavior which Balzac sketched out for Vernisset in that project—as he schemes to marry a rich heiress—explains his need of redemption at the hands of Madame de La Chanterie.

P. 44, L. 14. *the Countess de Cinq-Cygne.* The extremely romantic heroine of *Une ténébreuse affaire (A Shadowy Affair),* the Countess Laurence de Cinq-Cygne is one of the most fervent royalists of Balzac's aristocracy. In that novel, the countess becomes embroiled in a royalist conspiracy, with tragic consequences.

P. 46, L. 19. *"Saint Paul's Epistle on Charity".* Several of Paul's epistles discuss charity, but it appears that Balzac is referring here to the First Epistle to the Corinthians, including the well-known passage from chapter 13 in which the Apostle offers "a still more excellent way" of following Christ's example, through love, or charity. The Latin root of the word *charity, charité* in French, is *caritas,* or fraternal love; i.e., Madame de La Chanterie and her coreligionists express their Christian love of humanity through their charitable acts. "If I speak in tongues of men and angels, but have not love [charity], I am a noisy gong or a clanging cymbal" (1 Cor. 13.1) . . . "Love bears all things, believes all things, hopes all things, endures all things" (1 Cor. 13.7).

L. 24. *"the* Thousand and One Nights": This work enjoyed a certain vogue among the Romantics.

P. 48, L. 11. *Saint Vincent de Paul.* It was while serving as almoner to prisoners at hard labor that this priest was moved to devote his life to alleviating the misery of the poor. Saint Vincent (1581–1660) was the founder of the Congregation of the Mission and the Sisters of Charity *(see note for p. 15, l. 18, p. 213)*. He was canonized in 1737. Balzac insists on the physical resemblance between his character and Saint Vincent.

P. 49, L. 15. *Sterne's Uncle Toby:* Laurence Sterne's *Tristram Shandy* was a frequent point of reference for Balzac. Tristram's uncle Toby incarnates sentimentality, even passion, in opposition to his abstrusely intellectual brother Walter Shandy, Tristram's father.

LL. 22–23. *"'98, a time . . . survive":* Under the Directorate, 1795–99, the worst violence of the Terror of 1793–94 was past, but politics still made Paris a dangerous place; arrest and even execution were not unheard of.

L. 29. *1793:* the height of the Terror, with the execution of Louis XVI in January and Marie-Antoinette in October, the passage of the laws instituting the Terror, and the establishment of the infamous Committee for Public Safety in April.

P. 50, LL. 26–27. *the Grand Conseil:* another high court in the judiciary of the Ancien Régime.

L. 29. *gold* louis: a coin worth 24 francs in the late eighteenth century, fixed at 20 francs in 1803. Monsieur Alain's coins were worth 24 francs each.

L. 31. assignats: paper money issued by the Revolutionary government in 1789. Through the 1790s they depreciated dramatically; eventually they were worth next to nothing compared to gold and silver coin.

L. 32. *Les Grassins:* a *collège,* or secondary school, founded by a rich magistrate in 1569, situated in the Saint-Jacques neighborhood.

L. 34. *Monsieur Bordin:* Bordin appears in *A Shadowy Affair* as lawyer for the Simeuse twins, cousins and coconspirators of Laurence de Cinq-Cygne, who are arrested by the Imperial government *(see note for p. 82, l. 21, p. 224).*

P. 51, L. 9. The Marriage of Figaro: Beaumarchais's play, the sequel to his *Barber of Seville,* was a huge success, owing in part to the publicity it received from its initial interdiction by royal censors, including Louis XVI himself, who saw subversion in the anti-aristocratic comedy. Its début after more than five years' delay was a huge social and cultural event. Mongenod's attendance bespeaks not only a certain affluence and social position, but also liberal politics. Mozart's opera is based on Beaumarchais's play.

L. 21. *Voltairean:* It would be difficult to overstate the popularity of Voltaire among Parisian high society in the last decades of the Ancien Régime. The adjective implies skepticism, liberalism, and anticlericalism.

P. 52, L. 9. écus: The *écu* was worth three francs; the fact that the debt is in *assignats (see note for p. 50, l. 31, p. 218)* implies that the three-thousand-franc sum is grossly inflated.

L. 14. *General Mongenod:* Rapid rise in the ranks of the Army was not uncommon in the Revolutionary era. The most famous example, of course, is Napoleon Bonaparte, who in 1798 was not yet thirty but was already a national hero as a result of his victories in Italy.

P. 53, LL. 31–32. *"some Molière valet . . . doddering Géronte":* two characters typical of the farces of Molière (born Jean-Baptiste Poquelin, 1622–73), the great comic playwright of the seventeenth century. His masterpieces include *The Misanthrope* and *Tartuffe.*

P. 54, L. 10. *the Saint-Roch neighborhood:* around the church of Saint-Roch, just northeast of the Louvre on the Right Bank.

L. 11. *Citizen Mongenod:* The terms *Madame* and *Monsieur* being judged aristocratic, the Revolutionary custom of using *Citoyen* and *Citoyenne* (literally, "citizen" and "citizeness") as forms of address continued into the early years of Bonaparte's reign as First Consul.

P. 56, L. 11. livres: The *livre* was equal to one franc. The two terms were used interchangeably in Balzac's time.

L. 22. *the Châtelet:* Named after a former defensive fort on whose ruins it was built, the Châtelet was the site of a correctional tribunal under the Ancien Régime.

P. 57, L. 18. *"the King, I mean the Directorate":* Although officially a republic, the *Directorate* became increasingly dictatorial. Notoriously corrupt, the *Directorate* was swept away in the 1799 coup that brought Bonaparte to power.

P. 58, LL. 24–25. *a real Peru:* that is, a source of wealth, the mines of Spanish South America having become proverbial.

P. 59, L. 8. *Madame Scio:* Claudine-Angélique Legrand (1770–1807), a famous soprano.

LL. 22–23. *"a disastrous time for France's military ambitions":* The reverses experienced by Revolutionary armies in Germany and Italy were the beginning of the end of the Directorate *(see note above for p. 57, l. 18).* Young General Bonaparte would stage his successful coup in November 1799 *(see note for p. 60, l. 8).*

L. 24. *"the price of government securities"*: The *rentes*, as they were called, were the primary financial market in France at the time; the fluctuating prices of these securities served as a barometer indicating the health of the successive governments of the Revolutionary era.

P. 60, L. 8. dix-huit brumaire: November 9, 1799, according to the Revolutionary calendar, the date of the coup d'état in which Bonaparte swept away the Directorate and established the Consulate, which in a short time became a virtual dictatorship under the young Corsican general.

L. 10. *the battle of Marengo:* On June 14, 1800, this stunning victory over the Austrians in northern Italy solidified Bonaparte's position in Paris.

L. 15. *First Consul:* Bonaparte's official title reflected his superiority over the other two Consuls, Cambacérès and Lebrun, who were more like ministers to the *de facto* leader of the government.

L. 20. *Vlissingen:* a small Dutch port city.

P. 63, L. 24. *Monsieur Birotteau:* The perfume merchant is the hero of *La Grandeur et décadence de César Birotteau (The Rise and Fall of César Birotteau).*

P. 65, LL. 13–14. *"Only since 1815 . . . to travelers"*: The ultimate fall of Napoleon after Waterloo brought an end to the blockades the British had attempted to enforce on French-controlled Europe in an effort to strangle Bonaparte economically. British ships seized any vessels, notably those of the young and weak United States, suspected of trading with France or with nations under French control.

LL. 17–18. *"the unification of Holland with the French Empire"*: In 1810, Napoleon, enraged by the Dutch merchants who flouted his trade embargo against Great Britain, brought an end to the fiction of Dutch independence, which had existed since Revolutionary armies conquered Holland in 1795 and established a sister republic. Napoleon had installed his younger brother Louis as King of Holland in 1806, but Louis came to believe in his crown and sided with the Dutch against his brother. Louis fled to Austria when his brother deposed him.

P. 67, L. 21. *Popinot:* The saintly magistrate Jean-Jules Popinot plays a major role in the novella *L'Interdiction (A Commission of Lunacy),* in which we see him conducting his discreet charity. The Faubourg Saint-Marcel (or Marceau) was a working-class neighborhood on the east end of Paris, south of the Seine.

P. 68, LL. 35–36. Transire benefaciendo: from the New Testament, Acts 10:38: ". . . God anointed Jesus of Nazareth with the Holy Spirit; [and] he went about doing good and healing all that were oppressed by the devil, for God was with him"; roughly translated as "Go forth and do good works."

P. 69, L. 9. *the Baron de Nucingen:* the richest and most rapacious of Balzac's bankers *(see note for p. 20, ll. 30–32, p. 214).* Oddly enough, his twenty-five-million-franc fortune, while enormous, is relatively modest compared to those of the great bankers of Balzac's time.

L. 18. *Sardanapalus:* legendary king of the Assyrians.

LL. 35–36 *the influence of a given . . . inhabitants:* The physical resemblance between people and their environment is a frequent motif in *La Comédie humaine.*

P. 71, L. 13. *the Charenton asylum:* The most famous inmate of this mental institution just west of Paris was the Marquis de Sade.

P. 73, L. 20. *the crusade of Philippe Auguste:* King Philippe II Augustus (born 1165, reigned 1180–1223) led the Third Crusade alongside Richard the Lion-Hearted of England, against whom he would later go to war. He also greatly expanded the authority of the French crown against the great feudal lords.

LL. 23–24. *"our war with the principality of Hanover":* France went to war with the small German state of Hanover—ruled by the Hanoverian kings of England—during the Seven Years' War (1756–63).

LL. 29–30. *"the Bessin region . . . Caen and Saint-Lô":* This coastal region of western Normandy lies along the English Channel just west of Brittany.

P. 75, L. 5. *"women in those days":* raised their own children rather than sending them out to be nursed and raised by foster parents. Balzac himself was raised by a foster family until the age of four. The maternal trends of the late eighteenth century were generally attributed to the influence of Rousseau.

L. 11. *the National Assembly:* The Estates General convoked by Louis XVI in 1789 declared itself a National Assembly in June and soon imposed sweeping reforms on every aspect of French politics and society.

LL. 12–13. *"judicial posts acquired at so high a cost":* Under the Ancien Régime, judicial posts were among the offices sold by the Crown as a means of generating revenue.

L. 34. *"the overturning of the laws":* Among the laws overturned were those that regulated inheritance and preserved noble patrimonies.

L. 36. *the revolutionary tribunal:* The judicial instrument of the Terror, these tribunals were authorized by the Convention in Paris to try and convict those accused of political crimes, especially anti-Revolutionary activity. The sentence of death was almost invariable.

P. 76, L. 2. *the fall of Robespierre:* As Robespierre's increasingly dictatorial rule sent former allies to the guillotine, the different factions of the Convention united against him. He was declared an outlaw on July 27, 1794, and was executed the following day, in the coup known as *9 Thermidor* for its date according the Revolutionary calendar.

L. 10. *"a ruse . . . Madame de Lavalette":* In 1815, when her husband was imprisoned and condemned to death by the Bourbons for having rallied to Napoleon on his return from Elba, Madame de Lavalette visited her husband in his cell and exchanged clothes with him, enabling him to escape.

P. 77, LL. 22–23. *"the d'Esgrignon . . . the Nouâtres":* All these families figure prominently in the highest ranks of Balzac's invented aristocracy. Victurnien d'Esgrignon is the protagonist of *Le Cabinet des antiques (A Collection of Antiquities)*; Béatrix de Castéran marries the Marquis de Rochefide, is the heroine of the novel *Béatrix,* and plays a vital role in *Sarrasine;* Virginie de Troisville, as the Comtesse de Montcornet, plays a supporting role in many works, most notably *Les Paysans (The Peasants).*

P. 78, LL. 13–14. *"one of Louis XVIII's most active agents":* The exiled Comte de Provence (1755–1824), the younger brother of Louis XVI, declared himself King Louis XVIII upon the death of his nephew in a Paris prison in 1794. Before he actually returned to Paris to take power in 1814, many royalist agents were active on his behalf in France. He reigned in 1814–15 and from 1815 to 1824. The ingratitude of the Bourbons to those who served them during their years of exile is a recurrent theme in *La Comédie humaine.*

LL. 22–23. *"the cruelest tactics of the Chouans":* Balzac portrayed some of those cruelties—including those of the *Chauffeurs (see note for p. 80, l. 26, p. 223)*—in his 1829 novel *Les Chouans,* the first novel of what would become *La Comédie humaine.* Balzac returns to many of the same themes of that novel in this, the last novel of his massive cycle *(see note for p. 29, l. 36, p. 215).*

L. 24. *the Chevalier de Valois:* This secondary character appears in several texts. As his great name and minor title imply—*chevalier* means "knight"—this character claims descent from a royal bastard of King Charles IX Valois *(see note for p. 5, ll. 8–11, p. 210).* Balzac frequently blurred the line between his fiction and reality in this way.

P. 80, LL. 10–13. *"she felt a fanatical . . . wrongs of 1793":* This fanatical attachment to the Bourbons is typical of many of Balzac's aristocrats, and in this he is an accurate painter of the times. Laurence de Cinq-Cygne *(see note for p. 44, l. 14, p. 217)* displays these same sentiments in *Une ténébreuse affaire (A Shadowy Affair),* although her career is quite different from that of Madame de La Chanterie. [*T*]*he wrongs of 1793* refers chiefly to the executions of King Louis XVI in January and of Marie-Antoinette in October of that year.

L. 17. *the hostilities of 1799:* The counterrevolutionary uprisings of the Chouans and the Vendéens flared up in 1799 after several years of relative calm.

L. 26. *the Chauffeurs:* Taking their name from their use of fire as a means of persuasion—*chauffer* means "to heat," and the Chauffeurs often literally held their victims' feet to the fire—the Chauffeurs often practiced outright extortion, as Balzac portrays in *Les Chouans.*

LL. 26–27. *department:* One of the earliest acts of the National Assembly in 1789 was to create new administrative divisions called *départements* to replace the traditional provinces.

L. 29. *conscription:* The conscription required by the seemingly endless Revolutionary wars met sometimes violent resistance and contributed to counterrevolutionary sentiment in the provinces, especially in the west.

LL. 34–35. *"the holders of private and Church properties seized and sold off":* Church properties were nationalized in 1789, and the properties of those—mostly nobles—who emigrated or were otherwise judged to be enemies of the Revolution were seized throughout the Revolutionary era. These nationalized assets, known as *biens nationaux,* were sold to provide revenue for the government.

P. 81, L. 9. Le Moniteur: a quasi-official government journal founded in 1789.

LL. 22–23. *"Royalists ruined by the civil war of 1793":* The counterrevolutionary movements in the west and south and around Lyon had been brutally suppressed by the government of the Convention.

LL. 32–34. *"Lobau Island . . . Wagram":* In the 1809 war between France and Austria, Napoleon established himself on the island of Lobau in the Danube just west of Vienna. From there he launched the fierce battles of Essling (May 1809) and Wagram (July 1809). The results of these hard-won French victories were Austrian defeat and an alliance between the two Emperors cemented by the marriage of Napoleon to Maria Luisa von Hapsburg in 1810.

p. 82, L. 21. *the Simeuse trial:* The 1806 trial of the aristocratic Simeuse twins, cousins of Laurence de Cinq-Cygne *(see note for p. 44, l. 14, p. 217)* arrested for plotting on behalf of the exiled Bourbons, is recounted in *Une ténébreuse affaire.*

p. 83, L. 22. *Chevalier du Vissard:* The du Vissard family was to have figured prominently in the novella *Mademoiselle du Vissard,* which Balzac never completed.

L. 24. *the Emperor and King:* Napoleon had taken for himself the title not only of Emperor of France but also King of Italy.

L. 36–P. 84, L. 3. *a locale intimately... ransacked his coach:* This episode is depicted in *Les Chouans.* The woman leading this "band of brigands" is the fierce aristocrat Madame du Gua; the "infamous Marche-à-Terre," her brutal henchman, is known by his *nom de guerre,* as are the accomplices named in the bill of indictment that follows (the Bread Thief, the Grandson, et cetera).

p. 84, L. 20. *armies in Spain:* Napoleon's attempted conquest of Spain became a quagmire as his troops faced the relentless opposition of guerrilla forces and the invading English troops under Arthur Wellesley, the future Duke of Wellington.

L. 33. *the year VII:* According to the Revolutionary calendar—which began when the Republic was declared in September 1792—the year VII was 1799.

p. 85, L. 2. *the Fontaine division:* the division commanded by the Comte de Fontaine *(see note for p. 21, l. 10, p. 214).*

L. 5. *the Quiberon Expedition:* In the summer of 1795, a small émigré force, funded by the English government and transported on British Navy ships, landed on the Quiberon peninsula on the southern coast of Brittany, planning to unite with royalist *Chouan* troops in a counterrevolutionary insurrection. They were met and defeated by superior Republican forces under General Hoche, who was ordered by the government in Paris to treat the invaders with the utmost rigor; 743 émigrés were shot.

p. 86, L. 35. *nationalized assets:* See note for p. 80, *ll. 34–35, p. 223.*

p. 96, L. 18. *Walter Scott's Fergus:* from Scott's novel *Waverly* (1814). Scott's novels were immensely popular with the French public, including Balzac, and created a great vogue for the historical romantic novel.

L. 19. *Jacobite:* from "Jacobus," the latinized name of King James II. The Jacobites were followers of the Catholic Stuarts of England, deposed by the Glorious Revolution of 1688.

L. 23. *Diana Vernon:* another reference to Sir Walter Scott. Diana Vernon is the heroine of *Rob Roy*.

L. 33. *Bauvan:* For readers of *La Comédie humaine,* the name Bauvan recalls the Comte Octave de Bauvan and his wife, the protagonists of *Honorine*.

P. 97, LL. 14–15. *a young woman . . . with child:* It was customary in most of Europe for women condemned to death to be granted a stay of execution if they declared themselves pregnant.

L. 32. *the Count de Lille:* the name used by King Louis XVIII during his exile.

L. 33. *Contenson:* a name with great resonance in *La Comédie humaine*. Under his alias of Contenson and working as a ruthless agent of the police, Henriette's husband appears in *Splendeurs et misères des courtisanes (The Splendor and Misery of Courtesans)*. This late revelation is the only clue to his true identity.

P. 98, L. 33. *a true whited sepulcher:* a reference to the Gospel of Saint Matthew, signifying a beautiful appearance concealing an empty interior, i.e., a hypocrite.

P. 101, L. 1. *the Prince de Hatzfeld:* Governor of Berlin at the time of Napoleon's conquest of that city in 1807, Hatzfeld was discovered to be sending the Prussian forces information on French troop strength and position. He was condemned to death by the French but was pardoned when his wife made a personal appeal to Napoleon.

L. 17. *Doctor Guillotin:* The physician Joseph-Ignace Guillotin (1738–1814), as a member of the National Assembly, did in fact advocate and perfect the use of the machine that now bears his name as a humane means of execution, but he did not, contrary to popular belief then and now, invent the guillotine.

LL. 32–33. *Charrette* and *Georges Cadoudal:* leaders of the Chouans. François-Athanase de Charrette (1763–94) took part in early counter-revolutionary activity, then in the attempted landing at Quiberon, where he was captured and subsequently executed. Georges Cadoudal (1771–1803) was best known for his part in the attempts on Napoleon's life in 1800, then in another plot in 1803, when he was arrested and executed as well.

P. 103, L. 33. *the Beauséants:* This Balzacian family is represented in *La Comédie humaine* by Claire, Vicomtesse de Beauséant, who is the tragic heroine of *La Femme abandonnée (A Woman Abandoned)* and plays a vital role in *Le Père Goriot*.

P. 104, L. 26. *the accession of Louis XVIII:* The younger brother of the beheaded Louis XVI returned to Paris after the initial defeat of Napoleon in 1814. It would be almost a year before Bonaparte staged his dramatic return to France in March 1815. *(See note for p. 78, ll. 13–14, p. 222.)*

P. 105, L. 5. *First President:* "President," in this context, refers to a presiding judge.

L. 15. *the Duke de Verneuil:* another name from the larger *Comédie humaine.* The heroine of *Les Chouans* is Marie de Verneuil, illegitimate daughter of the duke, a daring adventuress who works as an agent for the secret police of the Directorate.

L. 30. *"the most curious trait":* This curious character trait is not unique to Louis XVIII in Balzac's world. The fate of the archcriminal Vautrin at the end of *Splendeurs et misères des courtisanes (The Splendor and Misery of Courtesans)* suggests that all governments are capable of this sort of cold-blooded pragmatism *(see note for p. 106, ll. 3–4 below).*

P. 106, LL. 1–3. *"Contenson . . . rooftops":* The criminal whose pursuit leads to Contenson's death is Vautrin, the archcriminal who casts his long shadow over *Les Illusions perdues (Lost Illusions), Le Père Goriot (Old Goriot),* and *Splendeurs et misères des courtisanes (The Splendor and Misery of Courtesans),* the novel in which Contenson dies.

LL. 3–4. *"Louis XVIII . . . police are concerned":* Napoleon's secret police was inextricably linked to the legendary Joseph Fouché (1759–1820), a former regicide and terrorist who was named Minister of Police and Duke of Otranto by Napoleon in spite of Fouché's bloody history and habit of conspiring against governments that employed him, including Bonaparte's. The implication is that Louis's employment of Contenson is morally equivalent to Bonaparte's employment of Fouché.

LL. 11–12. *Ronceret* and *Blondet:* two more names with associations in Balzac's larger fictional world. In this case, it is the sons of the two magistrates named who figure in many texts. Emile Blondet in particular appears frequently as a supporting player.

L. 17. *"heads rolling into the basket":* Such darkly humorous references to the guillotine became common in the Revolutionary era. This reference is to the so-called White Terror which took place under the Restoration, white being the color of the Bourbon family.

P. 108, LL. 13–14. *Swedenborg's doctrine on angels:* Balzac was fascinated by the theory propounded by the mystic Swedish philosopher Emmanuel Swedenborg (1688–1772) that between God and the world of man there exists a physical world populated by angels who live much as we do. Balzac's interest in Swedenborg and angels is evident in his philosophical novella *Louis Lambert* and even more so in his short story *Séraphita*.

L. 18. *Vicar of Wakefield:* title character in the 1776 novel by Oliver Goldsmith in which an unjustly imprisoned English vicar, Dr. Primrose, rises above his own misery in order to attend to the salvation of his fellow prisoners. Balzac cited Goldsmith's novel as an inspiration for his own *Le Médecin de campagne (The Country Doctor)*.

LL. 29–30. *"the Duchesse d'Angoulême . . . the Chancellor":* The *Duchesse d'Angoulême* was Marie-Thérèse, the daughter of Louis XVI and Marie-Antoinette, who escaped the Temple prison in Paris and later married her cousin, the Duc d'Angoulême, son of the Comte d'Artois who would become King Charles X after the death of Louis XVIII in 1824, whereupon her husband became the Dauphin—heir to the throne—and the Duchesse became the *Dauphine.* An austere woman, the Duchesse d'Angoulême was known for her piety and charity. Her sister-in-law, the *Duchesse de Berry,* was left a pregnant widow when her husband, the younger son of the Comte d'Artois, was assassinated in 1820. Her son, called the Duc de Bordeaux, was heir to the throne and the great hope of the Bourbon family. The Duchesse de Berry became a heroine to the royalist cause in 1832 when she attempted to resurrect the old Vendéen spirit in an insurrection against the Orléanist July Monarchy. She was arrested and imprisoned, but she lost public sympathy when it was learned that this twelve-year widow was pregnant. The *Archbishop* in question was probably Louis-Hyacinthe Quélen (1768–1839), who was Archbishop of Paris from 1821 until his death; and the *Chancellor,* the equivalent of a Minister of Justice, may refer to any number of incumbents in that office under the Restoration.

P. 109, L. 18. *Job:* the Old Testament figure who was the victim of every imaginable suffering, inflicted by God as a test of his faith. Job eventually revolts, renouncing his faith and cursing his birth, before ultimately acknowledging that God's ways are unknowable to man and accepting his fate as God's will. This submission earns him God's blessing, and prosperity is returned to him.

L. 28. *Saint Paul's Epistle on Charity: See note for p. 46, l. 19, p. 217.*

SECOND EPISODE. THE INITIATE

P. 115, L. 1. *Parnassus:* the mountain in Greece dedicated to Apollo and sacred to poets since the classical era.

P. 116, L. 2. *communist doctrine:* Early communist theory, which utterly horrified Balzac, became widespread throughout France in the 1840s. Balzac wrote to Madame Hanska that communism was a doctrine that "consists of turning everything upside down, *of sharing everything.*" When the first installment of *The Initiate* appeared in the *Spectateur républicain,* Balzac included the following note:

> In spite of our well known aversion for personal notes, current events force us to point out that this work was begun in 1840, and that the installment published today, written in Russia, near Berditcheff, last year, was only reread by us yesterday, 30 July [1848], the manuscript having been given such as it was to the printer. Current circumstances had no influence on this prophetic phrase. In any case those who will have done us the honor of attentively reading the first portion of this novel, *Madame de La Chanterie,* published in 1845, will recognize the logical connection of the observation made here with developments of the first part of the novel.

Berditcheff was the village closest to Madame Hanska's estate of Wierzchownia, in Ukraine.

P. 117, L. 9. *arrondissements:* These divisions of Paris were among the many administrative innovations of the Revolutionary era that continued into the Restoration and beyond. In the 1830s, Paris was still divided into twelve *arrondissements;* today there are twenty.

L. 32. *Rue d'Enfer:* By coincidence or irony on Balzac's part, *Enfer* means "Hell."

P. 119, L. 1. *"two perfect men":* Regarding Judge Popinot, *see note for p. 67, l. 21, p. 220.* The "country doctor" is the protagonist of *Le Médecin de campagne (The Country Doctor),* who through rational and authoritative humanitarianism revitalizes an impoverished district in the Jura. Balzac wrote *Le Médecin de campagne* in part as a political tract, and it contains perhaps the best expression of his political philosophy. Balzac felt strongly that his novel should have been awarded the Montyon Prize, a prestigious monetary award bestowed on works of art and science that contributed to the moral and material betterment of the common people of France.

P. 120, LL. 6–9. *the idea of association . . . over the State:* This paragraph reflects Balzac's essential conservatism, perhaps expressed most concisely in that 1842 preface already mentioned in the note for p. 6, L. 33: *J'écris à la lueur de deux Vérités éternelles: la Religion, la Monarchie, deux nécessités . . . vers lesquelles tout écrivain de bon sens doit essayer de ramener notre pays.* ("I write by the light of two eternal Truths: Religion [and] Monarchy, two necessities . . . to which every writer of good sense must endeavor to return our country.") While recognizing a certain level of elective democracy as both useful and necessary, limitless democracy was merely "government by the masses . . . in which tyranny knows no bounds." This is what happened in 1792, when the increasing democratic fervor of the Revolution brought down the monarchy, established a republic—the Convention—and eventually culminated in the violent excesses of the Terror. This triumph of the "Individual" over the "State," as Balzac describes it, was in his view the unhappy triumph of the secular Enlightenment and its blind faith in individualism. Balzac declares in the same preface his firm belief that "the Family, and not the Individual" was the true "social element," the necessary basis of a healthy society.

L. 22. *French Charbonnerie:* The Charbonnerie was an Italian import inspired by the Neapolitan *carbonari;* both groups sought to advance liberal politics. The French Charbonnerie was influential in bringing about the July Revolution of 1830, and many of its members joined the Party of Movement *(see note for p. 9, ll. 29–30, p. 212).*

L. 23. *Champ d'Asile:* This American colony was formed in Alabama by a group of self-exiled liberals and Bonapartists; they named their new "state" Marengo *(see note for p. 60, l. 10, p. 220),* and its capital was to be Aigleville, the eagle being one of the chief symbols of the Empire. The colony ultimately failed, in part, as Balzac states, because of fraudulent subscription drives.

L. 28. *the Hansas of the Middle Ages:* the Hanseatic leagues of the German trading cities and their dominant merchants.

P. 122, L. 29. *the Chaumière ball:* a public ball held regularly at the Chaumière café in the Boulevard du Montparnasse. Originally intended for the working class, it became popular with bohemians and upper-class youth.

LL. 29–30. *the Pontine marshes:* a notoriously insalubrious—and thus underpopulated—region of swamps on the Italian coast between Rome and Naples.

P. 124, L. 33. *Sunday and Monday:* the "weekend" for the working classes in early nineteenth-century Paris. Balzac paints the mores of the working classes in the wine shops and cabarets of the *faubourgs* in his long introduction to *La Fille aux yeux d'or (The Girl with the Golden Eyes)*.

P. 125, L. 12. *Monsieur Barbet:* Among Balzac's usurers, Barbet specializes in the world of writers and publishing; he appears in *Illusions perdues (Lost Illusions)*.

P. 128, LL. 12–13. *Don Quixote* and the *President de Montesquieu: Don Quixote* is of course the hero of Cervantes' mock epic, an impoverished, deluded knight-errant on a vain quest for glory. Charles de Secondat, Baron de Brède et de *Montesquieu* (1689–1755), a presiding judge in Bordeaux, is best remembered as a writer and one of the earliest thinkers associated with what is now known as the Enlightenment. He was the author of the 1721 novel *Les Lettres persanes (The Persian Letters)*, a lively indictment of French society through the eyes of two imagined Persian diplomats in contemporary Paris; he also wrote the very different *De l'esprit des lois (On the Spirit of Laws)*, his *magnum opus* which appeared in 1748 after twenty years of research, meditation, and writing. In this massive work, a study not only of law but of politics and society, the author distinguishes among three types of government and the virtues (or "spirits") necessary for each: republics of virtue, honorable monarchies, and fear-based despotisms. Despotism is obviously horrible, and republics must be small, so necessarily the best government for a large modern state like France is the honorable monarchy, supported by an enlightened and active nobility. Montesquieu's ideal was the English constitutional monarchy, with its parliamentary checks and balances moderating royal power. Although conservative compared to the revolutionary theories that took hold later in the eighteenth century, these ideas were considered radical in mid-eighteenth-century France. Montesquieu is considered one of the founders of classical European liberalism.

P. 130, L. 11. *a Pole:* The political and cultural ties between the French and the Polish—whom Balzac sometimes called "the French of the North"—date from the early eighteenth century and continued throughout the political turmoil in both countries during the Revolutionary era. In the French Revolution, many Poles saw a parallel with their own struggles against the Austrians, Prussians, and Russians who had carved up Poland for themselves *(see note for p. 166, l. 31, p. 234)*. Napoleon earned the loyalty and military service of many aristocratic Polish patriots with vague and ultimately unfulfilled promises of a restored Kingdom of Poland.

Balzac had personal reasons for flattering Poland and the Poles in his novels: He had since 1831 been engaged in a mostly epistolary love affair with Eveline Rzewuska, the Countess Hanska, daughter of an ancient family of the Polish aristocracy, who was married to an immensely wealthy Russian nobleman. Balzac and Eve met in Geneva in 1833, and then communicated mostly by letter until Count Hanski died in 1841. After continued correspondence and traveling together in Germany and Italy, they finally married near Eve's estate—where, in fact, Balzac had written much of *The Initiate*—at the village of Berditcheff in Ukraine in March 1850, then made the arduous trip back to Paris, where Balzac died in August, only a few months after the marriage. Eve survived him by some thirty years, dying in Paris in 1882.

P. 131, L. 23. *catalepsy:* a loss of voluntary movement in which the muscles remain fixed in whichever position they are placed, frequently accompanied by a loss of consciousness.

L. 28. *magnetism:* Balzac was fascinated by the theories of Dr. Franz Anton Mesmer (1739–1815), who believed, among other things, that illnesses could be cured by the properties of a magnet and the "magnetic fluid" in our bodies. Theories of magnetism continued to be popular in the late eighteenth and early nineteenth centuries. Balzac believed himself to be possessed of an exceptional degree of magnetic power.

L. 34. *Voltaire, Diderot, Helvétius:* three of the greatest names of the French Enlightenment. The towering figure of *Voltaire* (born François-Marie Arouet, 1694–1778), the author of *Candide* and *Les Lettres philosophiques (The Philosophical Letters)*, dominated the era. Less well known outside France, Denis *Diderot* (1713–84) was the editor of the *Encyclopédie* and the author of *Le Neveu de Rameau (Rameau's Nephew)* and of *Jacques le fataliste et son maître (Jacques the Fatalist and His Master)*. Claude Adrien *Helvétius* (1715–71) used his vast fortune to support the *Encyclopédie* project; as an author, he is best remembered for his essay *De l'esprit (On Wit)*, a rather brutal expression of the most radical elements of Enlightenment thought: atheistic and materialistic, it advocates moral utilitarianism and radical—for the time—social equality. Published in 1752, it was condemned by the King's Council and the *parlement* of Paris.

P. 132, L. 17. *hydrophobia:* not, in this case, rabies, but more literally an extreme aversion to water.

LL. 33–34. *Desplein, Bianchon, Haudry:* three doctors of Balzac's invention. *Haudry* is a minor character, appearing peripherally in a few works. *De-*

splein figures most prominently in *La Messe de l'athée (The Atheist's Mass)*, in which he is the atheist of the title. Desplein's student Horace *Bianchon* is the most frequently appearing character in the whole of Balzac's oeuvre; perhaps best remembered as a medical student and friend of Eugène de Rastignac in *Le Père Goriot*, he is also the nephew of the Judge Popinot who worked with Madame de La Chanterie to found the secretive beneficent order of this novel.

P. 133, L. 22. *Beaujon Hospital:* a hospital founded by the financier Nicolas Beaujon in 1784, located on the north side of Paris.

P. 137, L. 18. *the Prince de Wissembourg:* This character, also known as Maréchal Cottin, bears a Napoleonic title. Only the highest ranking and most successful generals earned the title of *Prince*. Napoleon liked to give his nobles titles from foreign countries to emphasize the internationality of his empire and his conquests. (Ironically, the town of Wissembourg in Alsace would be the site of a Prussian victory over the forces of Emperor Napoleon III in 1870.) The Prince de Wissembourg plays an important part in *La Cousine Bette*.

P. 138, L. 18. *a sort of Jew:* Most of Balzac's usurers are some "sort of Jew." While not virulently anti-Semitic, Balzac was not above the prejudices of his time.

P. 143, L. 26. *Garde Nationale:* founded as a civilian militia early in the Revolution. Service in the National Guard was compulsory for all adult males meeting a certain level of taxation; to be an officer in the National Guard was thus a sign of good bourgeois standing. Balzac does not mean this as a compliment, however. He despised the National Guard, often refusing to perform his required service; in 1836, he spent a week in prison for evading his appointed Guard duty.

L. 27. *Monsieur Dimanche:* In a famous scene in Molière's *Don Juan*, the aristocratic hero snobbishly mocks Monsieur Dimanche, a pompous bourgeois to whom he owes money. *(See note for p. 53, ll. 31–32, p. 219.)*

P. 147, L. 9. *Prince Poniatowski:* a member of a leading family of the Polish nobility, several of whom were elected kings of Poland. The prince in question was Joseph Poniatowski (1763–1813), nephew of the last king of Poland before the final partition in 1795. Joseph Poniatowski joined the Imperial Army in the hope that Napoleon would establish the independent kingdom of Poland. Poniatowski drowned while crossing a river during the retreat from Moscow.

P. 150, L. 20. *a* liard: a coin worth a quarter of a *sou*. To be without a proverbial *liard* was to be flat broke.

P. 153, L. 10. *"Bossuet's glass of water":* In a famous sermon on charity, the great preacher reminded the faithful that Jesus asked not for great gifts, but merely for a glass of water for the thirsty or a *liard* for the poor. *(See note for p. 41, ll. 22–24, p. 216.)*

P. 154, L. 15. The Spirit of the New Laws: a title that the French would immediately recognize as based on Montesquieu's *De l'esprit des lois (see note for p. 128, ll. 12–13, p. 230).*

L. 17. *"far more than five [codes]":* that is, not merely the famous Napoleonic Code, but all the laws created by the many successive régimes from 1789 through 1830, to say nothing of the ancient legal traditions of France.

P. 156, L. 18. *Godefroid de Bouillon:* Godefroi de Bouillon (1061–1100) was a great nobleman, the Duke of Lower Lorraine, who sold his fiefs and lands to help fund the First Crusade. In the Holy Land, he was elected King of Jerusalem, celebrated by his peers for his humility and zeal in the cause. The word *bouillon,* in French as in English, denotes a clear broth; thus Godefroid's "little joke" about putting food on the table.

P. 157, L. 1. *the Laocoöns:* The Trojan hero Laocoön, son of Priam, angered the gods, who punished him by sending sea monsters to strangle him together with his two sons.

LL. 7–8. *Tallement des Réaux:* Gédéon de Tallamant des Réaux (1619–90). His *Historiettes* (literally, "Little Histories"), a collection of anecdotes about Paris under the reign of Louis XIII, were published in 1834–35. The sick woman in question was diagnosed with the "mal de mère"— literally, "the mother's disease," or hysteria.

P. 159, L. 32. *arras:* so named after the northern French town of Arras where many such tapestry hangings were produced.

P. 160, LL. 4–5. *the finest quality and the highest price:* Critics have noted the parallel between Monsieur Bernard's generous deception of his daughter and the similar situation in Charles Dickens's *Cricket on the Hearth.* In that 1847 novella, an impoverished toymaker lets his blind daughter believe that they live in comfort rather than the squalor of their actual surroundings. Balzac read Dickens's story in the summer of its publication and declared it "a flawless masterpiece."

P. 163, L. 3. *Rubini:* Giovanni Battista Rubini (1795–1854), an Italian tenor who enjoyed great success in Paris and throughout Europe from 1825 through 1845.

L. 3. *Théâtre des Italiens:* a fashionable opera theater featuring a resident company of Italian singers and offering a repertoire of works by Italian composers.

P. 164, LL. 9–10. *"Lablache . . . I Puritani"*: all recollections of Balzac's own attendance at the *Italiens,* as the theater and its company were known: *Luigi Lablache* was a bass; *Rubini, see note for p. 163, l. 3, above; Tamburini* was a baritone; *la Grisi* may refer to either of two Milanese sopranos, sisters Giula and Giudetta, who found enormous success in Paris; Bellini's *I Puritani (The Puritans)* débuted at the *Italiens* in 1835, and Balzac considered Vincenzo *Bellini* (1801–35) the only composer who could compare to Rossini.

L. 25. *"leave for Algiers":* The French colonial adventure in Algeria began with the conquest of Algiers in 1830.

P. 165, L. 19. *a portrait of Madame Bernard:* another apparent error on Balzac's part. The portrait is not of Monsieur Bernard's wife but rather his married and widowed daughter. On these frequent if minor inconsistencies in detail, see *note for p. 34, l. 17, p. 216.*

L. 21. *Géricault:* French painter Théodore Géricault (1791–1824), considered a precursor of the Romantics. His most famous painting is the 1816 *Radeau de la Méduse (The Raft of the Medusa)*, a dramatic depiction of a raft carrying the survivors of the shipwreck of the French vessel *Méduse.*

P. 166, LL. 25–26. *Monsieur Maistre:* Count Joseph de Maistre (1754–1821), a counterrevolutionary who advocated archconservative positions such as ultraroyalism and papal infallibility; Balzac especially approved of the former. In de Maistre's eyes, all men were sinners, all destined to suffer divine punishment.

L. 31. *the division of Poland:* The kingdom having been weakened by internal divisions, Polish territory was carved up by Prussia, Russia, and Austria three times in the late eighteenth century: in 1772, in 1793, and finally, following a doomed nationalist revolt, in 1795 in a partition that wiped Poland off the European map, with Russia taking the largest share. At the 1815 Congress of Vienna, the European powers were forced to recognize the Russian czar Alexander I as king of a rump Kingdom of Poland.

P. 167, L. 27. *"Nathan's newest novel":* Raoul Nathan is one of many writers in

Balzac's fictional cast. He plays a prominent role in the novel *Une Fille d'Eve (A Daughter of Eve)*.

P. 168, L. 35. *the Polish emigration:* In 1830–31, Polish aristocrats and nationalists fled Russian reprisals following still another doomed rebellion, brutally repressed by Czar Nicholas I, who then annexed outright what had been a nominally autonomous kingdom under a Russian viceroy.

P. 169, L. 20. *the revolutionary Lelewel:* A professor of history in Vilna and War-saw, Joachim Lelewel (1786–1861) was a leading advocate of the 1830 in-surrection that led to the brutal repression of Polish nationals and the annexation of Poland to Russia.

P. 170, LL. 21–22. *Saladin* . . . *The Talisman:* still another reference to Sir Wal-ter Scott. In this 1824 novel, the chivalrous Saracen Sultan Saladin (1138–93) cures the illness of his enemy, the Crusader King Richard the Lion-Hearted of England (born 1157, reigned 1189–99), by wiping his brow with a small purse filled with curative herbs and soaked in water. Scott's tale may have been based in the legend that during the Third Crusade, Saladin sent snow to Richard in order to cure the latter's illness caused by the Mediterranean heat.

L. 28. *homeopathy:* This medical therapy was first advocated in Europe by the Saxon physician Samuel Hahnemann (1755–1843). Ill-received in Germany, he married a Frenchwoman and moved to Paris, where his theories found wider acceptance.

LL. 30–31. *Hédénius of Dresden, Chelius of Heidelberg:* both real doctors, who treated Madame Hanska *(see note for p. 130, l. 11, p. 230)* while she was trav-eling in Germany. In Heidelberg in 1840, Chelius treated her for arthri-tis; in Dresden in 1846, while traveling with Balzac, she suffered the miscarriage of a child who would have been Balzac's only son, and was cared for by Hédénius.

P. 171, L. 26. *the Baron de Nucingen:* the richest man in Balzac's fictional Paris *(see note for p. 20, ll. 30–32, p. 214)*.

P. 172, L. 6. *Prince Poniatowski:* Joseph Poniatowski, a leader of the nationalist movement in Poland *(see note for p. 147, l. 9, p. 232)*.

LL. 18–19. *"that idiot . . . Catherine the Second":* an unusually harsh judgment of Poniatowski. Catherine the Great was Empress of Russia at the time of the Polish partitions of the 1790s.

L. 34. *Huret* and *Fichet:* well-known Parisian locksmiths and safemakers of Balzac's time.

P. 176, LL. 8–9. *"the Banque de France . . . sadly corrupt":* The publishing industry was in fact notoriously corrupt in Balzac's time. Balzac had a number of conflicts regarding copyright and payment with several publishers, who were not always in the wrong. Balzac was the founder—with Sand, Hugo, Dumas, and other prominent writers—of the *Société des gens de lettres (The Society of Writers)* to defend the rights of authors and to fight against unlicensed printings and sales. Balzac was the first president of the *Société*, which still exists today.

P. 178, L. 14. *Saint Cecile:* also called Saint Cecilia; the patron saint of musicians.

L. 15. "The Prayer of Moses": from Rossini's opera *Moses in Egypt*.

L. 17. *Chopin:* The great Polish pianist and composer Frédéric Chopin (1810–49) fled Poland for Paris in 1831. In 1836 he began a famously tempestuous affair with the flamboyant novelist George Sand (1804–76) which lasted until Chopin's death. Balzac and Sand were well acquainted, and Balzac and Chopin knew one another as well.

P. 179, L. 11. *Rossini:* Balzac's favorite composer, Giacomo Rossini (1792–1868), is a frequent point of reference in *La Comédie humaine*. The two became acquainted in the 1830s.

L. 22. *Hoëné Wronski:* a Polish mathematician (1778–1853) who had lived in France since the 1790s.

L. 23. *Mickiewicz* and *Towianski:* Adam *Mickiewicz* (1798–1855), a Polish poet forced to flee Warsaw because of his nationalist activities, arrived in Paris in 1840. He became a follower of *Towianski*, a proponent of magnetism *(see note for p. 131, l. 28, p. 231)* after the latter cured Madame Mickiewicz.

P. 180, L. 4. *Augustin:* here, a diminutive of Auguste.

P. 181, L. 3. *the Society of Jesus:* better known as the Jesuits. In the early nineteenth century, the Jesuits were widely suspected of secret political activities. Balzac plays on this theme in *Les Employés (The Clerks)*, and the best-known example is Stendhal's *Le Rouge et le noir (The Red and the Black)*. The suggestion here that the Jesuits' secret activities were of a charitable nature is rather atypical.

L. 21. *"Two days later . . ."*: According to the chronology suggested earlier in the novel, Halpersohn should in fact have arrived for his appointment the next day. On these frequent if minor inconsistencies in detail, *see the note for page 34, l. 17, p. 216.*

L. 34. *"your one hundred francs"*: On p. 172, Halpersohn's fee is given as two hundred francs. On these frequent if minor inconsistencies in detail, *see note for p. 34, l. 17, p. 216.*

P. 184, L. 15. *the Polish plique:* Although most doctors of the time considered *plica polonica,* or trichoma, to be a fairly minor condition typified by matted hair and an inflamed scalp, Balzac's imagination was captured by those who believed that these were only symptoms of a far more serious disease that could produce the dramatic ailments manifested by Vanda. In particular, Dr. Knothe, Madame Hanska's physician *(see following note),* is thought to have given the author much of his information on the plique. Subsequent studies have in fact suggested that the condition now known as *plica neuropathica* manifests itself in patients suffering from psychiatric disorders such as schizophrenia and hysteria, and has also been associated with hysterical paralysis. The fact that the Polish plique was thought to be peculiar to Poles allowed Balzac to lend an air of exoticism to the disease and to the diagnostician, and also to explain why such brilliant doctors as Desplein and Bianchon were unable to help Vanda. In fact, the plique was common among nineteenth-century Poles owing to a combination of hygiene, custom, and superstition.

L. 17. *"I am the only doctor living today":* The exotic Halpersohn, the Wandering Jew who possesses mysterious knowledge, is modeled in part on Dr. Knothe, Madame Hanska's physician, who treated Balzac when the author was staying at Wierzchownia. Balzac, fascinated by the doctor's brusque personality and use of mysterious folk remedies, considered Knothe a medical genius.

L. 20. *"a grande dame—a Baroness de Nucingen":* The characterization of the Baroness as a grande dame is rather curious: the bourgeois-born Delphine Goriot qualifies only inasmuch as she is married to the richest man in Balzac's Paris. This comment probably reflects Halpersohn's values rather than Balzac's.

P. 186, LL. 1–2. *"under the name of Monsieur Nicolas":* The reader may remember that on page 29 it is the Marquis de Montauran who is named Nicolas, and the former judge Lecamus is named Monsieur Joseph. Again, such minor inconsistencies are not uncommon in *La Comédie humaine.* We can attribute this one to the three-year gap between the composition of the first and second episodes of the novel. With this mistake, however, Balzac may have been returning to his historical sources: three generations of Lecamus, all named Nicolas, served with some distinction in the Paris *parlement* in the seventeenth century.

L. 28. *Clichy:* debtors' prison formerly located on the Rue de Clichy in the north of Paris.

P. 189, L. 12. The Spirit of the Modern Laws: still another of Balzac's characteristic errors. On page 154 Monsieur Bernard says his work is entitled *The Spirit of the New Laws.* On these frequent if minor inconsistencies in detail, *see note for p. 34, l. 17, p. 216.*

P. 190, L. 23. *Fouquier-Tinville:* Antoine Fouquier-Tinville (1745–95), the ruthless prosecutor of the Revolutionary Tribunal in Paris. He was himself arrested and executed after the fall of Robespierre.

P. 197, L. 14. *the bluecoats:* the police.

P. 199, L. 31. *the Conciergerie:* the infamous medieval prison, on the Île de la Cité, in which those condemned to the guillotine during the Terror, including Marie-Antoinette, were confined.

P. 203, L. 14. *Cavalier and Company:* These publishers are an invention of Balzac's.

P. 204, L. 14. vous: the formal second-person form of address, indicating the stern old man's loss of affection for his grandson.

P. 206, L. 28. *"If you hope . . .":* In the original French, the old man here uses the familiar *tu* form in addressing his grandson; whether out of continuing anger or residual affection is not clear.

P. 207, L. 3. *Baron de Bourlac:* This is the only time that the "de" is used with Bourlac's name, and it is a rather surprising error on Balzac's part. The so-called nobiliary particle, especially when used with the title of "Baron," would suggest that Bourlac was a member of the old nobility, like Monsieur de Montauran and Madame de Cinq-Cygne. Bourlac, the one-time "twin of Fouquier-Tinville," received his title under the reign of Napoleon, and there is a vast gulf between his nobility and that of the Baroness de La Chanterie. Balzac's own family adopted the "de" in the 1820s in order to improve their social position.

P. 208, L. 9. *Madame Élisabeth:* Élisabeth de France (1764–94), the faithful sister of Louis XVI, who followed her brother and his family into the Temple prison, and was executed on the same day as Marie-Antionette.

[faint offset text from facing page, partially legible]

READING GROUP GUIDE

1. In his Translator's Preface, Jordan Stump praises Honoré de Balzac's narrative structure and the "perfect coherence that lies behind its apparently disordered surface: two equal halves telling two very different stories, revolving around two very different sorts of Parisian boardinghouses that mirror each other in subtle and intriguing ways" (xxiii–xxiv). Can you describe and compare these two boardinghouses and the inhabitants of each?

2. What levels of society do Madame de La Chanterie, Father de Vèze, and Messieurs Alain, Nicolas, and Joseph come from, and what is their current social standing? Why do they now perform anonymous acts of charity?

3. A. S. Byatt described *The Wrong Side of Paris* as "a stringent inquiry into our ideas of good and evil, virtue and vice." After reading this novel, how would you characterize Balzac's views on morality? Which characters best represent the extremes of good and evil? Do any characters represent both extremes?

4. "Each does what good he can in his own way, and believe me, there is a reason for my avarice," says Moses Halpersohn to Godefroid

on page 172. What do you suppose is the reason behind Halpersohn's method of selecting his patients? And what do you think of Balzac's depiction of the Polish Jewish doctor?

5. In his Introduction, Adam Gopnik compares Balzac to "late-twentieth-century South American writers García Márquez, Vargas Llosa, and even Borges—all those other masters in whose work folktale and the modern novel and outright fantasy coexist in a way that seems to mirror the condition of their countries and peoples better than a narrowly realistic novel ever could" (xviii). Drawing on examples from *The Wrong Side of Paris*, can you support Gopnik's theory?

6. How does this newly rediscovered novel, written near the end of Balzac's long, prolific career, compare with other novels in *La Comédie humaine*, such as *Cousin Bette*, *Père Goriot*, and *Lost Illusions*?

ABOUT THE TRANSLATOR

JORDAN STUMP is an associate professor of French at the University of Nebraska at Lincoln. He has published articles on the Marquis de Sade, Georges Perec, and Raymond Queneau, among others; he is also the author of *Naming and Unnaming: On Raymond Queneau*, and has translated novels by Marie Redonnet, Eric Chevillard, Patrick Modiano, Antoine Volodine, Jean-Philippe Toussaint, and Christian Oster. His translation of Claude Simon's *Jardin des Plantes* won the 2001 French-American Foundation Translation Prize. His recent translation of *The Mysterious Island* by Jules Verne is available from the Modern Library.

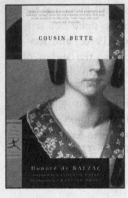
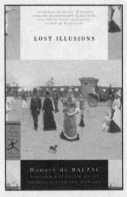

MODERN LIBRARY IS ONLINE AT
WWW.MODERNLIBRARY.COM

MODERN LIBRARY ONLINE IS YOUR GUIDE TO CLASSIC LITERATURE ON THE WEB

THE MODERN LIBRARY E-NEWSLETTER

Our free e-mail newsletter is sent to subscribers, and features sample chapters, interviews with and essays by our authors, upcoming books, special promotions, announcements, and news.

To subscribe to the Modern Library e-newsletter, send a blank e-mail to: sub_modernlibrary@info.randomhouse.com or visit www.modernlibrary.com

THE MODERN LIBRARY WEBSITE

Check out the Modern Library website at
www.modernlibrary.com for:

- The Modern Library e-newsletter
- A list of our current and upcoming titles and series
- Reading Group Guides and exclusive author spotlights
- Special features with information on the classics and other paperback series
- Excerpts from new releases and other titles
- A list of our e-books and information on where to buy them
- The Modern Library Editorial Board's 100 Best Novels and 100 Best Nonfiction Books of the Twentieth Century written in the English language
- News and announcements

Questions? E-mail us at modernlibrary@randomhouse.com
For questions about examination or desk copies, please visit
the Random House Academic Resources site at
www.randomhouse.com/academic